# Hunting Michael Underwood

## L. V. Gaudet

To Cara

keep reading and let the darkness in.

LV Gaudet

This book is a work of fiction. Names, characters, places, and events are products of the author's imagination or are used fictitiously. Any resemblance to actual events, locales, or persons, living or dead, is entirely coincidental.



ISBN 978-1718796447

ISBN 1718796447



Second edition published September 2018

Cover photo by Benjamin Lambert on Unsplash

Discover other titles by L.V. Gaudet:

Garden Grove
The Gypsy Queen

The McAllister Series:
Where the Bodies Are
The McAllister Farm
Hunting Michael Underwood
Killing David McAllister

"Michael Underwood walked
out of that prison
and off the face of the earth,
taking our only witness with him.
I will find him and bring him down."

"Who the hell are you?"

To sleep more deeply is to dream more deeply.
In the darkness, where the nightmares live.

Table of Contents

# Part One

# Free Pass

# 1 Insanely Guilty

The steady drone of the tires on concrete should have lulled Detective Jim McNelly into a false sense of normalcy. Nothing will be normal again. Not for him, or for anyone else.

His fat jowls work as he clenches and unclenches his jaw, his thick hands gripping the steering wheel hard. His bulk is more than ample enough to fill the driver's seat of the ancient brown Oldsmobile, almost spilling over into the passenger side.

The McAllister murders.

They are eating away at his gut, tormenting his sleep, and torturing his heartburn. They are victims he failed to save.

The phone call that brought him speeding towards the prison had shattered his morning.

Earlier:

It is Jim's day off, but his conscience isn't having it.

*Michael Underwood vanished along with our only living witness to the McAllister murders,* Jim thinks, pouring himself a cup of coffee.

*Michael visited McAllister in prison after the guilty verdict came down on Jason T. McAllister. That was the last time Michael Underwood and our only witness, Katherine Kingslow, were seen.*

He takes a sip of coffee, his unkempt moustache soaking up some of the brew.

The phone rings.

"McNelly," he answers it gruffly.

"Jim, have you heard the news?"

He recognizes the voice immediately, Lawrence Hawkworth.

*It was thanks to Lawrence's investigation that we discovered the identity of the killer.*

*Hawkworth, that buzzard-like creature who has no shame when it comes to digging up and publishing dirt for the InterCity Voice. He's the most notoriously underhanded investigative reporter in town, but he is effective. Otherwise, Jason McAllister would still be an unknown perp.*

Lawrence Hawkworth is also his long time friend.

"No. I haven't turned on a radio or T.V." He'd had enough of the news long before the trial finished.

"This hasn't hit the news wires yet. It's more rumour than news."

"What is it?" Jim frowns, sipping his coffee.

"The judge is cutting Jason McAllister loose."

Jim's grip on his coffee mug tightens and he scowls.

"What do you mean, cutting him loose? He's being shipped today to a high security nut house. It's not a real sentence, but at least he's locked up for now."

*His sentence will be determined on a month-to-month basis by a board of psychiatrists and the suits that run the place.*

The idea infuriates Jim. Not guilty by reason of insanity, that was the trial verdict. Instead of hard time in a penitentiary, he's doing not so hard time in a psychiatric facility. How long he serves depends on his behaviour.

"That's been put off. His lawyer managed to get the appeal date pushed up, fast tracked because someone at the top just wants it to go away, I'm sure of that."

"I'm not surprised. He used the media to get the public to sympathize with McAllister while he filed his appeal against the guilty but insane verdict. The moment the verdict came down the media switched from portraying McAllister as a monster to calling him an innocent victim railroaded by the police without proof, almost in the same breath. It will be impossible to find another jury that hasn't been tainted by the media for another trial."

"It's gone past that now. I doubt there will be another trial, not even a trial by judge."

"What do you mean?"

"Rumour has it the judge is releasing McAllister pending a new trial when the appeal comes before him. The appeal is just a formality. It's already decided."

Jim flinches, freezes, a stone cold statue. "You're joking. It's not funny."

"It's no joke. Jason McAllister will be standing before the judge within the next few days. He's walking out of that courtroom a free man."

Lawrence's words hit Jim like a physical blow, rocking him as hard as it did when the verdict came down.

His coffee cup explodes against the wall in a shower of broken ceramic fragments and coffee erupting and splattering out from the wall like dull brown blood.

*It's all too convenient. McAllister is too insane to be found guilty of kidnapping and murder, but not insane enough to be a danger to society. McAllister has just been handed a free pass, a get out of jail free card. Do not pass Go and do not collect your two hundred dollars, just go and run. Disappear.*

"What secrets do you know McAllister?" Jim mutters under his breath.

"What are you going to do, Jim?"

"I'm going to get the son of a bitch."

Present:

The road continues to roll under the ancient Oldsmobile's tires.

*Cassie*. The name is a whisper in his mind, haunting him.

A car horn blares rudely, bringing Jim's attention back to the road. He grips the steering wheel harder in his meaty hands, swerving to avoid a head-on collision. He was so engrossed in his thoughts he wasn't paying attention to the road and drifted across the center line.

The other driver gives him the middle finger with an angry glare as he passes.

Jim's mind keeps working, moving the puzzle pieces around in his head.

*When an unidentified woman was found savagely beaten and barely clinging to life, no one imagined it would be only the beginning. She was just one victim with no name or past and an unknown assailant.*

*With the Jane Doe kept sedated in an induced coma, we couldn't question her. All attempts to identify her failed and there was no missing persons report that matched her description. The best we could hope for was that whoever assaulted her and left her for dead would come back to finish the job.*

*Detective Michael Underwood was placed in position undercover disguised as an orderly to watch the victim during hospital visiting hours.*

Jim makes a sour face, the name tasting foul on his tongue even without voicing it. His eyes narrow with hatred.

*Then another body showed up.*

*More bodies showed up, each provoking the media to a bigger frenzy, and Katherine Kingslow went missing. The evidence pointed in one direction, that they were victims of the same killer, Katherine probably the next body to appear.*

*Serial killer began to be whispered around and the media picked up on it.*

*It was supposed to be a simple serial killer, not that a serial killer is simple, but complicated doesn't even begin to describe this case.*

*Suspicion that Jane Doe was the one victim who survived made her more valuable. She was our only living witness.*

*Then the killer did exactly what we were counting on; he showed up at the hospital to finish the job.*

*We completely botched it. Instead of catching McAllister in the act, we dropped the ball and he kidnapped Jane Doe and just walked out of the hospital with her in the middle of a lockdown and massive search.*

"That still burns me," he mutters. "It's still a mystery. How does a man who is the subject of a massive search by officers and hospital security swarming a hospital on lockdown just walk out with a woman in a hospital gown who could not have walked on her own, and no one saw anything?"

*Jane Doe was never found. Her body is no doubt rotting away in some secret grave somewhere. Only her hospital gown and intravenous tube and needle were found at the McAllister farm.*

*Jane Doe's identity is still a mystery.*

*It was Lawrence who found the farm. The McAllister Farm was passed down in the McAllister family for generations. Jason McAllister returning at that moment, decades after the family abandoned the place, was no coincidence. Except we had no proof, only a reporter's hunch.*

*We confirmed McAllister was the perpetrator when we searched the farm and discovered Katherine Kingslow held captive in the farmhouse and the evidence that places Jane Doe there. Molly, the missing nurse from the hospital, was found there too, putrefaction already begun, in the trunk of a stolen car parked in the driveway.*

*We had a new living witness.*

*There was one big problem with the case, our only witness.*

*We only had circumstantial evidence. There was no concrete evidence placing McAllister in the area in the days leading up to his arrest at the McAllister farm and we were up against a credible story of his arriving just that day. We needed that witness testimony to seal McAllister's fate.*

*Katherine Kingslow would not talk. She was damaged goods; damaged in a way that most victims will never recover from, even with years of intensive therapy.*

*Jason McAllister was convicted on loosely held circumstantial evidence based on his presence at the farm when we raided it. There was no substantiated evidence against him.*

*That leaves the much bigger mystery an unsolved case. The graves.*

Jim's hands squeeze the wheel harder. He grits his teeth, glaring down the road ahead of him as it passes continuously beneath his car. He realizes his hands are still gripping the steering wheel as if he is trying to strangle it and forces himself to loosen his grip, bringing the color back into his knuckles that had turned white with the vicious grip.

"Michael Underwood," he refers to him by both names, like a criminal, "was at the McAllister farm when I showed up to search it."

*I got there before my backup did to find Michael already on site. Only, he was oblivious to my attempts to contact him to meet me there.*

*Michael Underwood, or whatever his real name is, duped us all. He came into our building as a transfer from another department. All his papers were in order. Everything about him seemed legitimate. No one thought to dig deeper. There was no reason to. These transfers are common.*

*All my attempts to investigate Underwood's background after he vanished came up empty. The man never existed before that first day he set foot in my office. He isn't even a ghost using a deceased person's identity.*

*Michael Underwood is a likeable guy and that only makes it burn more.*

*I have no proof, but I know Michael was somehow involved in the McAllister murders.*

*The day after the guilty verdict came down Michael visited McAllister in prison. I had confirmation of that meeting from the guard on duty at the prison. I also learned a little of the conversation that happened behind that closed door, but very little.*

*Michael raised his voice in anger, demanding to know where she is, Cassie. The guard heard the name through the door.*

"Who is Cassie? She's a new piece of the puzzle."

*After that, Michael Underwood walked out of that prison and off the face of the earth, taking our only witness with him. Surveillance footage outside the prison shows them together. She waited outside for him.*

*I will find him and bring him down.*

*Is the witness still alive? If Katherine can place Michael as an accomplice to Jason McAllister, then Michael had a good reason to get rid of her. Most likely she's dead, her body decomposing in some hidden grave somewhere.*

He keeps coming back to that thought, hidden graves. "More victims I failed."

He is almost there. Jim turns his rusting brown Oldsmobile, a relic and an eyesore against the sleeker newer vehicles on the road, and heads down the last stretch of road to the prison.

*If I'm right, Jason T. McAllister could be the most prolific serial killer the world has ever seen and Michael Underwood may be his partner. But there is so much more to this story than that. There are still the bodies.*

*The search for the killer responsible for women turning up brutally beaten to death, and the search for Katherine, would never have been anything more than one man responsible for multiple homicides. It was those hikers discovering a gruesome find in the woods that was the catalyst to a much bigger discovery that rocked the world.*

*That remote area of forest beyond the McAllister Farm hid a big secret, a hidden graveyard with the remains of hundreds of bodies that have been buried there for generations.*

*Thanks to them, we turned up something much bigger than a few missing and murdered women, bigger than the most notorious serial killer ever known. The proximity of the graveyard and farm and the evidence suggesting the recent victims were buried and dug up, pointed to them possibly being the missing bodies from the few empty graves. The connection can't be dismissed.*

*I know Jason T. McAllister has something to do with that graveyard and its long buried residents and Michael Underwood has a connection to McAllister.*

*I just can't prove it. Yet.*

*I couldn't pin the graves on McAllister. We couldn't nail him for the missing and murdered women. There was no proof that could be undeniably held against him. He could have gotten the death penalty, or at least life.*

*All we had him on was kidnapping the Kingslow woman and Jane Doe, and the nurse, Molly. His lawyer denied it all, of course, arguing he was an innocent victim caught up in an unknown assailant's crimes, charged only because he happened to own the abandoned property.*

*When it looked like he would lose, his lawyer turned to the insanity defence.*

*He was found guilty, determined so by a jury of his peers. What a joke.*

The words still thunder in Jim's head, "Not guilty by reason of insanity. The defendant is considered to not have been of sound mind at the time the crimes were committed."

*The insanity defence; everyone is insane when they are guilty. There was no evidence pointing to unbalanced behaviour. It makes no sense.*

*Still, our only witness, Katherine Kingslow, wouldn't talk. The shrink said it was useless, she was too damaged, lost within her own tortured mind from the years of abuse she had suffered at her boyfriend's hands and then the kidnapping and being kept prisoner in a dirt floored cellar beneath the old farmhouse.*

Jim turns into the prison driveway and into the visitors' parking area.

# 2 A Visit to the Clinker

The clanging of metal doors echoes through the building, joining their footsteps in a jagged staccato echoing down the hall.

Detective Jim McNelly wonders as he always does, *why do they make these places like this, so every sound is a loud amplified clang and echo? Is it done on purpose as a daily reminder to the prisoners that they are nothing more than animals in cages? Or is it to remind the guards that?*

He follows the guard escorting him, his large frame too wide to make walking abreast comfortable in the narrow hallway. They would have had to walk so close they might as well have been holding hands.

The guard stops at the door to one of the small interview rooms used for inmates' meetings with their lawyers, meant to afford them a small measure of privacy.

It's one of the rooms Michael Underwood met with Jason McAllister in after the trial.

"Here he is," the guard says, slipping his key card into the box outside the door. The red light flashes to green and the door unlocks with an audible sound.

Jim half feels like something is missing without the large ring of jangling keys old prison movies bring the image of to his mind.

"I'll be right outside." The guard points to the small mesh reinforced window in the door. "Wave or bang on the door when you are done. I won't be able to hear you at normal conversation level, but if he tries anything just yell, I'll hear that."

"He won't try anything."

The guard opens the door and lets Jim in. The door closes solidly behind him, shutting out the nonstop echoing noises of the prison to distant phantoms.

"Jason T. McAllister," Jim addresses the man sitting in a chair on the other side of a table. A chair waits for him on the near side. Jason is wearing wrist and ankle shackles that are attached to a chain, chaining him to the wall like a vicious dog.

Jason does not look like a serial killer, but then they rarely do. He looks like he would have been big and bulky in a muscular way in his prime when he was burgeoning into a young man, a labourer's body, a farm boy who grew up on hard labour and continued with it through his adult years. Age and lifestyle had thinned him down and he has lost weight in the months spent in a cell. His age-worn face is weathered from years working outside, giving him that ageless look of a man who looks older than his years. His hair that was beginning to salt and pepper has grown saltier during his brief incarceration.

"You wanted to see me?" Jason says with a smirk.

Jim takes the seat across from him, leaning back in the chair. He would have liked to lean forward, but you never lean forward when sitting across from a suspect.

"So, you managed to get a pass out of this place into someplace more accommodating," he says, feeling Jason out.

"I'm crazy, you know."

Jim nods. "I bet you are."

"Did you just come here to wish me luck?"

"No. Now that the death penalty and spending the rest of your useless life in prison are off the table, I thought you might like to help me out a little."

"I'll help you with anything I can." Jason smiles. The smile does not reach his eyes. This is not a man accustomed to smiling.

"Michael Underwood came to see you after the conviction came down," Jim says.

"Yes he did. I guess he wanted to say goodbye before I got the death penalty."

"He wanted to say goodbye all right. He's gone missing. You don't know anything about that, do you?"

"He is? I don't have much access to what goes on outside these walls." Jason waves his shackled arms to indicate the prison walls. The chains jangle as a reminder of who he is to the man sitting across from him, an animal and a killer.

Jim is full of questions, but he has to move carefully. Jason has no reason to cooperate with him.

"You knew Michael, didn't you?" Jim asks. "Before this whole thing." He waves his hand to include the prison, meaning the arrest and the missing and murdered women.

Jason just smiles. He doesn't need to answer. The detective already knows the answer to the question. He is not going to admit anything.

"What's his real name?" Jim asks. "Michael Underwood is a fake name, his identity a lie. We both know it. Who is he really?"

"That, I can't tell you." Jason's expression remains unflinchingly casual.

Jim can see the underlying tension beneath the façade.

"You can't tell me or you won't?"

"You got me there." Jason smiles again. "Both."

Jim looks at Jason pointedly. The man is playing games with him.

"Where is the Jane Doe?" Jim asks.

"You have to ask her that," Jason says with his irritating smile.

"Where is Michael Underwood?"

Jason shrugs. "I have no idea."

"Where is Katherine Kingslow? Is she alive? What did Michael do with her? Did he kill her?"

"You have to ask him that." Jason is staying calm and casual against the onslaught of questions. He isn't worried.

*There's nothing new here. No questions I didn't expect. The detective knows only what he knew before, nothing. He's just trying to goad me into a reaction and I'm not going to give it to him.*

"Where are the bodies, Jason?" Jim demands, his voice low and cold. "Do you know where the bodies are? Where are Jane Doe and Katherine buried?"

Jason just stares back calmly.

*I'm getting nowhere and it's time to play my Ace,* Jim thinks. *I'm bluffing, of course. I have no Ace, just a name. But like a game of poker, it is that seed of doubt that will win or lose your hand; make the other player sweat and fold over what he thinks you have.*

He stares hard into Jason's eyes, his expression serious and his voice low and steady, revealing nothing.

If there is one thing Jim can be accused of, it is having a good poker face.

"Where is Cassie?"

Jason just stares at him, but there it is. Jim catches it, that fleeting shift of the eyes, the almost imperceptible tensing of the muscles, the start of the jaw clenching before Jason can bring his reaction under control.

*Jackpot.*

Jason feels the room jolt like a physical blow with the words. 'Where is Cassie?' His muscles tense, his jaw clenches, and immediately he fights to keep them loose and casual.

*How did he know?*

"Yes, I know about Cassie," Jim says, watching for Jason's reaction. "Michael isn't as clever or as careful as he thinks he is. He let it slip. Either he didn't realize it, or he hoped I didn't notice, but it slipped out."

"Maybe he just threw that out there to mess with you." Jason smiles. "A made up name to put you off."

The underlying tension and the strain in Jason's voice confirms Jim's suspicion.

*Whoever this Cassie is, she is the key to discovering what the relationship between these two men is and that is the key to finding Michael.*

Jim's mind works quickly, juggling the names and the pieces. *Jane Doe, Katherine Kingslow, Cassie. Two of them are complete unknowns. Is Cassie another victim? Is she one of the hundreds of still unidentified bodies still being exhumed from the massive hidden graveyard in the woods? Was she buried somewhere else? I suspect she and Jane Doe could be buried in the same place, somewhere far from the graveyard. Most Likely Katherine is there too.*

*Concentrate on just one name, one name only,* Jim cautions himself. *If I slip, one wrong word could reveal to McAllister that I'm just grasping, hoping to make him reveal something.*

Jim shakes his head slowly at Jason, a slow predatory smile creasing his lips.

"Cassie," his voice is almost a whisper. "I know." He taps his temple for emphasis. "I'm going to find her."

Jason's mind is whirling. *What does he know? Is he just playing me? Plucking a random name for one of the bodies from nowhere to see how I react? Was it the name of one of the many victims buried over the years? I never knew any of their names, except for the ones I killed myself. But why did he use that name of all possible names?*

Jason's confidence is slipping. No, it is shattering. *McNelly knows something. But what? What the hell does he know about Cassie?*

Jim leans forward now, breaking the cardinal rule against putting yourself in harm's way. Jason needs only to lash out quickly enough, wrap his shackled arms around his head and, straddling the table, throttle him. Jim would be defenceless. If his shackles could reach.

Jim is aware of this, but he sees the shock in the other man's eyes, that his mind is busy working over what he may or may not know. He is in total control, the aggressor.

"What do you know McAllister?" he hisses. "What do you have and who do you have it over? How did you get the death penalty dropped? How did you get life changed to a quick stint in the nut house? How are you getting released so fast now?"

He leans back again, conscious of the danger he put himself in, but confident McAllister is too smart to make a move.

"What do you know?" he asks again.

Jason pushes the fear down. He looks at his enemy across the table and smiles casually. It's a forced smile.

"I know where the bodies are," he says, laughing at his own joke.

He winks at Jim.

"Everybody knows where the bodies are now," Jason says.

"You won't stay free for long. I'll be digging into every pile of dirt in your background, every piece of trash you have ever discarded. I will find out where your family went when they fled town so many years ago. They did flee, didn't they? Now why would that be?"

Jim pauses, not quite giving him time to answer. He isn't looking for an answer. "Who is still alive? Your father? Mother? I will track down and talk to everyone who ever knew your family."

Breathing heavier, Jim leans in again.

Jason feels his warmth of his breath on his face, smelling the stale stink of coffee and cigarettes.

"I know you and Michael have a past, that you both are somehow involved with the graves. How far back does it go? Who else is involved? There are more graves than two people could dig in a lifetime.

I will prove that you and Michael are behind the graves and they'll give the both of you the death penalty. But if you help, they'll consider giving you life instead. If you help me, I'll help you. They'll go easier on you."

Jason chuckles. "What makes you think life like this would be preferable to death?" Jason holds up his shackled hands.

"Where are Katherine and Jane Doe? Is either of them still alive? Help me find them." Jim isn't begging.

*I would never stoop to begging one of these animals,* Jim thinks. *I just hope appealing to any shred of decency that exists in him, if there is any at all, might help. If there is even the smallest shred of hope Jane Doe and Katherine are still alive, I have to find them fast.*

"Help me find them before Michael kills them. If they are already dead, then help me bring closure to their families."

"I can't help you," Jason says.

Jim pushes himself up off the chair, frustrated.

"I will find them. Katherine Kingslow. Jane Doe. Cassie. I will find all three and, if they are dead, you and Michael will die with a cocktail of government approved drugs dripping into your arms.

He narrows his eyes meaningfully.

"It isn't always the fast death they promise."

Jason smiles. *McNelly just slipped up.*

Jim turns and bangs on the door, impatiently waiting for the guard to open it. The inmate's smirk is pushing him towards the urge to beat the answers out of him.

Jim pauses in the doorway on the way out, turning back to Jason.

"I will find them." It is a promise to Jason McAllister, to Michael Underwood, and to himself. It is a promise to the three women, Katherine, Jane Doe, and Cassie. It is a promise to his wife.

Jim lets the door bang loudly closed behind him and walks away, lumbering up the hallway away from a killer of unimaginable proportions.

Jason just sits there smiling at the closed door.

"You had me there for a moment," he says, thinking about the panic he felt when the detective mentioned the name Cassie. "You know nothing."

# 3 Looking to the Past

Jim returns to his office on a mission. Beth is at her desk when he walks in and the third desk in the shared office sits conspicuously empty. Detective Michael Underwood's position has not yet been filled.

Beth turns and scowls at Jim.

"Jerry LaCroix stopped in. He's trying for Michael's job. If he gets it, I quit."

Being a civilian employee, she can't simply transfer to another shift or department.

"He won't get it." Jim pauses, reconsidering what he is about to ask, and decides to go ahead. *I'll take any blame.*

"Beth, I need your help."

"With what?"

"Underwood. I need everything you can dig up on him. I don't care how trivial it seems, I want everything. I want a copy of his personnel file, memos and emails, a trace on where the email came from confirming his transfer. It had to come from somewhere outside of the department. I want copies of his phone bills, his rental contract, talk to his landlord and neighbours. I want to know if he so much as borrowed a book from a library and where he bought his groceries. You get what you can and I'll do the legwork and interviews."

"That's a tall order. This is an internal affairs investigation, not ours. We shouldn't be touching it."

"We're investigating the hidden graveyard in the woods beyond the McAllister farm and the two missing women from the McAllister case. He's a suspect like any other."

"If you say so," Beth sighs. "We really need that other detective."

Jim waves it off. "I'll get to it."

"What will you be doing?"

"Reviewing all his case notes and the case notes for the cases for the missing women and the graves, especially for Katherine Kingslow and Jane Doe. And digging up anything I can on Jason McAllister and his family."

"Speaking of digging in the dirt, Lawrence Hawkworth was looking for you."

Beth doesn't like the reporter. Everything about him rubs her wrong, from his buzzard-like appearance to his borderline illegal investigative techniques that too often cross the line, to his tendency to dig up the dirt on people for his stories whether they deserve to have it put out there for the world to see or not.

"I'll track him down later."

Jim digs out a pile of files, plops them on his desk with a loud thud, and settles his large frame into his chair with a grunt to start going through them.

"The answers are hiding somewhere, probably where I would least suspect, and I'm going to find them."

# 4 Lawrence Talks to Cliff Hofstead

Lawrence Hawkworth rubs his eyes wearily. They are dry and aching from the dust and hours spent searching through microfiche of old newspapers in the dingy basement of the newspaper building.

Anything more current is available on computer, but not going back to the 1980's. Attempts to convert the old microfiche to digital images had stalled from lack of manpower committed to the task.

He stretches wearily in the uncomfortable metal folding chair, getting to his feet stiffly to stretch more.

"I learned a bit about the local history of the area and the McAllisters," he says, satisfied, putting away the microfiche he has out.

"With this and my notes from re-interviewing the people I talked to chasing down leads on the serial killer before we identified him, I'm ready to dig deeper. I just have one more person to talk to. Cliff Hofstead. I never got to talk to him before."

He collects his notes and leaves.

Lawrence drives out of town to a farm not far from the city. The farmyard is what he expects. An older farmhouse squats in the yard with a wide parking area next to it. He can see where additions were build on, enlarging the house, despite attempts to make them fit seamlessly with the older home.

The wide expanse of yard is a tidy mix of neatly mowed lawn a large fenced vegetable garden on one side, and the rear yard a barren quarter down gravel appearing almost as concrete. One side has a row of silos and the other a large workshop garage that would fit two large tractors of the sort that would be used for large crop fields and the farmer would have to access by climbing a ladder up to the cab.

Parking near the house, Lawrence goes and knocks on the door.

A man answers.

"Cliff Hofstead?" Lawrence asks.

"Yes sir, what can I do you for?"

Lawrence holds out his large hand, long fingers splayed, for a handshake.

"I'm Lawrence Hawkworth with the InterCity Voice. I'm doing an article on the McAllister Farm and I've been talking to people who have lived in the area when the family still lived at the farm."

Cliff's face puckers into a disapproving look.

*I hope that look doesn't mean he won't talk,* Lawrence thinks.

"I saw the Hofstead name on the farm on the current tax rolls and going quite a way back. Your family has been farming here a while?"

"We've been raising cattle for a while. The farm has been in the family a few generations," Cliff says. "My grandfather left it to my father and I inherited it from him."

"So, your family is still raising cattle here."

"Yes sir."

"You grew up here?" Lawrence asks. "You must have gone to school with Jason McAllister. What do you know about him as a boy, and his family?"

"I was older than the McAllister kid," Cliff says. "There was only the one school, so yeah; we went to the same school. I didn't hang out with Jason. Barely knew him to say hi and I wouldn't have bothered even if the McAllisters did associate with anyone outside their family. Those kids weren't in school half the time anyway; Jason even less than his sister."

"What can you tell me about the McAllisters and the rumours around them back then?"

"They kept to themselves; didn't go to church or anything in town. Hardly ever saw the kids' mom. Everybody figured they weren't allowed to have friends or talk to anyone. Their old man was strange that way.

I heard the rumours about the McAllister family. Everyone who grew up in the area in that generation heard the stories. They'd sooner shoot you than talk to you if you step on their property. They've always been odd. Funny, they've been here more generations than anyone else, but they've always been more outsider than anyone who moved in new. It's no wonder everyone thought

William McAllister had to be behind girls disappearing and showing up dead."

"Do you think he was behind it?"

"I did. I guess not. The sheriff arrested someone else for it and he went to prison. That didn't stop the town from blaming William McAllister. A bunch of them even went to the farm to take matters into their own hands when the sheriff didn't seem to be doing anything about it."

"A lynch mob?" Lawrence almost chuckles. "That sounds so old West."

That's what it felt like back then. The older generation, my generations' parents, they know more."

"That's proving a little harder to find," Lawrence says. "I tracked down some people who lived here then. A lot of the closer farms are gone now, part of the city."

Cliff nods. "The town exploded seemingly overnight and was re-branded as a small city some years back. The police force expanded to more than a sheriff with a few men working out of a single building into a municipal force with a couple of stations. The old tags like Sherriff were dropped, the officers' titles changed to be in line with other urban municipal forces. Can't help but think it still feels like a small town, though."

"Do you know where I can find some of these older people?"

"The old hardware store is still around and it's still the hangout for the old farmers and town men who were around when the building boom started."

"Is there anything else you remember?"

"Amy Dodds."

Lawrence looks at him questioningly.

"She was a kid Jason's age. She went missing around the time of the others. The only kid too. Amy was never found."

Cliff shrugs. "Again, I don't know a lot. Didn't really pay much attention. I had other interests back then. The older generation would know more."

"Where do I find this old hardware store?"

Cliff gives him directions and Lawrence is on his way back to his office.

# 5 Lawrence

Lawrence shifts in his chair and looks again at the phone on his desk, waiting impatiently for Jim McNelly to call him back.

*The discovery months ago of the mass graveyard in the woods exploded on the news wires in a media frenzy immediately after I put up that first report about it,* he thinks.

For that brief moment, Lawrence had thrilled with basking in the glory that he had the lead on it, had been the one to break the story of the century. But, like all big stories, the momentum quickly died with nothing new to report and the story sank to the dark underbelly of the media world where common everyday atrocities steep quietly without breaking to the public while newer and flashier stories make the headlines.

*It's all about selling the news. Shock and awe sells, and the more exciting feel good stories. Even the same old political stories tossed out there with new shocking headlines sells. Depressing stories without the thrill of new shocks only depress the readers. They don't sell papers or advertising slots.*

*My editor told me to leave it alone, but I can't.*

*No one doubts there is something big behind the graves. They just doubt anyone will find out what it is soon enough to keep anyone interested in the story.*

*I will find it.*

*Somehow, the history of the McAllister Family and their farm holds the secret and Michael Underwood is somehow connected to both the farm and to Jason McAllister. I just have to find that missing link.*

Frustrated with waiting for McNelly's call, Lawrence pushes his chair away from his desk and gets up. He grabs his leather case with all his files and notes on the McAllisters and the town history and heads for the exit.

He is ducking past his editor's office when his editor, Paul Giovanni, calls out, waving him back. "Lawrence, get in here."

Lawrence thinks about not stopping, just pretending he didn't hear.

"I know you heard me," Paul calls.

Lawrence turns, caught, and stops in his boss's doorway.

"You aren't wasting time on that graveyard thing are you?" Paul warns.

"No, absolutely not."

"Or the Jason McAllister thing?" Paul eyes him warily.

*I have no doubts Hawkworth is doing exactly what I told him not to do. The man is a brilliant reporter, but he is an odd bird too and never plays by anyone's rules. I would have fired him years ago if he wasn't such a good reporter.*

"No sir," Lawrence smirks. He can't help it, the grin just came out. It's a nervous response to knowing he is doing something his boss had expressly forbidden. He isn't lying, of course. You only waste your time if you chase down a story that doesn't exist, and he knows the story behind the graves and the McAllisters is just waiting to be uncovered.

"Good," Paul says. "I have a couple stories I want you to work on. I sent them to your phone."

Lawrence's blank look says it all.

"You forgot your phone." Paul is bordering on exasperated. They are probably one of the last newspapers to equip their reporters with smart phones, except maybe the small town rags. Hawkworth is the only one of his reporters who can't seem to get on board with it.

"Go get it and don't lose it," Paul huffs.

Lawrence nods and ducks out of his office, returning to his desk. The phone is in the third drawer he checks. He tries turning it on and nothing happens.

"Must be dead," he shrugs.

Lashaya snickers from the next desk. "You have to hold the button down for a few," she says, teasing.

Lawrence smiles and nods. He knows he is the joke around the news office over his failure to learn how to use the phone.

Holding the button down, he waits the interminably long few seconds it takes for it to turn on and boot up. Finally, it blips at him.

He glances at the screen, sees the number 56 on the mailbox and 25 on the text box, 34 on the little phone for missed calls, and shoves it into his pocket without checking any of the messages.

He hurries out of the office before his editor can stop him again.

"I hope the old regulars are hanging around that old hardware store."

Lawrence is driving to the old part of the small city where the hardware store is when the sudden rude and unexpected intrusion of his phone ringing makes him almost jump.

With his focus half on the road, Lawrence fumbles for the phone, finds it, fumbles again for the answer button, and almost drops it before finally holding it to his ear.

"Hawkworth, InterCity Voice. You bury 'em, I dig 'em up."

It's his own private joke, that no matter how hard you bury the bodies or evidence, he'll find it, dig it up, and write about it.

"Lawrence, Jim here, what do you want?" McNelly's voice sounds like he is trapped somewhere in a deep hole far away.

"Jim, I'm on my way to talk to some old-timers at the old hardware store. I'm digging into the McAllister family's past. Do you want to come?"

"I can't make it there now," McNelly says. "I'm on my own thing right now. Meet me at the pub tonight."

"All right, but you don't know what you are missing."

"Yeah, a bunch of old men shooting the shit over the old days." McNelly laughs. "I can miss it."

"Tonight then." Lawrence fumbles for the button to disconnect the call, the car swerving as he takes his attention off the road and narrowly misses taking out the side mirror on a parked car. He drops the phone on the passenger seat and focuses on the road again, searching street signs.

When he finds the place, he parks and hesitates before getting out. This is the oldest part of town. Some of the buildings received facelifts over the years, but the predominant architecture here is from the nineteen-sixties and older. The buildings are all small and rundown, the odd newer building making a mockery of its neighbours with its glass walls and bright neon glowing signage.

The front of the hardware store is lined with battered old pickup trucks. He gets out and heads for the door to the hardware store.

The paint is peeling on the outside, the steps are cracked and sagging to one side, and the door looks like it had been yanked from the nineteen-fifties.

"This place must have been old in its prime."

From the outside, the building belongs in a small town in another era.

He pushes the door open with a creak of its hinges, an old-style spring-loaded closure pushing back against him. The old bell over the door jangles sickly.

Lawrence steps inside and looks around, the bell jangling again as he lets the door close behind him. He just stepped through a time warp back to the past.

Everything about the place is stuck in the past, from the old worn wooden floor to the old worn wooden counter. The shelves, clutter of old-style general use and household products piled and hanging everywhere, and old signage meant to give the store a rustic look, all adds to the dated feel.

The clincher is the row of stools pulled up to the L-shaped counter where wrinkled prune-like faces, skin yellowed and leathery from a lifetime in the sun and wind and cigarette smoke, stare in mute curiosity at the odd tall buzzard-like man who must have walked in by mistake.

The elderly clerk standing behind the counter leans against the counter. The dated but modern by comparison cash register is the one thing that doesn't fit with the rest of the picture.

Lawrence studies the men out of the corner of his eye like escaped zoo animals that must be approached carefully. Not dangerous animals, mind you, more of the slow-moving sloth variety that might skitter away if startled. He wanders idly, pretending to be interested in what might be on the shelves.

He can feel their stares on him.

Finally, Lawrence picks up a strange looking object, its purpose and use a mystery to him, and goes to the cash register.

"Found what you are looking for?" the old man behind the register asks with a crooked half smile.

"Yes, I think so." Lawrence puts the object down on the counter between them.

The old men at the counter all snicker.

"Yup, I think he got what he came for," one of them says.

"You even know what that's used for?" the clerk asks with an amused grin.

Lawrence looks at him with a blank expression, trying to come up with his best guess.

"You ever even been on a farm?" one of the men teases.

"No." Lawrence turns to him. He looks back down at the object, trying to figure out what use it could possibly have.

The old men just laugh harder at his expense, their shoulders shaking.

"Okay, I give up," Lawrence finally cedes. "I don't know what this thing is."

He picks it up and holds it in front of his face, inspecting it. "What's it for?"

The old men laugh so hard that Lawrence half expects them to fall off their chairs.

He looks at them quizzically.

One raises his fist in a squeezing gesture and the others break into a fresh fit, laughing so hard that one has to wipe a tear from his eye.

"It's a ball crusher," one of the men laughs as the clerk makes a slicing and squeezing motion at his genitals.

"Castration," the clerk laughs, "crushes the bull's balls." Emphasizing their great size, he mimics the treacherous act committed against the bulls' most private of parts with his hands before Lawrence's face as he says this.

Lawrence pales and feels sick. He puts the offending object down in a hurry, feeling the taint of its gross purpose forever staining his hands. He has to wipe his hands on his pants as if they have somehow been dirtied.

The old farmers roar with laughter.

Lawrence suspects he may never know the truth of the object's real purpose, but now that they had their fun at his expense it is time to get down to the real reason he is there.

He moves away from the old-style hand juicer, avoiding looking at it again.

Lawrence tries to look properly sheepish, but it's a look he just can't pull off with his skinny face and long buzzard beak-like nose.

"You got me," he chuckles. "I didn't really come here for that thing. I came to talk. I want to ask you a few questions."

They look at him with a mix of curiosity and suspicion.

"Cliff Hofstead sent me."

The announcement is met with a round of "Ah, Old Hofstead's boy," "How's the kid doing?" and, a debate as to just when old man Hofstead passed on.

The "kid" Cliff Hofstead is no kid at sixty-five years old.

"So what do you want?" the clerk finally asks.

Lawrence's expression sobers up and he turns to them, trying to be casual and friendly.

"I want to know about the McAllisters."

The name drops like a stink bomb; sobering up the old men, drying out their tears of laughter, and making them scowl.

One of them twists his face up into a disgusted pucker and is about to spit his distaste on the floor, but is stopped by a look from the clerk.

"Don't you go spitting on my floor," he warns.

"What do you want with the McAllisters?" one of the other men asks suspiciously.

"I want to know everything about them." Lawrence looks at him hopefully. "I'm investigating Jason McAllister's background."

"Are you a cop or something?" one of them snorts.

"They say that boy was behind all those bodies found in the woods past the old McAllister place."

"Humph, they're chasing down the wrong McAllister," the one who almost spat on the floor complains. "That boy was never nothing but a punk kid. It's the old man they should be after, William McAllister, that's who had to have buried all those bodies up there. The whole bloody clan of them McAllisters going all the way back are suspicious, if you ask me."

"Are you a cop?" the clerk repeats the other man's question, staring Lawrence down as if daring him to say yes. "They already tried to lock the McAllister boy up, but it didn't do any good. They say he kidnapped and murdered those women. Heard he's getting off scot free, moving him to the nut house. He won't even be getting any prison time."

"Scot free," one of the old men chuckled. "Free as a Scotsman and just as guilty."

The old man sitting next to him jabs him in the ribs with an elbow, scowling, the old Scotsman not finding the joke very funny.

It's a private matter between the two, and a long-standing sore spot.

"I'm not a cop," Lawrence confesses. His lips turn up into a sly grin and he leans forward conspiratorially. "Worse, I'm a reporter."

The old men look at him with an odd look until recognition dawns on one of their faces.

"Hey, I know you!" he declares. "You're that reporter from The Voice!"

The others look at him with confusion.

"You know who he is," the old farmer insists, turning to Lawrence eagerly. "You got that Durnst guy convicted for killing that kid! He got off on all these burglaries and assaults and finally on killing this teenaged kid. Said it was self defence when he shot the kid. You dug up shit that got that bastard put away."

The other old men stare at Lawrence with a new interest.

"You are going to get that Jason McAllister put away too, aren't you?" The old man who a moment ago almost literally spat out his distaste at the lanky man before him is now staring at him in awe.

"I'm going to try." Lawrence is pleased that he has won these old men over, even if it was initially at the expense of his wounded pride.

"You should get that William McAllister too," the old Scotsman mutters, shaking his head. "I just know he got off on a lot of bad stuff; always secretive those McAllisters. Didn't associate with anyone or let anyone on their property."

"So, what do you know about the McAllisters and their farm?" Lawrence asks.

The clerk shuffles out from behind the counter, waving him to follow.

"Let me show you something."

Lawrence follows, the other old men shuffling along behind them. They crowd into a little office where the clerk proudly displays an old aerial photography map that covers much of one wall.

"Not what it was anymore is it?" he mutters as they all study the map that all of them except Lawrence saw many times before.

The aerial photograph is of a small town surrounded by farms and a few scattered unidentifiable buildings. It's this same town before the construction boom made it quickly quadruple in size, turning it into a small city.

"This is us here, the hardware store. This is the old McCreary place. This is the Hofstead place." He goes through more names, pointing out the various farms surrounding the town.

His finger settles on one place towards the edge of the map and stays there after tapping it a few times with a finality weighted down with a heavy heart.

"The old McAllister place."

"It looks further on the map than it seems." Lawrence absorbs it all, taking in the map as a whole and mentally comparing it to what he knows of the area.

"That's because all this area here is now city." The clerk motions to the area between them and the McAllister Farm that the map shows as mostly fields of farmland.

"It's hard to believe this used to be just a small town with only a couple of businesses," Lawrence says.

"It's a small city now," the clerk shrugs. "When the building boom hit, it just kind of kept going. A lot of these farms aren't there anymore. Got eaten up by the developers and split up into housing lots." He sounds regretful, like something that mattered had somehow been lost when nobody was looking.

"So, you want to know about the McAllisters," one of the old men says, turning to Lawrence.

"Everything you can tell me," Lawrence smiles, his lips cracking into a predatory grin.

# 6 Peabody's

Jim is sitting in Peabody's, the beer on the badly used round table before him staring back at him. The jar of questionable pickled eggs on the bar across the way mocks his roiling gut as the acid in his stomach is pushed up in a wave of heartburn.

"Hours spent going through files and I found nothing", he laments quietly. "Beth, didn't find anything either, except . . .."

He shakes his head.

"How she did the impossible, I don't know. Only Beth could get her hands on a copy of the signed transfer for Underwood. It all looks legitimate. Even the names and signatures are what they should be."

Jim scowls at his beer.

"I was counting on it proving to be a fake transfer request. How did he do it? How did Underwood fake his way into the police department and get transferred to my unit? Why?"

Lawrence walks in. He looks around, gets his bearings, and spots Jim. He heads over.

"Jim," he says as he sits down.

"Lawrence." Jim reaches for and takes a swig of his beer.

The waitress spots Lawrence and starts in their direction. He signals to her, pointing at Jim and himself, and she turns around, heading back towards the bar. She knows what he wants.

"Find anything good?" Lawrence asks.

"Can't say, police stuff," Jim mutters around the beer glass at his lips. "You?"

"Can't say, confidential informant."

Lawrence smiles and nods at the waitress as she arrives and sets down their drinks. He watches her walk away to stalk other customers to serve.

Formalities out of the way, they get down to business.

"This little town sure grew fast," Lawrence says. "I saw an aerial photo today of what it used to be. I think we're sitting in a pig farm right now."

"What did the old goats have to say?" Jim asks, pun fully intended.

Lawrence grimaces at the bad joke.

"They had a lot to say about Jason McAllister and his family. Unfortunately, they were long on talk and short on facts. But that's gossip, the truth behind the truth, just without the facts."

Jim snorts. Gossip is anything but truthful. He can't deny, though, that too often there is that grain of truth behind the gossip. Gossip is often the only lead he has to go on. From that, he has to ferret out what is real from what is made up, but it usually eventually leads to facts and evidence after sorting out the lies.

"The old farmers think McAllister senior is the one behind the graves in the woods," Lawrence says.

"Is the old man even still alive?" Jim asks. "They might be right; partially right. The graves go back further than William McAllister's lifetime. Odds are Jason McAllister learned from someone, and that person could well have been his own father.

"I don't know." Lawrence takes a sip of his drink, grimacing. "There were some young women murdered when the McAllisters lived here when Jason was just a kid, some that were never found, and a kid vanished. William McAllister was the only suspect as far as the town folks were concerned. The whole community decided he was guilty.

Only the Sheriff wasn't convinced. They called him that back then when it was just a couple guys working out of a small office. Everyone knew William McAllister was guilty except the sheriff." He looks down at his notes, "One Sheriff Rick Dalton, refused to arrest him.

That's when some of the people around town decided to take matters into their own hands. Things got a bit crazy. The whole town had William McAllister convicted without a trial and a group showed up at the McAllister farm intent on tearing the place apart. They were determined they would find the bodies of the missing girls there or something that would put McAllister away."

"A lynch mob," Jim mutters, "sounds like a scene out of a bad western."

"McAllister took off with his family then. Just drove off and vanished. They were run out of town."

"Or running from the law. So, he got away with murder." Jim shakes his head.

"I'm not so sure. The old men at the lumber store think so. They were insistent William McAllister was guilty of the killings happening in the area at the time. At the same time the McAllisters vanished, the sheriff arrested someone else for the murders. They never got him on the child that vanished, but the murders were solved."

"But the old men don't agree."

Lawrence shakes his head. "They still think William McAllister did it, even though someone else was convicted."

Jim nods. "With what we know now about Jason McAllister, I'm not surprised. I remember some of these unsolved cases. Local cases of unsolved murders and missing persons were the first thing I checked when we discovered the graves in the woods.

There were a few women that were never found. Those are still unsolved missing cases. A child too, Dodds I believe the name was."

"That's the girl the old men said was never found," Hawkworth says. "Amy Dodds. Twelve years old. Apparently, Jason McAllister had a thing for her. They were the same age."

He pauses to swallow some of his drink, grimacing at the burn and unpleasant taste of the bourbon.

Jim files this piece of information.

"This is an interesting coincidence. If Jason McAllister or his father had anything to do with the Dodds girl's disappearance, it might just be Jason's first introduction to murder. Thrown out there at the right time, this might put McAllister off and make him slip up."

"The oddest part is there have been just these couple of blips," Jim adds. "A rash of kidnappings and killings over a very short period of time back then; and then again now. Otherwise, this is the safest place around because nobody goes missing under suspicious circumstances."

"I have more locals to interview," Lawrence says. "I'm betting there is still someone alive who knows something we don't already know about the McAllister family history."

"Maybe someone will know where the McAllisters went," Jim says. "I don't think Jason McAllister is going to cooperate and tell us."

"I doubt it. Sounds like the McAllisters really kept to themselves. I think there will be a better chance of finding where they went by searching for anything that could lead to them everywhere but here."

"That's a pretty big area to search," Jim snorts. "Just search the world except this one place."

"People will surprise you with the trail they leave behind without knowing it," Lawrence says with a sly grin. "Whatever they did, if they were involved with the bodies buried in the woods, it all centers right here. Work outward from the center and sooner or later something will stand out."

"You do have a knack for finding things nobody wants found, no matter how obscure or hidden."

"People aren't very good at hiding things," Lawrence smiles wryly. "Like your boys trying to keep the location of the graveyard in the woods secret."

He chuckles. "It wasn't exactly hard to find. All anyone had to do was drive up the road past the turnoff to the McAllister farm and watch for cars and flashing lights."

"Yeah, well, nobody really went up there."

"There must be a lot of gawkers up there now. Our generation never even heard of the McAllisters until the Jason McAllister trial. I still don't get why nobody ever went up that way."

"I guess nobody thought of it. A casual hiker could easily get lost up there. There are no trails."

Jim downs his beer and looks sadly at the empty glass.

"She's already gone through it a few times, but I'll get Beth running everything she can on the name McAllister again. With luck she'll find something, anything, a driver's license or vehicle registration. Maybe even a criminal record," Jim says.

He looks at Lawrence with a serious look.

"You were right. McAllister is being cut loose." His voice is heavy. "The judge is cutting him loose pending the outcome of an appeal."

"That man has something on someone important, doesn't he?" Lawrence shakes his head in disbelief.

"If there are any more bodies to be found, if anyone knows where the bodies are, it's him. This might be a good thing," Jim says. "I'm going to keep a very close eye on him. If that bastard so much as sneezes wrong, I'm going to know about it."

Lawrence nods. "Chances are if he has any family he'll try to contact them. Then we know where he's been."

"He might contact Michael," Jim says, an edge of disgust in his voice at the feel of the name on his tongue.

Lawrence raises an eyebrow at this. "Why do you think so?"

"I let a few things slip. I told him Michael wasn't as smart at keeping things to himself as he thought. I also let on I know about the three missing women associated with the two of them."

"Three? There are only two, Katherine Kingslow and the Jane Doe."

"I've got a name of a third, Cassie. No last name."

"Who is that?" Lawrence is already chewing on the name in his mind.

"Hell if I know, but I'm going to find out."

# 7 It's A Beautiful Day to Be Free

"It's a beautiful day to be free," Jason McAllister says as he is escorted down the hallway of the courthouse in cuffs and chains.

His armed escort only scowls without looking at him, one on each side, and keeps going down the hall.

They shepherd him into the courtroom and to the prisoner's box, which isn't really a box at all. It's just a chair a few feet out of reach of the table where his lawyer sits waiting.

The guards seat him and stand to each side, ready to take him down if he so much as breathes funny.

The nearly empty courtroom is anticlimactic for the seriousness of the proceeding. In attendance are Jason McAllister, the two officers escorting him, two more guarding the door they entered, and another pair standing at the door the judge will enter by. The court stenographer sits at her little table pretending to ignore McAllister even as she can't stop sneaking peaks at the infamous killer. His lawyer nods at him with a look that is not entirely confident, and the prosecution sits smugly refusing to acknowledge his presence.

A few witnesses sit scattered in the mostly empty gallery in ones and twos, diehards who have little better to do than haunt the courtrooms to feed some strange need to be involved in the inner workings of the court system. Court groupies, they are mockingly called.

They have no idea what they are about to witness, or even what the case about to be presided over is about.

The proceeding had been kept secret, the court docket giving little clue what is booked in the courtroom at that time. The news will break later after the shocked witnesses spread the news.

A few of the witnesses perk up, recognizing Jason.

The guards at the judge's door snap to attention and the one on the right commands them all to rise. A heartbeat later, a judge in his long judicial robe enters regally.

He takes his time taking his position and settling himself before acknowledging the courtroom and allowing them to sit and the proceedings to start.

He surveys the nearly empty courtroom with tired eyes. He slept little in the preceding nights. What he is about to do weighs heavily on his conscience and in his heart.

*When I am done, I have a bottle of vodka waiting in the desk drawer in my chamber behind me.*

*When I finish that, I have a bottle of port waiting for me in my desk drawer in my home office. Next to that bottle is a loaded revolver. If the drive home doesn't kill me, I will empty first the bottle of port, and then the revolver.*

*I am about to do the unimaginable. This is not my choice. I was ordered to do it. The hollow pounding of my gavel echoing through the courtroom closing the proceeding I am about to start will signal the end of my career.*

*I won't bother with a note. There is no need. As soon as the news agencies start to run with this, there will be no wondering why. After decades of being married more to my job than my wife, affairs, and the cold indifference that has become my childless marriage over the past twenty years, it seems pointless to bother saying goodbye now.*

He bangs his gavel and the sound echoes in the courtroom, bringing the small shuffling sounds to silence and marking the beginning of his end.

"Be seated," he commands the room.

Half an hour later the boom of the gavel echoes again through the room to the shocked gasps and outcries of the few witnesses in the public seating and Jason McAllister smiles.

An hour after that Jason McAllister is walking down the courthouse steps looking up at the bright sunshine, smiling, a free man.

"Yes, it is a beautiful day to be free," Jason says.

# Part Two

# Talking to One's Self

# 8 Talking to Crazy

Kathy Kingslow looks out at Michael through the glass patio door. He is in the backyard, sitting in a partially broken lawn chair that was left behind by some previous tenant, drinking a beer, his back to the house. Scattered empty beer cans litter the ground around him.

The sight sends the stiffness of dread through her, the memory of her ex-boyfriend Ronnie's drunken violence haunting her. She knows Michael isn't drunk. The empty cans have collected over the past few days.

Something about the rundown cheap rental house seems to suck the will out of them both, with it the will to pick up after themselves. The house is as depressing as the neighbourhood is and the clutter of empty cans and other trash is beginning to pile up.

The yard is not large, carpeted with a mix of half dead grass and bald patches and partially shaded by a large sickly looking tree. The cracked and peeling fence is long past the point of needing repairs and needs to be torn down and rebuilt. A few sections were repaired at one point by stapling haphazardly stretched out chicken wire to the boards that look like they had been partially consumed by either termites or a rather angry large squirrel.

Michael puts his beer down on the ground next to the chair, talking to himself again. Not really to himself, but rather talking to someone who is not there.

It makes Kathy feel sick in the way that fear of a danger you cannot hope to escape makes you feel sick, that strength sapping, soul draining kind of sick feeling.

"The first time I noticed it was outside the prison where he visited Jason McAllister before we left. He looked down and reached out as if to take the hand of someone who was not there and said something.

"Everything is fine," he said to me. "Let's go."

But then he said something else. He looked down, reaching out, and said "Everything's going to be just fine Cassie, you'll see."

It wasn't me he was talking to. He tried to cover it up, pretend it was me, but I saw. I knew.

I let it slide; trying to convince myself that I only imagined it. I can't pretend anymore.

Michael tries to hide it, but he is talking to this imaginary person more and more. He is being secretive too, acting like he is hiding something."

She can't say the next thought out loud.

*I know about the other women, the women he stalked, kidnapped, and murdered all in the search for her.* Even thinking it, she puts that special emphasis on 'her'. She is another woman and a special kind of threat to Michael and herself.

*I finally understand who she is; the woman Michael was so obsessed with finding. She was his younger sister who died as a child. At least, Michael said he believed she died back then, but he could not let go of his guilt and needed her to be alive, to be able to protect her and keep her safe. He was driven to find her even though everything he knew told him she was long gone.*

*But, then it turned out that she was not dead. He found her. Jane Doe, they called her. His sister, Cassie.*

*Now Cassie is probably dead for real, taken, Michael is sure, by Jason McAllister. I still don't know who Jason McAllister is to Michael. I only know that he's a killer.*

"Michael is going crazy," Kathy whispers. "If he isn't, then I am. Or his crazy is just going to drive me crazy. Either way, it's not good."

Her thoughts turn back to the life she now finds herself trapped in. She feels exactly that, trapped.

*It's like the world suddenly snapped shut on me and I'm stuck here all alone with no escape. No one knows I'm here. Just like the farmhouse basement.*

*We kept our first names after we left. Michael said they are common enough first names. But we had to take on new last names, new identities.*

*We are getting married soon, after we move again, and Michael says we have to change our names again before the wedding. He knows a guy who can get us legitimate identification, even set up officially in the government's computers. We will be real people again; real people with fake pasts. New schools, new birth places, and new birth parents.*

The thought of getting married should warm her, but it doesn't.

Michael doesn't even know who his birth parents are, so it doesn't matter to him. But, for Kathy it is a sharp pain in her heart to know she can never contact her mother again. Her mother will never know if she is alive and she will not be able to invite her to their wedding.

She has to push these thoughts away. They are too depressing.

Kathy turns her attention to Michael again, watching him talk to nobody.

It feels like watching a crash about to happen that you can't stop. The tightness of stress fills her until she feels it will snap her in half.

Michael starts turning around in his seat and she quickly slips out of sight past the edge of the patio door.

He looks at the house. He has that vague feeling of being watched. No one is there.

Michael turns his back to the house again, facing straight ahead. Cassie stares up at him, her expression serious. She is angry with him. Little Cassie, who is so pretty even when she is so angry, still the little girl after all these years.

Kathy peeks out again to see Michael turned away and talking again.

A shiver shudders down her spine and she suddenly feels an uneasy feeling rush through her.

*A premonition? That's silly, I don't believe in nonsense like that.*

She turns away, going into the kitchen. She can't watch any longer.

Michael pleads with Cassie to understand.

"I did my best to protect you, I really did. There was only so much I could do."

"But you didn't protect me, did you?" Cassie accuses. "You didn't protect me ever, David."

"Don't call me that," Michael says defensively.

"You let him take us David. You let him take us and kill our mother. You let him keep us and hit us."

"Don't call me David," Michael repeats. "That's the name he gave me."

He can taste the resentment of the name 'David' on his tongue as he says it.

"You ran away and left me behind," Cassie accuses. "You left me alone with him."

"No I didn't," Michael says. "You are lying now. You were already gone when I ran away. You were the one who left me alone with him."

"You made me go, David. They were not very nice people who took me in after. I went to foster homes. You know all about foster homes, don't you David? You know because you knew lots of runaway kids from foster homes. You heard the stories about what they do to kids in foster homes."

"No," Michael shakes his head. He is starting to feel sick. He doesn't like this conversation. "You didn't go to foster homes. You were adopted. You found a good family who took care of you."

"That is what you want to believe. I went to foster homes first, before I finally got adopted."

She looks down at her feet sadly, scuffing the dirt with a toe.

"They were not very nice people, any of them. I was better off with him."

"No, don't say that," Michael whines. He is starting to sound like a little boy. He feels like a little boy, overwhelmed with a world that is so much bigger than him.

Cassie looks up at him again, her eyes burning with resentment.

"Then you let him take me again. You were supposed to protect me. Always, you promised to protect me always."

"No, you were gone," Michael moans in despair. "You ran away. I found you. After years of searching, I finally found you. And you ran away from me. He couldn't have taken you again. You ran away."

"You know he did, David."

"Stop calling me David!" Michael snarls. "That is not my name!"

"Then who are you, David?" she asks, now mocking him. "Michael Underwood? Michael Ritchot? How many names have you had? Do you even know your real name? Do you even remember? David McAllister. That is who you really are. It doesn't matter that is not the name you were born with. You are a McAllister, just like him. He raised you to be just like him."

"No!" Michael yells, half standing up. He makes himself settle back into the chair.

Kathy hears Michael yell from inside the house and pushes away the urge to go see what is happening.

*Don't torture yourself by looking.*

"I am nothing like him," Michael hisses angrily, leaning forward threateningly.

"Day-vid," Cassie taunts in a sing-song voice, dragging out the sound. "Day-vid, Day-vid, Day-vid."

Michael lunges up from his chair, grabbing the chair in a fit of rage, the world around him fading, being pushed away to a distant place and replaced with the black fog of anger. He swings the chair viciously at Cassie and smashes it against the ground.

"You hurt me David." But it isn't Cassie's voice now. The voice is not that of a small child.

Michael spins to face Jane Doe and blanches. His mind compartmentalized his sister, needing to separate the two of her into separate people. Cassie is the little girl, the innocent he needed to protect. Jane Doe is the woman, the stranger Cassie became, the woman who fought against him and ran away.

"You took me and you hurt me David," Jane says, her calm voice slicing through his heart in a way anger never could. "You hurt me and locked me in the cellar and you killed me. You were supposed to protect me David."

"No!" Michael cries. "I did not kill you. You are still alive. I know it and I will find you. Wherever you are, whatever he did with you, I am going to find you."

"No you won't, David." She coos at him. "You are bad. You are very bad. You were bad as a boy and you are bad now. I don't want you to find me."

Michael is stunned. *How can she not want me to find her? I have to keep her safe so the bad thing can't happen to her.*

"I will find you, I promise," he whispers. "I will keep you safe from him."

"Who will keep me safe from you, David?" she asks. "Who will keep me safe from David McAllister?"

"Stop calling me that," he growls. "I am not David. I am Michael. Michael."

He blinks. Jane Doe is suddenly gone. He turns in confusion.

Cassie is standing behind him, watching him.

"Cassie," he begs.

"You hurt me David," she says quietly, her voice small. "You tried to kill me."

"No," he says hoarsely.

The flutter of a curtain in the window of the house next door catches his attention. He sees it out of the corner of his eye. Michael looks and the curtain is still, but he knows it moved. The neighbour next door is spying on him.

With a sinking in his stomach, Michael realizes that he had been yelling. He groans.

He goes into the house looking for Kathy.

Kathy is trying to make herself busy tidying up, although she finds the task almost impossible to force on herself, the heavy weight of unhappiness dragging her down.

"We have to go soon," Michael says. "We have to move on, find a new place. We have to keep moving. Just for a little while."

Kathy stops tidying, looking at him.

"That's good. I don't like this house." She doesn't tell him she is embarrassed and uncomfortable knowing that the neighbours see him talking to nobody in the back yard, that they know just as she does that he is crazy. Something is broken inside him and it is making him behave in ways that scare her.

She won't leave him. She still harbours that fear inside that she just can't let go. She knows Ronnie is dead, but that nagging doubt keeps pushing at her. What if he isn't? What if Ronnie is somehow alive and comes after her?

Besides, Michael would never hurt her. He will hurt others, but never her. He even killed Ronnie so that he could never hurt her again.

# 9 A New Home, For Now

Without any fanfare, Jason McAllister is dropped off at his new home by his social worker. He was released after a few hours of assessment in the mental institution. That was only a formality.

Jason is an outpatient, living on his own under a strict curfew and regular checks with his social worker. Normally, this would have been the final step after years of therapy in the institution followed by a period of time living in a halfway house meant to help the mentally ill learn to live on their own.

Jason has been granted his freedom in unprecedented time, almost freedom. They will be watching.

He gets out of the car with the small bag that contains his worldly possessions, and looks up at the house.

The car drives away without a wave goodbye from either him or the driver.

It is a two-story rectangular house with a narrow front, stretching long towards the back of the narrow lot. The front door is on one side of a not-so-large living room picture window. The house sports a tacky paint job that needed to be scraped off and re-painted at least ten years ago, and an over-grown lawn that is more weeds than grass. A rusting motor-less grass cutter that works by the wheels turning the blades leans against the fence. The blades look too dull and eaten by rust to cut grass.

The little porch sags and the railing looks like it will collapse if anyone leans on it. The windows are grimy and a second floor window has a crack running across it that would have glinted in the sunlight if it were not so dirty.

The little white picket fence surrounding the yard is missing a few boards. A few more are hanging half off and leaning drunkenly. The gate is nowhere to be seen, rusting hinges half peeled away and bent, probably from when the gate had been savagely torn off.

The low strains of country music can be heard coming from one of the rooms inside the house.

"Home sweet home," Jason says with a grim smile.

He approaches the house and mounts the wooden stairs. Looking down a hole in the porch, he can see the old concrete steps that came with the house originally. The door sticks and, for a moment, he worries it is locked. His social worker told him the landlord said it is supposed to be kept locked but he would leave it open for him.

Jason pushes harder on the door and it pops open with a groan of the swollen wood doorframe releasing the door.

The inside is dingy and full of shadows and an unpleasant smell. The decor is as outdated as the house is neglected.

He is in a narrow entrance. Directly ahead is a narrow staircase pressed against a wall that would have been better suited to allowing a window to let some light inside. Next to the staircase is a short hallway. To his right a double-width doorway opens to a living room with furniture that looks like it had been pulled out of someone's trash.

A dead plant sits forlornly on top of an old tube television that he suspects probably quit working in the 1970's, and drapes that look like they housed a multitude of moths over the decades hang in all their ugly glory from a slightly bent curtain rod in front of the window. Out-dated chairs and tables are barely visible.

The room is sparsely furnished, but cluttered with garbage, dirty dishes, and discarded clothing, making him suspect someone is living in that room.

Jason moves past the living room, deeper into the house, and as he does the unpleasant smell grows stronger.

Past the living room, a door opens to one of two communal bathrooms. He peeks in and backs away with revulsion. The grout between the tub tiles is cracked and falling away in chunks, allowing the mould to flourish in the wall behind the yellow-green tiles that remind him of some rather nasty vomit. Some of the tiles are cracked. The sink is stained orange and a steady drip from the faucet is already pressing on his nerves.

Beyond the bathroom is the kitchen. The cupboards and counters look like they have never been upgraded or replaced, and the fridge and stove are so old he wonders if they work. One cupboard is missing a door. Multiple holes are chewed into the wood where it had apparently been re-screwed on a few times before someone gave up on it completely.

Jason flips the light switch on and catches the quick scurry of a cockroach fleeing the light.

The table is scarred with childish attempts at crude artwork scratched into the surface with various utensils, and the legs are misshapen and bent. The one chair that has not been stolen has an ugly orange and yellow flowered vinyl seat from the thirties that is split wide open down the middle. The grey stuffing is spilling out and missing in the middle, revealing the rough wood beneath that would probably leave a splinter in the seat of anyone who sits on it.

On the wall, which is the backside of the stairs leading up, is a door that presumably leads to the basement. The door is padlocked and has a dark stain splattered on it.

"I don't even want to know what that stain is."

Jason leaves the kitchen to the cockroaches, turning the light off as he leaves, and mounts the steps to the second floor. They groan under his weight.

The second floor has another hallway, this one filled with doors. This part of the house had been renovated, making the rooms even smaller so that additional rooms could be squeezed in. There was barely any effort made to cover up where walls were moved. Wires hang from the hallway ceiling where a smoke detector was once wired in and at some point had been ripped out.

The stairs turn and go up another level again, even narrower, to the attic space above.

Jason looks up the stairs curiously. He didn't think there was a third floor from looking at the place from outside.

A door opens and he turns to see a dishevelled couple come stumbling out. They pause to lock the door behind them before coming towards him.

"Don't go up there," the woman giggles, "the crazy guy lives up there."

"What's up there?" Jason asks.

"The attic." He gets an unpleasant whiff of unwashed bodies as they get close and is glad when they squeeze past him and start down the stairs.

"What's his name?" Jason asks.

"Who?" The woman seems to have forgotten who they were talking about. Then she remembers. "Oh, crazy guy!"

"Don't know, don't care," the man says gruffly, and they are gone from sight down the stairs. Jason hears the front door open and close, their voices and laughter outside fading quickly as they walk away.

Jason turns away from the stairs and moves down the hallway past their door. None of the rooms have numbers on the doors.

He finds the other shared bathroom and looks in. It is just as bad as the one downstairs; only this one is missing the showerhead. Water drips from the pipe coming from the wall in the shower, the swivel ball of the missing showerhead still screwed on, the head broken off at the ball hinge that once allowed its aim to be adjusted.

He passes the closed door with the country music playing inside, silently dubbing the unknown resident as "The Cowboy".

His room is the only one with the door left open. He finds it from the description his social worker gave him. He steps inside. The room is at the front of the house. The only window is the cracked one he saw from outside, giving him a view of the front street.

The paint on the walls is bubbled and peeling in places and the front corner near the floor where two outside walls meet is blackened with mould. If there ever was a carpet, it had been ripped out years ago without bothering to refinish the ruined hardwood floor beneath. The floor is worn and stained, missing most of the wax that would have protected it.

The furnishings consist of a small scratched and dented dresser missing half its handles, a single battered looking wooden kitchen chair, and a rollaway cot with a mattress that would be better off burned. There is no pillow or bedding.

That's all the furniture that can fit in the tiny room.

The room is filthy and he is pretty sure those are rodent droppings on the floor.

This is home for now and exactly what he expected of a rooming house where people living well below the level of poverty can live for a day or a lifetime in a single rented room.

The keys were left on top of the scarred dresser, two keys, one for the room and one for the main door.

"It will do," Jason says. He snatches up the keys, plops his bag on top of the dresser, and locks the door on his way out.

"The first thing I need to do is buy some bedding and cleaning products and make this room liveable."

Jim's phone rings and he answers it.

"McNelly."

"He's all settled in," the voice on the line says.

"Good," Jim grunts. "I'll give him a few days to get comfortable."

He hangs up the phone.

"A few days to get comfortable, and then I'll be watching Jason T. McAllister very closely."

# 10 Investigating the Investigator

Jim parks his ancient brown Oldsmobile in the only spot available on the street, the engine ticking away almost as soon as he turns it off as it begins cooling.

The temperature gauge on the dash is running high.

It matches his mood.

The door squeals when he thrusts it open and the shocks groan with the shifting of his weight as he pulls his obese frame out. He takes a slender well-used leather case with him.

He doesn't bother locking the door when he closes it behind him. He never does. There is nothing worth stealing. The radio is about as valuable as an eight-track and the glove box holds a handful of parking and driving infraction tickets. A few are his, and a few are tickets he wrote against offending drivers and stuffed in his glove box instead of handing over when the driver reacted by rudely yelling their indignation.

He would nod his head at them, tell them he's letting them off this time with a warning, and stuff the ticket in his glove box. Let them pay the bigger fine, he would muse.

He does let the odd one off with just a warning, the ones who make a good show of being apologetic or seem genuinely remorseful.

Jim walks around the car to the sidewalk. His breath whistles in and out unhealthily as he walks the distance to the corner, turns, and heads up the next street. Halfway up the block is his destination, the precinct Michael Underwood transferred from.

He enters through the front doors and pauses to take in the room and get his bearings. He heads for the reception desk.

The young officer looks up. Everything about him screams green recruit. He is probably one of the unlucky ones, the most recent class graduates who were sentenced to spend a year on desk duty before being put on the streets.

Jim is huffing from the walk as he approaches the desk. "Detective McNelly," he announces, "I want to talk to the man who does the transfers."

"That would be Sergeant Reagers."

"Is he in?"

"He is." The young officer picks up the phone and calls the officer in question, talking quietly into the phone for a few moments. He hangs up and addresses Jim.

"He'll be with you right away."

Jim grunts and turns away, dismissing the young man's presence. He studies the entrance, assessing how easily someone who does not belong might be able to get in and access areas that are not open to the public.

"Detective McNelly," a balding man in his forties with a slight paunch announces as he enters from the back hallway, "I'm Sergeant Reagers. How can I help you?"

"You transferred a man to my department a while back, Detective Michael Underwood," Jim says.

Sergeant Reagers rolls the name around in his head, finally answering. "The name doesn't sound familiar. Why are you asking?"

Jim glances at the officer at the desk and turns his attention back to Sergeant Reagers.

"We need to talk in private."

Sergeant Reagers nods. "This way." He leads the way back the way he came and to his office, closing the door behind them.

"Sit," he waves Jim to the two chairs before his desk and moves to sit behind the desk.

"Why do you want to know about this Detective Michael Underwood?"

"You transferred him to my department," Jim repeats. "Turns out he wasn't such a good fit."

"Personality issue?"

"He's not a cop."

Sergeant Reagers raises his eyebrows in surprise. He smiles.

"You are pulling my leg. Who put you up to this? Murphy?"

Jim shakes his head.

"I'm investigating Michael Underwood for kidnapping, murder, fraud, providing false identification, and impersonating an officer. The list goes on."

Sergeant Reagers looks stunned. He takes a moment to absorb it.

"This detective is from our precinct? I don't remember the name."

"You signed the transfer. It came from the fax machine in this building."

Sergeant Reagers gets up, shaking his head.

"If I did, I'll have a copy in his personnel file."

He goes to the filing cabinets, opens a drawer, and starts thumbing through the files. He frowns.

"Underwood?" he asks.

Jim spells it.

Sergeant Reagers shakes his head again and turns to him.

"I have no file on an Underwood, Michael or any other Underwood."

"That's because he's a fraud," Jim says. "It's not his real name. Michael Underwood does not exist and yet somehow a transfer with your signature for a Michael Underwood was faxed from this building to mine."

"How do you know? If I signed the transfer paper, then he must be real." Sergeant Reagers says.

"I talked to people who would have been in the same class. Not a single one recognized the name or his face. His badge number doesn't exist either. It starts with the right number for the class the year he claimed to graduate, but it's past the sequence used. He's two numbers higher than the number of recruits in the class."

"Do you have a copy of the transfer?" Sergeant Reagers asks.

Jim pulls pages out from his leather bag and hands them to him.

Sergeant Reagers takes them and studies them.

"The transfer paper looks legitimate. That's my signature." He mulls it over. "I remember that class. We had one drop out last minute. Another was kicked out and one failed. So, that would make this the next sequential number, adding one to the class."

Jim nods.

Sergeant Reagers flips to the next page, a printout with Michael Underwood's police I.D. photo and his particulars. His photo looks like the kind of mug shot of a suspect that would be used in a briefing, like all the officers' I.D. photos. He studies the face.

"I've never seen the man," he says, shaking his head.

"That's what I thought," Jim says.

"Let's show this around the building," Sergeant Reagers says, indicating the photo sheet. "See if anyone else recognizes him."

When Jim leaves the building later, it is with the sickening feeling of being right. The photo will be shown later to the other officers who were not in the building right now and passed around the other shifts, but he knows it will be the same.

Not a single person will recognize the face.

Michael Underwood never existed before the day he walked into Jim McNelly's office and his life.

Thanks to Beth's clever research, he knows Michael's rental references didn't check out. His bank accounts hold no prior history. Even his insurance and driving records seem to have just suddenly appeared.

"Who the hell are you?" Jim mutters angrily as he drives away.

# 11 Secret Rendezvous

"Where are you going?" Kathy asks. She is nervous whenever Michael leaves her alone.

"I told you, I don't know yet. I'll be stopping in different towns to see what's there" Michael says, shoving a few changes of clothing into a bag."

"Do you have to be gone so long? Why can't I come with you?"

"You just can't." Michael turns to her. "I'm looking for a new place for us and a job. I'll only be gone for a few days."

Kathy is unsure. *What if he never comes back? What if he just abandons me here? Who was he talking to on the phone before he started packing? He arranged a meeting with someone. I know it, but he won't admit it. I know I should trust him, but I'm afraid to let him go.*

"If you are going looking for a new house, then why can't I come with you?" she asks.

Michael hates the begging tone in her voice. She is weak, helpless, and needs to be protected. It makes him feel bad for leaving her. He wishes she was stronger, less dependent on him. Sometimes her weakness grates on his nerves.

*I have enough to deal with without having to always be her anchor.*

"It's going to be boring," Michael says. "I'll just be driving around, checking areas out, see what's around, and sleeping in the truck. I'll have to drop into places and see if they're hiring. If I find a job, then we'll get a place in the area.

We'll stay there as long as we need, then move on. I want to get further away. We need to keep moving for now."

"You aren't meeting someone?"

"No," Michael lies. "I have got to go."

He grabs his bag and moves towards her. Pulling her close, he wraps his arms around her, leans down, and kisses her.

"Don't worry. I'll always keep you safe."

He releases her and she is torn. She wishes he hadn't let her go and yet does not want him touching her right now.

With that Michael is gone, heading out the door.

Kathy goes to the front window, watching him get into his truck and drive away. His absence leaves a cold chill of dread inside her.

"Who are you meeting Michael?" she asks the departing truck. "I know he's lying. I heard him on the phone. He's meeting someone. He's been acting secretive all week. He's hiding something."

The loneliness begins to set in before the truck is out of sight.

*I have no friends, no one but Michael to talk to. I have nowhere to go. He doesn't even want me leaving the house. I'm so lonely. I want desperately to call my mother.*

She looks at the phone longingly.

"No, I promised Michael I wouldn't. He warned me that if I call my mother or anyone else from my past life, the call will be traced. The police will be on us before we can run and he will be locked away.

Maybe if I go someplace else? Find a pay phone? I don't even know where to look. I can't remember the last place I've seen a pay phone. Everyone has cell phones now. Except us. Michael says they would use it to find us.

No. I can't even use a pay phone. They'll still trace the call to this town and find us."

Kathy goes to the sofa and sits down to wait.

"I feel bad for lying to Kathy," Michael says, staring at the road before him. "She deserves better. I have to bring her fully into who and what I am. It's the only way. But, I have to do it slowly. You can't be married and keep a big secret like this."

The long drive gives him too much time to think.

When he was a child he had vague memories of his real father, but even those mostly faded over the years. Then he blocked it all out, pushing his past and all the unpleasant memories behind a curtain of fog.

Now he has only the memory of having the memory. Memories he can't tap into.

Thinking about his childhood makes the memories stir, ugly memories. He doesn't want to remember.

"No," Michael says. "Think about something else."

He forces himself to think about the future.

"We will have to move a few more times, changing jobs, homes, towns. We need money. It costs a lot of money to not be found. I need to go back to work.

I need a job for a cover. Just like the McAllister Farm was for generations of the McAllisters, a cover to keep the neighbours from getting too nosy.

Papa, Jason, told me how little his family worked the farm when they lived there when he was a boy. It was little more than a front for what his father really did."

Michael swallows the sour ball in his stomach that feels like it's rising in his throat.

"As much as I despise it, I was raised a McAllister and I can never run away from that no matter how hard I try. Damn you Jason McAllister." He pounds the steering wheel with one hand. He tries denying it to himself, but when it comes to needing money, it will always be there waiting for him.

So will the McAllister Farm.

The drive wears on endlessly, his mind eventually numbing into a void without thought.

Finally, he pulls into a little roadside restaurant on the edge of nowhere.

Michael parks on the edge of the parking lot, out of sight from anyone looking out the front windows of the restaurant, and sits there.

His heart is racing and he is sweating. I have to get myself under control. I have to be completely calm when I walk in that door.

No fear.

Michael studies the place, the cars, and the people coming and going. He concentrates on breathing slowly, trying to slow his racing heart.

When he finally feels like he can go in without panicking, Michael gets out of the truck and starts walking towards the restaurant. He concentrates on his feet, keeping from stumbling and his pace steady. His legs are chunks of wood. They have no feeling.

He enters the restaurant and pauses, waiting for his eyes to adjust. It is dark inside compared to the bright sunlight outside.

There are a few scattered tables with people at them.

Michael looks around, spots a man sitting in a back booth, and approaches the table hesitantly.

The man sits there ignoring him and idly stirring his already stirred coffee as if that will somehow make it taste better. He is middle-aged with thinning hair cut in a business style. He is wearing a cheap suit jacket, trousers, and dress shirt with the top two buttons undone and no tie.

He is as average and nondescript as they come.

*Any witnesses wouldn't even remember this man was here. He's the sort they never seem to notice in the crowd,* Michael thinks.

"Anderson?" Michael asks. He has never met him before.

"Sit," the man says without looking up.

Michael slides in across from him.

Anderson finally stops stirring his coffee and sets his spoon down on the table.

Seeing Michael, the waitress prowling the restaurant is on him in seconds with a half-full coffee pot in one hand and a tired smile on her lips.

She reaches across Michael without asking, turning over the second cup that sits upside down on a small plate in front of him, and pours him coffee.

"Anything I can get you?" she asks, eying him appreciatively. "The Danish here is divine."

"No, thank you," Michael manages, feeling awkward.

"The pie here is pretty good too," Anderson says with a nod to the waitress. "We're good here, thanks."

Deflated with the knowledge that no meal means a much smaller tip, the waitress turns and walks away to stalk the restaurant, always ready to leap into action the moment a customer might need something. She works hard to earn her tips, unable to live on the meagre hourly wage they pay her.

Michael is nervous. *What if he isn't Anderson? What if it's a setup?* He pushes the thought away. *It's impossible. They are too well organized for that.*

He consciously stops himself from looking at the man sitting across from him as he pours sugar in his coffee.

"Cream?" Anderson asks, indicating the little bowl of sealed creamers.

"No thanks, just sugar," Michael says, stirring the sugar into his black coffee.

Michael sets the spoon down and looks pointedly at the man sitting across from him.

The man meets his gaze.

"Mr. Anderson?" Michael asks again. He needs to be sure.

"Yes," Anderson says with a slight nod.

"I'm-,' Michael starts and is cut off.

"Nobody," Anderson interrupts him.

Michael nods sheepishly.

Anderson casually sips his coffee, watching Michael over the rim, weighing and judging the younger man sitting across from him. He counts down all the things he knows about him.

*I don't know the man, but I know enough about him. He is a McAllister, if not by blood then by association. David McAllister, Michael Underwood, and currently Michael Ritchot.*

*I know Michael's past. I know all the aliases he used over the years. Jason McAllister had no kids, and yet raised two children. Michael ran away from Jason McAllister and spent his teen years running and hiding, living on the streets by whatever means were necessary. Before that, Jason groomed and trained the boy he called David as a McAllister.*

*I know who is responsible for the discovery of the graveyard that had been kept hidden in the McAllister family history for generations. Michael nearly murdered his own sister as a child when he had his first taste of blood, and that he is now crazed with the obsession of finding and protecting her. He has been for a very long time.*

*These things alone should have sealed Michael's fate long before it came to this point, long before he came to sit across from me in a diner in the middle of nowhere.*

*Michael should have been put down long ago. Why are they giving this jerk a chance? It's beyond me. If it were up to me, I would follow him out right now and make him disappear.*

*The McAllister farm hides secrets that Michael might know.*

*Michael is a loose cannon, just like Jason McAllister was when he was younger, and in some ways still is.*

*Damn, I'd like to just get rid of this bastard now. I can't. Why'd they put me on this, instead of someone else? My job is to determine just how much of a threat Michael is, and whether he has to be dealt with. My job is to be unbiased, but I am biased.*

His name is not really Anderson, of course. Anderson is the title given to the disposal experts' handlers. But he isn't that either. He is the Andersons' Anderson, the handlers' handler. He is here to assess Michael before deciding whether to kill him or hand him off to a handler. It's as good a name as any for Michael. Michael does not need to know the truth.

Anderson nods finally.

"I have a job for you," Anderson says. "I'll give you the general area and a time and place to get the details. The rest is up to you."

"Will I be working with you?"

Anderson shakes his head. "I'm temporary until we know where you will be working from and can set you up with a permanent handler."

Once assigned a handler, it is a relationship for life. A truly till death do they part arrangement. The handler and his charges must have absolute trust in each other, and you don't get that by switching handlers.

Michael nods. He understands what that means. *He doesn't trust me yet. They don't trust me yet.*

"You can count on me," Michael says.

"I hope so."

Anderson stands up, pulls out his wallet, and leaves money on the table, enough to cover his bill and an average tip. Waitresses don't remember the guy who leaves an average tip, but they always remember the cheapskates and the generous ones.

He nods goodbye to Michael and leaves.

Michael sits alone sipping his coffee. After waiting the required time, he puts his own money on the table with enough for an average tip, pauses, remembering the sad tired eyes of the waitress and is tempted to leave an extra tip, and changes his mind.

Michael slips out, leaving the waitress to clear the table and sulkily pocket her small tip.

"You never get tipped good just for coffee," she sniffs unhappily.

Michael checks his surroundings as he approaches his truck, making sure nobody is following or paying undue attention to him. He looks around before getting in.

*Where would he have put it?* He wonders.

For a moment Michael is on the edge of panic. *If I don't find it . . ..*

He opens the truck door, looking inside before sitting, and finally gets in.

He hears the crinkle of paper.

Michael feels around beneath him even though the seat was empty, and behind him. Finally he jams his fingers into the crack between the seat and its back. He feels the paper.

Struggling to grip it between the tips of his fingers, he pulls it out.

He turns it over. It has a single word on it.

Michael nods understanding.

"I have a house and a job to find," he says as he puts the key in the ignition and turns it, the engine roaring to life.

Michael pulls out of the lot and turns onto the highway going further away from home. He drives for some time before stopping to find a phone.

Kathy has not slept. She is still sitting on the couch waiting for Michael even though she knows he will be gone a few days. She just can't bring herself to go through the pretence of putting on pyjamas and crawling into bed knowing she won't sleep anyway.

The house is dark, just the light from the bathroom filtering from the open door and the moonlight coming in the windows to light the room.

The ringing of the phone startles her. Her heart races and she jumps. She stares at the phone as it rings again, afraid to approach it and pick it up.

Its insistent jangle shakes her nerves again.

Kathy blinks at it, trying to convince herself to move, that it's okay.

The next ring brings her to her feet and rushing across the floor to scoop the receiver off its hook.

"Hello," she breathes timidly into the phone.

"Kathy, you are still up," a male voice says, sounding tinny and far away. "You should be sleeping."

"Michael," Kathy says, relieved. "Are you on your way back?"

"No, babe. I'm going to be a little longer than I thought."

Kathy's heart sinks and she looks down at the floor that swims before her. Tears burn at the edges of her eyes.

"I won't be too long," Michael says. "I have a line on a place for us and a job. I'll just be a few more days."

"Okay," Kathy says quietly.

"Goodnight," Michael says. The dial tone moans in her ear.

Kathy blinks back tears as she replaces the receiver and returns to sitting on the couch in the darkness.

# Part Three

# Discovery

# 12 It's All About the Kids

Lawrence Hawkworth has an uncanny ability to dig up the unfindable. He seems to have a sixth sense for evil. It is an ability that makes him a great investigative reporter.

The tall lanky reporter who resembles a buzzard would have been a cop if he had not been turned down flat. He could not pass the basic requirements. Among other things; he is color blind.

He can sit in the scene of a crime and play it out in his head, imagining what he thinks could have happened, playing out the most probable to the impossible, getting a sense of a line that usually crosses somewhere down the middle between the two.

Clues overlooked because they were too obvious or unlikely stand out to him. Leads that went nowhere are rediscovered. And sometimes the impossible would quite literally fall in his lap.

Lawrence is sitting moodily staring into the amber liquid in his glass on the worn table before him in the dimly lit pub. He can still taste the unpleasant burn of the last sip and has no interest in touching it again.

It is there as a reminder.

He scowls at the glass, his wide mouth in a sour downturn.

*The more I dig into the McAllister's past, the more elderly people I interview who were here when the McAllisters lived on the farm, the stranger it all becomes.*

*The town was plagued briefly by a serial killer when Jason McAllister was just a boy. Before that, murders and disappearances were conspicuously absent. At least, they were absent when the McAllisters lived at the farm. Somehow the area had bucked the national trend and was an unusually safe place to live.*

*William McAllister was the prime suspect in the murders and disappearances of young women and teenage girls. The only reason anyone had to suspect him was his eccentric ways, his aloofness, and complete separation from the community.*

*The McAllister family vanished and the killer was identified in the same day. It was not William McAllister, but the people I interviewed all refuse to believe William McAllister is not guilty.*

*I poured over the transcripts from the trial and there was undeniable irrefutable proof the sheriff had the right man.*

"So why did they run?" Lawrence asks his glass. "If William McAllister was innocent, then why did he pack up his family and abandon the farm?

The attention on the family must have been unbearable, but enough to make a man just up and run? Not even selling the property?"

He can feel the papers in his pocket like a physical presence without moving to touch them. It is a copy of the land title for the McAllister Farm.

The name on the title is William McAllister.

"William McAllister is still alive," Lawrence mutters. "He has to be, or his name would not still be on the title for the McAllister Farm."

"Where are you William?" he asks as if the ghost from the past might actually answer. "Where did you go when you left?"

Lawrence grits his teeth, clears his throat, and makes himself take another swallow of the amber liquor. It burns unpleasantly as it slides down his throat and he bares his teeth at the unpleasant taste, making him look predatory.

He runs through the interviews and the old news clippings in his mind.

*Anecdotal stories are not proof, but they often prove to hold the seed of truth.*

Lawrence picks up the glass again, tosses the rest of the liquor down his throat, coughs on it, and hurries out, leaving money on the table to pay his tab.

He gets into his car and drives. It doesn't take long to find himself heading out a lonely road leading away from the small city.

He drives on, turning down a gravel road that eventually turns to mud. If it rains he will be stranded, the mud road turned to slop his car could not possibly make it through without getting stuck.

"How do farmers do it?"

Finally, Lawrence turns into an overgrown trail through a tall-grassed field that was once the long driveway leading into the McAllister farm.

His car rocks and bounces over the rough terrain, long grass swooshing against the undercarriage.

He stops in front of the old farmhouse and turns the engine off, just sitting there.

He can hear the hissing clicking of insects somewhere.

Lawrence looks around, taking in the scene.

He plays it out in his head, the townspeople trespassing with their guns, searching the place, a lynch mob. Marjory McAllister and her kids alone on the farm against a mob, frightened.

*No, Marjory wasn't as frightened as she seemed. She had an inner strength in her. She would have bravely stood up to them, shielding her children.*

*But the boy, Jason, was a kid with an attitude bigger than his size. He got into fights and got into trouble. He would have tried to act the man of the house in his father's absence.*

*Together, woman and boy would have stood their ground, looking at each other from across the yard, full of the strain of fear and either one ready to snap.*

*The townspeople were bent on tearing the place apart to prove William McAllister's guilt. Their daughters were going missing and turning up dead and they were afraid and they needed a monster. They chose William.*

*But William showed up. After that the stories became sketchier.*

Lawrence jumps with a yelp at a sudden explosion of sound and motion next to him, in the car with him, flailing his arms instinctively to protect his head.

He looks around wide-eyed, taking a few moments for the fluttering at his window to register.

He was startled by a bird that suddenly flew by very close, its wings brushing the window in a brown blur with the loud fluttering of its wings and voicing its complaint over his presence.

Lawrence shakes his head and looks down at his trembling hands, feeling the fear that still clings inside him and the fast pounding of his heart in his rib cage.

"Just a bird," he mutters and silently wonders, *what happened to the chickens and other farm animals after William McAllister and his family abandoned them.*

After sitting there for a while longer, Lawrence gets out and starts slowly roaming the yard.

He wanders to the edge of the trees and tries the shed door. The latch that once allowed it to be padlocked had been pulled out on one end and dangles loosely with the rusting padlock still locked.

Lawrence tries the door and it has a little give but is stuck because of the rotting wood of the door sagging on the nails holding it to the hinges. He pulls up on the door, lifting it to swing it open enough to peek inside. The dark interior is filled with dusty cobwebs. He spies a large fat wolf spider sitting in one and feels a pang of sickness in his stomach.

Lawrence lets the door sag back down, its corner resting on the ground and leaving it open, turning away. He moves off across the yard, passing the remains of what had once been a chicken coop, the wire fence torn and sagging, half of it lying tangled in the long grass. He passes the now empty goat pen, its fence boards mostly eaten by rot, many fallen to the ground to be claimed by the grass and weeds. He moves on towards the barn.

The whole barn sags towards one side, matching the trees that grow as if perpetually blown in that direction. The roof sags in the middle as if it were slowly melting into itself. The windows are cracked and mostly broken out, and there is little peeling paint left to suggest what color it had once been.

Lawrence hesitates before going inside the barn, pushing back a fear that it will collapse on him.

"If it stood this long, it'll stand another hour."

The inside of the barn is musty with dust and mould. Even after all these years you can still detect the faint odour of manure and moulding straw.

The small tractor parked inside the barn would have made a valuable addition to an antique collection if it had not been left to rust when William McAllister abandoned the farm.

Lawrence pulls up the memory of the interviews, cracked old voices whispering and angrily charging William McAllister with the most heinous of crimes.

The barn is the only building on the lot where a man with a family might have had some privacy to do foul deeds without being interrupted.

He tries to picture it in his mind, the farmer with a young woman tied up, probably gagged, while he mercilessly mutilates his victim. She would stare at him with terror-filled eyes, pleading for her life, haunted with her pain. His wife would be in the house, perhaps baking bread. The kids would be in school.

Lawrence's head is filling with cotton. It turns to water, too heavy, freezing to ice, sending blinding hot agony through the center of his head.

He feels like a scarecrow, hollowed out and stuffed with sawdust and straw, his skin pulled too tight, overstuffed to the point he might burst.

The barn darkens and Lawrence swoons. He staggers.

The image of William McAllister torturing young women will not come.

Lawrence staggers across the barn to a worn and stained workbench.

Pain-filled eyes stare up at him from behind a dirty bloodied gag, desperately pleading. She is not a young woman, but a child.

"The boy," her voice whispers in his head, almost too softly to hear.

He shakes his head hard.

"No, this isn't right," he mutters.

The smell of old manure and mouldy hay becomes marginally stronger. Stronger yet is the smell of a freshly oiled tractor. Then the other stench engulfs him, the air reeking of blood and fear.

Lawrence has to focus. *This is about the McAllisters, William and Jason, and coming up with an idea that might lead to finding Michael Underwood, or whoever he really is.*

"Whatever William McAllister was, he was not a monster. He was not guilty of the mutilation and murders the townspeople had been so convinced he was guilty of. I feel it in my very core."

Lawrence leaves the barn and wanders the yard, picturing William McAllister and his family. His wife, Marjory, is hanging laundry on a clothes line. The little girl, Sophie, is playing in the yard with a dog. The boy, Jason, is walking across the yard to whatever chores a boy on a farm does. The girl's laughter dances in the air as William drives his tractor in a distant field.

Chickens cluck and scratch at the dirt and goats stare at him through the fence of their pen. A cat suns itself lazily, its ear twitching to show that it is paying attention to the sound of a mouse rustling in the straw of the goat pen.

Lawrence wanders into the house, tearing off one side of the police tape blocking the unlocked door and leaving it to flutter in the breeze. He moves from room to room, the life of the family surrounding him in the tidy home filled with furniture that was already old when they lived here.

He pauses in the doorway to the small storage room, the trapdoor to the dirt-floored cellar laying flipped open, the blackness below yawning up at him.

He stares at that square hole. He senses desperation and fear down there, terror and hopelessness. Many invisible hands clawing at the light above that they can never reach.

A dread chill shivers through him with a sick feeling and he turns away, wandering back outside to the yard.

The yard goes sullenly silent and still, empty between scenes of the McAllister generations living here.

Lawrence pictures Jason McAllister, now the young man whose face stared back at him in a grainy photo in an old newspaper, going about puttering around the farm he came back to reclaim.

The laughter of a child trickles into the scene, a little girl. The ghost of a boy's voice echoes, barely heard.

"Don't do that, you'll make him mad." He can hear the anxiety in the voice, the pleading warning.

He has a sense they are not Sophie and Jason McAllister.

Lawrence blinks, looking around and feeling stunned, although none of it comes as a surprise to him. It is what he already knows from the interviews.

There is no doubt in his mind. Jason McAllister, the man who never married or had kids, had two children, a boy and a girl.

"Where did he get them?"

# 13 Cleaning House

Jason McAllister stands in the open doorway looking in at his handiwork. The tiny room that is to be his home still looks depressingly uncared for, but at least it is now clean.

He had rearranged the narrow cot, dresser, and single chair in an effort to make the most of what little room he has and sunlight now dazzles in through the once grimy window, brightening the previously gloomy room. The crack in the window is a bright slash of refracted light.

The mould stains are gone from the wall, though the paint is permanently discoloured. The dresser and chair have fewer stains, what remains are too ingrained into the warped wood to scrub out.

The floor is scrubbed and polished, and all traces of rodent feces are gone.

"I don't think I will ever get the unpleasant smell out of the room."

Finally, Jason carefully sets and places a couple of mousetraps and roach traps against the wall where the pests prefer to travel, one of each under the bed and by the dresser.

This is only the beginning of the job. There is still the rest of the house. The whole place is infested with the grime of tenants who think they don't have to care because they live in poverty. Their individual rooms are their domain, and they don't care what happens outside their door. It isn't their problem.

"It's just my luck to get roomed with people whose lives of poverty have beaten them into uncaring slobs," Jason mutters, taking his bucket of cleaning supplies.

He moves on to the second floor bathroom, scouring the tub and sink. The ever-present strains of country music come from The Cowboy's closed door. Chunks of grout break off between the tiles on the wall surrounding the tub with the effort of scrubbing them. He picks the chunks up and tosses them on the bathroom floor.

When he finishes cleaning the bathroom, Jason descends the stairs to the stink of burnt food and rotting garbage.

Moving down the short hall, he enters the kitchen where the smell is the most powerful.

The light coming in the kitchen and back door windows is softened by the layer of grime coating the windows.

It's a cockroach's paradise. The sparse counter space is filthy with remnants of past meal attempts and littered with food wrappers and packaging. The stove is so thick with grease and food spatters that he wonders how anyone can cook on it without it catching fire. Someone left a communal pot tossed into the dirty sink. Jason walks over to it and peeks inside. The pot is ruined with what appears to be burnt-on macaroni and powdered cheese product. A large plastic trash pail in the corner is missing its lid, allowing flies and roaches full access to the decomposing trash overflowing it.

The back door with its smudged six-pane window beckons him.

With a frown at the filth and stench, Jason unlocks the back door and tries to open it. The door refuses to budge at first, but pops open with a good tug.

The fresh air is a welcome relief.

Jason breathes in the fresh air and looks outside. At that moment a neighbour comes out of her house into her back yard. The line of yards all back onto an alley where the driveways and the occasional garage are.

He watches the woman. She partially disappears from view as she turns back to lock her door, reappearing when she walks through her yard to the cracked concrete of her driveway.

The all too familiar heat burns in his stomach as he watches her.

*Not now,* Jason silently chastises himself. *You've been good this long. Don't ruin things now.*

He pushes down the desire to see her eyes staring back at him, so expressive with the fear and pain filling them, begging him to save her even as he torments her; the feel of her warm blood caressing his hands.

She gets in her car and drives away out of sight to his relief.

*Haven't done that in four years,* Jason reminds himself silently. *A few more will be easy. You have to stay low, behave.*

He turns his attention to the filthy kitchen.

Two hours later the kitchen is clean, the open door still airing it out and the sun flows in through the clean clear windows. The strong lemon scent of the disinfectant cuts through the foul smell of rot that still lingers.

Jason is just coming in from taking the garbage out when he hears the noise of the toilet upstairs flushing, followed by the shower running.

"Must be The Cowboy," he mutters with a glance at the ceiling.

The couple from the hallway earlier come banging in the front door. He hears the man grunt and the woman giggle idiotically.

He can smell their approach. The stench of skunkweed and other intoxicants cling heavily to them along with body odour and her cheap perfume.

Jason steps to the kitchen doorway and peers out, watching them stagger to the stairs. The woman hangs off her companion to keep herself from falling off her feet.

They stumble and stagger up the stairs, one of them falling near the top with a thump. The floor above creaks with their weight and their shoes clomp noisily. There is a thud, presumably one of them falling against the wall, the rattle of the loose doorknob as it is unlocked, and the door banging open heavily against the wall when someone falls into the room.

The door slams shut and muted thuds can be heard then silence.

Jason packs up his cleaning supplies. He is beat.

"The rest can wait," he mutters, thinking of the living room.

A door upstairs opens the moment Jason puts his foot on the first step.

He is halfway up the stairs when he hears the muffled sounds of gagging and moans of disgust.

"Seriously?" the woman's voice is slurred and dismayed.

She is pounding on The Cowboy's door by the time Jason reaches the top of the stairs.

The Cowboy's door opens, releasing the country music, and he pokes his head out. Even after showering, his hair still looks greasy. He has done a sloppy job of shaving his sparsely bearded face. His chin and Adams apple jut out at her and he stares at her groggily as if he is either half asleep or pretending to be in an attempt at looking cool and casual.

"Are you fucking kidding me?" she shrieks at him.

"What?" He seems totally oblivious to her problem.

Her bracelet bobbles jangle on her wrist as she points at the offending bathroom.

"The bathroom!" Her voice is shrill, annoying. "Gross!"

"So?"

She huffs in exasperation at him. "Well, I ain't cleaning it up," she complains.

Jason pauses at the top of the stairs, observing this exchange.

*They're like a couple of bloody teenagers.*

He comes down the hall towards them, seeing more of The Cowboy when he gets to his door. He is shirtless and wearing worn jeans that are overdue for the laundry. He is scrawny, his limbs seeming longer for it, probably eating at most once a day. Jason suspects he is behind the burnt pot left tossed carelessly in the sink. Behind him, his room is tossed like a salad of clothes and litter. A pair of worn cowboy boots lay carelessly on the floor and a misshapen cowboy hat sits on the dresser.

He has every hallmark of a wannabe a cowboy of the worst kind; the kind who uses it as an excuse for being a useless jerk, a pretence of being too tough to care.

*Hell, that old goat we had would eat him up and spit him out*. Jason thinks back to that cranky old animal he had the misfortune as a boy of having to care for and try to milk every day.

He moves past the scene in the hallway and reaches the bathroom. He smells it before he reaches it. Jason stops at the bathroom doorway, halted by what he sees.

The man exploded on the toilet. The foul spray spewed backwards, splattering the toilet, floor, and wall behind it with sickly brown liquid feces. Fouled toilet paper drapes one side of the toilet seat and the brown sludge sits mockingly in the bowl.

He hadn't even bothered to flush.

The Cowboy made no effort to clean his mess other than to shower his feces off his own backside. The shower curtain and wall is smudged with a few brown smears. The smell of rotting intestines and shower steam still fills the bathroom.

The woman is screeching at The Cowboy to go clean up his mess, swearing at him and calling him insulting names.

The Cowboy is just standing in his doorway, smirking that lazy sleepy half smirk as if she is describing some incredibly boring event in her life to him.

Jason's stomach twists at the revolting scene in the bathroom.

"Go clean it up!" she screeches again.

"Not my problem," The Cowboy drawls, his voice sounding as fake sleepy as he looks.

He moves backwards as he closes the door.

Jason's hand firmly on the door stops it.

"What?" The Cowboy sneers, somehow looking annoyed, casual, sleepy, and alarmed all at once. He looks at Jason.

The woman steps back; unfortunately not far enough to take her unpleasant odour out of Jason's nose.

Jason stares The Cowboy down, his eyes hard and face expressionless.

"It's not my problem, man," The Cowboy mutters in his defence.

"Clean it up," Jason says, his voice low and level with just the barest edge of warning behind it.

The woman stands back, looking smug.

The Cowboy stares at him defiantly, looking a little less sleepy.

"Not my problem," he repeats and attempts to step back and close the door again.

Jason steps forward into The Cowboy's space, straddling the doorway and pushing the door open against the scrawny man's attempts to close it.

Alarm flashes across The Cowboy's face.

"Hey, get outta here man," he squeaks, trying to sound tough. "What's your problem?"

"Clean. It. Up." Jason's voice is low and clipped.

"Bugger off," The Cowboy squeaks. "You clean it. It's not my problem."

He quickly changes tactic at the flash of anger in Jason's eyes.

"They got someone that comes in to do that stuff," he complains.

Before The Cowboy knows what hit him, Jason's hands punch forward, grabbing him roughly and tearing him from the safety of his room. Jason spins them both around, using his momentum to keep The Cowboy off balance, and slams him into the wall across from the doorway hard enough to make the scrawny man wheeze for air.

The Cowboy tries to shrink down, but is held in place by his attacker.

The woman stares in shock, trembling with excitement and fear at the sudden unexpected burst of violence.

"Clean. It. Up." Jason repeats softly. He releases The Cowboy and turns away, walking past the soiled bathroom to his own room.

The pair in the hallway stare at him mutely while he unlocks his door, goes in, and closes it behind him.

Minutes later Jason hears the muffled sounds of The Cowboy gagging on his own filth as he fights back tears while he scrubs his feces from the bathroom.

The stinky woman retreats to use the bathroom downstairs, hoping to sneak back into her room without having to see either man.

The Cowboy disgusts her. The other man sent a sharp cold dread through her.

Jim dials a number and waits through a few rings before a voice answers on the other end. It's a bad connection and it's impossible to tell what gender the recipient of the call is.

"Hey, it's Jim. What's he doing?"

"Cleaning," the voice says, followed by a chuckle.

"He sick?"

"You bet. They don't screen these places or the tenants. Hey, how long do I have to stay here and watch him? This place is disgusting."

"It won't take long. I'm going to put the pressure on, force him to make a move. When he moves, I'll be on him. He's going to lead us to Michael Underwood, or whoever the hell he really is."

"Make it fast. I'm going to have to be deloused when I leave here."

"Couple days, that's all," Jim says and hangs up.

# 14 Only More Questions

Lawrence Hawkworth is sitting on the couch in his apartment. The large coffee table in front of him is covered with copies of news clippings, reports, and his notes. He is staring intently at the mess before him as if the answer will somehow seep from the pile of papers into him.

The only thing he is getting is more questions.

*Who is Michael Underwood and what does he have to do with Jason McAllister?*

*Where did the McAllisters go when William took his family and vanished? Where are the rest of the McAllisters now? William is alive, but his wife Marjory could be dead by now. They could be locked up in some seniors' home. What happened to the daughter, Sophie?*

*There have been no attempts by any of the McAllisters to contact or visit Jason McAllister after his arrest. None showed up to the trial.*

*It's as if none of them exist, or if they do, they are either unaware of what happened or for whatever reason chose to stay far away. The world knows about the women, the graves, and the trial. Have they disowned Jason for some reason? Completely blocked him from their lives?*

Lawrence's thoughts keep coming back to one thing, the kids.

*More than one witness claimed that Jason McAllister returned to the McAllister Farm as a young man some years after their family abandoned it. No one knew how long he was there before anyone noticed. That was agreed on.*

*The next question is not so simple. They didn't know when the rumour started or who started it, but whispers began spreading in town. There were two children living at the farm with Jason McAllister.*

*The old sheriff, Rick Dalton, visited the McAllister Farm to find out. Apparently he found no children, but the rumours persisted for years.*

*If Jason did have two kids living on that farm, nobody has actually seen them that I could find, and they did not exist legally.*

*The young Jason McAllister was just as reclusive and protective of his privacy as his father had been. No one dared go down that stretch of road towards the McAllister Farm.*

*It would not have been hard to keep two children secret. But why? Where did they come from?*

*They were real. They were there. Every way I play it out in my mind, every imagined possibility to explain why he returned and what he was doing there, every vision I run through my head of the adult Jason McAllister living on the farm, those two kids are like ghosts haunting my thoughts. A boy and a girl; just like the McAllister children.*

*They were there. It feels right.*

"Who are they and where did he get them?" Lawrence asks the papers spread before him.

He has a thought. "Were they his?"

The thought starts to grow. On a hunch, he gets up and goes to the coat closet by the apartment door.

Opening the closet door, he studies its contents. It is filled with banker boxes. The boxes are filled with copies of reports, statements, newspaper clippings, and interview notes; a treasure trove of saved research from a lifetime spent as an investigative reporter.

These are files Lawrence inherited.

He studies the boxes thoughtfully.

"I have the feeling that somewhere hidden in the past is the answer. There is no better place to start."

# 15 Proof William is Alive

Lawrence has spent hours searching through the boxes of old files looking for any references to missing children and feels drained and wrung out, his head in a fog of names and dates and dated photos.

The buzzing of the door buzzer interrupts him like a rude alarm clock. Not expecting it, Lawrence looks up with a startled expression to stare at the door.

He gets up stiffly and goes to the intercom on the wall, pressing and holding the button.

"Hello," he says into the intercom, then releases the button.

"It's Jim," a voice crackles at him through the poor intercom feed.

Lawrence presses and holds the button down. "Come up." He presses the other button and holds it for a few moments. Downstairs, the inner door at the main entrance unlocks while a buzzer bleats.

Minutes later Jim is knocking on Lawrence's door.

Lawrence peeks out through the peephole even though he knows who is on the other side before opening the door.

It takes him a few moments to unlock and remove the assortment of locks, bars, and anti-home invasion devices.

Jim eyes the security features as he closes the door behind him.

"You've gotten more paranoid since the last time I've been here," he says. "You added a few more."

Lawrence shrugs. "Some people don't like the questions I ask."

Being an investigative reporter, Lawrence gets the odd threat against his well-being. Being an investigative reporter who has a tendency to dig a little too deep, take his investigations a little too far, and write stories without bias or consideration for whether it's moral, he sometimes gets more than the average number of threats. This is probably not a good thing, since Lawrence is also a coward.

Jim nods to the mess. "Research?"

Lawrence nods. "I'm sure Jason McAllister had two kids. They would be adults now. Coffee?"

Lawrence is already moving towards the small kitchen.

"If you don't have anything stronger," Jim says.

"There's no record of him ever having kids," Jim says doubtfully.

"I'm trying to find out where he got them," Lawrence calls out from the kitchen. "More than one interviewee told me about a rumour that started some months after he came back to the farm the first time. A rumour he had a couple kids there."

"So where do you think they came from?"

Lawrence refills his cup and pours another for Jim. The coffee in the pot is hours old and will taste burnt from sitting on the warming element too long.

"They could be his or a girlfriend's kids. I can't find any record of his ever having any, but that doesn't rule out a girlfriend."

Lawrence returns to the living room, handing Jim a coffee. Jim scowls at it before he even takes a sip.

"My best guess is he kidnapped them or got stuck with them unintentionally and didn't know what to do with them," Lawrence continues. "I just don't know why. It doesn't seem to fit the man."

Jim raises an eyebrow. "He doesn't seem the daddy type to me. Do you have any theories why he would kidnap a couple of kids?"

"I doubt it would have been on purpose. Do you remember the murders and disappearances of young women in the area when Jason McAllister was just a kid? The townspeople were convinced his father William McAllister was guilty. The McAllisters fled and the sheriff caught the killer. It was not McAllister."

"Okay, so?" Jim's curiosity is piqued now.

"Check that file there," Lawrence points to a stapled set of papers. They are crisp white against the age-yellowed papers around them.

Jim picks it up and starts skimming through it.

"What's this?" he asks, although it is all too clear what it is.

"An autopsy report," Lawrence says.

Jim skims through the report with a puzzled frown.

"The body is described as being so decomposed there was little more than a few bits of bones and hair fibres. The body was carefully wrapped; almost lovingly. The report describes the remaining shreds of cloth wrapping it. To their joy there had been remnants of hand

and foot bones with nails still intact. That joy quickly faded when bacterial analysis and microscopic study failed to find any viable evidence under the nails. They had resorted to testing the soil itself. No cause of death could be discerned."

"So what's your take from this?" Jim asks. "Why this report? This girl?" The girl is a young woman, barely out of her teens.

"That's one of your graveyard bodies from the woods." Lawrence points at the report in Jim's hand. "She is one of the missing women from back then who was never found."

He pauses. "I guess someone has to break the news to her family."

"How did you get this?" Jim looks up at Lawrence. The other victims of the decades old serial killer case had been exhumed from their family plots after the discovery of the graveyard in the woods to be re-tested for whatever traces the magic of modern science can discover.

Lawrence shrugs. "I have my sources."

Jim humphs. *Someone leaked the report to the reporter against department policy.* This is a new question for Jim now.

"Another man killed the women who disappeared around town back then. There was no connection between him or his victims to the McAllisters, except for unfounded suspicions. Jason McAllister was a child then. The killer dumped the bodies carelessly, sloppily. So why is this one body different? Why was only this one body so carefully buried in the massive hidden graveyard in the woods beyond the McAllister farm?"

"Could he have left the body too close to the farm, forcing William McAllister to dispose of it? What was he hiding up there besides that graveyard? Odds are, if the body was left dumped in those woods, the graveyard would never have been found and the body scavenged by animals until there was nothing left."

"Where are you going with this?" Jim asks.

"I was looking for another body; one that has not been found yet."

"Who?"

"Amy Dodds, the only child that vanished around that time."

"The profilers didn't think the kid was a victim of the same killer as the women."

"Neither do I."

"What are you thinking?"

"What's the difference between that woman in your hand and the others who local to the area?"

Jim thinks about it, sifting through notes in his mind, trying to pull up the memory of those cases from well before his time. He had pulled the files and gone over them after the discovery of the graves in the woods. The first thing he did was investigate any disappearances and murders in the area going back decades.

Jim looks up at Lawrence.

"They were sloppy," he says. "Every one of them, the bodies, the dump sites, the burials even, were sloppy. The killer made some efforts to cover his tracks and lead investigators in the wrong directions, but it was done so haphazardly that a child could have done better. He left clues and evidence all over the body dump sites and the bodies themselves.

The very first notes on the case by Sheriff Rick Dalton are his opinion the killer was a man with a low IQ."

"This one," he waves the report in his hand, "is different. The body was buried in the hidden graveyard. The disposal was expert, like the rest of the graves."

"Exactly!" Lawrence squawks excitedly, his hand snapping out to point at Jim. "Someone covered up this one killing, but only this one. Why?"

Jim shrugs. "We know Jason McAllister has to have some connection to the graves. We just can't prove it. Most of the graves were dug before his time. Before his father's time even."

He thinks it out, shifting pieces of the puzzle around in his head, rearranging them.

Jim meets Lawrence's eyes again.

"He learned it from the master. This woman vanished when Jason McAllister was just a child. She was expertly buried. There's no way a child could have done that."

"Exactly!" Lawrence crows. "His father!"

Jim nods, "So William McAllister was connected to the graves long before his son. We suspected that."

Further understanding dawns in a natural sequence of events.

"The bodies were dumped randomly around the area. I'm willing to bet this body was dumped too close to the McAllister farm. William McAllister could not risk the police searching the area with the secret graveyard beyond his farm and who knows what could be hidden on his property, so he disposed of the body where he assumed it would never be found again."

He frowns.

"But none of the bodies exhumed could be linked to either McAllister. They were apparently burying the bodies, but they were not killing them."

"Except one." Lawrence pauses to give it time to sink in. "Amy Dodds."

"You think William McAllister killed Amy Dodds?" Jim asks doubtfully. "It's possible, but why her? Why only her?"

"Jason McAllister," Lawrence says with a wolfish grin. "His father may have only buried the bodies, but I think Jason is a killer. I think the Dodds girl was his first. That's why the McAllisters ran."

Jim studies him.

"What do you know?" he asks.

Lawrence digs out sheets of notes, eager to share what he learned. He thrusts them in front of Jim, pointing at them.

"I managed to trace some of Jason McAllister's movements over the last fifteen years. Tracing credit card and bank withdrawals, I was able to pinpoint not only where he lived but also where he travelled. He's moved around a bit, never staying in one place for more than a few years. He shows up and then vanishes again, on and off the radar up until four years before Jane Doe showed up. All of a sudden he vanished completely.

He doesn't take them from close to home, that's too much chance of getting caught. He's not dumb, but obviously not as smart as his father was. Where he goes women tend to vanish, everywhere he goes except close to where he's living at the time."

He stares at Jim expectantly.

"So you think Jason has been kidnapping and killing since he was a boy," Jim says. "But why take the kids? Usually a man who wants to pass on his legacy also wants his own son to pass it on to. There are enough people out there that he could have easily found some woman to have kids with."

"I don't think it was intentional. I think he kidnapped a woman, however he did it, and accidentally took the kids too.

I don't think he planned on the kids. And, for whatever reason, he couldn't just get rid of them. He ended up keeping them."

"That's pretty farfetched," Jim frowns.

"But it feels right."

"How do you expect to find out?"

"I need to find a missing woman and kids from around the right time. But it could be from anywhere. It's one of his missing blocks of time when he was off the radar, right before he appeared back at the farm." Lawrence looks eager at the prospect.

"You may never find it."

"That's why I think in the meantime we should ask."

"Ask? Who?"

"William McAllister."

Jim grunts. "Good luck. He's probably dead."

"He's alive. We just have to find him."

Jim becomes more alert at this news. "How do you know?"

"He still owns title to the McAllister Farm," Lawrence says.

Jim shakes his head. "Paperwork that wasn't updated. It could be impossible to find him, if he's even alive. How did you manage to trace Jason's movements?"

Lawrence just smirks.

"I'm starting with the address on the land title," Lawrence says. "The document was sent care of a post office box. Even if it's no longer used by McAllister, there has to be some old records, maybe a forwarding address. Somewhere, William McAllister exists and I'll find him."

Jim's phone rings.

"McNelly," he answers it gruffly. He listens, nodding, and scowls. "Thanks. Keep an eye on him. I'll get inside and check it out."

He turns to Lawrence. "I have to go. Jason McAllister is on the move."

Lawrence nods. "And I have a couple of kids to find."

"Do you think you'll be able to find them?" Jim asks, eyeing the mess of scattered reports. "Those are his files, aren't they?"

Lawrence grins. Even his happy grin looks sinister, wolfish.

"If there is a report on a missing woman or kids from that time, it will be here. He was very thorough, obsessed, about missing person reports."

A flash of sadness crosses his face and Lawrence quickly pushes it away. The man he inherited these boxes from had been obsessed with something he would not speak of. He would only say it was big, very big. All Lawrence knows is that the files include the most extensive collection of missing person files he has ever seen. They cross both continents and generations.

*What were you looking for?* He silently asks again. But the dead don't answer.

"See you later," Jim says, breaking the thought.

Lawrence nods as Jim leaves and returns to searching the files.

As Jim rides the elevator down, he keeps turning it over in his head. *William McAllister is still alive.*

"I have to find him," he says, although he knows it will probably be Hawkworth who finds him. *He may be a reporter, but Hawkworth has a knack for finding people and things that mean to not be found.*

"I have to find out what William McAllister knows about his son Jason and Michael Underwood's relationship."

As soon as the elevator doors open, Jim steps out and dials his phone.

"Beth," he says, "I need you to find someone. Start with the deed on the McAllister Farm. I need you to find William McAllister. If he's alive, he may be in a seniors care home."

He pauses, listening.

"Thanks Beth." He disconnects the call.

*If Lawrence does not find William McAllister, Beth might. Despite his lack of a personable personality, Lawrence Hawkworth is able to dig up almost anything and convince almost anyone to give him information they shouldn't.*

*But if a record exists anywhere on a computer linked to the internet, Beth is probably the best chance to find it. Lawrence is a technophobe.*

Huffing and out of breath, Jim heads out to find his car.

# Part Four

# The Next Life

# 16 A New Name and a New Start

"Have you thought about a name you like?" Michael asks. "Make it something you'll remember easily. We have to decide this now so I can get things in motion. It's time for us to move on. As soon as we have the documents with our new legal names and our new backgrounds in place, we'll go. You'll like the new place better, you'll see."

Kathy doesn't quite see.

*We changed our names so many times I don't even know who I am anymore,* she thinks. *Every place we stayed in on the way to where we are now has been as depressingly shabby as this one. Our neighbours always argue a lot, the kids are rude and disrespectful and too often living through a childhood of rebellious desperation. Some of the neighbours and neighbourhoods we've stayed in are downright scary.*

*Michael always chooses quick turnover rentals that he pays cash for and uses a false name. He doesn't even use the alias he's living under at the time to rent them. They are the sort of places the landlords don't bother trying to keep up with repairs on and don't care that they know you are probably giving a fake name as long as you pay cash in advance. They don't expect the tenants to stay a second month and don't care because there are enough people living below the level of poverty desperate for even their crappy house with affordable rent that they never stay empty long.*

*They are the kind of places that a person can get lost in.*

"Why do we have to change our names again?" Kathy asks.

"To keep us safe," Michael says.

"Can't I keep my first name again?" She looks at him sadly. There are too many reasons to be attached to her own name.

*It's the only thing I have left that my mother gave me*. Like all of them, she keeps this thought to herself.

Michael shakes his head. "We are making a clean break this time. We leave nothing to trace us by when we move on."

He points to the front door for emphasis.

"Starting the moment we walk through that door, Katherine and Michael no longer exist. We are new people."

He studies her. Kathy has her eyes down, looking at the floor and feeling cornered.

"Elaine Carver?" Kathy asks finally, looking up at him.

"Are you asking me?" Michael says with a playful smile.

Kathy fidgets. "No, I think that's the name." She still sounds unsure.

*Elaine is my mother's middle name at least*, she thinks.

"It's a beautiful name, like you," Michael says, moving closer and taking her in his arms.

Kathy always feels safer in his embrace and gratefully leans into it.

"Have you thought of your name?" she asks.

"I'm still thinking," Michael says, bending down and kissing her. "I'll come up with something by the time I see the guy to get our new identities made."

"What about David?" Kathy asks. "I've always liked that name. It sounds like someone who is nice."

Michael stiffens and releases her, stepping back.

Kathy tenses, feeling him stiffen. She watches him anxiously.

*Is he angry? But why?*

Michael paces away, stops, and turns on her on the verge of anger. He pushes down the rage rising inside him like a heat in his suddenly sour stomach. He struggles to control his expression, tries to smile, and fails.

"Where did you get that name?" he asks coldly.

Kathy senses the cold rage in his voice and immediately recognizes the danger.

She learned to be good at recognizing the kind of rage that brings on violence when she was with Ronnie. Michael saved her from Ronnie, taking her away from his drunken abusiveness. He killed Ronnie and she is grateful for that too. She doesn't have to spend the rest of her life looking over her shoulder in fear that Ronnie is walking up to her right at that moment. That doesn't stop her from sometimes being overwhelmed with that fear now and then, even knowing she does not have to be afraid.

Suddenly she feels that same old fear now, only this time afraid of the anger she senses in Michael.

"I don't know," Kathy says quietly. "It's just a name. You don't like it, that's okay."

Michael stares at her.

"Don't ever call me that," Michael wants to scream in her face, clenching his jaw to keep the words from coming out.

He pushes the red heat of anger down, forcing himself to be calm.

*She doesn't know about David McAllister*, he reminds himself. *I killed and buried him a long time ago; when I ran away as a kid and lived on the streets under the dark cloud of that name, always afraid and running, knowing he would find me.*

*I thought I saw him a few times, Jason McAllister, the man who pretended to be my father. I'd be running again. Finally, I got smart and let go of my past, who I was, my everything. I abandoned the only name I knew myself as when I ran away, the name Jason McAllister gave me years before when he took Cassie and me to live with him, when he killed our mother. After that, it was easy to walk away from my life, my name, and start a new life with a new name whenever I needed to. I never felt the need to look back or hold on to any part of my new past.*

*You are dead David McAllister. I told myself when I dropped that name for a new one so many years ago. I have killed you. You are dead.*

He snaps out of it, pushing his thoughts down with the anger.

Michael doesn't like thinking about his past. It makes ugly memories well up, vile and dark.

"It's okay." He manages a gentler tone, seeing the tension in her body and the fear in her eyes. His voice still holds the undercurrent of the rage he is barely suppressing. He can feel that rage beginning to drain away.

"It's only a temporary name anyway, until we get married. Then we change our names again. I'll be Ryan Crowley," he says.

Kathy stands stiffly looking at him. She wants more than anything to look away, but can't.

*How does he go from happy and loving one moment to dangerously angry the next? It's like a switch just got flipped.* It's not the first time she asked herself this question.

And the switch is flipped again.

Michael smiles and relaxes, stepping forward and taking her in his embrace again, leaning down to kiss the top of her head tenderly.

Kathy does not resist despite feeling tense and afraid still.

He seems oblivious to the stiffness of her body that gives away her uncertainty about him.

*I'm safe with him,* she tries to tell herself, *safer than anywhere else.*

"I'll go get the paperwork and our new lives started," Michael says, smiling. "It shouldn't take long, a few weeks at most. Then we will make the move."

"This place we are moving to," Kathy asks, her voice holding a slight tremor, "where is it?"

"You'll find out when we get there," Michael says. "It's rural, lots of open space and no city."

"How rural?" Kathy asks, her curiosity helping the fear to slip away just a little. She almost asks if it's a farm and thinks better of it. She hopes not. She is terrified of the complete isolation, of feeling trapped like she did on the McAllister Farm.

Kathy is filled with a sudden icy chill washing through her like a wave, drowning her, making her legs weak. She feels faint and sick.

She wants to scream. *Please don't let it be a farm.* Horrid memories of being locked for endless hours in the root cellar of the McAllister Farm press against her, making blackness close in.

The terror and loneliness. The hunger. Thirst so desperate she thought her tongue would swell up until she could no longer breathe. The hopelessness, knowing she would die but not knowing when. Wishing he would just get it over with.

The sick feeling of gratefulness that went against every other emotion tormenting her, grateful to the man, her tormentor, for kidnapping her, for the death he will soon give her, for freeing her from Ronnie. The terror every time she heard his footsteps above, terror that filled her to bursting and tore her apart when he brought another victim home to the farm.

The icy chill continually washing through her in waves becomes a welcome thing. She embraces its relief against the heat of emotions and fear.

"Kathy," Michael's voice comes from far away, sounding anxious, afraid, repeating her name over and over.

"Kathy! Kathy! Are you okay? Kathy!"

Kathy is confused, her mind fuzzy. She blinks, unsure where she is.

For a brief moment the chill clinging to her is the cold damp root cellar floor. The hardness pressed against her backside is the hard floor of the living room in the little farmhouse where she had collapsed after being forced to leave the root cellar to clean for him, weak with hunger and thirst after he had mostly forgotten to feed her.

Kathy looks up into the eyes of her kidnapper and terror rushes up through her. His eyes are filled with remorse, pain, and worry, just as they had been that day when he finally saw her for the weakened gaunt creature she had become under his neglect. The terror is pushed out by confusion.

"Kathy, are you okay?" Michael asks again, holding her in his arms as she lay on the floor, staring worriedly down at her.

Kathy blinks her eyes again, trying to focus on her surroundings. She is in a dingy little house, neglected and overused, like she feels.

"Michael?" she whispers weakly. "What happened?"

"You fainted," he moans into her hair as he pulls her closer and holds her like he is afraid he is about to lose her.

After a long moment passes, Kathy tries to pull away, to get up. She's weak and her limbs don't cooperate.

"No, just rest," Michael says. "Lay still."

"I-I have to get up," Kathy says weakly, feeling waves of nausea and weakness flowing through her. She starts shivering.

"Shhh, it's okay."

"No." Kathy pushes against him weakly. She starts to feel panic with the surging nausea. "I'm going to-."

Before she can finish the words, her fear comes rushing up her throat, washing them both with hot vomit.

"Throw up," she finishes weakly.

Michael only holds her closer, making soothing sounds. He can feel her shivering like she is cold, but knows it is shock from fainting. So is the vomit they are both now covered in.

He picks her up gently and carries her to the bathroom. He strips them both and lifts her into the tub with him.

Turning the shower on, they are both blasted briefly with ice cold water and he tries to shield her from it, taking the brunt of it with his own back.

Michael gasps with the sudden icy blast.

The water warms in moments and he lets its warmth wash over them both, gently washing the vomit off Kathy.

By the time he's finished washing them both Kathy is still weak but able stand on her own, leaning on the shower wall for support. Michael lifts her out of the tub and dries her off as she stands there. He carries her to the bedroom and lays her on the bed, covering her with blankets.

"I threw up on you," Kathy says, her voice still shaking. "I'm sorry."

"It's okay," Michael says gently. "It's not your fault. It's the stress. We're going through a big change. Everything will be great, you'll see. You rest. I'll go clean it up. Then I'll go see the guy about getting our new lives started."

He leaves her alone.

Kathy lies there, huddled under the blankets and wishing she was warmer. The warmth is coming back to her beneath the blankets, but slowly.

She can hear the sounds of him cleaning, scrubbing the floor and rinsing out their clothes.

Michael wrings the clothes out and bundles them up. He finds the bag they use for laundry and comes back into the bedroom, pulling clothes from the hamper and stuffing them into the bag.

"I'll stop at the laundromat and do a load," he says. "I don't want to leave the puke the dry on."

He stops by the bed, kisses her on the forehead tenderly, and leaves.

Kathy listens to the front door close and lock. A moment later his truck fires up and the pitch of the engine changes, telling her he is driving away.

Still feeling weak and shaky, Kathy gets up and wraps herself in a housecoat. She goes to the living room. Pausing, she looks at the floor where she vomited. Michael did a thorough job of cleaning it up, even sprinkling carpet deodorizer on the floor for the smell.

The white patch of deodorizer stares back at her; a reminder of the memories that flooded through her, causing her to faint.

Kathy turns away, feeling her stomach lurch with nausea again. She goes to the front window and looks out.

*Soon Kathy won't exist anymore, like I'm dead and they just haven't found the body yet. I'll have lost the only thing I have left of who I was, the last piece of my mother who is probably grief-stricken with worry not knowing what happened to me.*

"She might even think I'm dead."

"No," she decides, "Mom would cling to my memory and refuse to believe I'm gone forever. She will always watch for me in every crowd, waiting for me to be found and come home. That's the kind of person she is. She'll never give up on me, not until they show her my dead body."

Knowing the torment she is putting her mother through, especially after being kidnapped and found again, makes Kathy feel wretched.

She wishes more than anything in the world to call her mother right now.

She turns to the phone, not letting herself think about anything. She isn't going to call. She's just picking up the phone. She picks up the receiver, her mother's number itching at the tips of her fingers. She puts the receiver to her ear and is met with silence. She frowns at the phone and taps the hang-up button a few times. Nothing. The phone is dead. Numbness fills her.

"Michael knew I would weaken. He disconnected the phone," she whispers.

She sags and tears slip down her cheeks. She looks at the clock.

"How long will it take to stop at the laundromat to wash and dry a load? Two hours? An hour and a half? How long to change our lives forever?

It must cost a lot of money to buy fake identities complete with legitimate documents and a past that will show up in any search or background investigation. Where does Michael get the money from?"

For the first time since running away with Michael, Kathy feels the overwhelming urge to flee from him.

# 17 Peek-A-Boo Neighbour

Jason McAllister is sitting in his room watching out the window. There is little else to do in a tiny single-room apartment with barely enough room to fit a narrow bed, small dresser, and single wooden kitchen chair.

He sees the brief flutter of the upstairs window curtain of the house across the street. He has seen it on repeated occasions.

Across the street, the man in the upstairs window is looking out. He sees the man in the upstairs window of the rooming house looking out his window. He's often seen him sitting for long periods just watching out that window.

He lets the curtain drop, pulling his arm back and bolting to huddle in the corner.

"He's staring at me again," he says, his voice jagged like his nerves. It is beyond his comprehension that the man could just be staring out at nothing, watching the occasional car and pedestrian go by out of boredom.

He forces himself out of the corner. He has important work to do. He gets back to business.

Today he is busy plastering all the windows of his little room with layers of newsprint soaked in water and baking soda, creating a papier-mâché barrier. Unfortunately, the smooth nature of glass makes it a less than perfect perch for the slimy paper that keeps sliding down the slick surface.

He keeps at it, determination fuelling his energy with a rough buzz, his movements jittery.

"He won't be able to see in through my windows and walls anymore when I'm finished." He has already half finished re-wallpapering the inside of the outer wall with tinfoil to block the man's psychic stare.

Jason is feeling too cooped up to just sit in his room any longer.

*The neighbour lady has been doing a pretty good job avoiding me, which is just as well. Seeing her stirs urges that I can't risk answering to right now.*

He leaves his post at the window and goes downstairs. For the first time, he enters the living room.

The room is dark and gloomy, the lights out and curtains drawn closed.

Jason stands just inside the doorway surveying the room. There are plates, clothes, and garbage cluttering the room. The foul smell of rotting food, dirty clothes, and human over-habitation fills the air.

He flips the light switch on the wall a few times. It does nothing. He pulls the curtains open, letting the sunlight in through the dirty window.

The brightening of the room does nothing to brighten its appearance. The furniture in the small room looks sadder in the light.

Jason looks around. The dead plant still sits forlornly on top of an old tube television, the moth-eaten drapes hanging from a slightly bent curtain rod, ugly and discoloured from years of tobacco smoke. The walls are also stained from the smoke residue, looking as if nicotine infused condensation had sometimes trickled down the walls.

He shakes his head at the mess.

"There is no reason to live like this," he mutters.

Jason starts picking through the litter, collecting whatever dirty dishes he can find in the filth. There isn't a lot. The house has few dishes that are supposed to be available for all its residents. Apparently they are all here.

He dumps the dishes in the kitchen sink and picks up the garbage can, carrying it back to the living room.

Jason picks through the rubble, tossing the garbage into the can and the clothes into a pile. Some might have been clean, it doesn't matter. Cockroaches skitter away in a panic when he picks some items up.

"There must still be a bloody nest of them somewhere," he mutters, certain the still unseen living room resident is the main reason they are still flourishing despite the poison traps. He glances in the direction of the kitchen where the basement door resides, although it isn't visible from here.

For a brief moment he pictures swarms of the pests slithering endlessly over each other down in the basement with a dry rustle that never stops. He stomps his foot quickly, crushing one bug attempting to make its escape.

When he's done, the garbage can is full and the pile of clothes is surprisingly small. He carries the trash can back to the kitchen and retrieves the cleaning supplies he left under the kitchen sink. He isn't worried his housemates will steal them. None of them seem to care less about the cleanliness of where they live.

Digging out the vacuum, another barely functional resident of the rooming house, he drags it along with his armload of cleaning products to the living room.

He turns the vacuum on and it comes to life with a sickly growl, making unpleasant crackling sounds as it sucks up dirt and chip crumbs from the carpet as he moves it back and forth.

Jason spends a good hour cleaning that living room. He discovers the bulbs in the lamps had been loosened so they won't turn on. When he finishes, it smells much better and the discarded clothes are tied in a garbage bag in the corner. If they remain untouched, he will put them out with the rest of the trash.

Jason spends another hour with the ancient television pulled out and its back removed, trying to see if he might be able to repair it.

Giving up on the television for now, Jason takes out the trash again and washes the dishes. Finally done, he parks himself in the sole kitchen chair and just sits.

A few hours later the front door crashes open and the stinky couple come staggering in. They bounce drunkenly off the wall, hanging on to each other to keep from falling. She giggles, but it sounds off. Something is upsetting her.

Jason hears them both gasp in shock. He smiles. *They saw the living room.*

"What the hell happened here?" The woman's voice is shrill with surprise and unexpected pleasure. "Oh my gawd!" He can hear them muttering, their words slurred.

Her boyfriend's tone of voice is rude, annoyed. Jason can't make out what he said to her, but it sounds harsh. She hushes up quickly and they head for the stairs together.

As they ascend the stairs, Jason gets a glimpse of her face. It is puffy and swollen looking, splotchy from the tears she already shed. Their eyes meet for that brief heartbeat as she passes out of sight. Hers are a bottomless pit of unhappiness, outlined with red from the tears that threaten to come again. Bruising stains her cheek.

"Someone roughed her up," Jason says quietly.

He is tired. He gets up to head up to his own room, glancing briefly at that padlocked basement door before leaving the kitchen.

Halfway up the stairs he can hear the stinky couple arguing in their shared room. He pauses, looking up towards the sound, and continues on to the second floor.

Jason stops outside their door, listening to the angry voices. There is a thump. It could be a body falling or something else, then snoring followed by soft sobbing.

It's a usual day for The Stinkers, as he mentally calls them.

Jason goes to his own room, closing the door behind him. He lies on his bed for a long while before finally dozing off.

Jason's snoring sputters and stops and he opens his eyes. It's the middle of the night. He was woken by the pressure in his bladder. He gets up and stumbles out of his room to the bathroom, bleary eyed and more asleep than awake.

He groans with the relief as he urinates, tucks himself away, flushes, and steps back into the hallway.

Jason stops, listening. He heard a sound. It takes a moment to place it. *Downstairs.*

Fully awake now, he treads softly, moving down the hall to the top of the stairs and peaking over, looking down.

He listens to the sounds of someone moving around, swearing quietly. He is sure it's coming from the living room.

The main floor is in darkness with just the weak light of the moon and stars coming in the windows giving enough light to see shapes without any real details. Whoever is down there hasn't turned on any lights.

Jason starts creeping down the stairs, staying low and against the wall to stay out of sight. He stops at the bottom, crouching pressed against the railing.

*It could be a burglar, but not likely. There is nothing here to take and someone robbing the place wouldn't waste so much time in one room or be moving things and swearing.*

He hears now the sounds are coming from the kitchen.

Looking through the stair railing to the kitchen doorway, he watches for any movement. The figure shifts, just a sliver of them in view at the edge of the kitchen doorway, moves away, and then walks past the doorway to vanish again.

Jason leaves the stairs, moving quietly into the dark living room. He looks around to see if anything looks out of place. The garbage bag of clothes is ripped open and the clothes spilled out carelessly on the floor where they were left after being rifled through.

He hears footsteps. The intruder is coming down the hall.

Jason presses against the wall by the living room doorway, holding his breath, waiting.

The intruder steps into the living room, dressed in dark clothes; a black hoodie with the hood pulled over his head hiding his face. He gets only the smallest glimpse of the pale flesh of the face, not enough to judge age, sex, or any other characteristics. The intruder is shorter than average height and skinny.

He watches the intruder stare down at the clothes.

The intruder starts turning towards Jason.

Jason pounces before the intruder has a chance to see him, lunging forward to take him down in a tackle, letting his weight and the force of his momentum take them both to the floor, grabbing and pinning the intruder's arms.

They hit the floor with a thump that should have woken the household, the intruder's cry of surprise cut short quickly with the collision with the hard floor and Jason's weight working together to knock the wind from his lungs with a sudden wheeze of the air being forced out.

The intruder is a lightweight compared to Jason, and easily overpowered. Jason is fit and strong still, his muscles accustomed to hard labour.

The intruder gasps and gags; coughing and trying to suck in air that will not come at first, impotently trying to struggle free.

Jason gets up, yanking the intruder with him, standing him up and then shoving him roughly down into a chair.

He steps forward, reaching out and roughly yanking the hood back to reveal the intruder's identity.

Jason blanches, tries to hide his shocked reaction, and stares back at the terrified face staring up at him.

*David.*

He almost says it, catching the name before it slips out. *Of course it isn't David. David is a grown man now.*

A rush of emotions flows through him, surprise, shock, fear at what he had done so many years ago. He feels weak suddenly, dizzy, the room darkening.

The frightened boy staring up at him can't be any older than David was when he ran away.

Warily, watching for any movement that might signal the boy is about to bolt, Jason reaches and flips on the light switch, bringing two table lamps to sallow life.

"What are you doing here?" Jason demands, his voice rough and angry, trying not to let the emotions tearing around inside him show.

The boy swallows the lump in his throat, staring up in mute terror. He cannot make his jaw work to make any words come out.

"I asked you a question. What are you doing here?" Jason repeats.

He studies the boy. His pant legs are rolled up and bunched around his ankles so he would not be walking on them and he seems even smaller inside the hoodie that is sizes too big. His worn runners look like they must flop on his feet with every step, much too large like the clothes. His hair is greasy and unwashed and needs a haircut. His face is pale in a sickly way, washed out with fear and probably ill from not eating anything but junk and not getting enough sunlight.

He steps back so the boy can see the clothes on the floor. They are oversized for the boy, like the clothes he wears now. Most likely they were stolen from some machine in a laundromat or grabbed quickly at some homeless shelter without checking sizes in a hurry to flee before they call the authorities to collect the under-aged boy.

He thumbs towards the clothes on the floor. "That yours?"

The boy nods. He looks around the room, eyes as big as saucers.

"You've been living here, haven't you?" Jason asks.

The boy nods again.

"Can't speak?" Jason asks. "Speak, talk."

"Y-y-yes," the boy manages to stammer out, working his mouth hard to force the words out through his fear.

"You are too young," Jason shakes his head. "They don't let kids in a place like this. We got a cowboy junkie, a hooker, and a loser. No kids."

The boy moves his arm hesitantly, pointing and motioning upwards. "The attic," he mumbles.

"What about it?"

"And the crazy guy in the attic."

"Yes; and the crazy guy in the attic." Jason pauses. "And someone is living in here." He indicates the living room.

The boy looks sheepish.

"What's your name?" Jason thinks better of it. "Forget it. I don't want to know your name. I don't even know you are here, you got me?"

The boy just stares at him.

"Why are you here? Go home kid. Go home to your family."

"I can't."

The boy's eyes hold a troubled faraway look.

*This kid is running from something, maybe from someone,* Jason thinks.

"Why not? Just go home. You have no business here. Does anyone even know you are here?"

The boy shrugs. He is used to meeting fear and confrontation with a blank stare, his body turning numb to mute the trembling that might have given away the sinking sick feeling inside him, and has gotten pretty good at hiding his emotions.

He thinks he is better at it than he really is.

"They don't pay attention," he says. "The other people here don't even use the living room. They don't care."

"I haven't seen you before," Jason says. "I've seen The Cowboy and The Stinkers."

The boy almost grins at that, but he's afraid of the man confronting him despite his attempt at showing bravado.

Jason continues.

"I've seen your filth piled up in here. The others don't seem to know or care who is living in here. How come nobody sees you?"

"I only come at night. I leave early. I go where I got to go."

Jason knows what that means. The boy hides somewhere else during the day. Somewhere that probably isn't safe or warm at night. By his pale flesh it's probably someplace underground, a parking garage or basement, something like that.

"So you decided to hole up here," Jason says.

The boy nods. "It's shelter."

Images of David and the other street kids he hung around with after he ran away from home come to Jason. He had followed David, keeping tabs on him, making sure he was all right.

He knows the kinds of things these street kids do to survive on the street and it makes him feel sick. It made him feel sick then too; knowing the hell David was going through. But every time he got close enough to try to bring the boy home, he ran again. He could have just taken David home by force, but he knew David would have just kept running away.

He would have had to keep him locked away in the cold dark root cellar to keep him there. He couldn't do that to the kid.

*It was just something that was in David, the need to run. The memories, long suppressed, of a life before. David knew he didn't belong to me; didn't belong with me.*

*And there was what happened to Cassie.*

Her smiling face floats up in Jason's memory, so small, her innocence. He pushes that painful memory back too. *I can't think about that right now. I have this other problem to deal with.*

Jason studies the boy again.

*He's terrified. Not just of the man who just attacked him in the dark. Not just of being discovered squatting in the living room of an un-cared for rooming house where the tenants keep to themselves and don't see or care about anything else.*

*The boy is scared of being taken back to wherever or whoever he is running away from.*

*It's the same fear I saw in David's eyes.*

Jason steps forward, grabbing the kid by his hoodie's neckline, bunching the fabric in his fist just below the boy's throat, and pulls him roughly to his feet. He pulls the boy close, their faces almost touching.

"Look kid," Jason says quietly, a warning, his breath warm on the boy's face. "You don't live here. I don't care if you crash here, but you don't live here. I don't see your clothes, I don't see your garbage, I don't see your dirty dishes, and I don't smell you. This is a living room, not a rodent's den. Respect it."

The boy is frozen in fear.

Jason releases him with a rough shove, making the boy step back or fall on his ass.

"If you get caught living here it's not just your ass that will get locked up, got it? You will be sent back to wherever you came from and so maybe will everyone else living here for harbouring a runaway kid. This isn't a hotel. Every one of them has a record. They will all go to jail over you." He motions towards the floor above.

Without another word, he turns away and mounts the stairs to go back to bed.

# 18 Slaughterhouse

It doesn't matter to Michael where he works or what he does. He did a lot of things to survive since he ran away as a kid. He did a lot of things that would shock most people, things a kid has to do to survive on the street.

He did a lot of things before he ran away too, things his father who is not his real father made him do, but those are memories he does not let himself think about.

For now, he has taken a job in a slaughterhouse under the identity of Ryan Crowley. If he was a different sort of person he would never be able to eat meat again after working in a slaughterhouse and witnessing firsthand what goes on there.

Michael is at work, his dark blue-grey coveralls covering him from the neck down, heavy steel-toed work boots protecting his feet, and a large black rubber apron covering most of his front. He wears heavy rubber work gloves. His protective hat that he is supposed to wear is tossed into a corner.

Large goggles with a single unbroken lens of tempered glass protect his eyes from splatter.

He is covered in the gore of the assembly line victims that passed through his hands over the past hours. The work is exhausting, both of body and spirit.

Michael wipes the spattered gore off the lens of his goggles with his sleeve as he presses the button and his victim is dragged away by the heavy chain it's hooked on.

They each have their own workspace inside the large warehouse building, the killing pits. The walls and floors are gouged and stained with feces and blood.

Metal railings create pens that are packed so tight with cattle that the animals are pressed together and unable to move.

Often that is the only thing keeping the weakened beasts from collapsing and being trampled to death beneath the hooves of their pen mates.

Some still manage to slip beneath the hooves of the others where, desperate to stay on their feet, the other cows low mournfully as they are forced to step on their fallen pen mate, stumbling. The animal on the ground would kick and try to get up, but it would be useless and she dies beneath the sharp hooves stepping on her and the sheer mass of cows bearing down on her, broken and suffocated.

Between the pens is a network of paths for the movement of the animals to the killing pits, gates placed where they want them to stop to better control the beasts.

The building is forever filled with the loud moaning of desolate animals calling mournfully against their cruel treatment.

The animals themselves are so despondent and weakened with illness, neglect, and abuse by the time they arrive at the slaughterhouse from the farms that mass produce them that they could not fight back even if the will had not already been beaten out of them before they arrive at the slaughterhouse yard.

The shear senseless violence and brutality of the slaughterhouse sickens Michael. Yes, even him, the man who committed the same sick violent brutality on so many women for not being her, Cassie.

The men he works with sicken him too.

One man, in particular, is especially bad. Trevor Mitchell. Not only is he the angriest, most hate-filled man Michael has ever met, he thrives on it.

All day, Michael watches Trevor in the next killing pit as he himself mechanically drags in and slaughters animal after animal, impaling the dead beasts on the hooks that are dragged by on heavy chains suspended from the ceiling, hoisting them up with the winch, and pressing the button that works the machinery that drags the carcasses on to the next step in the assembly line slaughter and brings a new hook for the next cow.

Cries and thrashing of tortured cows comes from the other pits at times.

Sometimes it takes too many shots to the head with the bolt gun to kill them, the men aiming carelessly, oblivious to the torment of their dying victim as the cow gives a few weak kicks in a final moment of mindless jerking spasms and confused pain.

Michael watches the dead cow in his pit drag away on the chain then turns and makes his way through the maze to the pens.

After hooking his cow to be dragged off, Trevor goes through the maze of metal fencing and gates and opens the gate to one of the pens with cattle packed in. Some just stand dumbly, other animals roll their eyes in their heads and try to shift away but have no place to go and are too defeated to really try.

Michael enters a pen and takes a cow by the head, leading her with the ease of a man who grew up working cattle and knows how to handle them. He has no use for force or abuse. She obediently moves where she is guided.

In the next pen, Trevor yells and swears at the cattle, grabbing a hook similar to an elephant hook, and using it to pull at one cow. She shudders at the painful barb of the hook, eyes rolling and lowing pleadingly as she tries to move away from the pain. Unfortunately, that movement brings her closer to him.

He hooks her again, yanking viciously on the hook, making her take another unwilling step away from the safety of the herd. There is no safety for any of them here, only pain and death.

She moves forward and stumbles.

Trevor switches from the hook to the cattle prod, jamming it hard into her ribs and rump, holding it there with electricity biting the animal's flesh with burning pain long after it is considered allowable by their employer to inflict this torture on the beasts.

The cow bawls and the smell of burning hair and flesh makes the other frightened cows tremble. The whole place terrorizes them, filled with the stench of blood, death, and fear.

He swears and rages at the beast, beating her mercilessly with the cattle prod until the already broken animal moves.

She does not know what to do or where to go. She only wants to please the humans so they stop hurting her.

Trevor drops the prod and grabs her tail with both hands, pulling on it painfully with all he has; all while yelling and swearing all his hatred at the world out at this helpless beast.

When she clears the gate, he closes it, keeping the rest of the slaughterhouse victims in the pen.

He moves the cow along the fenced path to his killing pit, punching, kicking, electrocuting, and beating her as they go even though she is moving obediently. At one point he winds up and gives the cow a head-numbing roundhouse kick, laughing callously as he staggers and almost falls on landing. He calls out to the others proudly, as if to display his prowess.

"Did you see that one?" He looks around to make sure they were watching. They look disinterestedly. A few laugh dully. It was nothing special. It's something they all do for kicks.

Michael's eyes narrow as he watches, keeping back and slowly leading his cow on.

Trevor beats and torments the cow all the way to his killing pit.

For some reason none but Trevor himself could know, this particular forlorn animal is drawing out of him a particular viciousness.

With his victim in place, Trevor thrills in beating and torturing the helpless animal.

The cow only stares back, suffering the abuse, her stomach heaving with the deep lowing calls of distress, not attempting to either escape or defend herself in any way.

Michael brings his cow into his pit and gets her in position.

Trevor finally tires himself out beating the cow. He drags the meat hook down and impales her on it, hoisting her up with the chain and winch without the consideration of slaughtering her first.

The tortured animal cries out long and low and can then only twitch and low mournfully.

The killing floor men are to move them into place, shoot three or four bolts into their brains through their thick skulls, and put them on the hooks to be dragged to the next room where they are disembowelled and bled in the next step of the butchering process. If the animals are lucky, the bolts do their job and they are dead before being impaled on the hooks.

Fast movement of cattle is expected and they aren't always dead by the time they are sliced open in the next room to let their intestines fall wetly to the concrete floor.

Watching the torture with a sick feeling, Michael envisions at that moment Trevor being the one dragged in, beaten and tossed around, and then impaled alive and aware on a meat hook to be butchered while still alive.

He turns away from his own animal, bolt gun in hand, and walks over to Trevor's killing pit.

Michael walks up to the suffering animal and her torturer stops and looks at him in surprise. The cow turns her head to stare at him with pain-filled broken soft brown eyes.

He sees the intelligence there even through the haze of pain and shock and sickness.

Placing the bolt gun to the cow's head he shoots off four bolts in quick succession, putting her out of her suffering.

Trevor turns to him angrily, raising his fist and taking an aggressive step towards Michael.

Michael raises and points the bolt gun at Trevor's forehead, only inches away, mimicking the pullback of his arm from the air-powered kickback of the gun and making the poof sound of it firing a single shot. He turns away without a word and returns to slaughtering animals in his own killing pit.

Trevor stares after Michael, his face drained of color and trembling. The threat is clear. Finally, he moves woodenly, pressing the button and having the dead cow dragged away.

He does not yell or swear at or hit another animal for the rest of his shift, struggling to move the animals he has no idea how to handle. He watches Michael warily each time he moves a cow to his killing pit, nervously slaughtering them with what might almost resemble an attempt at mercy.

Michael ignores him as he slaughters cow after cow, mechanically moving and killing them with assembly line precision.

The other slaughterhouse killers keep their distance, their own vile abuse of the animals they slaughter muted for the rest of the shift, uncomfortable with the man who threatened one of their own.

When the shift finally ends and the last carcasses are dragged off, the slaughterhouse men hose down their areas; water, piss, shit, blood, and gore spraying to the gutters where they run in rivers of death draining out to a sewer.

They move to the change room where they strip off their heavy rubber aprons and gloves, tossing them into large bins. They strip off their bloodied coveralls, tossing them in too. The bins will be dragged out later, the aprons hung and hosed off and left to dry, the coveralls and gloves laundered in a futile attempt to wash the death off them.

The men shower the gore splatters that inevitably find its way to their hair, face, and neck, and the stink of sweat and bovine fear off before dressing in their own clothes. The clothes they wore on the floor under their coveralls are bagged to take home to wash. They bring a fresh change for the end of the day, their clothes soiled with blood despite the coveralls and aprons. They change their boots, leaving their blood-soiled work boots in their lockers for their next shift and putting on their regular shoes.

In his exhaustion and sickness at the other men's callous viciousness, Michael forgets to grab his clean clothes before showering.

Getting out of the shower, he looks down at the blood soaked clothes with a heavy sigh and pulls them on. Now that he is showered and back in the soiled clothes, he doesn't have the will to do what he knows he must.

Michael glances back at the showers as he walks away, gets his stuff from his locker, and leaves, following most of the others, who are moving faster than him.

More cattle are already being forced into the indoor pens for tomorrow's shift, packing them in painfully tight. The animals look around unhappily, calling out, afraid of the smell of blood, fear, and death. They are desperately hungry and thirsty, but they will not be fed or watered today either. They are not thought of as living things, but as products void of the ability to feel physically or emotionally.

The slaughterhouse men are heading out, chatting and joking about the abuse inflicted on the cows that day, muted by the shock of Michael's actions. Some make plans. They head for their vehicles.

Trevor Mitchell glares at Michael, filled with hatred for this new guy.

Michael ignores him, getting in his truck and driving away.

"Stupid," Michael mutters at himself, angrily thumping the steering wheel. "Threatening the guy with a bolt gun? Just stupid! Bringing attention to yourself. You know about bringing attention to yourself. If he reports it, I could lose this job. Worse, it could be reported to the police."

Slaughtering animals all day doesn't bother Michael. But the nonstop unnecessary abuse the others inflict on the cows does.

When he arrives home, he parks on the street and just sits there for a long moment. Finally, he gets out and goes into the house.

Hearing the door, Kathy goes into the kitchen before Michael enters. That's one of the things he insists on. When he comes home from the slaughterhouse, he doesn't want her coming out to see him. She can go in the kitchen, the bedroom, or the back yard, but she is not to come out until he is in the shower. She stirs the pot cooking on the stove.

Michael goes straight for the shower. He doesn't want Kathy to see the blood he imagines he comes home wearing every day. Even when he's sure he got it all in the shower before leaving the slaughterhouse, even with the change of fresh clothes he had not bothered with today, he is always worried there is still more on him.

No matter how well you wash, you still have the taint of blood on your hands.

He has a separate laundry bag just for the clothes he wears to the slaughterhouse. He will wash them himself, without her. She can wash the rest of their laundry, but he does not want her to be upset by the blood and bits of brains that inevitably end up on his clothes.

Stripping off his clothes, he drops them on the bathroom floor. The bottoms of his pants legs are dry where they were tucked into his boots. From the knees to the boot tops are soaked and slap wetly on the floor where they hit. His shirt lands silently on top of the jeans, mottled with wet splotches, mostly around the collar. The red doesn't show against the black fabric of the shirt, looking only wet.

He picks them up and shoves his bloodied clothes into the laundry bag, taking care to wipe up all traces of blood the clothes leave on the floor.

Turning on the shower and stepping in, Michael stands there letting the hot water rain down on him. He leans forward wearily, pressing his head against the wall in front of him. His hair leaves a bloodied mark on the tile, leaving bits of gore behind when he pulls his head back again. He raises his face to the shower head and lets the water pour over it.

Either he had not washed it all out of his hair today or he had transferred gore from his shirt while pulling it over his head. At this point Michael doesn't know or care which.

He stands there for a long time before finally picking up the soap and beginning to scrub.

With the gore washed from him, Michael turns off the shower, steps out, and dries off. He wraps the towel around his hips and leaves the steam-filled bathroom behind.

The rest of the house feels chilled after the steamy bathroom and goose bumps raise instantly on his skin.

Kathy is waiting for him.

It's a very small house, old, with a single bedroom, on the edge of a very small town plunked down in the midst of nothing but farm fields and other scattered small towns for at least a hundred miles. But it is better cared for than the places they have stayed before. Like the others, it's a rental, paid in advance in cash. Unlike the others, the owner is an elderly woman, a widow, who could no longer live on her own. She moved into a seniors' home with partial care, the rental income helping to pay the high cost of being in a facility.

Michael sweeps Kathy into his arms and holds her tight.

"I'm home," he murmurs and bends down to kiss her.

"Dinner is almost ready," Kathy says.

Michael releases her and goes to the bedroom to get dressed.

*I really like this little house, he thinks. Nice little town, quiet, a place we can spend a long time in without ever being found, I think. We can make a good life here, Kathy and me.*

He smiles ruefully, silently chastising himself. *Elaine Carver,* he reminds himself. That's how I have to think of her now. *Elaine Carver and Ryan Crowley. Can't slip up on the names.*

He leaves the bedroom feeling content. They have a new home, new names and a new start. Life is good.

# 19 A Visit and a Reason to Move

Jim's ancient brown Oldsmobile comes to a stop against the curb in front of the two-story rooming house. He looks up at the dilapidated house.

It seems somehow less tired looking than the last time he saw it. Someone made an attempt to cut the grass and the sun no longer highlights the dirt-clouded nature of the windows.

It takes him a moment to realize the glass is actually clean, the sun glinting off the crack streaking across one of the front upstairs windows.

Jim pushes the driver's door open on squealing hinges and shifts himself to get out. The car leans with his weight as he shifts it to the apex of climbing out. Swinging his legs out and using the door to pull his large bulk up, Jim climbs out of the car. The car rocks from the motion, settling gratefully back, now sitting level without him weighing down one side.

Jim is not fat. According to his doctor, he is obese and it is going to kill him very soon. If the unhealthy affects the excess weight have on his body doesn't kill him, then his unhealthy diet will.

Suffering from chronic insomnia, he roams the streets at all hours of the night in his ancient car. He haunts hole-in-the wall after-hours bars and clubs where he has the unpleasant habit of eating things best left displayed in their dust-caked jars like oddities in a curiosity museum. Then he finds himself hunting for all-night pharmacies in search of relief from the heartburn eating him away from the inside.

He can't sleep because his victims keep him up.

They are the victims of his cases, the victims the police failed to save; the victims that he himself failed to save. They come to his desk after it's too late for anyone to save them, but he still feels the guilt. If he could, every one of the degenerates committing the atrocities he sees every day would be caught and put away before they can harm a single victim. Unfortunately, it doesn't work that way.

He could not save Michael's victims, but he will stop him before there are more if he can. First he has to find him.

Jim turns and closes the car door with a screech of the hinges and a bang, and heads for the rooming house.

This is his third visit. The first one was to scope the place out before McAllister was released from prison.

The second visit was when he got the call that Jason McAllister was on the move while he was at Lawrence's apartment. He has no reason to expect him to run yet so, as planned, the person he has watching him followed McAllister while he went to the house.

It was easy enough to break into this old house without damaging the door or lock. It was also easy to break into McAllister's room without leaving any visible evidence.

He searched the room thoroughly and was gone long before McAllister returned. There was nothing to find. The man could not have been cleaner.

This time it's a social call.

Following protocol, Jim mounts the stairs and pauses at the front door, raising a fist to knock.

The door is yanked open before his knuckles can touch it.

The couple exiting stop and stare at him in surprise, not expecting to come face to face with anyone.

Jim is immediately assaulted by the smell of unwashed body and cheap perfume.

He steps aside and the pair passes, not caring to ask him who he is or who he's there to see.

*They opened the door and granted me entry.*

Jim enters the house, closing the door behind him.

He notices immediately that the place feels and smells cleaner.

He takes the few steps to reach the living room doorway and looks in. The old television is pulled out from the wall and someone is lying on the floor behind it. The back cover is removed and leaning against a wall. Otherwise the room is tidy, a surprising transformation from the filth pit it was before.

There is no way of telling who is behind the television.

Ready to reach for his weapon only a few inches from his hand if needed, Jim speaks.

"Hello."

"Detective McNelly, I guess you are here to see me," Jason says, sitting and then standing up and coming out from behind the television he is working on.

"I see you are keeping yourself busy," Jim says. "Trying to fix it?"

"Yes, not sure if I can though," Jason says. "As you can see I'm still here." He spreads his arms for emphasis. "I'm behaving myself."

He lowers his arms.

"The last time I saw you I was a guest in one of your institutions," Jason says. It is an intentional rub over the fact he's now free. "Now I'm here in this fine home where my social worker set me up in an accommodation paid for by the government, with a bunch of housemates in similar circumstances, the final step before complete freedom after whatever crimes we are each accused of."

He tilts his head curiously.

"I am curious to know what kinds of crimes my housemates were accused of and put away for. It takes something special to have to go through this multi-step process to freedom."

"You know I can't tell you that. If they choose to tell you, that's on them. I came to finish our conversation," Jim says. "Now that you are out of a prison cell, I'm willing to bet you've been in touch with a mutual acquaintance of ours."

"A mutual acquaintance," Jason says as if he's guessing. He already knew the moment he heard the detective's voice.

"You know who," Jim says sourly, hating to have to say the name. "Michael Underwood."

Jason seems to be thinking about it, and then looks triumphant.

"Is that the guy who showed up at the farm before all the other cops? He was your partner, wasn't he?"

Jim grinds his teeth at that. *Underwood was no partner of mine. He was no cop. He was nothing more than another degenerate criminal who kidnapped and murdered innocents.*

"Who is he really?" Jim asks. "Don't play games." He looks around. "We're not in jail, not in an interview room. There's no one listening. It's just you and me, off the record.

I'm going to find him anyway. If you help make that happen faster, maybe you can get your total freedom faster. No more social workers checking in."

"I have no problem with social workers. Mine is actually a nice lady once you get past her attempt to seem hard. Not bad to look at either."

The thought comes unbidden to Jason's mind, his social worker, her suit askew, skirt pushed up to reveal more of those legs. Her hair is mussed like she had gone to sleep with that tied back and up hairdo and just woke up with it half falling down, and it makes her look more attractive. Her blouse usually has the top couple of buttons undone to reveal just a hint of cleavage and her always tasteful necklace. But in his image she has a couple more buttons undone, popped off and missing from the strain against the fabric of her blouse.

She is tied up by her hands and feet, sitting in a corner on the floor, frightened eyes staring at him over the gag in her mouth. A trickle of blood from her nose is already drying, her mouth puffy with swelling from where she had been punched, mashing her lips against her teeth.

He can feel the silky feel of her pantyhose as he runs his hands up her legs, hear the shredding tearing of them as he pinches and grips them, tearing them away to leave her legs bare. He feels the smooth shaved skin of her bare legs.

And that will be as far as it will go. It's only a tease, to bring out greater fear in her before he really begins to play.

But it hasn't happened. He hasn't touched her. Not yet.

Jason pulls himself back to the present, regretfully leaving his fantasy behind.

Jim thinks he's likely thinking it over, the comment about the social worker just empty posturing.

"You help me and maybe I can help you," Jim says. "Just tell me where Michael Underwood is. What's his real name? He won't even know it came from you."

Jason smirks.

"You sound like you think I should be afraid of your partner," he says. He chuckles.

Jim scowls. *It's time to stop playing good cop.*

"I was going over the interview notes from Michael's debriefing after your arrest at the McAllister farm." He pauses to let Jason think. "I talked with the others who interviewed him, everyone on his shift who knew him, his neighbours. I even talked to the clerks at the store where he bought groceries and the regulars at his gym."

He pauses again.

"Michael Underwood is not as smart as he thinks he is. He let more slip than just in the interviews with me. The man has a loose tongue.

You would be surprised what you can piece together from all these different conversations with different people."

Jason's heart beats faster. *David has always had a reckless streak in him, even as a boy. What could he have said?*

He plays casual, telling himself the detective is just fishing, that he has nothing.

"It's no matter to me, he's your partner," Jason says.

"It's his connection to you that interests me; his connection to the McAllister Farm, the graves in the woods, and to Jane Doe."

Jim watches Jason carefully, reading his responses, the dilation of his eyes and tension in his jaw.

Despite Jason's best effort to not react, he can't stop the involuntary responses of his body. Those responses give him away.

*You are just grasping,* Jason says silently, keeping the words to himself. *You know nothing. You are just trying to get at me.*

He shrugs noncommittally. "Means nothing to me."

"And Cassie," Jim throws the name out there. The name Michael was overheard yelling behind closed doors when he met with Jason McAllister in prison after the conviction came down; the same day Michael vanished. The name that brought out a reaction in Jason before.

Jason feels the name like a physical blow. *Cassie, sweet innocent little Cassie.*

The name brings up a well of pain from deep inside him.

*I never wanted kids,* he thinks. *I never expected kids. They were an accident. A mistake. I should have just ditched them someplace far from both home and the farm. They could have said anything. At their ages they would have not been able to tell anyone where they ended up. They never would have looked in the right place.*

The image of Cassie comes, unwanted, her little body so frail, full of blood and dirt.

The memory pushes on him.

He came home that day to find David and Cassie in the barn. David had done unspeakable things to her. He had beaten and tortured her.

Little Cassie, so small and frail; the sight of her, ruined, filled him with pain; waves of sickness washing over him, making him feel weak.

David, a thin slip of a boy, looking at him in shock at getting caught, covered in his sister's blood, his eyes burning and breath coming fast with excitement repulsed him.

Even more unsettling was the memories of his own childhood that welled up as he stared at them; torturing the pretty little female coyote, the coyote pups. The knife sliding into the rabbit, its warm wet blood and absolute surrender to its fate. Amy Dodds.

After that things went a bit dark, fuzzy, his mind blocking out the details of that long ago moment in a fog of pain and anger.

When David hurt Cassie, he moved mechanically, wrapping Cassie and covering her face. He had been sure she was dead.

He remembers the trip to the woods vividly, hiking through them with her almost weightless body slung over his shoulder, David struggling to keep up with the unbearable weight of the shovel and his deed.

Watching David's feeble attempts to break ground and finally taking over to do it himself. The agony of every shovel full of dirt as it plops on Cassie's lifeless body.

David frantically attacking the partially filled in grave, clawing at the dirt with his bare hands and pulling her out. David holding her lifeless body in his arms, cradling her and sobbing over his sister. David's eyes staring up at him, accusing, as if he was the one who had done this to the little girl. The fresh anguish of seeing her dirt and blood smeared little face.

David running off, tormented by his loss and the horror of having murdered his own sister.

Walking away, lost in anguish over the little girl he raised as his own, over the ruination of the boy, David, and knowing it's his fault. He did this. He turned the child into a monster.

When he knelt to wrap and rebury Cassie he saw a flicker of life. After all that she still clung to life, barely. He had to finish that job too. He couldn't. He couldn't strangle her with his own hands; see that glimmer of her looking at him through mostly closed eyes while the last of her life fled her broken body.

He needed something to finish David's mess, tarps and another shovel. He would cave her skull in, one quick hit, or shoot her, but he couldn't look at her. He had to pretend she was something else.

When he returned to the open grave Cassie was gone.

He remembers the numb shock, thinking David took her, realizing it was not possible. Searching the woods, growing more frantic with each heartbeat, and finally stumbling to the road just in time to see a couple putting her in their car and driving away.

He pushes the memories away, coming back to the present. He is filled with revulsion and sorrow at what David had done.

*I should have killed David then. I tried to protect them, to look after them. I failed.*

Jason struggles to lock his jaw from clenching, to keep it loose, unconcerned. He tries to keep his eyes steady.

Jim sees the shift of his eyes, the clenching of his jaw, and the grinding of his teeth. He smiles inwardly.

"I learned more about Cassie," Jim says, pressing his advantage, pushing the man closer to the precipice.

*Jason McAllister is nothing but a cold-blooded killer; him and Michael both. I'll push as hard as it takes. If I can break the man, I will do it with pleasure.*

He switches gears, leaving Jason to stew on the other thoughts, trying to keep him off balance.

"What did Michael do with Katherine Kingslow? She vanished the same day he did. She's dead, isn't she? Where's the body?"

"I wouldn't know." Jason's voice has an edge to it despite his attempt to keep it sounding casual.

"I'm very close to learning the rest," Jim presses on. "The pieces of the puzzle are all falling together. The bodies, the McAllister Farm, Michael, you… Cassie."

He is careful not to reveal anything.

*Just stick to the names, no details. Any slip could blow the whole thing, letting McAllister know that I'm as blind as a titmouse with its head taken off by the owl hunting it.*

Where the hell did that come from? He wonders briefly of the comparison to the mouse and bird.

"I know all about your family," Jim presses it home, "the trouble your family had. I talked to the sheriff at the time, Sheriff Rick Dalton."

He hadn't. He hasn't even located the retired sheriff and doesn't know if he's dead or alive. Jason McAllister doesn't need to know that.

"I know about the women, the murders," he pauses, enjoying the game. "Amy Dodds."

The name comes like a blow out of nowhere, knocking the wind out of Jason. He almost staggers, but manages to hold his body firm, if only barely.

*Amy Dodds. I haven't heard that name in decades. Haven't even thought of her until today.*

He feels dizzy suddenly, sick.

"I know what happened to Amy Dodds." Jim steps closer to close the gap, using his bulk to make Jason feels closed in, trapped, in the small living room.

*Amy Dodds is a wild card, Lawrence's guess. The body has never even been found. The only links we have is that she happened to be Jason McAllister's age, went to school with him, the possibility they were friends and that he may even have had a crush on her, and that the McAllister family vanished soon after her disappearance.*

*There are so many other mitigating factors that point to other reasons for them to run. The McAllister family had good reason to leave because of the harassment and threats directed against them for crimes committed by another man which the town blamed William McAllister for. Jason was only a child at the time and child killers are extremely rare.*

*These are good reasons to believe Jason McAllister and his father had nothing at all to do with the Dodds girl's disappearance. But, Lawrence's instincts are rarely wrong.*

Jim sees Jason's eyes shift, looking for an escape route.

He has him.

"I only have one more person to talk to," Jim says, "your father, William McAllister. I'm going to visit him next week."

He sees Jason swoon and thinks he might faint. He presses deeper.

"I learned some interesting things about the McAllister family, very interesting things. About your mother Marjory, your sister Sophie," he pauses, "your grandfather."

Jason McAllister is not hearing him anymore. He is a caged animal. *I have to get out of here right now.*

# 20 Trevor Swears Revenge

The other guys at the slaughterhouse show Michael, Ryan Crowley to them, a new respect since he threatened Trevor with the bolt gun. They show their victims a new respect too, warily glancing at Michael as they handle the animals.

Trevor keeps glaring at Michael with an intense hatred that would make anyone else cringe.

*Ryan Crowley, you bastard,* Trevor fumes silently, *you will pay for threatening me. You think you scare me? You are the one who should be afraid.*

Trevor can't focus on his job with the anger burning through him. With his mind elsewhere, he manages to get his foot stepped on by a cow and gets pinned between another cow and the rail, bruising his ribs. He doesn't dare abuse the animals with Ryan in the next killing pit. He's afraid of him, but he will never admit it even to himself.

Michael doesn't seem to notice. He just goes on mechanically slaughtering cow after cow.

# 21 Michael Goes on a Trip

Michael is shoving clothes into a backpack.

Kathy leans against the bedroom doorway, watching him. "Do you have to go?" she asks unhappily.

"I won't be gone long. Four days."

"Why? I thought we were settling in here."

"It's just something I have to do. I told you that from time to time I would have to go away on a little trip."

*He's keeping a big secret from me,* Kathy thinks. *I can feel it and I don't like it. Is it another woman? No, I don't think so. He goes to work and comes home. He never goes out. He never does anything to give me reason to suspect he has another woman. He has been acting so strange. Maybe there is another woman. I know who, but, she's probably dead.*

"It's her, isn't it?" Kathy asks.

Michael stops packing and turns to her, surprised.

"What? No." He says it too quickly, making Kathy think he's lying.

*It is her. I'm sure of it now.* She looks down at her crossed arms. Kathy doesn't know where to go from here, or what to say.

Michael comes across the room to her, stopping in front of her and trying to look into her eyes.

She won't meet his gaze.

"It's not her," Michael repeats.

She finally looks up to meet his eyes. Her eyes are clouded with uncertainty, his pleading for understanding.

"You want to find her again," she says.

"I don't even know if she's alive," Michael says. "She's probably dead."

"You can't let her go."

*It's true. He can't let her go. He never will. I see him talking to someone who's not there when he thinks I'm not looking and I know it's her, Cassie.*

*Jane Doe might have been her, probably was her, but he lost her again. He will never give up searching for his sister for as long as he lives.*

*Even if he finds her, he may never be able to give up the ghost of the sister that was. He may always doubt it's really her.* The idea terrifies Kathy.

*It was this obsession with his sister that drove him to kidnap those women, including me. A grown woman can never be the little girl he lost. Even if he finds her, that doubt will always be there. It was that doubt that drove him into the blind rages that made him kill those other women.*

*It could happen again.*

Michael hates that Kathy looks so troubled and uncertain.

*I wish I could take her with me, keep her at my side and protect her. I never want her to feel fear or uncertainty.*

He looks into Kathy's troubled eyes and pulls her into his arms.

"I have you," he says into her hair and kisses her gently on the top of her head. "I wish I could take you with me. Maybe soon. Maybe the next time I have to go."

Kathy stiffens. *The next time?* She pulls away.

"This isn't just one trip? There will be more?"

Michael feels guilty for not telling her the truth.

*I can't tell her the truth yet about the trips. I will have to sooner or later, but not yet. She isn't ready. I'm not ready. I don't know yet if I can trust Anderson.*

*Jason McAllister, the man who posed as my father, had his own Anderson. The man who would have been my grandfather, William McAllister, had an Anderson too. From what Jason told me, his father's Anderson encouraged bringing the wife and kids into it.*

*They are all called Anderson. Just that; one simple name for every man who holds the same position in the organization.*

*It's traditionally a family business and the organization is big on traditions.*

*Family members who might not approve are considered a threat. Kathy has to be in one hundred percent or she won't be trusted. They have to find her to be trustworthy beyond a doubt and following the rules.*

*Things are very different times from when Jason was a boy learning the business from his father. People are different; their attitudes and beliefs. It seems like life must have moved much slower then, more relaxed and trusting. Nobody trusts anyone anymore.*

"We discussed this. This is only the first trip," Michael says. "There will be more, I told you that. I just don't know when or how long it will be between trips. I'm doing this for us.

It will be a good thing for us. We'll never be able to settle down if I have to keep going from odd job to odd job. This will make our lives stable. We can find a safe place and settle in to make our lives there. No more moving around. We'll be safe."

*Of course we will be safe. We will be on the inside of a very underground group that stops at nothing to keep all of its trusted members and their families safe. Anyone looking for us would be made to stop before they can ever get close, including the police.*

"You won't even tell me what this business is. Are you doing something illegal?" Kathy looks up at him anxiously.

"You don't need to worry about that. I have to go," Michael says gently. "I won't be gone more than four days. I'll call you. Once I've got the business established I can start to bring you along if you want to come."

He gives her a parting kiss, quickly finishes stuffing his clothes in the bag, and hurries out the door before he changes his mind.

Kathy accepts the kiss stiffly and does not respond. She just stands there looking at the empty bed where the bag had been, trying not to cry.

Michael has to stop himself from looking back as he drives away, wracked with guilt.

Michael is getting closer to the place he is to meet with Mr. Miller. With each mile that passes beneath his truck's tires, his stomach roils and sours more. He is so nervous that he has to urgently find a toilet to release his watery bowels on.

He spots an older gas station with outside entrances to the bathrooms on the side of the building and turns sharply into the lot, driving too quickly to the side of the building. The box of the truck has five large sealed plastic barrels. They wobble, threatening to tip on the turn, but righting themselves without falling.

Putting the truck in park and shutting off the engine, he races for the bathroom, ploughing into the immobile door.

Locked!

"Damn!" he mutters.

*I would prefer to avoid going inside. They will have security cameras trained on the door to catch every person who enters. I hope if the equipment is working, it's on an old-style tape loop that will be recorded over within days, and that the tapes and equipment are old enough to make the video quality so bad it would be useless.*

Those extra wasted moments might also be the end of his pants.

His stomach clenches with the lurching pain of his unhappy bowels and he moves quickly, roughly shoving the door of the station open before him as he rushes for the counter, his hand reaching ahead of him by the time he gets there.

"Men's key please," Michael says urgently.

The guy behind the counter is little more than a kid. He snickers at the panicked look on Michael's face and takes his time fetching the key from under the counter.

"Thanks," Michael says, irritated, snatching the key quickly and charging out the door.

The kid behind the counter gives his retreating back a rude smirk.

Michael rushes to the bathroom, fumbles in his urgency to unlock the door, and would have missed locking it if it was not a self-locking door.

His stomach lurches at the sight and smell of the small bathroom.

There is a single toilet, sink, broken paper towel dispenser, and a large cracked garbage pail. The mirror over the sink is either very dirty, stained, or both. It's chipped along the edges as if it regularly gets bumped, although that seems impossible where it's located.

With a feeling of revulsion, Michael wonders when the last time anyone cleaned the toilet was.

Not wanting to touch it with his skin, he snatches at the toilet paper dispenser, yanking out the too small squares of pre-cut rough paper and scattering them over the toilet seat. He barely manages to sit before his nervous bowels explode in a wave of foul smell and sound and a cold sweat washes over him.

"What the hell! This has never happened to me before. This is not my first job."

"Get a grip man," Michael mutters. "You've never been this nervous for anything, and you've done a lot of shit in the past."

But Michael knows why this time is different. For the first time, it's not just himself he has to worry about. He has Kathy to keep safe and this is a dangerous life.

He lived a life filled with this and worse. He has done this job before, and there were the things he did for survival as a runaway kid on the street. And there was his childhood. Growing up on the farm with Cassie; raised by a deranged killer who made him help dispose of the bodies.

They weren't only Jason McAllister's victims either. The man who raised him and Cassie took them both on his special trips. Trips where he would leave them huddled hiding in the truck while he met with people in remote motel rooms, then led them to an even more remote location where they would swap the bodies from one vehicle to the other. Then there was the long drive to the woods where he and Cassie would have to walk for miles following him as he lugged the bodies to bury them where no one would ever find them.

Cassie hated it and always cried on these trips. She cried over the putrid stench of the dead bodies, over her fear that she would be one of them one day, and over the dead themselves.

They had no mother anymore, no one at the farm to look after them, so Jason McAllister took them with him.

Michael and Cassie learned about death and dead bodies very young. Jason McAllister murdered their mother.

For Michael, these are memories he'd kept locked away behind a dark shroud in his mind for years. Many of them only recently came flooding back with his confrontation with the man he had worked so hard to forget.

Michael swoons and the room darkens as weakness washes over him and an icy sweat chills his body, making him shiver with shock. A memory teases and prods against the dark curtain of haze that still locks away so many memories of his childhood.

His mother's voice echoes in the tiny bathroom, coming from far away, angry sounding, hurt. He can hear the tears cracking her voice while she tries to sound strong and angry.

Then a man's voice, anxious like a child who just got caught doing something bad.

Michael doesn't know what they are saying, but it's something bad. The man did something bad.

The man is not Jason McAllister.

"Dad da," Cassie says softly, tugging at Michael's sleeve.

His eyes are hot and wet and the tiny bathroom is blurry. Michael rubs his eyes with his fist and looks down at little Cassie.

She stares up at him, so little and frail, her face frozen in a look of fear and sadness, eyes large and watering with the tears she is too confused to cry.

She is a toddler, not the little girl he remembers. He pictures her sitting in a booster chair coloring at the table while their mother cooks their breakfast. She can say very few words but loves to sing when music is played.

"Dad da," she repeats quietly, her word for daddy. The world is large to Michael's child's eyes.

He looks down at her little hand on his thick arm, so small against the muscles bulging tensely beneath his sleeve.

"No, this is all wrong," Michael moans, confused.

He stares at her little hand on his arm, the arm of a grown man who has worked at hard labour. But I'm just a boy. How?

Michael blinks hard and shakes his head, trying to find sense where there is none.

The small bathroom rushes back in around him with a suddenness that leaves him reeling, overwhelming in the complete clarity of the cramped space in all its nasty filth and smell.

He barely manages to spin around, squatting in front of the toilet to vomit into the vile mess already in the bowl, gagging more at the sight, smell, and just the thought of puking into his own shit.

His stomach keeps heaving, the whole disgusting nature of his position making his stomach keep cramping with nausea.

When he finally manages to stop and look around, Michael is confused to find himself alone, but doesn't know why he is confused by it.

*Of course I'm alone.*

The sound of pounding seeps into his awareness.

He looks up in confusion, taking a moment for it to register that someone is banging on the door and yelling.

"Hey buddy, what the hell are you doing in there?"

The pounding on the door, its echo filling the small room, almost drowns out the voice on the other side.

"Give me a minute!" Michael yells, feeling weak and strange.

He hurriedly cleans himself up, not bothering with the splatter on the toilet from erupting at both ends, stumbling to the sink to quickly wash his hands and splash water on his face, and stumbles for the door.

He opens the door to a waft of relief in the form of fresh air only to come face to face with an angry man who looks like he has been driving for a very long time.

Behind the man is a small boy who is holding himself and doing the pee-pee dance. Behind them is a station wagon with a harried looking woman in the front seat, three more kids in the back, the rear hatch packed to the roof, and a large hairy dog slobbering on the nearest back seat window.

They saw Michael going into the bathroom as they pulled in, so didn't bother going inside to ask for a key. The man had rushed the boy out of the car, nearly losing the untrained dog in the process, and rushed him to the bathroom door to wait impatiently.

Less than a minute later he was already banging and yelling at the door while his son whimpered that he is going to pee himself.

"S'cuze me," Michael mutters, annoyed by the man's rude impatience. He steps into the man's space, making him take a step back before stepping past him, giving the door time to close while the man stares him down roughly.

The toddler manages to squeeze past the adults and narrowing gap of the door, finding himself all alone in the strange bathroom as the door clicks closed behind him, locked.

He looks around at the gross bathroom and pinches his nose at the awful smell.

"Dad-da?" He calls. "Daddy!"

Realizing too late that the door closed and locked, the father pounds even harder on the bathroom door in frustration, terrifying the toddler inside who doesn't connect the pounding with his father on the other side of the door.

Michael rushes back inside the gas station, depositing the key on the counter with a curt nod and quickly retreats outside to his truck.

The little boy starts crying and screaming for his mommy.

The father looks around a moment before it clicks on his exhausted brain that the boy is locked inside.

He stops pounding and looks at the door in a mix of anger and despair.

"Open the door," he calls through the door, but the child just keeps crying.

He swears and runs for the gas station door. "The jerk didn't even give me the key. I just hope to hell they have one inside or I'm gonna bust that damned door in," he mutters more in fear over his son being trapped than his quickly deflating anger.

Michael is long gone by the time the family gets on the road again.

Down the highway Michael finds what must be the last motel on the planet.

*It has to be for anyone to stay there by choice,* he thinks. 'Roach motel' pops into his mind, but doesn't even come close to summing up what the place looks like.

*If a health inspector ever took a look inside, the place would be immediately shut down and condemned to the demolition crew. I've stayed at some pretty bad places over the years, but this is possibly the worst I've seen.*

Michael takes a drive around the building, casing it out.

There are only two vehicles in the lot. The parking lot is poorly gravelled, the rocks sinking into the mud to leave large areas that are more mud than rock. It is rough with ruts and potholes that formed in heavy rain and grew worse over years of neglect.

Parking, he gets out and approaches the door for the room number he was given.

He looks around furtively, knocks on the door, and waits.

Michael senses movement inside before a shadow crosses the peephole. Someone is looking out.

Michael tries to look casual, but not friendly. He wants the person on the other side of that door to fear him. He has no idea who it is, has never met the person, and may never meet them again. But, he needs them to trust and obey him without question.

The door opens a crack, hesitates, and then opens a little more.

A youngish middle-aged man's face appears in the crack and Michael immediately thinks nerd.

"Mr. Miller," Michael says.

The man nods nervously and swallows a knot of fear in his throat, opening the door a little wider.

Seeing more of him gives Michael just as much of a nerd vibe.

Michael nods. "Let's go, let's get this done. You followed all instructions?"

Mr. Miller nods anxiously.

"All of them?" Michael presses. "Told no one? How to prepare and wrap the package? No devices, cell phone or anything else that might ping a location?"

The man nods again.

"Can't talk?" Michael jokes. "Relax. Let's just get this done and you can go back to your life. Follow me. Follow all the rules of the road. Do not speed or run a sign for anything. If you get too far behind I will stop and wait for you to catch up. Just keep going on that road."

For just a moment the temptation to play with the man comes over Michael. To lead him out and purposely lose him, let the man panic while he loops around to come up on him from behind.

*I have to stay professional. I don't think Anderson has a sense of humour.*

Michael turns and heads for the parking lot.

The wind changes direction and suddenly he can smell the man's car. The odour is strong. It reeks of that special smell that can only come from one thing, a decomposing body.

Michael swears and speeds up.

*We have to get out of here before anyone notices the stench of corpse, if they haven't already.*

He gets in his truck and is already heading for the parking lot exit before Mr. Miller is in his car.

Mr. Miller is panicking before he gets his car moving; worried he is going to lose the man who is here to get rid of his problem. He drives too fast out of the parking lot, racing to catch up.

Michael glances in his rear view mirror.

"Keep your distance," he complains at the car driving too close behind him, although Mr. Miller can't possibly hear him.

Michael is cautious to choose a route that avoids going too close to any homes where the residents might notice the smell.

He finally pulls over and waits on the edge of a narrow dirt road.

Mr. Miller pulls up and stops on the side of the road behind him, getting out and approaching the truck.

Michael gets out and walks back to meet him, shaking his head.

"Trunk to tailgate," he says. "I'll turn around."

He gets back into the truck, drives forward and does a three-point turn in the narrow road, leaving just enough room to transfer the cargo.

He gets back out and walks up to Mr. Miller.

"It stinks," he says. "You didn't follow instructions." He points to the trunk.

"I tried," Mr. Miller stammers apologetically.

"Open it up. Let's just do this."

Mr. Miller opens the trunk, his keys jangling with the trembling of his hand.

The stench that wafts out of the open trunk is overwhelming, making Michael's eyes water. He turns to the truck and scowls.

He drops the truck's tailgate and grabs a large plastic barrel by the edge, dragging it closer. He pulls it out onto the ground and pries the lid off.

"Put the package inside," he says.

Mr. Miller looks at him as if he had just spoken some strange language.

"Come on," Michael says. "You know how it works. I don't touch the package."

Mr. Miller looks like he is going to vomit. His face is waxy and pale. He makes a move towards the trunk, but can't bring himself to touch its contents.

"Really?" Michael says. "You got it in there and you can't get it out?"

He gives Mr. Miller a look of disgust and returns to the truck's driver's side door.

Mr. Miller almost chases him, panicking, thinking he is about to drive away and abandon him with a rotting corpse in his trunk.

Michael reaches in behind the driver's seat and pulls out a pair of disposable plastic coveralls, gloves, goggles, and face mask. They are the kind of thin disposable coveralls that cover you head to foot, including your shoes. He pulls the coveralls on carefully, not wanting to tear it, and walks back to the car. He puts on the gloves, mask, and goggles, and then reaches into the trunk and grabs the wrapped bundle inside, pulling it up to lift it out.

There's none of the expected stiffness of rigor mortis or even of a body that has gone past that stage to become pliable again.

The contents slither wetly inside the wrapped bundle. It's like trying to handle a human-sized mass of gelatine that has been wrapped in burlap and left out of the fridge too long.

He can feel the bones sloshing inside, but that's the only still solid part of the body.

Disturbing it only makes the stench worse. Michael gags at the putrid fumes wafting up at him. The smell is so bad he can taste it. He wants to work his tongue to get the foul taste off it. Michael imagines this is what it would taste like to lick a rotting corpse.

Mr. Miller turns away, looking pale and green and making retching sounds.

"You puke and you are going to clean it up," Michael warns coldly, "every last drop. No evidence gets left behind. Not even here."

Jason McAllister's often repeated words echo in Michael's head as he struggles to lift the liquefying corpse out of the trunk and into the barrel.

You never touch the package in Mr. Miller's presence. As far as Mr. *Miller knows, you never touch it, ever. The only evidence on the package is whatever he left behind. If he ever thinks of giving you up, he has to know beyond a doubt that you will never be linked to his mess. Don't let him play at it being too disgusting and gross. Whatever he did to that body before he killed his victim is probably a lot worse than just moving a dead body.*

*As my father would have said; he made the mess, he has to clean it up.*

*Your father was wiser than me,* Michael thinks as he works grimly.

Mr. Miller stands by, watching anxiously as Michael struggles with his package.

Michael gets the package over the mouth of the barrel. Just as he is starting to put it in the burlap bursts open, releasing its contents in a rancid gush of putrescence that fairly erupts from its confines. It splashes over both Michael and the barrel, raining wetly to the ground, a gelatinous mass of soft tissue, slimy skin, and bones. Luckily most of it sloshed into the barrel.

Michael glares at Mr. Miller, whose face drains of all color as he stares back with a look of terror.

"How the hell long has that thing been in there?" Michael growls, looking down at himself with disgust.

*I'm going to stink of rotting corpse for days now,* he thinks.

His motions rough with suppressed violence, Michael angrily grabs a shovel from the back of the truck and starts scooping up contaminated dirt, jabbing and scraping at the hard-packed dirt in an effort to get it all. He dumps the dirt soiled with bodily fluids into the barrel.

He picks up bones that landed on the ground next to the barrel, holding a femur like a club that he might beat Mr. Miller with.

At that moment both Michael and Mr. Miller have a similar vision flash in their minds; Michael of the satisfaction of pounding the man senseless with the bone, and Mr. Miller of being on the terrifying end of a vicious assault.

Michael tosses the bone into the barrel and scrapes and scoops the dirt where the bones had lain.

When he's finished, Michael puts the lid on the barrel, pounding it on tight. He carefully peels off his mask, goggles, gloves, and coveralls. He takes care that the coveralls come off inside out, trapping the gore splattering them on the inside. He wraps the goggles, gloves, and mask inside the coveralls and puts them and the shovel inside a second barrel. He grabs a rag and spray bottle and cleans up any spatter he can find on the vehicles. He tosses the rag in the barrel with the coveralls, sealing it closed.

The stench of decomposing corpse still hangs heavily in the air. It's the kind of stink that takes a while to leave, that you can taste on your tongue. It will be burned into his nostrils and taste buds for days.

Michael grabs one side of the barrel holding the liquefied corpse and looks at Mr. Miller.

Knowing what he wants, Mr. Miller cringes away.

"Help me lift it in," Michael growls at him.

Mr. Miller blinks at him, thinks through a list of excuses, starts to complain about his back, and is quickly silenced.

"My ba-," Miller whimpers.

Michael glares harder at him.

Miller snaps his mouth closed unhappily and reluctantly takes the other side of the now heavy barrel.

It weighs less than Michael expected with the soupy contents and added roadside dirt and would weigh even less if Mr. Miller actually put some effort into lifting it.

Together, they lift it to the tailgate and shove the barrel in. Michael turns his attention to Mr. Miller's trunk.

He looks at Mr. Miller with disgust.

"If you can't clean it up right, then you have no business making the mess in the first place."

Mr. Miller looks down sheepishly.

The fabric lining the trunk is wet and stained with the slowly oozing mess that had been wrapped and left in there too long. The trunk has scattered evidence of the person the victim once was. The contents of a purse are spilled all over the trunk. Hair is caught in the jack where her head had banged against it.

With another look of disgust directed at Mr. Miller and a shake of his head, Michael grabs the barrel that he put his coverall in and yanks it out of the back of the truck and moves it aside.

He grabs a third barrel and drags it out, setting it on the ground. Prying off the lid, he starts grabbing everything out of the trunk and dumping it into the barrel. The jack lands in the barrel with a heavy thud.

"My jack!" Mr. Miller complains, reaching as if he might actually try to take it back.

"It's covered in her hair and blood," Michael glowers at him.

Mr. Miller takes a step back and shuts his mouth unhappily, standing back to just watch.

He cringes when Michael starts violently tearing the fabric lining out of the trunk. Michael jams it into the barrel too.

After a careful inspection to make sure he got it all, Michael turns his attention to the rest of the car.

He finds more evidence that he tosses into the barrel.

The longer this takes, the angrier Michael is getting at the man's sloppiness.

*It's not my responsibility to clean up his mess. If he gets caught because his car is a mess of evidence that's his problem, not mine. My job is only to take the package and make it disappear so it will never be found.*

Finished with the car, Michael seals the barrel.

He jumps up into the truck box and drags a fourth barrel over to the tailgate. This barrel is heavy. The truck shifts with the weight being dragged across its bed. Jumping down again, he pulls it to the edge of the gate.

Popping the lid, Michael takes a length of thick flexible tube and places one end in the barrel. The other end he sucks on until the liquid comes up and over the lip of the barrel, gravity pulling it down the rest of the tube.

Before the contents can fill his mouth, Michael shoves the other end of the tube into the trunk, letting the unpleasant smelling liquid spray into the trunk. He holds the tube there, moving it around to let it wash over every surface inside the trunk.

Mr. Miller watches unhappily.

"My own concoction," Michael says.

It will seep out on its own, and is already dripping out onto the ground.

Finished, Michael pulls the tube out of the barrel and puts the lid back on. He pushes the barrel back and loads the other two, shoving the tubing into the box and closing the tailgate with a loud bang.

"What's the other barrel for?" Mr. Miller asks, his voice shaky.

Michael's look answers the question without words. The last barrel is for him if he messes up.

Mr. Miller swallows hard.

"A-are we done?" he stammers.

Michael steps forward aggressively.

"Go home. You don't know what you are doing. If I ever see you on the other side of that door again," he points to the remaining barrel, "I'll finish cleaning up the mess."

Mr. Miller can't get out of there fast enough.

Kathy is getting ready to go to the laundromat when she is startled by a knock at the door.

"Who can that be?"

She goes to the door and hesitates, hand reaching out just a little. She almost doesn't open the door.

Opening it nervously, she looks down into the faces of two school aged girls sporting some sort of scout uniform and looking up at her hopefully with boxes of cookies thrust out towards her.

"Do you want to buy some cookies?" the braver of the two asks.

Kathy hesitates then smiles uncertainly.

"Sure, I'd love some cookies," she says. She quickly retreats inside to find her purse and some money. She buys a box from each girl.

She watches them happily go on to the next house and looks for any sign of a parent. She sees none.

"They really let them go alone?" She is incredulous. "I guess it's safer in a small town," she shrugs.

Kathy grabs her purse and the bags of laundry and soap. Locking the door behind her, she heads out to walk to the laundromat to do the laundry.

Trevor is sitting in his truck up the street watching the house. He raises an eyebrow at the woman who answers the door when the kids go to the house selling cookies.

He followed Ryan home the other day to find out where he lives and if he has any family, a wife or kids.

"So, he's got a woman," Trevor says thoughtfully. "Ryan doesn't talk to anyone. He shares nothing of who he is. Nobody knows anything about him."

He watches the woman exit the house carrying a larger sack and a smaller plastic bag. He waits for her to get some distance before starting his truck and following. He drives past her, watching her in his mirrors to see where she is going.

Trevor follows her to the laundromat. He sits in his truck, watching her through the large picture windows at the front of the building.

"This is going to be fun. I'm going to hurt her to get even with Ryan. But first I will play."

His thoughts turn to his situation.

*The slaughterhouse job is perfect. I love to inflict pain, to cut up and torture living things. I just started working at the slaughterhouse two weeks before Ryan and it was going great until now. I had to leave where I was living before and move far away. Too many people there suspected I was the one behind their pets vanishing.*

*Animals are easy.*

*There are always cats' owners who allow them to roam freely as if they're immune to the dangers out there. Cats tend to be skittish and not trusting, not taking my food offerings, but there are always some that trustingly walk right up to me with their backs arched in anticipation of having their back scratched.*

*Dogs are easier. They are almost always so trusting, even the ones whose owners abuse them. Even the skittish ones almost never turn down food. Sometimes I give them hunks of raw ground beef laced with broken glass, razor blades and needles, then hide to watch them suffer. They cry and yelp in pain even as they can't stop themselves from eagerly devouring the treat that is already killing them.*

*The owners come out and cry in their confusion, having no idea what is wrong with their precious pet.*

*Other times it's just laced with poison.*

*The best are the ones I steal right from their yard to take home and play with.*

*Ryan Crowley's wife or girlfriend, or whatever she is, won't be my first human plaything.*

Trevor is lost in his fantasy thoughts, time passing unnoticed, when his daydreaming is interrupted. The woman comes out of the laundromat, bags in hand, and is walking away. He almost misses her.

He watches her retrace her steps.

"She's going home."

He starts his truck and pulls out, passing her and beating her home. He is already parked, engine off, when he sees her coming up the sidewalk.

She goes into the house and closes the door.

Trevor considers his next move.

*Should I knock on the door? What would I say? I don't see his truck, so Ryan must be out somewhere, but he could show up any time.*

The door to the house opens and the woman comes back out.

Trevor has the urge to slink down guiltily in his seat, thinking she must have seen him spying on her and is coming to confront him.

Instead, she cuts across the street and over a set of train tracks.

*Wherever she's going, it can't be far if she's walking. Should I follow her in the truck again? No, I'll have a better chance of getting close to her on foot.*

He gets out of his truck and follows at a discrete distance.

Kathy walks to the grocery store oblivious to the man following her. She turns and looks behind her just as she is about to enter the store, feeling a creepy sense of being watched. She shrugs at her own foolishness and enters the store.

Kathy picks out the things they most urgently need, buying only what she can carry in the small grocery basket. She stops at the meat cooler, searching the meats for an inexpensive cut of beef that is not too tough. She wants something special to have for dinner when Michael returns.

*Ryan*, she silently reminds herself. *You have to think of him as Ryan now.*

She moves on to the fruits, where she selects a small ration of a few different fruits.

Finished her shopping, Kathy takes her over-filled basket to the checkout and heads out with her groceries.

She is just walking out of the grocery store lot, laden with paper grocery bags, when a man comes running up to her.

She is immediately anxious, wondering what he wants with her. There can be no doubt she is his intended target with his persistent gait and eyes focused on her.

*Go away; leave me alone*, she silently pleads.

He comes alongside her, smiling at her.

"That's a lot of bags," he says. "Here, let me help." He holds out his hands to take some of the bags.

The word "no" is on her lips. She wants to pull the bags away, to keep walking and ignore him. She feels trapped into being polite.

She doesn't stop him or say anything when he takes some of the bags from her and starts walking beside her. She feels awkward about it.

"You're Ryan's, aren't you?" he says, his voice and face friendly. "I mean, you're his wife or girlfriend."

"His girlfriend, I guess." Kathy is unsure what to say.

"You guess," he chuckles. "You aren't sure? He seems pretty sure about you."

Kathy looks at him in surprise. "You know Ryan? You know me?"

"Yes, oh sorry, I guess I should introduce myself. I don't think we've ever met. It feels like we have because Ryan talks about you so much. He showed me your picture too, that's how I recognized you."

He shifts the grocery bags to hold out his hand, stopping so she can shake it.

Kathy tries to shuffle her bags awkwardly to free a hand and manages only to sort of stick a hand out while using her arm to pin the bags against her body.

*I didn't know Michael even had a picture of me,* she thinks, feeling off balance by the situation.

The man takes her hand in his. His hand is warm and a little rough with calluses, his touch gentle.

"Hi, I'm Trevor Mitchell. I work at the slaughterhouse with Ryan."

Kathy nods at him.

"What was your name again?" Trevor asks. "He told me, but it's slipped me right now."

"Uh, Elaine," Kathy says, almost slipping and giving the wrong name.

Trevor starts walking again and Kathy has to follow or be left behind, standing there foolishly while her groceries go on without her.

After a brief pause staring after him uncertainly, she hurries those few paces to catch up and walks with him, still anxious.

Trevor talks all the way to the house, telling her stories about the guys at the slaughterhouse, keeping the topic light and far away from what actually goes on there.

He is so friendly and personable that Kathy is feeling at ease by the time they reach the house.

She unlocks the door and opens it, turning to take the grocery bags from him.

"I'll help you bring them in," Trevor says, moving past her as if it's the natural thing to do.

"Where's the kitchen?" he asks, even though he spots it as soon as he enters.

"This way." Kathy follows him in with a sense of unease and shows him the way.

Trevor sets the bags on the counter and starts going through them, putting groceries away as if it were his own home, not hers.

It's a familiar gesture that at once is both awkward and comforting for Kathy.

"So, when is your man coming home?" Trevor asks. "I was actually on my way here hoping to catch him when I saw you with all these bags."

"I'm not sure exactly," Kathy says, still feeling a little off over this strange man putting her groceries away for her.

"Maybe I can wait?"

*No, I don't think that's a good idea.* The words come to Kathy's mind, but not to her tongue.

She doesn't know why, other than to blame it on the absolute loneliness she feels. Instead, she says something totally unintended, something she does not want to say and yet does.

"Would you like coffee?" Kathy asks. "I have some cookies too."

"Scout troop cookies?" Trevor asks hopefully. "I love their cookies." He laughs. "No, of course you don't. They only go around selling them once a year or something."

Kathy blushes, thinking how it's almost like he knew.

"Um, I do have some scout troop cookies," she says shyly. "I don't know what troop they are, but a couple girls came by earlier selling cookies. I bought a couple boxes."

Trevor smiles even bigger. "Wonderful!"

He watches her while Kathy self-consciously puts coffee on. She gets cups and they sit in awkward silence while the coffeemaker gurgles and dribbles its brew into the pot.

When the coffee is finally done, they sit at the kitchen table with their coffees and a box of cookies.

Trevor seems to have no limit in coming up with things to say. He keeps his distance, staying friendly and casual, and showing no undue interest in Kathy. They have a second cup of coffee and she is feeling totally at ease with her new friend.

Trevor looks down regretfully at his empty second cup.

"I really should be going now. Tell Ryan to give me a call when he gets in."

Kathy blushes guiltily and looks down, her hands fidgeting. She looks up at him again.

"When I said I wasn't sure when Ryan is coming back, I meant I'm not sure what day. He said maybe four days, but it could be longer."

Her eyes are pleading with him to not be angry with her for the little lie by omission.

His expression is understanding.

"You just moved here, no family. No friends either, huh? You must be feeling pretty lonely, especially if he's gone for almost a week."

Kathy nods, feeling a little sad now.

"Don't worry," Trevor says. "Ryan is my friend and that makes you my friend too."

He gets up to leave, pausing to look at her.

Kathy gets up to show him out.

"I'll be back to see that everything is okay," he says. "I'm sure Ryan would do the same for me."

Once he is gone and the door is closed behind him, Kathy peeks out the window surreptitiously, watching him walk away.

Michael pulls into the parking lot of a truck stop diner just off the highway. There is nothing else there; just a diner with an over-sized parking lot to accommodate all the big rigs next to a gas station. His truck box is empty of the large plastic drums.

There are half a dozen semis in the lot and a couple of scattered cars and trucks.

Michael walks into the diner and looks around, spotting Anderson sitting at a small table against the wall near the back.

The waitress sees him and starts in his direction, but Michael redirects her. He nods to her and points to the coffee pot sitting on the burner, then continues on towards Anderson's table. She is an older woman, matronly and plump.

He takes the empty seat.

"How did it go?" Anderson asks.

"The man has no business in this," Michael mutters. "His car was a mess. He was a mess."

He pauses, looking up to see the waitress approaching, and waits.

"You want anything with that coffee?" she asks as she pours the coffee into the cup on the table. "Breakfast? Lunch? Danish?"

"No, just coffee is fine thank you," Michael says.

Her expression changes. He catches her disappointment and changes his mind.

"No, wait. Actually I'll take a sandwich. Roast beef or pastrami or whatever you have on rye with mustard and one of those Danishes too. That sounds pretty good. Just wrap it to go at the counter. I'll grab it on my way out."

She smiles and nods, going away happily.

Anderson watches her go. *Keeping the waitress happy,* he thinks. *She won't be thinking later about the guy who came in just for a coffee. Meal is a bigger tip.*

He turns his attention back to Michael. "So, it didn't go so well?"

"The package was past ripe," Michael says with a scowl. "He wouldn't touch it. I had to do it all myself. I had to clean up his car too."

Anderson shrugs. "Maybe you should have just left it. Let him go down."

"I should have."

"Are you still holding the package?"

"I've already taken care of it."

Anderson nods.

"I'll contact you when I have another job for you Michael."

A warning bell goes off in Michael's head. They don't use names. Anderson would know that.

*He's toying with me.*

Anderson pauses, studying Michael's reaction.

"Oh, but you go by Ryan Crowley now. I'll remember that." It's a dismissal.

Michael bristles at that. Someone could overhear the name and repeat it to the authorities if questioned. He carefully keeps his expression bland.

Michael gets up, leaving his half drank coffee, and heads for the counter at the front. He grabs his sandwich and Danish, paying the waitress and leaving an average tip, and leaves.

He gets in the truck and starts the long drive home, wishing he's already there, thinking about Kathy there all alone.

"Soon. A couple more jobs, then I can ask Anderson about letting you come."

Anderson's use of his name and the intended jab letting him know he knows Michael's current alias hovers at the back of his mind.

*He's putting me on notice, letting me know he's thoroughly checked me out. And that he's not above cutting me loose too maybe.*

Kathy keeps looking at the door.

*I need to find something to do to keep myself busy. I have nothing. The house is spotless. I already cleaned and re-cleaned it.*

*I miss Michael. I'm so bored and lonely.*

*Ryan. He's Ryan Crowley now. Remember that. You have to start thinking of him as that all the time now. Me too. I'm Elaine, always Elaine Carver now.*

Worse than forgetting to think of them as their new identities, is that her mind keeps turning to Ryan's friend Trevor.

*He is so friendly and nice. I like him.* She is thinking of him in a friend way.

The thought makes another come unwanted, the vision of Trevor leaning down to her, his lips touching hers. She pushes it away, knowing it's nothing more than a product of her loneliness. She has no desire to either cheat on or lose Ryan, and has none for his friend.

Elaine gets up and walks to the window, looking out for Ryan's truck for what she thinks must be the millionth time since he left. She makes herself turn away and go sit on the couch. He won't be home for a few days still.

She looks around the fairly empty room.

"Maybe I can talk to Ryan about getting a TV."

She jumps at the unexpected knock at the door.

Elaine approaches the door warily.

*Michael would not have knocked. Ryan,* she mentally reminds herself yet again.

*Trevor?* Her heart quickens at the thought and she catches herself smiling.

She opens the door and there he is.

"Hi, just checking up on you like I said I would," Trevor says.

Elaine only now realizes how much she missed Trevor since meeting him. Has it really been only two days?

"I brought you something," Trevor says, pulling something from behind his back with a smile.

"I saw it and I remembered that you said you liked it and haven't had it in a long time."

Elaine looks at the bag in his hands uncertainly.

*What could it be? I don't remember telling him about anything in particular, but we talked about so many things. It felt like talking to a long-lost friend.*

He holds it out, urging her to take it.

Elaine takes it and opens the bag.

The picture of golden sponge-cake with soft gooey creamy filling oozing out where it is cut open and the rich chocolate icing coating is like looking at a moment of pure happiness.

She squeals with delight and hurries to the kitchen with her prize.

"I'll make some coffee," she says.

Trevor reaches behind him to grab another bag on the ground and brings it in, taking it into the kitchen and putting it on the counter.

"I know it's not easy getting around to do your groceries on foot," he says. "I brought you a few other things too."

"I-I don't know what to say," Kathy stammers in shock. "Thank you. Tell me how much I owe you and I'll pay you."

"Nothing. Just helping out a friend. Excuse me a minute, I need to use the bathroom."

Elaine nods as she happily digs into the bag on the counter. There are things in here she would not have thought to buy, not when they have to watch every penny. She feels spoiled and it feels good.

Trevor slips into the bathroom and closes the door with an audible click. He opens it slowly, careful to be silent, stepping out and peeking towards the kitchen. The bathroom is only a ruse.

He watches to make sure Elaine is busy putting the groceries away while the coffee brews, silently closes the bathroom door, and slips into the bedroom. He looks around and quickly spots what he's looking for.

Trevor digs through her dirty laundry. Picking out a pair of her underwear, he brings it up to his nose and sniffs it long and slow, then pockets it and returns to the bathroom, silently slipping inside and closing the door. He flushes the toilet and runs the water so Elaine thinks he's washing his hands.

Trevor returns to the kitchen.

The coffee just finished brewing and Elaine is pouring two cups at the small kitchen table. They sit across from each other, talking over coffee and golden sponge cake.

Elaine can't stop smiling.

Trevor is almost giddy with excitement and has a hard time controlling himself.

*Stay calm, be casual,* he keeps reminding himself while he shares cake and coffee with the woman who belongs to his enemy.

His cup empty, Trevor quickly makes excuses and leaves when Elaine moves to fill it again.

"I have to go. I have some errands to run," he says, getting up from his chair.

Elaine sees him out, a little sorry to see him go.

*It's going to be a long lonely wait for Ryan to come home,* she thinks.

Ryan stops at a burger joint in a medium sized town halfway home. He needs a break from driving so he goes in to eat instead of ordering to go. After hungrily devouring the grease-sodden burger that sits too heavily in his stomach, he decides to go for a walk to stretch his legs. He feels stiff from the long hours spent driving.

"I have a reborn appreciation for those guys who do long distance driving for a living."

He walks aimlessly to the corner, crossing the street and heading down another street with no destination in mind.

That's when he spots her.

He stops.

"Cassie."

"No, it's not her. It can't be. She's gone."

She is skipping along the road humming to herself, long hair bouncing behind her. She is the age Cassie would have been the day he ran away from the McAllister farm if she had not had that accident a few years before.

The Cassie he has never seen. She has grown in those few years, but she's still so small and frail looking.

The world fades away, leaving nothing but the girl.

Ryan is Michael again, watching the two girls play hopscotch as the little dog jumps at them. Cassie is younger. He doesn't recognize the other girl.

Michael is David again, a child himself. He is confused.

"Where are we? We're going to be in a lot of trouble. We're not allowed to leave the farm."

He starts walking faster.

"I have to get Cassie and get us both back to the farm before he finds out we're gone."

The other girl and the dog are gone. The hopscotch crudely drawn in chalk is gone. The street is gone. Cassie is bigger again and the street is different. He doesn't recognize it. Cassie is skipping happily along by herself down the street away from him.

He blinks in confusion.

"Where did the other girl go? The dog? Never mind, I can't worry about that right now. I have to get Cassie and find our way back to the farm fast."

The girl pauses in her skipping down the road when she hears a noise behind her. She turns and sees the man walking towards her. She would have thought nothing of it, but he has a strange look on his face, determined, and he's staring right at her.

Cassie turns and looks directly at him, seeing him, but he sees no recognition in her eyes.

The girl has an uneasy feeling. She turns back and picks up her pace. She hears the man behind her speed up too.

Ryan who is Michael who is David wants to call out to her, but has a sense he shouldn't.

*What if he's around here somewhere? Papa. He'll catch us away from the farm and punish us.*

She looks back at him again, walking faster.

Cassie speeds up and he does too.

*She's playing games with me, trying to stay ahead of me.*

She turns and looks behind her again and starts jogging.

"Cassie, stop it," he mutters under his breath, gritting his teeth and speeding up.

She looks behind her again and the look on his face sends fear racing through her, her heart beating fast. She heard about kidnappers. Suddenly she is absolutely certain this man means to hurt her. She starts running, tears streaming down her cheeks.

He runs too.

She puts her head down, trying to run faster.

He puts on an extra burst of speed, closing the gap.

She feels the sharp jab of pain in her side from running and almost trips. She is gasping, winded from both fear and the run, gulping mouthfuls of air.

*He's going to catch me! He's getting closer!*

She has only a vague idea of the things strangers do to kids they kidnap. Most of it was left to her own imagination, but she has a feeling there is something much worse that the adults do not tell you about.

She passes a large RV blocking the view of the houses up the street on that side and sees a man in a yard wearing heavy work gloves and a baseball hat shovelling gravel from a wheelbarrow onto his driveway.

She almost cries out with relief. She doesn't know him, but she recognizes him as the dad of one of the boys two grades higher at school.

She changes direction, running for him, sobbing so hard she can't talk.

The man looks up to see the girl running at him, tears streaming down her face with a stricken look that raises an instant alarm in him.

She is gulping air and coughing and crying, almost collapsing when she reaches him. Her voice is coming out cracking unintelligible sounds.

"What's the matter?" he asks, looking past her and half expecting to see a dog chasing her or a gang of kids tormenting her.

She blubbers and gasps, unable to make any words come out, and points.

Ryan comes running past the RV and skids almost to a stop, staring at the girl.

The girl jerks her arm back and forth, pointing at him. Her meaning is clear.

"Is that your dad?"

She shakes her head "no".

"Do you know him?"

Again, she shakes her head "no".

The man shovelling clenches the shovel tighter in his fists and steps forward menacingly.

Ryan who is Michael who is David stumbles towards Cassie in confusion.

*This is all wrong.*

He sees the man with the shovel tighten his grip on it. There is violence in the man's body language and a threat in his expression as he steps forward.

"What do you want?" the man with the shovel says in a cold voice.

"I-I just," Ryan manages, his mind unable to figure out what to say. He looks past the man to Cassie and is drawn back to the man.

"Who are you?" the man demands. "I haven't seen you around here before."

"David," Ryan manages. He looks down, scuffing his toe, and stops to stare at his own feet in shock.

*They are so big! My legs too.* He holds out his hands, staring at them. *They are big! A man's hands!*

"But, but," he stumbles the words out, finishing in his mind… *I'm just a boy.*

The man with the shovel watches the stranger scuff the ground with a toe and can't help thinking the man is like a child. A chill goes through him as he watches the man inspect himself with a lost look of confusion.

"Enough of this," he mutters.

Holding the shovel threateningly, he takes another step forward.

"Get out of here, buddy," he growls, "or you are going to get this." He raises the shovel to make sure his meaning is clear.

*Did I say my name is David?* Michael thinks. He looks around, turning back to the man, unsure where he is. *Why is that man holding a shovel and looking at me like he's about to beat me with it? Ryan, I have to remember to say Ryan. That's my name now.*

The man steps forward again, ready to swing the shovel.

Ryan sees the girl standing behind him now, shaking and pale, tears flowing and staring at him in fear.

He turns and runs back the way he came, back towards his truck, his legs shaky and weak and his stomach sick.

*What is going on?* he thinks wildly.

He is out of breath when he reaches his truck. He gets in and tears out of there without looking back to see if the man with the shovel is chasing him. He can't get to the highway fast enough.

Once he is on the highway he can finally breathe again, his breath coming in ragged gasps as he tries to catch his breath. He grips the steering wheel too hard, knuckles white and hands trembling.

"Okay, breathe, calm down," he pants.

He looks at Cassie in the passenger seat beside him. Little Cassie.

*How did I ever think that other girl is her? She is older than Cassie. I followed that girl, but I don't know why. It's like it all happened in a fog now.*

"You have to stop doing that," Cassie says.

Ryan turns his attention to the road ahead, but he can feel her eyes boring into him.

"You have to stop thinking they are me," she says. "I'm gone. I'm dead."

"No, you are not," Ryan says. "You are not dead and I'm going to find you again. I just have to find out what he did with you."

"Where are you Cassie? Where did he hide you?"

He looks at her.

"I'm dead," Cassie says. She is Jane Doe, the adult woman he thought was little Cassie grown up. She stares at him with those empty eyes, lost in a haze of the drugs the hospital had given her. She is wearing the hospital gown, her hair dishevelled and an intravenous tube trails from one hand.

Ryan turns his attention back to the road.

"I know who might know where you are."

"Who?" Cassie asks and she is the little girl again, his Cassie.

"His father, William McAllister."

"Maybe," Cassie says. "If he's still alive."

"He's still alive."

"What if he won't tell you? What if he knows, but refuses to tell you?"

"I'll make him tell me. If I have to go after his wife, I will make him tell me. I know where she is too."

"You wouldn't really hurt her, would you?" Cassie's voice is small. "I always wanted a grandma. She's like my grandma."

"She is not your grandma and he is not your grandpa. He is not our father, not our real father. You just don't remember our real father. You were too little."

"If you hurt them, grandpa and grandma, I will not forgive you."

Ryan doesn't want to talk about it anymore. He clenches his teeth and stares straight ahead, driving on.

All he wants right now is to get home to her, Kathy. *Elaine,* he reminds himself.

# 22 Next Door

Jim McNelly is leaving Jason McAllister's rooming house feeling more satisfied than he should be. He is confident he has forced McAllister's hand.

*McAllister will stew on it a little, worrying over it, doubting, and then he will have to check and find out what I know. Then I'll have him. He will lead me either to Michael Underwood or to the still missing Jane Doe or Katherine Kingslow. Maybe to William McAllister. Better if it's Michael Underwood.*

He gets in his car and notices the police car parked just a few houses up.

He has a bad feeling about it. It isn't the best neighbourhood, and crime and police cars are expected, but it's just too close to this particular house.

His phone rings. He looks down at the number and answers it.

"McNelly."

He listens.

"Ok, I got it, thanks." He hangs up.

He gets back out of the car and waddles heavily to the house a couple doors up. It's the house the woman Jason has been watching lives in.

He walks in the front door without knocking.

Two uniformed officers are standing over a distraught looking man sitting in a kitchen chair. One of them is busily scratching in his note pad.

The man looks up at the fat detective with the same hollow-eyed look he has seen too many times. He looks trauma stricken, eyes red-rimmed and afraid. Seeing Jim does not put him at ease.

Jim pulls his badge out and flashes it perfunctorily.

"Detective Jim McNelly," he says. "Let's start at the top. When was the last time you saw your wife?"

Jason McAllister retreats to his room the moment Jim leaves. He feels shaken. Sick.

"I have to get out of here."

*McNelly is going to talk to my father.*

Even at his age, his father now a withered old man, the thought strikes a chord of fear in him. He is still, after all these years, afraid of his father, William McAllister.

*Worse, he might go so far as to visit my mother. Who knows what she might say.*

Jason goes to the window to watch Jim leave. Jim gets in his car, but instead of driving away, he gets out a moment later and starts walking.

He is out of Jason's line of sight by the time he reaches the far edge of the frontage of the house next door. It doesn't matter. Jason knows where he's going.

He smiles shakily.

"That will keep him busy." He pictures a route in his mind, himself slipping out the door, staying close to the house and ducking low as he moves past the house on the other side. A few houses down and he will be able to cut across to the next street and he will be gone.

*McNelly will never see me go. Everyone knows the first twelve hours in a missing person case are the most important. If they don't find the missing person by then, their chances begin to drop exponentially.*

He smiles as he hastily packs a bag.

*It doesn't matter. They'll never find her.*

# 23 Ryan Comes Home

Ryan pulls up in front of the small house, home at last.

He's almost giddy with eagerness to see Elaine. He wants to tell her all about how the job went, about Cassie, and about his idea of going to see William McAllister in the hope he'll tell him where Cassie is.

He shakes his head. "No, no, no, you can't tell her," he cautions himself. "Not yet."

He walks up the uneven sidewalk to the door and grips the doorknob to open it.

Elaine hears a noise outside and her heart races. Her first thought is that it's Trevor. She mentally chastises herself for feeling excitement at the thought, but she can't push the feeling aside.

She goes to the door and reaches for the knob.

Ryan opens the door to a rush of surprise at finding Elaine standing on the other side staring up at him.

A look of disappointment flashes in her eyes in the moment it takes her brain to register that it's not Trevor, and then for her mind to flip over to the realization that it's Ryan.

The thrill and relief that Ryan is finally home rushes through her and she almost throws herself at him.

But something in his eyes stops her. Her smile falters just a little.

Ryan saw the flash of disappointment and it cut him deep inside. He doesn't understand that it's a product of her loneliness and not knowing when he will be back, a part of her deep down inside her questioning if he will even come back. Or that it's that brief heartbeat it took her to realize he really is back at last and his coming back makes her happier than she could possibly have been if it had been anyone else at the door.

All he knows is for that brief moment she was disappointed to see him.

The question flashes in his mind. *Who was she expecting? Her mother?* The idea scares him. *What if she contacted her mother while I was gone?*

*That's it; I have to tell Anderson on the next job that I can't leave her alone again. She'll have to come with me after that. Anderson might not feel confident about her, but I know she can handle it. She's strong enough.*

*And if she did contact her mother, then I'll deal with that. We'll have to move and change identities again, but we'll get through it.*

"You didn't break down and call your mom while I was gone?" he asks, scared of what the answer will be.

"No. I promised I wouldn't."

"You didn't contact anyone at all?" He studies her reaction. "Because, you know what that would mean, right? Your mom, anyone else, they probably have their phones and everything tapped. They will trace it to us and arrest me. Maybe you too for being with me."

He looks at her searchingly.

Elaine is shaking her head, feeling like he doesn't trust her.

"I promise, I didn't call anyone."

He pushes his worry aside, drops his bag on the floor, and takes Elaine in his arms, holding her tight.

"I'm back."

"Finally," she whispers in relief.

They hold each other for a long moment and she finally pulls herself away and looks up at him.

"Your friend from the slaughterhouse stopped by a few times to see you. I didn't know when to tell him you would be back."

"Friend?" He has no friends there. He can't think of a single man there who would have any reason to come to the house looking for him.

"Trevor Mitchell."

Ryan stiffens at the name, his jaw clenching and eyes narrowing.

"Did he say what he wanted?"

"Only that he was stopping by to see you, the first time anyway. He said he would keep stopping by to check on me until you get back."

A cold chill slithers through Ryan.

He looks down at her with a frown. "He was checking on you?"

Elaine's expression falters, her smile slipping more. "He said you would do the same for him. I thought you sent him."

"No, I didn't."

His mind races with suspicion. He does not trust the man. *What is he up to?* He wonders silently.

Ryan keeps his concern to himself. Instead he looks at Elaine again, smiles, and sweeps her up into his arms, picking her up.

She squeals with delight.

"I'm home," he says.

# 24 Hawkworth has an Epiphany

The door closes on Jim and Lawrence seems to sag with it. He is exhausted after the hours he spent pouring through the boxes of old files on missing persons. Jim's visit reinvigorated him, but only for as long as the visit lasted. Now his whole being feels like it's made of lead.

He rubs a hand over his face roughly in an effort to make himself feel more awake. He isn't done yet.

Getting a freshly poured cup of coffee from the pot that sat warming too long in the kitchen, he returns to the boxes of files.

"I wish he made some kind of list indexing what's in these boxes," Lawrence mutters as he pulls yet another file from the box before him.

Like each file before it, he opens the file, making a quick glance first for any victim photos clipped to the first page, then the sex of the victim. The one thing his predecessor had done was organize each file in an identical way despite the disorganization of the files themselves within the boxes. Knowing the man who left him the files, he knows there has to be some point to the order they were placed in the boxes, but it's a secret that was taken to the grave with him. The first page of each folder contains a brief summary of the basic information and a photo if there is one.

*No photo in this file, male, not what I'm looking for,* Lawrence thinks, closing the folder and putting it aside.

He is reaching for another when his cell phone rings, startling him.

Lawrence has to fumble for a moment first to find it and then to take the call on the unaccustomed to device.

"Hawkworth," he says into the phone.

"Hawkworth," his editor's voice comes to him urgently, "whatever you are working on put it aside unless it involves murder, mayhem, or the downfall of someone rich and powerful." He sounds breathless.

"What do you have?"

"Missing woman," Paul says, "lives only a couple doors up from the rooming house Jason T. McAllister was placed in on his release."

Lawrence can see Paul's slow shake of his head as if in doubtful shock and the gleam of a hot by-line in his eyes through the excitement in his voice.

He can't help but grin mischievously.

"You can't be suggesting it could have anything to do with Jason McAllister, could you?"

He pictures Paul pursing his lips and crinkling his forehead in annoyance on the other side of the call.

"Don't even go there Hawkworth. I told you to leave off the Jason McAllister/Michael Underwood thing. That's old news. Hell, it wasn't even news when it was fresh. If there was a connection, don't you think the police would have charged him as an accessory? No connection, the man is gone, end of story."

"Whatever you say sir, you're the boss."

"I want you to find out what you can on the missing woman, any link she has to Jason McAllister. The public will eat this one up. Serial killer set loose kills again. Hang on a sec."

Lawrence can hear background noises in Paul's office, rustling, voices murmuring, then his editor exclaiming.

"Oh shit!"

His voice comes back on the line loud and clear, filled with a new level of shock and excitement.

"Hawkworth, check into the judge that let McAllister walk too. He was just discovered in his home office by his maid. We need a timeline. It looks like he may have gone home and killed himself after releasing McAllister."

Lawrence stares straight ahead with stunned shock.

"That's assuming he killed himself," Paul says. "You got all that?"

"Yes," Lawrence says, trying to let it sink in.

"All right, get on it." Paul hangs up the phone.

*Did the judge kill himself?* Lawrence mulls it over, turning the story over in his mind as he does with every story before tackling the initial investigation. The statement feels wrong to him. Something tugs at him, a feeling inside. He turns and looks at the boxes of files. Was there something in there that he skimmed in his search about another judge who committed suicide? It's the barest flutter of a feeling. And just like that it is gone.

Moments later it is completely forgotten.

"I need a break anyway," Lawrence mutters.

Hours spent pouring through the files turned up nothing.

His gut feeling is that these kids he pictured at the farm, kids Jason McAllister was rumoured to have in his possession, did not belong with Jason McAllister.

Lawrence heads out. His first stop is the missing woman's house. He parks up the street so he has to walk past the rooming house. It gives him a chance to get a look at the place and the area without being obvious about it.

He walks slowly up the street, taking in the neighbourhood.

Lawrence catches the motion of an upstairs curtain across the street from the rooming house.

*A potential witness. Those are often the best ones, the nosy neighbour who can't help but keep looking out their window at every sound. Once you get past the neurotic irrational obsessions that make them constantly peep surreptitiously on their neighbours, they are the witnesses who tend to see and remember the most detail. They're practiced snoops.*

Jim's car is parked on the street in front of McAllister's rooming house.

*This must have been the call he got. No, he said that McAllister was on the move. He must be there somewhere, maybe inside the rooming house checking it out.*

*Good. I can get answers better without him there.*

Lawrence keeps going. The rooming house itself sits silent and lifeless. *If anyone is home, they are probably hiding out in their sad little rooms, probably hoping the police won't knock on their door. Or, if they do, they will think they aren't there and go away. I'll come back to it later to check it out more thoroughly and see if I can get any information from the other residents.*

Lawrence turns up the walkway to the house two doors from the rooming house. It's a tidy little house, home and yard kept better than the rentals that surround it in this low income neighbourhood.

He mounts the steps, pausing in front of the door to raise his hand to knock even as he considers whether he should knock or just walk in, and the door swings open as if the resident was expecting him, startling the men on both sides of the door.

Jim takes in the tall lanky reporter staring blankly at a door that is no longer there.

Before Lawrence can register who is standing before him, Jim speaks. "No reporters," he says gruffly.

"Jim!" Lawrence says, collecting himself for the push he knows he will need to get past the fat detective.

Jim uses his greater bulk to force Lawrence to step back from the door and down the steps.

"That was fast," Jim says quietly so he won't be heard inside as he closes the door behind him. "How did you get word of this so quickly?"

He shakes his head. "No, don't bother to answer that. It doesn't matter."

He leans in toward Lawrence. "None of your usual reporter stuff, understand?"

"Funny how a woman a few doors from Jason McAllister goes missing just days after he's released," Lawrence says.

Jim sighs. *There's no use keeping anything back. Lawrence will dig it up anyway.*

"Everyone is assuming it was him, but it doesn't fit," Jim says. "In all the investigations digging into his past, it looks like he doesn't soil where he sleeps."

Lawrence knows what he means. *Just like an animal won't dirty the place it sleeps and eats with its own feces if it can avoid it, Jason McAllister is the kind of two-legged animal who does not kill where he lives. That would only increase his chances of getting caught.*

"So, you don't think it was him," Lawrence says.

"No, I don't. He's been watching her, probably made her feel threatened, but my person watching him doesn't think he had an opportunity. And, it doesn't fit his profile."

Lawrence looks down, thinking about it. He looks at Jim, opening his mouth to speak.

"I already thought of that," Jim says. "I don't think it was any of the other residents. They all have mental health issues of one sort or another, and have a list of charges behind them, prostitution, drugs, petty property and theft crimes. The only one with a history of sex crimes only goes after boys, young ones."

"I'd be suspicious you are telling me this so I stay away from your serial killer," Lawrence says, "except I think you are right. Do you think it's someone else in the neighbourhood?"

"Could be, if she hasn't just run off. Kidnapping is usually a crime of convenience or passion. Most of them aren't very well planned out."

Lawrence nods towards the house across from the rooming house.

"Notice the peeper up the street?"

Jim nods. "The curtain moved eight times since we stepped out here. Seems they're pretty nervous."

They both look up the street towards the house.

The occupant upstairs drops the rod he used to push the curtain open and steps back quickly into the darkened shadows of the corner, plastering himself to the corner, eyes wild like a caged animal. He breathes heavy and fast, trying to hold his breath as if the men up the street can hear him.

*It's them!* His mind reels. *No, it can't be. You are safe. It's at trick. They're just people. They're trying to trick you into thinking it's them.*

He starts chanting his litany in his head. It usually has a soothing effect.

*The walls are papered in tinfoil and papier-mâché made of my own mix and full sheets of newspaper. The shiny metallic foil blocks out the radio signals coming from the radio towers and satellites. The words on the newsprint block in the demons writhing inside my head. I built a papier-mâché wall in front of the window, leaving a gap between it and the glass. If it touches the glass it will shatter and they will get in. I cut a square flap out of the papier-mâché covering the window so I can open it and peak out to watch for them.*

*They sneak up on the house sometimes.*

*It's nerve-wrecking, but I have to reach through the flap to pull the curtain back to look out. I can feel the sunlight burning my flesh when the sun is out. The stars shoot little pinpricks of light through me like little daggers, trying to kill me. I have to keep my body protected when the stars are out. I have a special suit for that. The moon is the worst. The moon talks to me. I don't like what it has to say.*

*I'm not sure if they control the sun and moon and stars, or if it's the extra terrestrials trying to get at my demons from space.*

*They use the radio signals to try to control me, to try to talk to the demons inside me. The government wants my demons. They want them to escape from inside me so they can control them and do terrible things with them.*

*The demons do terrible things when they get out and I can't hear them anymore. I know. They whisper to me about it inside my head when they come back.*

It takes all his inner strength to force himself to move, to step forward towards the window.

His arm is trembling so much he can barely move it as he reaches out to flip the flap closed. He flips it quickly and it snaps closed as he yanks his hand back to the relative safety of the corner.

The room falls into darkness and he sinks weakly to the floor against the corner; sobbing woefully and moaning. In the shadows, his face is a mask of fear and absolute despair, his body thin with malnutrition and his clothes that once fit drape off his withered frame.

He starts the litany again, whispering it quickly and breathlessly, repeating it word for word.

Still standing in front of the missing woman's home, Lawrence and Jim turn back to each other.

"I thought you were checking out McAllister," Lawrence says.

"I was," Jim says. "I was just leaving there when I got the call and came here."

He looks pointedly at Lawrence.

"The last thing that man in there needs right now is a reporter in his face."

"I need enough to run the headline and summary."

"I'll give you enough for the headline, but that's it. I know I'm going to regret it. There is no story anyway. Not yet. We don't know anything except that she's supposed to be here and she isn't."

He looks up and down the street.

"It's not as if anyone is likely to have video surveillance on their house in this neighbourhood. And, anyone who might have seen anyone probably won't want to talk to us. This area is full of low end rentals and rooming houses, slumlords and bad tenants."

"Just the nervous guy up the street."

"Yeah, there is that."

"I guess I'm off to see about the judge then," Lawrence says with a small wolfish grin.

He counts mentally in his head. One … two … three …

And there it comes right on cue.

"Judge?" Jim scowls. By Lawrence's expression, he knows the reporter knows something he should.

"Kkkkddd," Lawrence makes a sound and a slicing motion across his throat. "Or maybe," he makes a popping sound and a shooting himself in the head motion.

Jim's eyes narrow. "What do you know?"

"The judge that let Jason McAllister walk went home and offed himself," Lawrence says with his best wolfish false innocence look.

Jim's phone rings. He pulls it out and looks at the number.

Lawrence nods and points at the phone. "There it is."

Jim eyes him suspiciously as he brings the phone to his ear and presses the button.

"Detective McNelly," he snaps.

He listens. "Got it. I'm on my way." He hangs up the call.

"How the hell do you do that?" he glares at Lawrence.

"Race you," Lawrence says, turning on his heal and walking nonchalantly to his car.

Jim huffs breathlessly as he follows. His car is closer, but with Lawrence's long legs and better health he can easily make it to his car first.

Lawrence arrives at the judge's house first.

A sleek vehicle sits parked crookedly in front of the house. Scrapes and dings mar the surface, one in particular gliding down the length of the passenger side with a bright paint transfer from whatever the vehicle scraped its side against. They provide ample evidence of a less than accomplished drive home.

From the inexpensive nature of the second vehicle parked discretely on the other side of the garage, its bumper just poking out into view, Lawrence pegs it as belonging to one of the hired help.

There are a couple of patrol cars sitting quietly, no lights, and no officers in sight.

"They must be inside guarding the scene."

Parking out of the way, he gets out and jogs around the house past the maid's car, looking for another entrance. A house this huge will have multiple, some less guarded and reserved for the hired help.

He finds one and slips inside, the door left unlocked as he expected.

Lawrence takes a moment to take in the grandeur of the place, thinking, *If I were a judge, where would my office be? Bedrooms would be upstairs. Main floor.*

He starts cautiously looking around for the office. It doesn't take long to find. It's the only door with an officer standing outside it. He spies another officer through the kitchen windows, guarding the rear entrance.

*Lucky I didn't go that way.*

Two more officers are standing inside the front entrance to the house, chatting. Up another hallway, he catches a glimpse of someone hovering in a doorway, trying to be invisible.

*The maid.* He slips down the hall.

He finds the trembling distraught mess of a too-skinny maid hovering in a doorway where she thinks no one will see her. She is surreptitiously peeking around the doorway towards the officers, looking terrified. She keeps weeping and clutching herself while muttering in a language that is unintelligible to Lawrence.

*Probably scared she'll be deported. Most likely she speaks little or no English and is paid accordingly.*

Lawrence moves in for the kill. She backs away fearfully at his advance, putting up her arms as if to block an attack.

"I'm here to help you," he lies. "I want to help." He backs her into the room, out of sight of the officers to get whatever information he can from her.

Minutes later with the help of the distraught maid distracting the officer away from the door, Lawrence slips quietly into the heart of the situation, the judge's home office.

The desk and room are tidy, the only items out of place are an empty bottle of port and a glass still a quarter full of the dark liquor;

and the dead man slumped in the luxurious leather chair behind the desk with his head hanging backwards over the chair back and a spray of blood and brains spattering the wall, floor, and chair back behind him. Blood dripped, then oozed, and finally congealed and mostly dried down the back of his ruined head, down the back of the leather chair, and pooled on the hardwood floor beneath him.

It isn't a large pool, only as much as could drain from the head and what the last few feeble attempts of the heart to keep pumping could push up into the cranium before it stopped beating.

Lawrence is standing there, taking it all in, quickly snapping a few pictures on autopilot and shoving his camera out of sight in his bag, his mind awash in a dizzying rush of possibilities as he plays possible scenarios through his head, when Detective Jim McNelly walks into the office and swears.

"Who's supposed to be guarding this scene?" Jim looks around angrily, seeing no one except one trespassing reporter.

There is a clatter of shoes running towards the room and a couple officers appear in the doorway looking sheepish.

"Get back on guarding this door and get him out of here. Damned scene has been compromised."

Lawrence steps back from the scene towards the large angry detective. "I didn't touch anything."

Jim scowls at him, waving him out of the room.

The two officers grab him roughly by the arms, escorting him towards the front entrance and handing him off to two more officers.

Lawrence grins, his grimace wicked and wolfish on his face as it is with every smile, as he puts his arms up in surrender to the large men who take over escorting him out. He's not capable of a disarming friendly smile. His features simply will not twist that way.

They give him an unimpressed look and escort him outside to his car, making sure he drives off the property.

The quest for answers at the judge's house will pit cop against reporter against family with what Lawrence suspects are hired security roughly removing him from the property and barring his attempts to re-enter if he comes back.

Lawrence isn't concerned. He managed to get a glimpse of the crime scene and that's enough for now. The office is only the visualization of the story. There is nothing more there for him. The police forensics can have it.

*He's been there for a few days before anyone discovered the body. Either the judge lives alone, his wife is out of town, or the married couple have become so accustomed to not seeing each other that it never occurred to his wife that his absence over the past few days meant anything, or to check his office to see if he's there.*

*The real story is the hired help. The maid, gardener, maintenance, cook, pool cleaner; the invisible people no one notices but keep a large home like this running. I'll come back to talk to them after the police are gone.*

*For now, I'll go back to searching for anything I can find that might point to how Jason McAllister may have ended up with two children. Someone was missing those children.*

Lawrence returns to his apartment, the adrenaline of chasing the two cases wearing off to leave him feeling like his body is filled with liquid lead.

He is beyond exhausted and hasn't slept in more than twenty-four hours.

By the time he pulls into his parking spot, Lawrence knows he's a hazard on the road and should not be driving so sleep deprived. He might have been alarmed for his own safety if he was not too tired even to feel that.

Lawrence leans against the elevator wall as he rides it up, stumbles down the hall when it reaches his floor, and leans on his door as he fumbles with the keys to open the various locks.

Stumbling into the apartment, he falls onto the bed in exhaustion, not so much as taking off his shoes, and is promptly snoring.

In the living room the sounds of life that never totally sleeps in an apartment building echoes down the hall and in through the open door.

Two hours later Lawrence wakes with a start. He blinks and rubs his eyes, obliviously pushing his glasses up to do it, trying to make his eyes come into focus. He feels like he had been drugged, but it's just the effects of exhaustion.

He fumbles on the night table beside him, looking for his glasses only to discover them on his face when he rubs it again in confusion.

Lawrence tries to focus. He feels off. Something woke him up.

The apartment is still. He sits up, listening.

Lawrence slides off the bed, wincing at the soft rustle of his clothes against the bedspread. Holding his breath, he grabs the only weapon at hand, a lamp. Holding it upside down, the shade wobbling with the movement and ready to swing it like a baseball bat; he creeps to the bedroom door. He stops there and listens before daring to poke his head around the doorframe to peer out.

There is no sound or movement.

Lawrence passes the open bathroom door, tensing and ready to leap back, and looks inside. It's empty. The bubbled partially frosted glass of the shower doors does not reveal the shape of an intruder hiding in the shower.

He moves on, stepping to the entrance of the living room. Lawrence immediately notices the open door with a dull edge of panic.

*Did I leave it open?* He thinks, trying to pull the memory into his mind of the moment he came home. It will not come. He can't remember most of the drive home.

He is filled with a growing sense of presence, that someone else has been there in his apartment, that he is not alone right now.

Lawrence swallows hard and grips the lamp tighter.

There isn't much left to check, just the kitchen and closet.

Almost losing to the urge to flee, he steps slowly and quietly towards the kitchen. Relief begins to flood him the moment he looks in and sees the kitchen empty of intruders, but then he's drawn to the closet.

*They always hide in the closet, don't they? In the movies they do.*

Strung tight with anxiety, Lawrence turns his back on the kitchen and moves to the closet. He checks the closet quickly in case he has to run. It's empty.

Stepping past the closet to the still open door, he cautiously pokes his head out, looking up and down the hallway. The sounds of the building echo hollowly in the hallway, but the hallway is otherwise still and silent.

He closes the door and flips just the one deadbolt locked, just in case he has to get out in a hurry. Lawrence backtracks, checking the apartment again, more thoroughly this time.

Finally satisfied he's alone, Lawrence returns to the living room where he puts the lamp down and locks and sets the rest of his security devices on the door.

He sits on the couch and looks around him, wondering what startled him awake. He can't shake the feeling that he is not alone.

"Must be the exhaustion," he mumbles.

Lawrence's eyes are drawn to the closet.

With no idea why he gets up and walks over. He stops. He looks up at the cardboard boxes on the top shelf. These are the oldest boxes. Their sides sag at the bottom as if too tired to stay firm.

Reaching up for a box on the top shelf, he grabs its bottom corners and pulls it to the edge. Sticking his fingers in the opening cut in the side as a handle, he tips it towards him with one hand, ready to catch its weight with the other. As the box tips, the lid slides off, bouncing off his head and falling to the floor.

He pulls on the box, dragging the front corners over the edge of the shelf, tipping it towards him more, its bottom sliding over the shelf edge so that he can grip the bottom. As he is taking it from the shelf, the aged box's cardboard gives, pulling apart in the near silent rip of rotten cardboard and the contents tumble, raining down on Lawrence. Pages tumble in clumps and flutter individually, folders spilling out their contents as they fall and plop to the floor with some pages holding fast to their fasteners and some breaking free. Almost the entire contents of the box now lays scattered on the floor around him.

With an unhappy groan, Lawrence pulls what's left of the box down and lets it fall to the floor with its last remaining contents. He sighs heavily, looking down at the mess.

Stepping carefully to not tear any pages, Lawrence removes himself from the center of the chaos inflicted on him by the ruination of time on cardboard. The papers show the yellowing effects of age, as do many of the other files in these boxes.

These boxes hold a lifetime of dedication to the fruitless search for an answer. One that started decades before Lawrence started on the same path as a reporter.

Finding another box to put the files in, he starts the long and meticulous job of cleaning up the mess. He starts with studying the scattered files and pages, trying to determine how best to bring them back to their original well-ordered files. By their placement and his memory of how they fell, he is able to quickly piece some files and groups of papers together.

The order of the files in the box is lost, something he tried meticulously to avoid mixing up in the other boxes until he can make some sense of the reasoning behind the order of the files themselves.

Lawrence starts the long slow process of reading the remaining scattered papers and files to determine what belongs in which file.

These files are all missing persons' reports. This box is so old that he didn't think there could be anything relevant to his investigation in it, so he had not intended on going through it.

About an hour in, Lawrence picks up a page, glancing at it to quickly find the information that will link it to a particular file.

He slides it into the folder with the matching name. Only half the contents of that folder spilled out, the rest having slid only half out. He slid them back in when he picked the file up.

He pauses, not letting go of the page, drawn to it.

A faint sound tickles his ear. *A child's laughter?* It is so faint that it could have been anything.

*It's probably just exhaustion buzzing in my ear.*

Lawrence shrugs it off, letting go of the paper and leaving the file in the box.

He turns to pick up another sheet, but is still drawn to that paper. He tries to push it away, to continue cleaning up the mess, and finally gives in.

Turning back to the box, he pulls out the file. Pulling out the report, he skims over it for the most pertinent details and is quickly devouring the details, reading them over and over.

His breath comes faster and his heart races.

"This is it! This is 'the' report." He has no reason to believe this, but he feels it in his gut.

The report itself reveals very little; the name of the victim, date of birth, sex, and residence. It lists the date the report was filed, who filed it, and the name of the officer who took the report. Anything else would be in the investigating officer's notes, which would not have been given out to a reporter unless he came by it through unconventional means.

Next to relationship to the victim is a single word typed in the same crooked old-style typewriter key-striking-the-page font as the rest of the report; "SPOUSE".

It's the notes jotted in the margins of the report by the previous owner of the files that pulls Lawrence in completely. He immediately recognizes the slanted mostly illegible chicken scratch of the reporter, his mentor, who had collected these files over a lifetime.

It brings to him full force the memory of the man's obsession over something big he was investigating and would never breathe so much as a word of, not even to Lawrence. This was something he held on a much deeper and more personal level. Lawrence had seen fear in his eyes those few times he questioned it.

Lawrence turns his attention to the cryptic notes in the margins, working at deciphering them.

Cop suspects husband

Other cop suspects jilted wife - revenge

Affair

Dead or alive?

Not husband?

Someone else. Who?

Why the kids?

The notes only lead to more questions.

Lawrence turns and stares at the papers still scattered on the floor. "There has to be more. You don't keep such detailed files through your whole career and not have investigated further, leaving only unanswered questions."

He gets down on the floor and starts going through the scattered pages methodically. Pressed with an unnerving urgency, he is soon pawing at them frantically; tossing aside anything that can't be part of the file. He skims the maybes before adding them to a growing pile to review again. He is determined to find those ever multiplying elusive answers that had evaded him from the discovery of the first body and only survivor of Jason McAllister – Jane Doe, who was left for dead, discarded with the trash.

*Was it Jason McAllister?* The thought comes unbidden and he pushes it away. *Of, course it was.*

Lawrence picks up a news article clipped from a newspaper, his mind pulled into contemplation, distracted by his own thoughts and looking at the article without really reading it.

From the start Lawrence sensed there was something much bigger and darker than a single serial killer behind the McAllister story and he was not going to stop until he broke it and found the truth. The discovery of the mass graveyard spanning generations in the woods past the McAllister Farm only reinforced that belief and his conviction to find the real story.

He almost tosses the paper in his hand aside to flutter down in the scattered mess of discards.

He pauses, bringing the paper back before him.

It has the typical shock and awe headline.

HUSBAND HELD ON SUSPICION IN DISAPPEARANCE OF WIFE AND KIDS

The article was written by his predecessor and mentor, the files' previous owner. The accompanying photo is of the mother and kids, a toddler and small boy, smiling into the camera.

Lawrence reads through the article, reading between the lines for the writer's own suspicions behind the story. *There is always so much the writer holds back for the sake of the article.*

The article details the husband's affair that ended his marriage, leaving his wife for the other woman. That day he and his wife planned a final outing as a family with the kids, supposedly to lessen the blow of the devastating news. That last fateful day they went to the zoo as a family.

At the end of the day they were to tell the kids together. Only the husband bailed, telling his wife at the end of the afternoon that his mistress was picking him up there. She would have to deal with the kids' confusion and heartbreak on her own.

That day is the last time anyone saw her and the two kids. They vanished forever. The article left more questions than it answered. The husband was held as a suspect. The article failed to say who filed a missing persons report or when it was noticed they were gone. The zoo trip was the last time anyone saw them.

From his predecessor's notes on the missing persons report, it was days later when the husband made his first attempt to contact his wife. Weeks later before he filed the missing persons report.

Lawrence mulls this over, trying to get a feel for how and where it fits in.

"The kids. Every time I try to figure out the Michael Underwood and Jason McAllister connection, I keep coming back to the same thing; the kids. Did Jason McAllister have kids? They weren't his; there would be records somewhere of them. It's only a rumour from a few elderly people who knew who he was back then.

It can't be connected. The kids and their mother vanished and are presumed dead. The father was a suspect, believed to have killed them because his marriage was breaking down."

# 25 Room Sitting

Billy, aka The Kid, is walking down the sidewalk of a busy street in what would have been a skyscraper-filled downtown in a larger city, feeling relatively safe lost in the flow of traffic and people. The creepy new guy who just moved in upstairs at the rooming house is gone. He has no idea where or for how long.

*It's weird,* he thinks. *First he attacks me and threatens me. Scared the crap out of me! Then he leaves me food and clothes that fit and other stuff. He even asked me stay in his room and said he'd pay me to watch the room. The whole situation feels unreal.*

*He's some kind of creeper,* The Kid decides, *a regular perv. He's trying to buy my trust, but I'm too smart. I'll take his money and the stuff, and maybe the place to sleep while he's gone. I haven't decided on that yet. But I'm not stupid enough to trust him. When I sleep, if I sleep in that guy's room at all, I'm going to wedge the chair under the doorknob so he can't come in while I'm sleeping.*

Late last night, when he snuck into the house to crash for a few hours, the creepy new man upstairs was sitting in the dark in the living room waiting for him.

His mind flashes back to that moment.

Earlier:

The kid skulks through the darkness outside the house, going to the kitchen window that doesn't lock. It's a little stiff in the frame, but he pushes it up with only a little trouble.

With a jump, he gets enough leverage to pull himself up and into the house. His entrance is ungainly, and he plops quietly on the floor and gets to his feet.

Trying to be quiet, he tiptoes into the living room, expecting to be alone.

The man's voice comes from the darkness, startling him, and he jumps and almost lets out a little yelp.

"Kid, I have a deal for you." It's the creepy new guy from upstairs, the one who threatened him.

His pulse is racing and he feels the urge to run. *How fast can I get out? What's the fastest? The window? Front door? Back? Can he outrun me?*

Jason stands up and approaches. The kid feels suddenly sticky with fear, frozen in place and wants only to bolt.

Jason reaches out to him and he is sure he is reaching to grab him roughly and rough him up again, maybe worse. He stares at the outstretched hand in terrified shock. It takes long heartbeats to register.

Jason is holding out a key to him and he knows what he wants. He feels physically sick.

*Some of the other street kids do that; for money, drugs, and stuff. Eventually it sometimes becomes a matter of survival. I managed to avoid it so far. Now he's going to force me.*

Jason takes the kid's hand and places his room key in it.

The kid stares down at it. The metal is slightly warm from being in Jason's hand and somehow that makes it all the more treacherous. That part sticks in his mind for hours after, the warmth of the metal.

Jason is talking, but he isn't hearing at first.

Then he realizes what he is saying.

"Look after the room for me," Jason says. I'm going away for a few days, maybe longer. I'm not sure how long. You can use the room while I'm away; I've got nothing in it anyway. There are just a few things there that I don't need. You can sleep there, hide out there, whatever. Just keep it clean."

He shoves money into the kid's hand and he almost drops it.

"That's for food and stuff," Jason says, "payment to look after the room. It has to look lived in by a man at all times. No kid stuff; none of your personal crap. If anyone ever goes into the room it has to look like I and I alone am living there, not a boy, not me and a boy. Got it?

It has to look like I'm there while I'm gone. Open and close the curtains at different times, turn the light on and off just like someone is living there. Stay away from the window. Make sure you can't be seen in the window at any time. Not even when you are moving the curtains. Keep the man clothes and stuff tidy and orderly, move them around a little every day as if I'm there using them."

He stares the boy down hard, giving him only a brief pause to let it start to sink in.

"And most importantly, never let anyone see you enter or leave the room." Jason stresses this, hoping the boy will understand just how important it is.

No one can know he's gone. He plans to be back long before his case worker and Detective Jim McNelly ever have a chance to suspect he's gone. He also isn't stupid enough not to expect the detective to at least do the occasional drive by to see if it looks like he's home.

"I'm going on a trip," Jason says. He leaves and is gone.

The kid stares down at the key in his hand. It is still disturbingly warm from the man's hand. He shoves the cash in his pocket.

*Whatever, it's cash. But I'm not doing anything weird or anything.*

He tries to settle in and sleep on the couch, but can't stop looking at the door. He half expects the guy to come back at any moment.

Feeing anxious and exposed in the living room where anyone who comes in will find him, after a few hours he sighs and gets up.

"What will it hurt?"

He waits a while longer to make sure the man isn't coming back and then goes up to check out the room, ducking down and sneaking past the other rooms as he passes them.

Just as the creepy man said, there are man-sized clothes in the dresser drawers, and a small bag with toothbrush, toothpaste, soap, and other shower stuff. A towel hangs on the corner of the chair back. The top dresser drawer holds a shaving kit and comb. On top of the dresser is a worn book.

On the bed is a bag with a note. It's addressed to "The Kid."

Hesitant and distrustful, he opens the bag. Inside, are a couple of used books and comic books.

*The kind a boy my age might be interested in if he lived in a regular family like they show on TV.*

There is also a used cell with charger. He flips through the books and comics quickly. Some of them are old comics he never would have looked at. He presses the button to turn on the phone and swipes to open it. The screen is locked.

"Figures. I can't even use it."

He goes to the door and locks it, returning to lie on the bed. He pulls out one comic book and looks at it. It is some kind of old western. Billy the Kid.

"Never heard of him."

With a shrug he opens the comic and starts reading it. As he reads and flips pages, something falls out; a handful of money and a prepaid card for the phone. Picking up the card, he looks it over.

"It's still useless without the code for the lock screen."

He picks up the note that had been on top of the bag, looking at it again.

"The Kid."

He turns it over. There is writing on the other side.

"For emergencies kidd."

"Kidd?" It strikes him as weird that the guy would spell it with an extra d. Then a thought hits him and he looks at the phone.

*Four digit code on the lock screen.*

He looks back at the note. Kidd. "It's worth a try."

He presses the button again to bring up the lock screen, keying in the four digits corresponding with the letters – K I D D. He is in.

"The Kid," he shrugs, feeling a mix of uncertainty and relief at breaking the code.

He looks at the comic again. "Billy. Billy the Kid."

The cover displays an old-fashioned looking graphic of a rough looking man snarling around a fat smouldering cigar, his clothes and face seeming to almost be melting into each other, his eyes dangerous. The ember on the end of a roughly rolled cigarette sprouting from the corner of his mouth glows bright red against the darkness of the rest of the picture. Twin barrels of a pair of Colt .45s seem ready to pop off the page, pointing at him with smoke curling from their muzzles. He's wearing the required bad guy black cowboy hat, the hat worn and misshapen as though it had been through a lot of fights.

The backdrop is a darkened saloon. Ladies in low cut floor length dresses and large hats cower back with shocked expressions. The men, all rough looking cowboys, are either diving for cover or dropping cigarettes from mouths and poker cards with frightened expressions. A tipping table is sending its drinks, cards, and poker chips exploding into the air.

He studies the main character's dangerous looking face.

"That's as good as any other name. I'll be Billy now, or The Kid."

Present:

The Kid is not paying attention, lost in his thoughts as he walks along the sidewalk of the busy downtown street.

He looks up and stops at the corner, waiting for the light change and the cars to stop, letting the memory slip and putting his focus now on the traffic and traffic lights.

He sees it. Across the busy intersection and a few buildings down. A white van.

Paling, The Kid turns and runs.

# 26 Plans and Counter-Plans

Trevor is in the change room getting ready for his shift along with half a dozen other guys. He almost jumps when Ryan walks in, startled by his sudden appearance. He feels the rush of adrenaline he always gets, worrying he will get caught. It's more than a worry; it's a fear, a challenge that is exciting. His whole body almost vibrates with it. The feeling clings to him.

*What will Ryan do here with all these witnesses?*

Ryan only goes to his locker, puts his personal stuff in, and gets his own coveralls on, ignoring Trevor.

Trevor can't help himself. He glances at Ryan nervously now and then. His hands are trembling and he turns to block them from the others. He doesn't want anyone to see his hands shaking.

Ryan still doesn't look at him.

Trevor looks around to see who else is there to witness anything Ryan does. Not all the guys are in yet. Those who are there are not paying either of them any attention. They are already dressed in their coveralls and leaving the change room for the kill floor.

Trevor pulls his coveralls on quickly, grabbing his goggles, gloves, and hard hat and hurries out of the change room to go to his killing pit. He silently berates himself for being so obvious. He doesn't want to be left alone in the change room with Ryan.

By the time he gets out to the killing floor, the other guys are already getting their first bawling victims of the day from the holding pen.

*All I did was talk to her*, he thinks as if that would excuse what he is planning to do.

Behind him he hears the voices of more men arriving for work.

Minutes later, when Ryan follows to his killing pit next to Trevor's, he only nods a curt noncommittal greeting at Trevor as if nothing happened between them and goes to work systematically slaughtering cattle.

Trevor does the same, turning his attention to slaughtering the cattle. He doesn't enjoy the job the same way, not since Ryan threatened him with the bolt gun. Now he is too afraid to get a little rough with the beasts, or to take out his anger on them or have any fun with them before killing them.

As the morning wears on, so does Trevor's nerves.

*What is Ryan waiting for?* He's regretting his decision to visit Elaine now, his legs and arms are lead weights with his fear of the man in the next killing pit.

Ryan keeps to himself all day, watching Trevor when he isn't looking. By the afternoon, Trevor is questioning everything he had been thinking.

*Am I making a mistake toying with Ryan and his woman? Is Ryan not going to say or do anything at all? Did Elaine tell Ryan about my visit?*

These thoughts come to him sporadically over the afternoon.

Ryan surreptitiously watches Trevor get increasingly nervous in the next killing pit as the day progresses. He is enjoying it.

He can tell when Trevor's thought process changes because his jerky nervous movements turn confident, cocky even.

By the end of the afternoon Trevor decides that Elaine didn't tell her boyfriend about his visits. He is wallowing in the knowledge that she kept it to herself.

*This is going to be even more fun,* Trevor thinks. *I'm not going to just play with them a bit. I'm going to have her. I'm going to use her behind his back, and when I'm done with her I'll drop whatever is left of her on his doorstep. Then I'll really have my fun. After I've broken her I'll come back for her. He will know it was me, but he won't be able to prove it. There will be no body, but I'll make sure he knows.*

Ryan sees Trevor's gloating looks and he smiles inwardly. *He's playing along. He's getting comfortable again.*

*Trevor did not show up at my house while I was away to check in on Elaine. He is no friend of mine and would not have come to visit me. How the hell does he even know where I live? He must have followed me home.*

*If Trevor is watching the house, it can't be for anything good. Soon, I'll find out what game he is playing at. Then I'll kill him.*

# Part Five

# William McAllister

# 27 Jason Visits his Father

The bus pulls into the bus station behind another bus, its brakes hissing and making high pitched farting sounds. The doors open and the occupants soon begin piling off the bus and queuing up to wait for the driver to release their baggage from the compartment beneath the seats.

Another bus comes in behind it, turning in to follow the same long sweeping driveway next to the building.

Jason McAllister gets off the bus in the midst of the crowd, carrying a worn duffel bag just large enough to hold a change of clothes.

He looks around the busy depot. Inside the glass doors are more people, benches, and the ticket counter with the board listing the city destinations of the busses.

Clutching his bag, Jason slips through the mob of people cluttering the sidewalk next to the bus and heads off across the lot.

*I don't know if he'll still be there or if he's still alive. It's been a few years since I looked him up, and even then I never went to see him. It could have been a bogus address then for all I knew.*

It takes some time to get there, by local bus, subway, and then another local bus. Finally, with no sign of his final bus coming up the road, Jason decides to walk the remaining blocks.

*It will give me a chance to scope out the area, taking a circuitous route to the address. There shouldn't be anyone watching, but my father taught me to always take those extra precautions.*

At last, Jason is almost there. He arrives at the street. The address is just across the street and a couple of buildings up.

He stops. There he is, across the street, sweeping the sidewalk pavement in front of the building with a worn straw broom. It's the kind of thing some old people do that doesn't really surprise the younger generation who think it's senseless.

The man who once seemed like he would be strong and proud forever is now a withered old dried up husk. Frail.

"Why does the old man bother? It's the sidewalk, for Christ sake."

His mind swirls with things he should say, questions he wants to ask. After a moment to gather his courage, Jason crosses the street.

The old man never looks up, not bothering to pause in his sweeping, his concentration on the sidewalk and appears to be oblivious to the middle-aged man approaching him. William McAllister has never been oblivious to anything happening around him.

Jason stops at the edge of the sidewalk, leaving space between them, a safety zone. He opens his mouth to speak but the words that were in his head a moment to ago have suddenly evaporated.

After all these years he is still afraid of his father.

William McAllister speaks, still sweeping and not looking up at him.

"I should have put you down that day with the rabbit. Should have put a bullet in your head that day we went to get rid of the coyotes. I knew then what you are."

Jason wants to say something. Hundreds of conversations had run through his mind for this first time seeing his father again after all these years. But now he is mute.

*He hates me. I knew it even then as a child, or maybe especially then. After Amy Dodds, Dad was never the same. He never forgave me for that or for being what I am.*

Jason can't find the words.

William sweeps on. He knows it's pointless sweeping a sidewalk that, by its very nature of being outside in a high traffic area, will always be dirty. It gives him something to do. It's all he has, the last visage of having something useful to do; a useless old man.

He finally pauses in his sweeping, but doesn't look up. His eyes are steady, staring at the concrete he was sweeping; his face void of the scorn Jason knows must be in his heart for him.

Jason wishes his father would look up, would look at him, but at the same time is relieved he doesn't. He doesn't want to have to meet his eyes.

"What did you do this time?" William asks, moving the broom slowly and deliberately again, sweeping much slower now as if lost in thought, or maybe in a torrent of memories from a past that has long ago moved on without him.

"I tried to help him," Jason finally manages. "I went to stop him finally, once and for all. I couldn't," he swallows, ". . . my own son."

William stops.

"He's not your son. He's another man's son. You took him, stole another man's son."

Jason wants to look away, but he is trapped. He can only stare back at the man who will not even look at his own son, feeling awkward.

"Why are you here?" William asks.

"They're coming, the police, to talk to you and Mom."

The old man finally looks up, hatred in his eyes.

"You brought this. You brought attention on yourself, on us, on her."

He spits on the ground as if he needs to get the foul taste of contempt out of his mouth.

"What do you mean you lost him?" McNelly demands. His fist tightens its grip on his phone as he listens.

He purses his lips and puffs out his moustache, making angry faces. If he could reach through the phone right now, he would throttle the person on the other end.

His stomach recoils sourly with a sudden urge to eat something rot-gut that he knows he shouldn't.

He shakes his head at the defeat, listening.

The person watching Jason McAllister at the rooming house has just broken the news to him that McAllister slipped out right from under their nose. No one has any idea where he went, only that he's gone and hasn't come back.

"No, just stay there. I think I know where he's going."

McNelly only has a hunch as to where McAllister is going, or rather to whom.

*My push worked. Jason McAllister is going to see his father. I was counting on him leading me to the old man. Then I would use the old man as leverage to find out where Michael Underwood is. That won't happen now.*

*Now I'll have to find his father without him. And, I'll run him in for breaking curfew and leaving the area.*

Billy the Kid's feet pound the pavement, his breath coming rough and ragged. He wants nothing more than to look back and see if they are still there.

He doesn't dare. Looking back will only slow him down. He skids around a corner and keeps running.

He thinks he got a glimpse of white out of the corner of his eye. He still won't let himself look.

"Come on, run!" he urges himself breathlessly, his heart simultaneously racing and choked in the tight fist of fear squeezing him.

He grabs a railing with both hands and vaults it, the stamina of youth giving him an edge. But that edge is wearing thin, the breath burning in his lungs and a painful stitch cramping his side. He leaps down the wide stairs that cut a path down a hill through a park and towards the next street, taking them in as many steps at a time as he dares.

At the bottom of the steps, he darts down a path to the left. He races into a parking garage there, not bothering with the door in the concrete frame and instead going over the fence made of steel tubing that would keep no one out. The fence is there in place of a concrete wall, allowing the exhaust fumes to dissipate into the air instead of trapping the lethal gas inside.

His slapping sneakers echo loudly in the parking garage and his arms are pumping furiously as he charges through the concrete structure to the other side.

Another steel tube fence blocks cars from driving over the edge where a ramp leads down to a lower level.

Billy drops and skids as he races full tilt at the fence, banging himself painfully on it as he slips beneath, almost losing his footing as he drops to the lower floor on the other side.

He puts his head down and charges on.

Tires squeal somewhere in the parking garage and an engine rumbles, the sounds echoing hollowly.

Billy reaches a door on the other side and pauses, finally letting himself turn and look behind him.

He sees no movement.

He opens the door carefully, cringing in fear it might make a sound.

It opens only inches silently and then lets out a loud metal-wrenching squeal of ungreased hinges.

Billy flinches and freezes. He doesn't dare open the door wider and make more noise, but is sure he can't fit in the narrow opening.

He tries anyway, hinges squeaking at the slightest movement, gripping the door and pulling it tight against him to try to keep it from opening wider. It threatens him with another loud screech, but he manages to keep it to a duller groan.

He carefully closes the door behind him, unable to stop it from banging as the door closer pulls against his efforts to close it silently, the door slipping in his fear sweat drenched hands.

Billy almost cries out.

He hurries down the stairs, trying to not let his feet pound loudly on them, his footsteps echoing up and down the staircase.

He goes through the door at the bottom, hearing the sound of a door opening a few levels above.

The parking garage is on the edge of a hospital complex made of multiple old buildings, each added on decades apart over time. These basement levels are a sprawling maze of tunnels leading between this and other parking garages and the different hospital buildings. Also down here are the maintenance and boiler rooms for the buildings, the hospital laundry, and other seemingly secret underground hospital rooms that he could not guess at their purpose.

Billy races through the tunnels, more lost than not, sure he can hear the sound of pursuit.

He hits a dead end and looks around frantically.

There is a service elevator, a set of double metal doors, and a large abandoned laundry cart on wheels filled with white towels and blue hospital gowns.

He tries pulling at the doors, but they're locked.

He presses frantically at the elevator button. The up arrow, the only button there is, blinks for a fraction of a second then shuts off. The elevator must be shut down. Then he spots the key hole next to the button and realizes that you must need a key to unlock the elevator.

With nowhere else to go, Billy sets his attention on the laundry cart. The idea is not appealing. *What kind of bodily fluids might be on that stuff in there?*

He climbs in, burrowing under the dirty laundry. He clutches at himself, trying to stay perfectly motionless, holding his breath that tries to force its way in ragged exhausted gasps.

He listens to the sounds that never die; the sounds of the bowels of a hospital.

The sound of echoing footsteps grows louder and he holds his breath harder, trying to let his breath out only in shallow breaths through his nose.

The footsteps come, pause, and leave.

Terrified, Billy stays where he is.

*How long should I wait?*

He waits a long time, hours, hiding alone and scared in that cart of dirty laundry that had been forgotten down there.

When he finally decides he can't wait any longer and climbs out, he feels shaky. All Billy wants now is to find someplace safe to hide.

He moves through corridor after corridor, turning down new routes in the endless rat's maze

"I've been down this way already." He jogs down more corridors, each looking familiar.

"I'm going in bloody circles." He's lost in the tunnels and panic washes through him.

"What if I'm trapped down here forever? What if they find me because I can't find the way out? What if I walk right into them?"

He jogs down another corridor and the discovery at last of a door marked "EXIT" with the glowing red letters comes as both a relief and a new wave of fear.

Billy stops and stares up at the sign, then at the door handle. "What if they're up there waiting? I can't stay down here forever."

He sucks in a breath and holds it, then opens the door and starts to make his way up the stairs and out into the night.

When Billy breaches the door above, he sucks in the fresh cool night air. He has no idea what time it is or how long he stayed cowering in the dirty laundry cart.

He keeps to the shadows, hiding wherever he can as he makes his way back to the only place he knows he might not be disturbed, the creeper's room at the rooming house.

He keeps vigilant watch for any sign of the white van.

It's not the first time he has seen it.

Rumours live on the streets like the rats, skulking in dark places where they thrive. The rumours of the white van are only one of them.

Jim heaves his frame breathlessly up the stairs of the precinct building. The streets are unusually quiet at this time of night. It always gives him an eerie sense, like it's so still and quiet because something is about to happen.

He reaches the second floor. The precinct is unusually quiet too. He passes the empty counter that serves as a place to greet visitors and take their complaints, and goes down the aisle between desks in the open room beyond.

He enters the back office. Michael Underwood's desk sits conspicuously empty, a constant reminder of the man who betrayed them all.

"Jim," Beth says from her desk, pulling his attention away from the empty desk. "I think I found what you are looking for." She looks triumphant but tired. She had been holding this announcement in for hours waiting for the chance to tell him.

"Which case?" He hopes it will be good news. "Jason McAllister's neighbour," he starts listing off some of his open cases, "the girl from the South end, or the missing pro?" That's his term for a prostitute. "There is also a runaway pre-teen boy, and now our favourite psychopath killer, Jason McAllister, has gone AWOL."

Beth waves her hand in a dismissive motion.

Jim stiffens, leaning forward.

"You found him?" he is almost afraid to say it.

"No, not him," Beth waves him off again, "not Michael. I think I found William McAllister."

Jim's stomach drops out from under him.

Beth smirks at the expression on his face. "You didn't think I could do it, did you?"

Jim realizes he is standing there dumbly with his mouth open and closes it.

"I could kiss you right now," he blurts out, his face breaking into a huge grin, excited over the news.

Beth makes a face showing her distaste at the idea. She knows he means it rhetorically.

# 28 Finding William McAllister

Beth's digging revealed that William McAllister is living in a single room apartment in a small decaying apartment building squeezed between larger buildings that were built around it when it managed to avoid the wrecking ball that took out the rest of the block for redevelopment years ago. The entire neighborhood is aged before its time and well worn with the abuse of decades of hard use.

Of all the low income housing available in the area, it is among the lowest.

Jim pulls into an open space up the street from the address Beth gave him. The car creaks and rocks on worn shocks and finally settles itself with a decided lean to the driver's side, its engine ticking as it begins to cool.

The door screeches as he opens it, the car tilting lower with his weight as he climbs out, and rocks back on its shocks to settle again, levelling out. The door hinges creak loudly with the effort of closing when he swings it closed.

Jim pauses, looking up and down the street.

He's not familiar with the city or the neighbourhood, but the neighbourhood looks rough. Graffiti tags businesses and apartment buildings alike, garbage litters the ground, and he instantly spots at least three derelict buildings that had been abandoned to the rats, feral cats, and homeless squatters.

A couple of homeless teen boys sitting three buildings up eye him warily. He notes they have their entire lives packed in a pair of large worn canvas army-style duffel bags that they probably got from an army surplus store and a morose looking dog with a heavy rope tied around its neck. Either the dog is used to its life as a hobo and has no interest or care in the world passing it by, or it is as hungry and tired as the boys look.

Jim knows the dog is most likely stolen. No one is going to give a pair of drifter kids living on the street a dog.

*It's not my problem. I'm here for more important things than busting a couple of runaway kids for canine theft.*

He knows the type all too well. They are on the move, travelling from one city to another for reasons only they know, always running from something.

He's not going to bother trying to pick them up either. They'd only run the moment he tried. He would never catch them. As much as it bothers him, he knows you can't save them all.

The boys get up, trying to act casual, grab their bags, and walk on the moment Jim starts walking in their direction.

Jim walks past William McAllister's apartment building, taking in its worn condition before entering it. The narrow space left between it and the neighbouring buildings is not wide enough to slide more than a hand or maybe an arm though. He is sure he can see the ledges of window sills, the adjacent buildings blocking off both light and escape through the windows.

The building is as run down on the inside as it is on the outside. It has the old urine stench of an old building that is not maintained. The mailboxes at the door look like they are broken into regularly; the doors and the entire front that swings open with the mailman's key are bent and twisted where they've been pried open. Some of the hallway lights are burnt out or outright broken.

As usual, Beth's investigation was beyond thorough. She did not stop at finding the address. She went on to dig into who the other tenants of the building are, just in case he needs some extra leverage against any of them to get them to answer questions.

*If she were ever paired up with Lawrence, they would make a deadly team,* Jim thinks. He can only shake his head in wonder at how she manages to find out so many details without apparently ever leaving her computer.

The other residents vary.

There is a drug addict who just came off his outreach program in a halfway house, sent out to fend for himself despite having the ability to do so on par with a child. He is already skirting returning to his former life of drugs and petty crimes to pay for the habit.

On the second floor is a prostitute who just gained temporary freedom from her pimp, who is currently incarcerated. Failing in her attempts to get clean, she is still plying her trade, the only thing she knows how to do. She is little more than a slave trying hopelessly to grasp that false brass ring of freedom that she can never have.

There is a newly separated man, kicked out of his home by his wife when she learned of his affair. To make things worse, now that he has no money to spend taking her out and buying her gifts, his girlfriend dumped him.

There is a single mother with a baby, struggling to survive and unable to work because she has no one to look after her baby and can't earn enough to support them on minimum wage.

Other apartments sit empty.

"Time to get to work," Jim mutters. "The first thing I want to do is learn more about the old man."

The first door he knocks on is the young mother. He can hear the baby wailing inside through the apartment door. It takes her so long to answer that he starts to wonder if the child has been left alone.

He knocks a few more times while waiting and finally hears movement on the other side of the door.

She opens the door just a crack, keeping the flimsy security chain on.

"Yes?" She peers out at him, looking a little frightened. The screaming baby is louder with the door open.

Jim decides to play straight up with her. He flashes his badge, knowing she's too nervous to pick up on it being for another city.

"Police, I would like to ask you a few questions about one of your neighbours."

She blanches.

"No, I can't," she whispers, trying to scan the hallway despite the almost closed door.

He knows her nervousness. She's afraid of what would happen; that he wants information on a neighbour she knows is doing something criminal, and that they will come after her for it.

"It's the old man," he says. "I'm checking on his well-being. His family is concerned."

Her fear slips away, but not completely.

"I didn't think he had any family," she says, closing the door and slipping the security chain off.

For that brief moment, Jim is sure she is closing him out, refusing to talk to him. But then the door opens.

She stands there, just a little bit plump, her clothes looking like she lives on hand-me-downs, the ill-fitting cast offs of others after they had been picked clean of any clothes purchased with any semblance of taste.

"Do you need to get that?" he asks, referring to the still crying baby. The non-stop screaming of the baby is wearing at him.

She glances back towards the baby somewhere in the apartment behind her and turns back to him. He can see the stress, the struggle of being a single mother. She shrugs.

"He won't stop until he falls asleep."

He wants to yell at her to go pick up the damned baby. The cries are turning to hiccupping cries now, the baby finally tiring himself out from crying.

Her eyes cloud for a moment.

"You guys were already here," she says, "you know, to check up on the old guy."

Jim is taken aback by this, but tries to hide it.

She picks up on his surprise.

"I don't think the other guy was a cop though. Was he family?"

"What did he look like?"

"Tall and thin. Kind of looks like a buzzard, you know, those big ugly birds that fly around in the sky looking for dead stuff to eat in the desert."

"Hawkworth," McNelly mutters under his breath.

"What?" she asks, not quite hearing him because he spoke too quietly. The baby's cries are muffled now.

He must have buried his face in his unhappiness, Jim thinks.

"Lawrence Hawkworth," McNelly repeats. *Hawkworth must not have told her he was a reporter. She would have remembered that.*

"He's a social worker," he lies.

The young woman nods understanding, thinking how the old man must need the help, being so old.

"Does he have any regular visitors that you are aware of?" Jim asks.

"No. I don't think he's ever had a visitor. He likes things quiet, doesn't like people coming around."

She ducks her head towards him conspiratorially. "He doesn't even like anyone else having visitors."

"How is that?"

"That other woman who lives here, she's a prostitute you know." She makes a face indicating her disapproval. "She was always bringing strange guys around. They wake my baby up. It takes me forever to get him back to sleep."

The dark circles and bags under her eyes are a clear indication that her sleep has not improved.

The baby's cries finally drop off, much to Jim's relief. He's asleep.

"These guys were always bugging me when they saw me," she continues. "Like they thought I'm like her." She says "her" like it's an insult. "They scared me. I didn't feel safe."

She points, indicating the other apartments.

"They're all kind of scared of the old guy. I'm a little scared of him too, I guess.

He started coming out and threatening these guys coming around here, her Johns I guess. He yelled at her too. She stopped bringing those guys around after that. I'm not sorry, though. I feel a lot safer here now she doesn't have these strange guys coming around."

"So, the old guy has no visitors, no family or anything coming around, checking on him or anything?" Jim presses for confirmation.

"None that I know of."

He nods. "Thanks, that's all I need. You take care now."

He turns and leaves, leaving her standing there wondering what it's all about.

She closes the door and locks it, going to sit down in the silence of her apartment now that the baby has finally stopped crying. She sags onto her couch in exhaustion and starts watching T.V.

Jim moves on to the next tenant on his list, the soon to be divorcee.

The man who answers the door has the haunted look of someone whose life has turned into chaos and they have no idea why.

He stares at JIM, his eyes both blank and angry and his face puckered into a permanent scowl as though the whole world is against him.

"What?" he says it insolently.

Jim flashes his badge.

"Detective McNelly," he introduces himself. "I'm doing a wellness check on the elderly gentleman. He's not answering his door. Does he have any regular visitors; friends, family, social workers? Anywhere you know that he hangs out regularly?"

The man's scowl deepens and his eyes get a wild look as if just talking to him or being in his presence somehow offends him.

"Gentleman?" he cries the word out indignantly, his face triumphant and angry. "That old geezer is crazy! He threatened me, do you know that? I told that other guy too, the tall ugly one that came around asking about him."

Jim only nods, the man is on a rant. He might get some good information letting the guy just go with it. More likely, though, anything he says will be tainted by his anger at the world.

"He tried to tell me how to look after my own kids. My own kids, like he knows better than me. He's always down there sweeping the sidewalk. And he doesn't like anybody.

If you have anybody come around he's watching. If he doesn't think they should be here, he's right in your face about it. The only good thing about it is at least that prostitute and the junky don't bring their low life people around anymore. He scared them all off."

"He's a scary guy, huh?" Jim says.

"That guy is creepy weird. Always watching like he doesn't approve, going on about family and keeping quiet and not bringing attention on yourself."

"He has a thing about that, does he? Not bringing attention on yourself?"

"He's crazy obsessed with it. That's probably why he doesn't have any family. He just hangs out down there sweeping the sidewalk and watching what everyone else is doing."

He looks distraught and lets out an animal sound of angry despair. Jim's automatic reaction the moment the wail starts is to wonder what the hell that was for.

"Auugh, he's just like my wife, telling me what to do, how to look after my own kids, where I can go and who I can see. He's going to get all in my face just for talking to you!

I don't deserve this! She kicked me out for nothing, just to be a bitch, took everything from me, all my furniture, my stuff, my house, my kids. I don't deserve this!"

Jim heard enough. The man is really grating on his nerves. He read Beth's report, and it was more in depth than needed. The man's wife had bagged all his belongings and dumped them outside for him to pick up. The separation and ongoing divorce are bitter and ugly.

*I guess she took offence to the girlfriend,* he thinks.

"That's all I need, thank you for your time." Jim turns and walks away, not giving the man the opportunity to try to keep him there. He can hear his tirade still going on, even though he no longer has an audience, all the way down the hall, even after the man had retreated to his apartment and closed the door.

Jim moves on to the second floor. It's too early to be claiming to be doing a curfew check. It doesn't matter. The prostitute and druggie both don't answer their doors.

His final stop is William McAllister's door. He doesn't answer either, although Jim thinks he hears movement inside. He waits, knocking on the door again, and finally has to give up.

He has the sense of being watched through the peephole as he walks away.

Jim returns to his car. He doesn't start it right away. Instead he pulls out his phone and dials. He waits, listening to the drone in his ear of the call ringing.

"Hello," the voice on the other end starts. Jim doesn't give him a chance to continue.

"Hawkworth, what are you doing snooping around William McAllister?" he demands.

Lawrence picks up immediately that Jim is pissed, both from his tone of voice and his use of his surname.

"Just following up leads," he says.

There is a heavy pause over the line, Jim breathing to control his temper and Lawrence knowing him well enough to give him that time.

"What did you find?" Jim finally asks.

"I might have a lead on William McAllister's wife, Marjory."

"Where do you want to meet?"

Lawrence gives him the name of and directions to a small corner pub.

Jason McAllister doesn't know what to do, so he hops the bus back home. His meeting with his father went as badly as he expected it to.

He warned him the police are coming to question him, maybe his mother too. But that's all he got out of it. That and an unpleasant bitter taste in his mouth from his father's open hatred of him.

*What was I thinking?* He asks himself silently, staring out the bus window at the fields going by. The bus is half empty and he has a seat to himself.

*Did I think we would have some kind of happy reunion after all these years? That he would greet me with open arms? From the man who has never been capable of showing any emotion except anger?*

*Did I think he would have forgiven me for Amy? For being who I am?*

Jason's thoughts turn to his mother, kept locked way in that home. He suddenly has the urge to go see her. He promised his father he won't. He made that promise a long time ago, the last time he had seen him.

*Maybe if nobody sees me? If she doesn't see me? No, I have to wait. At least until after they would have tried to talk to her. Then I'll go see her.*

Jason needs to blow off some steam in a bad way. He thinks about visiting the old farm property and thinks better of it.

*I could justify it, since it is my family farm. But that would not be smart. They'd be watching the farm. I have to find someplace else, someplace secluded.*

*Cities are full of secluded places, sometimes only feet away from a heavily populated building, street, or in the midst of a busy park. Sometimes it depends on the time of day or night. The right place at the right time.*

His bus pulls into the station at last, breaking him from his thoughts. He hadn't even realized they reached the city and he wonders when it happened, although being a small city it didn't take long to go from the surrounding farm fields to the center city bus depot.

Jason has no plan of action in mind when he disembarks off the bus except to return to the rooming house.

He does not make it there.

Billy's stomach lets out the distressed sound of gnawing hunger.

He is huddled on the floor in a corner with the blankets and pillow as shelter, eyes still wide with fear.

*Did they follow me? Are they outside right now watching? Coming up the stairs?*

*I didn't hear the door open downstairs or the creak of that step in the staircase that always creaks loudly under your weight if you don't know to step over it.*

He looks down at his empty stomach and clutches it. He is so hungry that he feels like he is going to vomit, but he's terrified of going back out there in search of food.

Finally, driven from hiding by hunger, Billy climbs out of the corner and dumps the bedding half on the bed.

He goes to the window, conscious of the creeper's warning never to be seen in the window, and pulls back the curtain just a little, looking out. He searches the street as far as he can see in both directions.

There is no sign of the white van or anyone watching the house.

He turns to leave and pauses at the door.

"No, better leave it like I found it." Returning to the bed, he tugs at the sheets, making the bed with an unpractised hand. He never bothered making his bed when he lived with his family.

It isn't the best bed-making job, but he feels better after it's done.

He pulls the curtain back again to look outside, spending a long moment studying the neighbourhood.

Still not feeling safe, he has no choice. "I have to find something to eat."

The hunger pain in his stomach gnaws at him in reply, sending another gurgle rumbling through his stomach.

Billy turns away from the window and leaves the room.

Across the street, a wild-eyed unkempt man watches through a little door flipped open in a room repeatedly wallpapered in newsprint and tinfoil. The room is dark, the only light coming from the night sky and streetlights glowing in that little door that opens to the glass window behind it.

He sees the curtain move in the upstairs window across the street and a face appear in the window. He leaps back, plastering himself against the wall behind him. He stares at the little opening as if he expects something or someone to lunge through it at him.

Trembling, he pushes himself away from the wall and cautiously approaches, making himself look again.

He watches the face in the window.

"No no no," his voice wavers. "You do not do this to me. You are not the man, you are the boy. How? How did you become the boy?"

He gasps, the realization horrifying, covering his mouth with his hands.

"You are a changer!" he sucks the words in as he speaks them as if that somehow will take away the truth of them.

The face vanishes from the window and he turns away, pacing the floor and poking his head hard with one finger.

"Think think think think," he chants.

It doesn't work and he starts hitting his head harder, open palmed, sucking those words back in and trying to blow out whatever is blocking him from thinking.

"If I blow hard enough, maybe I can push out whatever they put in my head to stop my thoughts," he pants

He paces frantically, smacking himself repeatedly.

"Think think think think!"

His eyes widen with a thought and he stops.

He rushes back to the opening to stare at the window in the second floor of the rooming house.

There is no face there.

He watches for what feels like forever and is reaching for the little door to close out the world, giving up, when the curtain moves again.

"There, the boy again, looking out. The man has become the boy. For how long?"

"You are weak like that, aren't you?" he hisses at him. What did you do to the boy? Eat him? Did you suck him up into your being? Consume him? Is he a dried shrivelled empty husk like the spider's victim, sucked dry of his life? Is he there, locked up somewhere?"

He hates the boy. But now that he thinks the man has done something to him, has somehow become him, he likes the boy.

"Poor boy," he says, shaking his head sadly.

He turns away, closing the little door and blocking out the only light in the room.

He starts pacing, holding himself and rocking, pacing harder.

"Nnnngh, nnnngh, nnnngh, nnnngh, nnnngh, NO!"

He groans and plasters himself against the wall, wild-eyed.

"No no no no, do not make me. No."

He looks wildly at the now closed little door.

"You are weak now. A weak little boy, not a man. I can stop you. I can kill you."

He flings himself at the door to what was once a bedroom, flipping locks open one after another after another and yanking the door open.

"If I get you before you become the man again I can kill you so you can't hurt anyone else."

He flies from the room, feet pounding down the hallway and down the stairs.

An elderly woman's voice calls to him from somewhere in the house.

"Nathan, what are you doing? What's all that stomping?"

"Nothing Mom, I'm going out," he calls back.

The elderly woman blinks in confusion in her chair in the darkened living room where she sits. The furniture is worn and outdated. It's impossible to tell if the house has electricity or not.

"Out? But he never goes out. Almost never leaves that room."

She struggles to push herself up from the chair, reaching for her walker and dragging it closer with one hand. Gripping it with both hands, she pulls herself up unsteadily.

He is already gone before she can stop him.

Billy pauses at the top of the stairs, looking down into the darkness below. The lack of windows here lets little light into the stairs and hallways.

He turns back to look at the creeper's door.

"What if something happens to me? Nobody will know."

Billy scurries back to the room, almost dropping the key as he fumbles it, and makes it back inside, locking the door behind him. He leans against the door in desperation.

"Come on man, you got to eat," he groans.

Afraid, he writes a note before leaving the room.

"If I'm not here the white van people got me," the note reads in jagged printing that seeps fear.

Billy leaves the note on the bed with his stuff. He thinks better of it, and pockets the phone. He cautiously unlocks the door and slips out, locking the door behind him.

He goes quietly down the stairs to the kitchen, careful to avoid the creaky step. He rummages through the kitchen, finding nothing to eat.

He inspects the garbage, reaching in and pulling something out. He sniffs it and pulls it away quickly with a disgusted look, tossing it back.

*Nothing.*

He goes to the front door, pauses to stare at it, and thinks better of it. He retreats back through the house to the kitchen and goes out the back door.

Keeping himself pressed against the house, Billy sneaks around to the side. He looks up when he realizes he's in the shadow of a frightening looking man towering over him.

Billy is frozen in terror, unable to move. He manages a dry swallow, staring up at the eyes that stare back down at him.

He finally breaks free of his paralysis and turns to run, but the man is faster. His arm snaps out and he grabs Billy. The grip is unbreakable, fingers digging painfully into Billy's shoulder.

Jim walks into the little corner pub and quickly spots Lawrence in a booth in a back corner. The place looks like it's trying to imitate the old sixties burger joints, or maybe once was one and never fully remodelled after it was turned into a pub.

He catches the bartender's eye and waves him over on the way to the table. There is no waitress in sight and he suspects there probably isn't one on most days.

Jim nods to Lawrence as he settles his bulk into the booth across from him. He barely gets himself in when the bartender is hovering and asking for his drink order. He orders and waits for the drink to come before turning his full attention on the reporter. He leans back, taking a long gulp with relief, and stares at Lawrence.

"So, dig up any bodies I should know about?"

"Funny you should ask," Lawrence says with a wry smirk. His expression grows serious.

"You know those killings way back when William McAllister and his family still lived at the McAllister Farm?"

Jim nods. "Yeah, some young women when Jason McAllister was just a kid. The town people were convinced William McAllister was the killer, ran him out of town with a lynch mob."

Jim's mind is already working the memory over. "There was the kid too, Amy Dodds. She was never found." He had gone back over what files he could find. He was lucky the files even still existed.

"The sheriff, Rick Dalton," the name springs into his mind. "His notes pointed to William McAllister as being good for the missing and murdered young women, but not the girl. Dalton had been unsure of her.

Right up to the end when the McAllister family vanished, William McAllister was his prime suspect. But his notes questioned that too. It was just too convenient, too many sloppy clues. He noted that William McAllister, in his opinion, was too smart to have left those clues. His suspicion that it was someone else, someone less intelligent, grew.

The file contained the note someone left him too, pointing Dalton to the murder scene, an abandoned farm that turned out to be the scene of multiple murders. It led to the arrest and conviction of another man."

"That's it," Lawrence says. "Usually when local people are this convinced a man they are this familiar with is guilty of something, it proves to be true."

"There was irrefutable evidence against the man they convicted."

"Yes, and I believe the locals are completely wrong about William McAllister being involved in the missing and murdered women then. I have no doubt the sheriff got the right man for that. But I just can't let go of the feeling that William McAllister is guilty of something."

"You think he's a killer," Jim says. He doesn't doubt it, but he wants to hear what Lawrence thinks.

Lawrence shakes his head.

"No sir, I do not believe he is a killer. I think his family is involved in something much bigger."

Jim arches an eyebrow in question.

Lawrence looks around the pub, empty except for the bartender some distance away, as if afraid someone might overhear.

He leans over the table to get closer to Jim and whispers.

"I think he was some kind of clean up guy."

Jim almost laughs. He wonders if Lawrence is trying to be funny. His smile slips away as quickly as it came with the dead serious expression on Lawrence's face.

"It makes sense," Lawrence continues. "The McAllister Farm never produced enough of anything to pay for itself, not as far back as records have been kept. He farmed enough to feed his family and a small herd of livestock, living off the farm, and that's it. It's been paid off for generations, no mortgage, so that would help. But I can't find any records anywhere of William McAllister ever selling a single unit of any kind of crop, not a single animal.

The man had no job, no income. He claimed enough on his income taxes to look like a legitimate farmer, paid his taxes on time and in full every year, but it's all false. So, where did his money come from? The man didn't even have a bank account.

Even the old farmers I talked to said no one thought there was any way the McAllister Farm could support itself with what he produced."

"I think you've spent too much time digging in dusty basements," Jim says. But he's thinking it over.

"I think the farm is a cover," Lawrence says. "It all fits, the family's reclusiveness, William McAllister's aversion to having any kind of attention drawn to him or his family."

"The boy was exposed to it," Jim says, seeing where Lawrence is going with this now. "William might have been grooming him even, training Jason to work with him. Or, he just let him hang around while he worked. Something like that sure would mess a kid up."

He looks pointedly at Lawrence, his eyes eager now.

"That's where it started for Jason. That girl, Amy Dodds, was probably his first victim. William had to dispose of the body, clean up his son's mess."

Lawrence is nodding.

"This could be…" Lawrence starts.

"…The link that ties both McAllisters to the mass graveyard in the woods," Jim finishes. "They're still excavating graves and processing bodies. They'll be at it for months yet, and they're still exploring for more remains. Who knows just how far this graveyard goes. Amy Dodds could turn up there yet."

Jim could have hugged the man right now. "What else did you find?" he asks, suspicious this isn't all.

"I don't know," Lawrence says, shaking his head and looking down. He looks up again.

"That means you have something. Out with it man."

"I don't know, it's a long shot, they all are, but I think I might have found two missing kids that vanished around the time people think Jason McAllister suddenly had two kids living at the McAllister farm."

"How sure are you?" Jim leans forward, his expression grave.

"Not sure at all," Lawrence says doubtfully. "Just happens to be around the right time."

Jim has a feeling he's holding something back. There is no point pressing it though. If Lawrence is holding something back, he won't give it up. Not until he's ready.

"You talk to the parents yet?" Jim asks.

"No. The mom went missing at the same time and the dad moved since. I'm still working on tracking him down."

"So what did the files say?"

"The detective listed it as a custodial kidnapping, the kids as being taken by their mother."

"You don't believe that."

Lawrence shakes his head. He has no reason to not believe it. His predecessor, whose files they were, didn't believe it. His notes on the report said as much.

"So, you canvassed William McAllister's neighbours," Jim says, changing the topic. "Learn anything I should know?"

"Not much. The other tenants are all scared of him."

"Yeah, I got that and I only talked to two of them."

Jim shakes his head with a smirk. "He's pretty old by now. I can't see him being all that scary."

"They say he's strange. Creepy. Doesn't like anyone coming around and is always out front sweeping the sidewalk. That must be the cleanest sidewalk in the city."

"Maybe he's lonely," Jim suggests. His own talk to the two tenants suggested the man is a recluse.

"Maybe he's watching," Lawrence says.

"For what?"

"That's what I would like to know; or maybe, for who."

"Maybe he's paranoid and needs to watch everyone coming and going. If he was what you think, he has good reason to be wary."

Lawrence shakes his head. "Wary, yes, I can give you that. Paranoid, no. I think he's too smart for that. I think he's waiting."

"For what?"

"I don't know."

After his meeting with Lawrence, Jim returns to William McAllister's apartment building.

This time as he approaches he spots a frail looking elderly man out front in an old work shirt, suspenders, and hat, standing there slowly and methodically sweeping the sidewalk.

He notices what he missed on his first visit; the stretch of sidewalk in front of the apartment building is a lighter color than the rest, the affect of years of daily sweeping slowly removing the grime that builds up and seeps into the concrete, permanently staining it over the building's lifespan. It is evidence of the old man's obsessive daily sweeping.

Getting out of his car up the block, he walks the rest of the way. He approaches the old man, nodding a greeting to him.

The old man sweeps, not acknowledging him.

Jim stops and watches him sweep for a few minutes.

"You sure keep that sidewalk clean."

The old man just sweeps on.

Jim holds out his hand, the universal symbol of offering a handshake.

"I'm Jim McNelly."

The old man's broom stops. He looks up; his eyes steady and hard as they stare back into Jim's.

"What do you want?" He makes no move to accept Jim's hand.

*Okay, so you want to be that way about it, do you?* Jim thinks to himself.

"Are you always out here sweeping?" he asks.

The old man just stares at him, not answering. There is no discernible reaction at all.

*He's good.*

"I can see you are a smart man. Let's cut to the chase." Taking a chance, he flashes his badge, hoping it's too quick or the old man doesn't care to look closely enough to see it's not local.

"I'm Detective Jim McNelly. You are William McAllister. I'm sure you know your son Jason has gotten himself into trouble."

*There it is; the flash of the eyes. He knows and he probably isn't going to talk. Play it cool. He doesn't like attention brought on him or his family. Play down Jason McAllister's part. Watch him carefully for any signs of reaction, no matter how small.*

"I'm not here for Jason. He's already been tried. I'm looking for someone else, someone your son knows. What do you know about a Michael Underwood?"

"Never heard the name," William mutters, his broom moving again in a slow sweeping motion. His attention is focused down on his broom against the sidewalk.

"Are you sure? Your son knows him well."

*Well enough to kidnap and murder women together.*

"Maybe you know him by another name. He is younger than your son, by about fifteen to twenty years. Someone your son knew who maybe was not the best person for him to hang around with."

"Doesn't ring a bell." The broom goes back and forth slowly against the sidewalk, deliberately, scritch, scritch, scritch.

"Mr. McAllister, William, I don't think you understand the urgency here. I need to find your son's friend. There are two missing women who I believe Michael Underwood kidnapped. If they are still alive, their time is running out for me to find them."

*There, a twitch in his arm, his muscles tensed. Make them real for him, give them names.*

"We have not identified one of them. He hurt her once already and he's taken her again. We called her Jane Doe. We couldn't let Jane go nameless. The other is Katherine Kingslow. Her mother is very worried. You've probably heard of them. They've been on national news. You've seen their pictures."

"Don't watch the news." Scritch, scritch, scritch.

The scratching of the broom on the sidewalk is getting on Jim's nerves. *Time to push it.*

"I was hoping you could save me a lot of work. If you can point me in the right direction, help me find Michael Underwood, you might just save those women's lives."

Nothing.

"If you can't help me out, tell me where I might find Michael Underwood, I'll have to dig deeper into Jason's life, and his past."

William tenses at that, anger flashing in his eyes before he controls himself again. His sweeping motions are more abrupt, harder, showing the anger seething beneath his forced calm.

*He's angry. You are a hard man, William McAllister. You are not going to make this easy. I'm going to have to push you harder if I'm going to get you to talk.*

"I'm going to have to talk to anybody else who might know. Your daughter, Sophie, and your wife, Marjory. I've already talked to neighbours."

William looks up from his sweeping finally, his broom still. For a span of racing heartbeats, Jim is sure the broom is going to snap up and strike him.

"It won't do you any good to talk to Marjory and Sophie hasn't talked to her brother in years. You'd be wasting your time."

"If you tell me what you know about Jason's relationship with Michael Underwood, I won't need to talk to them."

The threat is clear and hanging heavily between them. William meets his eyes, his own steady and hard.

"I never heard of him. I haven't seen my boy in years. You didn't notice that not one of us came to his trial? That boy is no longer part of this family, not since he was old enough to fend for his self."

Jim nods understandingly. "I see; you had some sort of falling out. It happens in a lot of families. It's a lot harder for a mother to turn her back on a child. I'm willing to bet they still communicate."

"It won't do you any good. She won't be able to talk to you."

"It's still worth a try, don't you think?"

William shifts position, his fists tightening on the broom.

*He's stronger than he looks, I bet,* Jim thinks.

"She's sick," William says, "dementia, doesn't know who anyone is. She's lost inside herself, can't talk to anyone anymore. You'll only frighten and confuse her."

William turns and stalks off, holding his broom like a staff, ready to defend himself. He walks back to the apartment door without looking back.

"Do you know about Jason's kids?" Jim tosses at his retreating back, a parting shot.

William doesn't even flinch, vanishing inside the building.

"That will make him think."

Feeling completely unsatisfied with the meeting, Jim returns to his car.

William holds himself in check, showing no reaction to anyone who might be watching, until he has retreated to the privacy of his small apartment.

Closing the door with deliberate control, he checks himself, leaning the broom against the wall with forced control.

"That boy," he says it like a curse, his eyes blazing with anger, "I taught him better than this. Always telling him, don't bring attention on yourself or the family. Stay clean, don't get into trouble. You stupid stupid boy."

His emotions run the range from anger to failure and back to anger again.

"I'm always cleaning up your messes. Should've put you down then, should've put you down."

William pulls an old battered suitcase from the closet and starts packing it.

"I put it off, gave you a chance to fix your own mistakes. It's time I clean up this mess too."

William stands there taking slow deep breaths, getting his rage under control.

"You killed her Jason, you killed her."

Taking the suitcase, he leaves.

# 29 The Boy is Trouble

Jason is walking down the street when he is stopped by an old man. He looks at the old man, thinking how he is easily as old as his father.

"You always were a problem," the old man says, staring at him with pale cold rheumy eyes. His lack of smile shows it's not a joke. His face is completely expressionless.

Jason studies him, the lined age-weathered skin, the age spots and skin discoloration, the thinning wispy hair that still mostly covers his head. The man is frail with age, in his eighties, maybe late seventies, but no younger than that.

"You bring too much attention to yourself," the old man says.

Jason stares into his eyes, eyes that are fading with age, clouded by cataracts, and as steady and bold as any man who fears nothing.

*I know you*, he thinks. Jason just can't place him.

*My father's words, don't bring attention to yourself, how many times have I heard him repeat that?*

It clicks.

"Anderson," Jason says almost proudly at having figured it out. This is the man he met in the diners with his father when they went on jobs together. He was a child then and he had always been terrified of this man; even more than he was of his father.

Then he feels startled. "You are still alive!"

Anderson ignores this.

"You make trouble," Anderson repeats, "for yourself, for him."

Jason knows he's referring to his father.

"For us."

Anderson blinks at him. Jason can't answer. He has no idea what to say.

"Everyone who gets close to you is in danger. But you still keep bringing them in." Anderson pauses, letting Jason think about it. "The boy. Where did you get the boy?"

*Boy?* Jason thinks, confused.

"There is no boy." The words are no sooner out of his mouth than he knows what boy Anderson is talking about; the boy at the rooming house.

"He's nobody; a runaway. The kid was already crashing there before they put me there."

"What are your intentions with the boy?" Anderson's stare is cold, calculating, weighing and judging his response.

Jason bristles at this, unsure what he is accusing him of. *Does he think I'm that kind of monster?*

"None. I was going to send him packing, but he's just a kid on the street. He's a problem and I don't want any problems, not that kind. Every person in that house can get sent back to jail for harbouring him."

Anderson nods. "Good. Your problem is gone."

Jason flinches. "Wait, what do you mean?"

"You aren't as smart as you think you are. The boy is spoken for, claimed property. Someone else already had their eye on the boy."

Jason pales, feeling sickened. He knows what that means. *The white van.*

The image of David the same age as the kid swims before him.

"Do they have to take that boy? There are so many others."

Anderson's hard stony expression doesn't change, although he is sickened too by it. *It's not my place to decide these things. Besides, I'm too old to get involved. Too old to be involved now.*

"The boy is gone by now. Don't bother going after him. You won't find him. The boy is better off. Is he dead? Probably, by now."

Jason feels the world closing in on him. *The boy, who is so much like David was at that age.*

"Why are you here, Anderson? Just to tell me about some street rat?"

"I know you. You are too soft, too sentimental. Something inside you is broken too. I came to warn you. You keep messing up and one of these times it's going to hurt people.

You just brought a big pile of crap on your family and I don't know if I can protect them. We can't control everyone, and a few of those we can't are asking too many questions and digging too deep. They are asking about their Jane Doe and Katherine Kingslow. But that is just an excuse. They are really chasing down the larger beast."

"That's David's doing."

"David nothing. He's your mistake, your responsibility."

There is a heavy pause, the silence hanging between them like a heavy shroud.

"Management knows. They're watching and when it comes down it's going to come down hard. That detective and the reporter are going to talk to your mother. You have to fix this before things go bad. Management will clean it up if you don't."

An icy sweat drenches Jason and he feels like a blast of freezing air is washing through him. He wavers on his feet, dizzy. He blinks, trying to straighten out his suddenly blurred vision. He closes his eyes.

"Anderson . . .." He opens his eyes. Anderson is gone.

Panic floods Jason, sending uncontrollable shivering through him.

"Come on, get it together." He tries to stop shaking, to slow his breathing that's suddenly coming in ragged gasps. "What the hell, I'm too old for panic attacks. Think about something else."

"Oh no, the kid."

Worry pushes everything else out of his mind and he bolts.

The trip home is painfully slow, jogging and running, bus, train, and the bus again. Jason is humming with nervous energy, bringing odd looks his way, anxious to get home fast.

*They took him. He's just a bloody kid. Why him? Why did they have to take him? It's my fault. No. Anderson said someone already had their eye on the kid. Who?*

These thoughts plague him all the way home.

Finally, Jason gets off a city bus a block from the corner of his street. His feet barely touch concrete and he's sprinting for the corner, head down and focused on one thing only, getting home. He reaches the corner and charges down the street, feet pounding the sidewalk.

It's a race against the past, knowing he was already too late when Anderson stopped him.

Jason is out of breath, gasping in great whooping breaths of air by the time he reaches the rooming house.

Staggering up the front steps, he digs out his key to the front door. He kept that key since the boy was already getting in and out of the house somehow.

His first try misses and the key strikes home on the second, turning it and opening the door with trembling hands.

Still gasping for air, he staggers up the stairs, moving down the hall past the ever-present country music coming from the Cowboy's room. Gripping his door knob, he tries to turn it. It is locked.

He grips the knob with both fists, leaning his shoulder into the door, legs pushing out, and pushes against the door. There is a little give, but it holds. He throws his weight against it harder, and again, harder, in a hurry to get in.

"It's not that good of a door," he mutters.

He steps back and gives the door a kick just below the knob.

The door pops open with the dull sound of crunching wood.

The room is empty. No boy.

"Did you really expect him to be here, even without Anderson's warning?"

Emptiness fills him like the day he discovered David ran away, a feeling of hopeless loss and helplessness.

He looks around, immediately spotting the bag on the bed.

"Did he even come in here? Did he touch the stuff at all?"

Jason moves to the bed, picking up the note on the bag.

"If I'm not here the white van people got me." The printing is a jagged scrawl, done in a hurry. It reeks of terror.

Jason's muscles tense into angry knots.

"Does Anderson have anything to do with this? My father?" he snarls. He is enraged. He paces the room, thinking.

"I have to find out who took him. Did they hurt him? They'd better not have."

He checks himself with visible effort, taking deep breaths, getting control. He calms down.

"It's not my problem. Not my kid."

The words are a lie meant to be obeyed. Even as he utters them he knows it will keep nagging at him.

# 30 Donald Downey

Lawrence is chewing over the missing person file of the woman and two kids who vanished years ago, quite literally. His jaw works as he thinks. He can't let it go. He feels driven. There is something about this particular file.

He is sitting in his car outside a house. It is an average looking house in an aging average middle-income neighbourhood, older and well-kept.

The investigating officer was a bust. He died years ago. There were some news articles, but no leads. The articles ran the gamut from pointing accusatory fingers at the wife's husband, blowing up in a thither over rumours of an affair, to accusing the wife. All other avenues of investigation came to dead ends. There is only one left.

"Ah, there he is."

A car pulls into the driveway of the house, the driver looking at him curiously as he turns past him. Lawrence gets out, his long legs bringing him to the car as the man is getting out.

He's an older man, approaching retirement age.

*Older than Jason McAllister,* he thinks. *The age is right.*

The man watches him approach curiously.

Lawrence has his hand out as he reaches him, offering a handshake.

"Are you Mr. Donald Downey?"

A flash of instinctive alarm crosses Donald's eyes and he stiffens, wondering how this odd looking man knows him. He hesitates to answer, taking the handshake awkwardly.

"Forgive me, I'm Lawrence Hawkworth." Lawrence sizes the man up, gauging his reaction.

*I will get nothing if he knows he's talking to a reporter,* he thinks. *From the articles I read, the news raked Mr. Downey over the coals pretty good when his wife and children went missing.*

Lawrence tries to give him his best disarming smile, but it comes off predatory. He does not do disarming well.

"Mr. Donald Downey, I'm investigating a cold case involving the disappearance of a Mrs. Madelaine Downey and her two children. Are you the same Mr. Donald Downey who was married to her?"

Donald stands there staring at him in stunned shock. It takes long moments for those words to sink in.

Lawrence gives him time.

Donald visibly sags with it when it finally does. He looks shaken.

"That was a long time ago," he manages.

"Yes sir, it was. The case was never closed." Lawrence lets that hang between them, letting him take from it what he will.

Donald tenses, going on the defensive.

"I had nothing to do with it. They tried pretty hard to prove I did and couldn't then. Madelaine took the kids and disappeared. Now maybe I deserved that, she was angry, hurt. I did not kill my wife and kids."

Lawrence looks up and down the street, making the gesture obvious.

"Maybe we shouldn't talk out here. Can I come inside? We can sit down. I think we have a lot to talk about."

Donald glances around quickly, spotting a neighbour watching them curiously from his yard.

"I have nothing to say. I think you should leave."

*He's still got a lot of anger. I don't blame him. The press found him guilty without proof and the notes on the interviews with the police looks like they didn't take him seriously at first. I'm going to have to break him. He deserves to know the truth.*

"You want to hear what I have to say," Lawrence insists, "and I don't think you are going to want the neighbours to watch."

Donald shifts his stance, ready to be more forceful to get rid of this guy.

*Who the hell does he think he is, digging up the past? That's gone and buried years ago,* Donald thinks angrily.

Lawrence sighs, acting defeated. He's grinning on the inside.

"Your wife didn't take your kids. I know who did."

Donald almost falls over.

# 31 Ryan's Trip

Ryan is packing a bag for another trip. Elaine watches him unhappily. By now she knows not to beg him to stay or let her go with him. She is quietly resigned to yet another lonely absence with nowhere to go and nothing to do.

"Have you thought about getting a T.V. so I can at least have that?" she asks.

Ryan doesn't look up from packing. *How do I tell her? It's not safe to have a T.V. She's not going to buy that. We would have to get a satellite or cable connection, and that means having a record of us. It's to keep us, her, safe.*

"I'll see what I can figure out," he says, putting off dealing with it for now.

She is crestfallen. She knows that means no. Another absence alone with nothing but the walls, a bird in a cage and nothing at all to keep her from going crazy.

"Hey, cheer up," Ryan says, looking at her with concern. "I won't be gone long."

Elaine just nods. She has nothing to say. Don't go. Let me come. At least let me get a job or get involved with something local, something. None of it will do any good. They've had that discussion too many times already.

She follows him to the door, accepting his kiss and barely reciprocating, and watches him leave in silence. She watches his truck drive away through the front window and the moment it is out of sight feels deflated. She blinks away tears.

"There has to be something I can do. I don't think I can take this much longer. All I do is sit here waiting for him to come home."

It's too early to do anything, so she starts dusting, although the place doesn't need dusting. She stops before she finishes, sitting on the couch and fighting back tears. By afternoon she is restless and feeling trapped. She has been feeling this more and more, even when Ryan is not gone on one of his trips.

Feeling braver and daring, she decides to go for a walk around town.

"Ryan won't like it, but what he doesn't know won't hurt him."

She spends the next few hours walking and just checking out the town. It is the first time she has been able to do this. She hasn't gone anywhere except the laundromat and grocery store. She walks aimlessly up and down different streets, absorbing everything.

Elaine feels invigorated by her daring adventure by the time she returns home.

She is barely home when there is a knock at the door.

She flushes with guilt, opening the door. "Ryan?"

Trevor is on the other side smiling down at her. "You look different, kind of glowing," he says.

Elaine blushes, deepening her flush, and he smiles larger.

"Ryan wasn't at work today. I guessed he's gone on another of his trips?"

"Yes, he left this morning."

Trevor shakes his head regretfully, but his grin is anything but. "If I had a lady like you waiting for me at home, I wouldn't be taking off all the time."

The compliment makes her feel awkward, but at the same time it feels good.

"Do you want to come in?"

"You aren't expecting him back right away?"

"Not for a few days."

Trevor grins and bows himself in.

"Have you eaten?" he asks.

"No."

He smiles disarmingly. "How about we go out to eat?"

Elaine frowns doubtfully. As much as she wants to, it would be wrong.

"I can't. Ryan wouldn't like it."

Trevor's grin turns mischievous. "We will be discrete. He will never know. We can get something to take out, or go to the next town."

"No" is on Elaine's lips. It's the right answer. But her desperate loneliness makes her reckless.

She nods hesitantly.

"Let's go," Trevor ushers her out before she has a chance to change her mind.

They sit in one-sided awkward silence in his truck as he drives to the next town. He's grinning hugely, while she is wracked with guilt.

Trevor glances over at her and sees her unhappy frown. "Hey, it's okay, it's not a date or anything. Just friends. Totally casual."

"I guess. It just feels different this time. Before, we just sat in the house. This time we're going out somewhere."

Ryan has finished the transfer of the package and he and Mr. Miller have gone separate ways. This time he has to meet his Anderson before he can dispose of the package.

He pulls into the truck stop, parking by the garbage bins behind the building. The barrels in the truck box are airtight, so he isn't worried about the smell. But the package was ripe and if anyone does detect an odour, they'll assume it's coming from the large garbage bins next to the truck.

Ryan sits there for a moment, just watching the parking lot.

He jumps when the back door of the building suddenly bangs open.

A man comes out dragging a wheeled cart with garbage bags piled on it. He blocks the door open with a cinder block before wheeling the cart across the concrete to the garbage bins.

Ryan sits motionless. Any movement will draw the man's attention to him. He can see only a straight hallway inside the door.

The man roughly manhandles the bags, tossing them into the bin furthest from Ryan, and wheels the cart back. Shoving the cart through the door ahead of him, he pushes the block away with his foot and lets the door close behind him.

Ryan waits another ten minutes before he moves.

Getting out of the truck, he walks around to the front, scoping the lot out as he goes.

Entering the restaurant by the front, Ryan takes a moment looking around before he spots Anderson.

He meets the waitress halfway to the table, ordering a coffee and apple pie and sending her on her way.

Anderson nods a greeting as he slides into the seat across from him.

"No problems?" Anderson asks.

"None. Everything went smoothly."

"I didn't think there should be any problems on this one. The customer is a long time customer."

Ryan is surprised. "You didn't set him up with his usual guy?"

"Unfortunately, we had a double booking."

The waitress comes with the pie and coffee pot, filling Ryan's cup and topping up Anderson's.

"Anything else I can get you gentlemen?"

"No thanks, we're good for now," Anderson smiles at her. They wait for her to be out of earshot.

"How are things at home Ryan? Are you and Elaine settling in nicely? No problems on the home front that I should be aware of?"

Ryan bristles at the use of their names. They are not supposed to use names. He tries to control it, keep his expression calm, no reaction.

*Why is he asking if there are problems at home? What does he know? No. He's testing me, trying to push my buttons, see how I react.*

"Everything is great."

"If there are any problems, I trust you will let me know."

"Absolutely."

"Good. I'll be in touch when there is another job for you."

It is a dismissal. Ryan puts money on the table for his coffee and leaves.

He gets in his truck and puts it in gear, pulling out of the parking lot onto the highway.

"The bastard still doesn't trust me. Well, I'm not giving him anything to prove him right. I still have the package to dispose of, and then home."

*Trevor is just being a friend. He has no ulterior motives,* Elaine tells herself again. So, why do I feel guilty? I'm not cheating on Ryan.

She is pulled out of her thoughts with an electric jolt when Trevor touches her hand.

They are sitting beneath a tree on the bank of a creek, watching the sunset where no one is likely to see them. Not that anyone would know Elaine. She has no friends and they haven't so much as talked to a single neighbour.

"You are deep in thought," Trevor says.

She looks up at him and her heart quickens.

*When did he get so close?*

The thought startles her a little. She can feel his presence like a physical force. She is so alone in the world that she can't deny the feeling rushing through her; the craving to be touched, for a physical connection pulling her back into the world that she has felt so detached from for the past months.

It brings with it unwanted physical attraction.

*He's a nice enough man, funny and kind, and nice to look at. But, he isn't Ryan. Ryan, who is at work for long hours, then away on these trips for days doing jobs, leaving me alone.*

The loneliness wells up in her, empty and painful.

*When Ryan is away, Trevor is here, and he's really here. He's not distracted or always talking to someone who isn't there. He's never shown anger. Ryan is so quick to get angry. Like Ronnie. No, don't compare the two, they're nothing alike. Ryan would never hurt me.*

Trevor brings his hand up and gently caresses her cheek, watching her for the telltale signs of her reaction. Her pupils dilate and her breath comes faster. It's the reaction he's looking for. He leans in to kiss her softly and she hesitates before pushing him away.

There is no denying her true reaction, despite her quaking heart and guilt.

She looks down and he pulls her chin back up.

"Don't say you didn't like it."

"I can't." She meets his eyes, hers full of the pain of loneliness, guilt, and need.

"He doesn't look after you like I could. He leaves you alone too much. He won't even let you go out and do anything, socialize. You haven't even left the house except to do his laundry and buy food for his meals, have you? You aren't meant to be kept a prisoner in his house."

The truth of his words slices through her and she tries to make excuses in her own mind for Michael.

He leans in again and kisses her gently, slowly. Again, she hesitates before pushing him away. She has to force herself to be indignant.

"I said no. I can't." She gets up. "Take me home."

Trevor looks up at her, hoping she will change her mind, and reluctantly gets up when she just stands there stubbornly waiting.

"Okay, I will take you home."

They drive back in silence, him giving her time and her trying to compose herself.

When they pull up in front of the house, Elaine starts climbing out and Trevor follows.

"You don't need to walk me to the door."

"What kind of gentleman would I be if I didn't?"

*I don't want you to walk me to the door,* she thinks. She's afraid he will try to kiss her again.

As she opens the door and turns to say goodbye, he leans in again, his kiss more passionate this time. Her body responds too eagerly, even as her mind recoils and pulls away, the two at odds with each other.

"Let me come in."

"No, you need to go."

He tries to gently push his way in, careful to not be forceful, trying to put his arms around her and kiss her again.

She has to turn and slide away to escape his embrace. Panic flutters through her. Not that he might hurt her, but that she might give in and do something she doesn't want to, something that she will regret.

*Ryan, Michael, where are you? I wish you were here right now, that you would walk up, rescue me from this, from myself. Make him go away and understand that this can't be because I am yours.*

Her thoughts, the need for him to come right now, feel like a physical force flowing out through her with such intensity that Elaine wonders if he can feel them.

She pushes Trevor away more forcefully, standing firmer this time. Her voice wavers and she despises herself for it, trying to sound firm.

"You have to go."

He steps back, giving her a reluctant look, and bows out. "You can't blame me," he says as he retreats to his truck.

She closes the door, leaving it open just a crack, watching him get in and drive away before she closes out that last chance for him to come back with the soft click of the latch.

Down the street, Ryan sits in a darkened car that is not his, watching. His jaw clenches and works angrily.

"I told you," little Cassie says, sitting in the front passenger seat next to him. "He is a bad man. He's tricking her, you know. He's going to hurt her, just like you did and there is nothing you can do to stop it."

"I won't let him. I'll kill him first."

"And what are you going to do to stop yourself from hurting her again?" Jane Doe is talking to him now, sitting where Cassie was a moment ago. "You are angry. I know you want to go smash that door in. I can see it. If you go in there now, the ugly blackness will take over, you will lose yourself to it again, and you will hurt her. You will kill her."

"No, I would never hurt her."

"You did once, you will do it again."

"Never again."

"Why do you torture yourself like this? Why do you lie to her and sit here watching, waiting for him to steal her away from you? You are looking for a reason to hurt her."

"He won't steal her. She would never leave me, definitely not for that guy."

"Why? She doesn't know what he is, that he is just like you."

"I'm not like him," Ryan growls angrily. "Why would you even say that?"

"You are the same. You both let your anger at the world control you. You both use it as an excuse to hurt people."

"It was a cow. He was torturing a cow, not a person."

"Animal, person, if he can do it to one, he can do it to another. Maybe he already has. It's too bad you don't trust Anderson enough to ask him to check him out."

"I don't need Anderson. I'll fix this myself. He's not going to hurt her. He's just messing around to get even with me. It's a big leap to go from an animal you are paid to kill to killing a person."

"She likes him," Cassie says.

Ryan turns, surprised. "Where did she go?"

"Jane left. She thinks you are being dumb. When are you going to let her know you are back?"

"Later. Maybe tomorrow. I want to watch him. Why do you think she likes him?"

"She let him kiss her."

He clenches the steering wheel harder, his knuckles turning white.

"Are you going to tell her you know?" Cassie asks.

"No. I need to see how this plays out. I need to know what he plans to do. I know he's up to something. What if he knows something? What if she told him about our past? She could have let something slip. I need to find out."

"Then what? Will you kill her? I like her. I don't want you to hurt her."

"No, I won't hurt her."

"What if she leaves you? What if she picks him? You should look after her better. What if she just leaves?"

"Where would she go?"

"She could go home."

"No, she can't. They will be waiting. They'll be watching."

"She's not the one who's running from the law, you are. She can go home any time she wants to."

Ryan leans his head against the steering wheel, trying to control the anger surging through him. He is in a car, temporarily 'borrowed'.

"I don't want to talk about it anymore. Leave me alone."

Ryan sits there as the sky grows darker. He didn't plan to come home until tomorrow. Tonight he planned to watch them both; see what if anything is going on. Now he knows.

"I could put off going home for a few more days to watch him."

The image of Trevor and Elaine is burning in his mind. Anger surges in him and blackness presses against the edges of his vision.

"Ah, I can't take it. I have to go in. I have to see her, talk to her."

The anger is building. He feels betrayed.

"No, she didn't do anything. She sent him away. But she was out with him. Who knows what they are doing while I'm gone."

With a snarl, he starts the car and tears off down the street.

Elaine is leaning against the door. She feels exhausted and overwhelmed; wallowing in guilt and confusion.

*I look forward to seeing Trevor because I'm so lonely, but I can't deny the attraction I felt. I wanted him to kiss me, even though I know it's wrong. I'm losing Michael. He's becoming more distant all the time. What happens when he's decided he's tired of me?*

The image of the McAllister farm comes to her, the women upstairs screaming and crying while she's locked in the cellar, helpless and terrified. Being brought up and made to clean up the blood after he killed them for not being her, his sister Cassie.

Her knees go weak and the only thing stopping her from falling is that she's leaning against the door. Her stomach swims with nausea and an icy sweat pours from her, sapping every ounce of strength with it. She has gone pale as death.

*He kills them. Every one of them.*

The angry roar of an engine and screech of tires outside startles her, making her jump with a yelp.

"Ronnie," she gasps, fear thrilling through her with the image of Ronnie barrelling in through the door, drunk and angry with that look in his eyes that always meant he's going to beat her. She looks around quickly for escape, her heart pounding in her chest.

"No, stop it, he's gone! Ronnie is gone forever! Michael made sure he could never hurt you again. No, Ryan, you have to remember to always call him that, always think of him as that or you'll mess up."

The color is coming back to her face. She looks at the door, shivering with shock, the color draining away again.

"Ryan. What if it was him? What if he saw?" She looks out the front window, seeing no sign of life. "No, it didn't sound like his truck. It was just a neighbour."

Exhausted from the emotions and too wound up from the stress, Elaine gets ready for bed and crawls in. She can only lay there sleeplessly staring at the dark ceiling.

Trevor is driving home feeling very satisfied.

"This is working out so beautifully. She's fighting it, but Elaine is falling for me more every time I see her. Ryan is only helping dig her grave, always going off and leaving her alone.

This is going to be so sweet. The first time I take her, I'll have her mind, body, and heart. I'll make sure he knows.

The next time, Elaine will learn fear and pain. And when I'm finished with her, I will dump what little is left of her at his door for him to try to piece back together. He will know it was me, but they won't be able to prove it. Then I will take her again and they'll never find the body. But he will know what happened, oh he will know."

The thought of it brings on a powerful urge, driving him.

"I can't wait for Elaine. I need to have some fun now."

He turns at the next street, heading out of town. He knows where there are easy pickings. He's been watching the house.

Billy's eyes strain to see through the blackness. It's exhausting and makes them hurt. It's dumb too, he knows. But his eyes keep straining to see, even though he has them closed tight.

The blindfold over his eyes is tied too tightly and, with a sack over his head, there is nothing but blackness when he does try opening them. The course fabric is scratchy on his eyeballs and he has to close them again.

He tries struggling and squirming again. His arms are twisted behind him and tightly bound. His legs are tightly bound too and pulled up behind him painfully. His bound hands are tied to his bound feet.

*If I can get my hands down over my feet, maybe I can manage to pick one of these ropes loose.*

He tries, and it feels like his shoulders are going to explode out of their sockets. The ropes feel like they are cutting through his skin. He whimpers through the gag with the pain.

He tries moving his fingers and feels the strain against his muscles. His arms are twisted in a way that makes it hard and painful even to move his fingers. He manages to finger one spot of rope with one finger. He feels the thin hardness of plastic. Hope fades.

*Zip ties. I can't untie zip ties.*

Billy lies still, waiting for the pain to go. It never goes; it just is either more or less. Every time he tries to move, his muscles feel like they are being torn from his limbs with a white flare of agony. When he lies still, it's an ever-tightening sharp pain of muscles and joints pulled and held in unnatural positions.

*Am I still in a car or something? I don't know. If I am, it hasn't moved for a long time.*

The terror of the past hours had his mind in a fuzzy panic, leaving him confused and unable to remember most of it. Except the fear. He can't forget that.

# 32 Meeting Marjory

"I don't like the look of this place," Jim complains.

Jim and Lawrence are sitting in Jim's ancient Oldsmobile, staring at the building.

Bayburry Street Geriatric Home. It looks like it was constructed with a half-hearted attempt to make it comforting and welcoming, more bed and breakfast-styled resort than hospital, and utterly failed. Worse is the attempt at Southern plantation charm.

The result is a subtly threatening monstrosity. A building trying to trick you with forced false charm.

"That place is as out of place as your car," Lawrence smirks.

Jim scowls at him.

"How is this thing even still on the road?" Lawrence digs in deeper. "They haven't even made these cars in decades."

"It's a classic. Don't make me regret letting you come."

Lawrence laughs. "This heap is no classic."

"I could see you in a place like this." Lawrence grins mischievously.

"Over my dead body. The place looks like a funeral home, not a care home for the elderly."

"Shall we go in?"

"Fine," Jim grunts.

The inside looks even more like a funeral home. Forced elegance and perfumed flowers give the place an untouchable air. It's as silent as a tomb and lifeless. The wear and tear of the decades is even more obvious on the inside.

"This place is as worn out as its residents," Jim whispers.

Lawrence stifles a laugh, feeling like any sound is vulgar. He suspects everyone must whisper quietly here.

"Can I help you gentlemen? I am Miss Krueger, the Director of Bayburry Street Geriatric Home."

The authoritative voice booming in comparison to the absolute silence a moment before startles them both. They turn like a pair of boys caught red-handed and unsure what they are guilty of.

The woman is past middle-aged, her hair looking a bit haggard in a bun that may have looked severe when it was fresh. The tired lines around her eyes make her look annoyed rather than softening the severity of her expression.

She is a bit frightening.

Jim manages to pull himself out of his shock, flashing his badge quickly and putting it away so she doesn't have a chance to look at it too closely. He is out of his jurisdiction. Puffing up his chest, he uses his best authoritative voice.

"Detective Jim McNelly, this is my partner. We are here to interview Mrs. Marjory McAllister as part of an investigation."

"I am afraid that is quite impossible," Miss Krueger says.

"We have a court order." Lawrence pulls out a folded paper, unfolding it and flashing it before her to reveal an official-looking document. He folds it up and puts it away without giving her the chance to inspect it.

She doesn't back down, shaking her head sternly.

"You are wasting your time gentlemen. You cannot question Mrs. McAllister. Are you aware that this is an end of life assisted living facility? Our residents require around the clock care and we do our best to keep them comfortable in their final days on this earth."

"Has she," Lawrence looks around, his birdlike mannerisms and large nose more resembling a confused vulture than the intended innocence, "passed on?"

"She is quite alive."

"Then we need to interview her," Jim insists.

"Fine, but you are wasting your time. I'm afraid Mrs. McAllister resides in our secure wing for those residents with mental infirmities. Physically, she is healthy for her age. But her mind and memory are completely gone.

She leads them through a set of grand double doors that hide the hallway and doors beyond.

Past the double doors all façade of grandeur is gone and replaced with architectural décor that screams mental hospital. The doors are reinforced steel and glass.

She pulls out a ring of keys. They jangle loudly in the silence. Jim thinks of a jail.

"Is that soundproofed?" Lawrence asks. "I expected to see residents walking around and at least hear them in a place this size."

"It is soundproofed. We don't want to disturb the residents in the other ward."

She unlocks the door, opening it and waving them through ahead of her. She makes sure it is securely latched behind them.

"It is not visiting hours. We normally keep this door locked outside of visiting hours."

Jim and Lawrence look ahead of them. There, a harried looking woman wearing a nurse's uniform looks at them with stunned surprise from behind a desk that looks like it belongs in a hospital ward. Next to the desk is another set of double reinforced steel and glass doors. They can hear the hint of sounds echoing from the other side of those doors.

"Karen, these gentlemen are detectives here to see Mrs. Marjory McAllister," Miss Krueger says, her voice as commanding as before. "Is she having one of her good days today?"

Jim suspects she's not capable of sounding soft.

"It's not her best day, but not her worst." Karen hurries to pull out a book and lay it out on the desk.

"I need you to sign in." She looks at them apologetically.

Jim and Lawrence exchange looks. They don't want to leave a record they were here. Jim shrugs and steps forward to sign. His writing is illegible. Lawrence follows suit.

Satisfied, the Director nods to Karen to allow them in.

She hurriedly grabs keys from behind the desk and unlocks the doors, opening them to unleash a cacophony of noises.

Somewhere within the lockdown wing a woman is wailing loudly in distress.

"This way gentlemen," Miss Krueger commands, leading the way. "For the most part, the residents in this wing are unaware, lost in their own fading minds. They have their good days and their bad. They can get confused easily, and that makes them frustrated and distressed. You are in luck. Today is not one of her worst days. She might even know who she is today. I do not want you to distress

Mrs. McAllister. It can take a resident hours to come down from that."

Their walk through the lock-down ward is an eye opening experience. Residents wander the halls, some seeming hopelessly lost. It's a noisy and busy ward.

On the way to Marjory McAllister's room, Lawrence looks into the open doorway of one of the rooms they are passing.

An elderly and very frail looking woman sits restrained to a wheelchair. She stares at him with fierce intelligence, not the blissful unawareness the Director implied all the residents have.

"Help me," she mouths to him. "Get me out of here. They are trying to kill me."

Feeling disturbed, he quickly moves on, catching up to Jim and the facility manager.

"There are no men here," Lawrence observes.

"We keep them in a separate wing for our residents' safety. Here we are," Miss Krueger says, stopping in front of a room. "Do not say anything to upset her."

She walks briskly into the room, putting a smile on that does not lessen the severity of her face.

"Mrs. McAllister, we have some visitors today."

The elderly woman sitting in an uncomfortable looking hospital chair in the small room looks up at them.

"Did we not get dressed this morning?" Miss Krueger asks.

Marjory looks down at her nightgown, then up at the two men and the Director. "No, I think I'm the only one who did not get dressed."

"Aren't we just the card today," Miss Krueger says.

Marjory frowns at her in response.

"These gentlemen would like to visit with you. Gentlemen, please introduce yourselves. There is no need for formalities here."

"Jim McNelly," Jim says, catching her meaning. He steps forward to shake her hand.

"Lawrence Hawkworth," Lawrence follows suit.

Miss Krueger nods at them to go ahead.

"Mrs. McAllister, how are you doing today?" Jim asks.

"I'm fine." She is sizing him up.

"I'd like to ask you a few questions about your son, Jason."

Marjory's hands come up in a nervous motion, and she lowers them again, resting them on her lap.

"What has the boy done this time?" she asks.

"Actually, we're more interested in his friend, Michael. Do you know Michael?"

Marjory frowns at them. "Michael? No, I don't know any Michael. Jason doesn't really have any friends. Whatever Jason and this Michael have done, we will deal with it when William comes home." Her hands flinch, touching each other. She flattens them on her lap.

"Michael Underwood, the name isn't familiar?"

"No, I'm afraid not. You did not say what this is about. Did something happen at school? I don't recognize you. Are you new teachers at the school?"

"We're police, Mrs. McAllister."

Her hands come up, holding each other in a nervous gesture. She looks alarmed. She starts wringing her hands.

"Where is Rick Dalton? Where is the sheriff? Why isn't he here? What has Jason done?" She is glancing around nervously.

"Do you know Katherine Kingslow?" Jim asks. "Have you heard the name?"

"No, I don't know the family. Is she a new girl in Jason's class?"

"Something like that," Jim says. "Mrs. McAllister, we are looking for Katherine Kingslow. She is missing and we believe she may be with Michael Underwood. Are you sure Jason never mentioned either of them?"

"No, he never did. Jason can't be involved in whatever they have done; he's been home with me. He's missed school again because there is so much work to be done on the farm and his father is away a lot. So, whatever these other kids have been up to, it's nothing to do with Jason. You need to go now. William will be home soon and he doesn't like visitors."

Marjory is wringing her hands anxiously in her lap now.

"Mrs. McAllister, we know that your son knows Michael and Katherine. We believe he knows where Michael took her."

"No, no, no." Marjory is wringing her hands harder, twisting them like she's trying to strangle them. "Jason is not involved." She looks around in confusion.

"Jason? Jason. Where is he? He's here somewhere, doing his chores."

She looks at them, her eyes muddled in a haze of confusion.

"Who are you? Where is William? William?" She looks around for him. She is talking to herself now, oblivious to the people in the room. "William does not like visitors. He does not like attention brought to the family. William is going to be angry. He is going to whip that boy like he has never whipped him before.

I burned it, I burned it, it's gone. No one will ever find his little treasure."

She looks up at them, suddenly realizing they are there.

"Hello?" She looks a little alarmed to see them there. "Why are you here?" She looks around quickly. "William will be home soon.

She frowns. "Where's Sophie? Sophie? I told that girl not to go into the woods."

She looks at Miss Krueger. "I don't know you. Whose mother are you?"

Jim and Lawrence exchange a look. Clearly the woman is too far gone to be of any help.

"I think we've heard enough," Jim says.

"Where am I?" Marjory asks. "How did I get here?"

"Mrs. McAllister, we've been over this many times," Miss Krueger says. "You are in a hospital."

"Hospital?" Some of the confusion melts away and sadness creeps in. "William never visits me."

Miss Krueger gives Jim and Lawrence a look that says she has heard this many times from all their residents. The old complain that family does not visit enough.

"You don't get visitors?" Lawrence asks.

Marjory is still looking around in confusion, not recognizing the place.

"Sophie?" she says, "Does Sophie come to see me?"

"Yes, Sophie visits you. Not very often," Miss Krueger says.

Marjory nods. "Jason visited me a few times. I remember. Until his father told him not to come back."

A cloud crosses her eyes. "I miss Jason, and Sophie. David came to see me once too."

"David?" Jim pounces on it. "Who is David?"

Marjory looks alarmed again. She is wringing her hands so hard that Jim is afraid she'll hurt herself.

Marjory looks up at him and he can see the lucidity in her eyes, the fog of confusion clearing away.

"William does not visit me." She looks around at each of them, repeating it louder. "William does not visit me. Why doesn't he come?" Her expression and voice are growing agitated.

"Where are my kids? Where are Jason and Sophie?"

She's struggling out of her chair, to stand, clearly not accustomed to doing it often.

"Mrs. McAllister, please sit back down or I'll have to call the nurses," Miss Krueger warns.

A look of fear flashes across Marjory's eyes, but then her expression sets with determination.

"You can't keep me here. You can't keep my kids away. You can't keep William away."

"Mrs. McAllister, sit down and calm down," Miss Krueger says sternly.

"I want out, I want to go home!"

Miss Krueger steps to the door, calling out to the hallway, "Nurse!"

They hear footsteps running and a look of fear flashes across Marjory's eyes again.

Two large nurses push their way in, grabbing Marjory and manhandling her down onto the bed. Marjory tries to fight them off, crying and wailing at the sudden attack.

Jim cringes at the way they roughly handle this frail looking old woman, watching as they hold her down while one stabs her arm with a needle, pressing the plunger home. He looks at Lawrence.

Lawrence is leaning forward, watching the nurses with alarm.

"Do you have to handle her so roughly?"

"The residents must be kept from getting too agitated," Miss Krueger says. "She will get the whole ward going."

Marjory's struggles are already growing weaker and her cries softer.

Miss Krueger is ushering Jim and Lawrence out.

"Her husband never visits her?" Jim asks as she walks them briskly down the hall.

"He visits her every day, she just doesn't remember. Most of the time she doesn't even know who he is."

"And her kids? They visit her?"

"Her daughter does, not often. I think her son did once or twice. He hasn't been here in years."

"What about this David she mentioned? Any idea who he is? Would you have a record?"

"We would if he has ever visited. But she has never had any visitors except her immediate family. We don't normally allow visitors outside of the immediate family.

Lawrence turns to look as they pass the room with the old woman strapped down to a wheelchair.

She stares into his eyes as they pass, her eyes still filled with a fierce lucid clarity.

The Director escorts them back through the secure door, past the reception there, and into the outer reception area.

The false funereal opulence makes the wretched inner sanatorium even more shocking once the silence settles around them once again.

"I hope you gentlemen aren't too disappointed," Miss Krueger says with a superior air. "I did warn you that you would be wasting your time."

"No, it was good. It crosses one witness off our list. Thank you for your cooperation." Jim nods his way out and makes a hasty exit, Lawrence on his heels and grateful to escape.

"Remind me never to get old or senile," Lawrence says as they walk quickly back to the car.

Jim turns to Lawrence once they are seated back in his car.

"Any ideas who this David could be?"

"None."

"Marjory is pretty far gone. She won't be any help."

"I have a feeling she isn't as far gone as she seems."

"You think?" Jim fires up the engine and starts pulling away.

"Any suspicions?"

"We know Michael Underwood is an alias." Lawrence nods to himself, thinking, running scenes through his mind, trying to imagine who David could be. He is tense and stressed, off. He was barely able to concentrate in the care facility, images bombarding him and trying to play out in his mind. He tries to sift through those ghosts of moments past in his mind.

One teases at him. It is an unfamiliar place. A boy, not quite a teen. His eyes are haunted. He looks like he probably hasn't eaten in days.

"Are you his mother?" the boy asks.

A woman turns around. Marjory, younger, past middle age.

"Who are you?" she asks. "Why are you here?"

The boy cringes, struggling with the words.

"David." He makes a face like the name tastes bad.

"Are you his mother? Jason McAllister's?"

"Yes. What do you want?" She is wringing a towel she holds in her hands, twisting it nervously.

"My sister…"

"Are you all right?" Jim's voice breaks the image. "You look like you just saw a ghost."

Lawrence's complexion is pale, grey and pasty. He looks shaken. He turns to Jim.

"David."

"Did you think of something?"

"He was a kid. Jason McAllister had kids he got from somewhere. It would make sense. Who doesn't bring their kids to visit their grandparents some time?"

"A man who has no kids; who kidnapped them and probably murdered their mother."

"What if he did, though? Marjory said David visited her once."

"What are you thinking?"

"Michael. The two kids Jason kidnapped. His age fits. I'd bet David is Michael, that that's what he called him. McAllister changed the kids' names after he ended up with them. He could have called the boy David."

Jim's jaw clenches. "And the girl. At the prison, Michael raised his voice when he went to see McAllister. He demanded to know where she was. He demanded to know where Cassie was."

He takes his eyes off the road, turning to look at Lawrence.

"Now I know who Cassie is."

"His sister," they say almost in unison.

"Now what?" Lawrence asks. "Marjory can't help us find Michael."

"We need to visit Auntie Sophie."

"Any idea where she is?"

"No."

The severe Director of Bayburry Street Geriatric Home purses her lips at the retreating detectives' backs as they make their quick exit, the heavy front door closing behind them.

"There's something off about that pair."

She turns away and returns to her office just behind the empty reception desk of the funereal entrance to the home.

In contrast to the elaborate display that greets visitors when they first walk in, her office is simply decorated without the attempt at looking like anything but a utilitarian office devoid of all personality. There are no flowers or pictures. Not even a single family photo.

She sits at her desk, making a quick call to summon one of the nurses to her office, and then waits with quiet reserve. Minutes later, the woman arrives somewhat breathless from running across the facility and looking ruffled.

"Have a seat," Miss Krueger nods her in. "How is our Marjory McAllister after her visit?"

"She is agitated and is in and out of cognizance. She kept going on, talking nonsense gibberish. She's talking about lost children, coyotes, little toes, and graveyards. I've never seen her in such a state. She starts, then she seems to realize we hear her and she clamps up. Something is really upsetting her. She had to be sedated a second time. She is sleeping now."

Miss Krueger nods thoughtfully. "When is the last time Mr. William McAllister was here to visit?"

"Three days. She's been growing more agitated each day he doesn't come." She pauses, unsure if she should say what is on her mind or not. She decides to take a chance. Concern has been eating at her gut for the old man who shows so much devotion to his wife.

"It's not like him. In the years Marjory has been here, he has never missed a day visiting her. What if something is wrong? I mean, he is pretty old. What if-?" she breaks off.

"If the old bird has passed on, then Mrs. McAllister will forget he ever existed. It's not pretty, but it is how the ailing mind works. She already doesn't know who he is most days. The outside world will forget she exists here too. Mrs. McAllister will while away her remaining years here in obscurity, blissfully unaware that her family has abandoned her like so many others have abandoned their elders to our care when they become too bothersome to visit."

The nurse frowns. She thinks it is deplorable how the elderly seem to be just dumped off and forgotten at their facility to spend their final years locked in a prison of both hospital starkness and their own minds.

But there are those few cases whose mental incapacity she doubts. Mrs. Marjory McAlister is one of them.

"Maybe we should make some effort to contact him," she suggests. She knows her boss will most likely shoot the idea down. She is pretty sure the woman has given up on their patients' families.

"I'll contact Mr. McAllister."

Miss Krueger's words shock her. They give her hope.

She swallows uncertainly. Something about the woman who is her boss has always terrified her. She just can't put her finger on what.

"Is there anything else?" Miss Krueger looks at her pointedly. She senses the nurse has something else to say.

"Mrs. Bheals got out of her restraints again," the nurse says uncertainly. "She was at it again, trying to escape." She pauses and almost holds the next bit back. "She's been unusually lucid."

Miss Krueger's lips are a grim tight line.

"Thank you. We will need to keep both ladies sedated. We don't want anyone hurting themselves. That will be all."

Dismissed, the nurse hurries out, regretting telling her boss about Mrs. Bheals.

*I was worried about Mrs. Bheals. I don't think she belongs here. It's horrible how we keep her tied down to a wheel chair. I've seen her in there, behind those eyes, intelligent and alert. I know she's in there, not like some of the others. There is no confusion there.*

*I think Marjory is in there too. She's upset and forgot herself today, but she seems so … careful … in what she says.*

She passes through the ladies lockdown unit, wanting to take another look at the two ladies. She stops at Mrs. Bheals's doorway and is heartbroken by what she sees.

The frail old woman is sitting in her wheelchair, slumped and staring off vacantly, her eyes unblinking and dry looking. A string of spittle hangs down from her slack mouth. She has been strapped down to the chair again, although in her state it is pointless.

She pulls a small bottle from her pocket, slipping into the room. Tilting Mrs. Bheals's head back, she quickly drops a few drops of saline into each eye. It's as much to help the old woman as to give her a chance to reassure herself that she's still breathing. The old woman is oblivious to her presence, but she feels her faint breath on her wrist.

She quickly moves on, finding Marjory McAllister's room down the hall. She stops in the doorway and looks in.

Marjory is lying on her back on the bed just as she was left when the nurses finished sedating her. Her nightgown is hiked up and her hair dishevelled from the fight.

She slips in, straightening the old woman's nightgown and trying to straighten her hair. She quickly drops a few drops of saline in each drying eye.

"They could at least leave her with a little dignity."

The drugs have left her in a state that is not sleep. Her eyes are half open, drugged into oblivion. She hears the rattle of the old woman's breathing. She grips her and rolls her onto her side.

Just as she suspected, her mouth is filling with drool. She would have eventually choked on it. It dribbles from the corner of her slack mouth, thick and stringy like the other old woman.

Tears burning at her eyes, she leaves the old woman.

"I wish I had some way to contact their families and tell them to take them out of here."

# Part Six

# Solving Problems

# 33 Old Men Talking

William McAllister shuffles up to the door of the little coffee house, pushing it open to the delighted jangle of a bell over the door. His arthritic hands are knotted with bulging veins, the bones showing through the age-spotted skin covering them.

He looks up in annoyance. *Damned bells, one of these days…*

Without pause, he shuffles down the aisle between tables towards the back.

"Afternoon, Harry. We haven't seen you in here in a while," a plump waitress calls out to him.

He grunts and waves in response, not turning to look at her.

He sits at a table at the back of the coffee house, joining another elderly man already sitting there drinking coffee and eating pie. He is slightly hunched over the table, his coat and hat from another era carefully hung on the coat rack near the table.

The waitress is on William by the time he settles himself.

"Your usual, Harry," she smiles, setting a small plate with blueberry pie and whipped cream in front of him. She turns over his cup, filling it with coffee before hurrying off.

"Anderson," William nods to the elderly man sitting across from him.

Anderson nods back.

"Just like the old days." Anderson's eyes crinkle with his smile and his grin is more toothless than toothy.

"Yeah, just like the old days." William sips his coffee and grimaces. "Coffee is just as bad too."

"That's why you always come here."

Anderson's expression sobers. "That boy of yours doesn't know how to keep a low profile, does he?"

"He's always had trouble not bringing attention on himself." After a moment of thought William adds, "And the family."

"He came to see you." It's not a question. Anderson knows about the visit.

"He came to talk about David. He took off with that girl. He's a bigger fool than Jason. The police are looking for them. Jason came to warn me they'd be coming to talk to me; to Marjory too."

"Are you worried?"

"A little. Some days she's more lucid, some days not so much. No way to know what she might say on a bad day. If they start talking to her too much, asking too many questions, she could go off into one of her fogs, reliving a memory."

"The organization is concerned about that too. We have other problems too. Your boy is getting into trouble again. He has another kid under his roof, a runaway. The kid was already there. I'm not sure if it's a setup."

"The organization?" William wrinkles his brow.

"The authorities. There is a detective on him who has gone off the grid. He is not following the rules. He is not one of ours, we don't control him. He is determined to bring your boy down, David too, no matter what it takes."

"That's a long stretch, don't you think? Them planting a kid in a place like that?"

"I don't think they planted him. The kid has no idea about what is going on. But the authorities knew he is there and didn't remove him. They're probably watching to see what happens."

"And Jason bit."

"He bit. He could have ignored the kid, or got rid of him. But he didn't, just like the other two."

"David and Cassie."

"The kid is a complication. He's going to bring too much attention if they bring Jason in for harbouring a runaway. The organization ordered him removed from the situation."

William's eyes drop, trying to hide the sadness. He knows what that means. The kid is a package.

"Do you know where David and Cassie are?" Anderson asks.

William tries to keep his expression unreadable.

"David, no. Cassie, I have a hunch. Are they…"

"Just David. He's back in the fold. The organization is watching him. It doesn't look good. They're assessing him. Jason didn't teach him well enough. He doesn't seem to understand how far the mess will reach, or the clean up."

"So, he's doing jobs."

"Carefully chosen ones."

"And Cassie?"

Anderson shrugs. "They aren't looking for her. Either they know where she is, or she's dead." He gives William a meaningful look. He thinks William knows where Cassie is.

"But you know where David is," William says.

"I do. He's holed up with that young lady, the one he didn't kill. They're testing him and I'm pretty sure the man deciding his fate is setting him up to fail."

William's jaw works. *Jason's foolishness in keeping those kids, his recklessness, is going to hurt others yet. I'm always cleaning up that boy's messes.*

Anderson looks at him levelly.

William looks away. He knows what is coming and doesn't want to hear it.

"William," Anderson says softly. It's the first time in the decades of their association that he has ever spoken William's name.

William looks at him, sees the pain in his eyes, the regret.

"It's time," Anderson says.

"No," William says. "Not yet."

"You need to clean up this mess before they do."

"Don't I always clean up my own messes?"

"You are not as young as you used to be."

"Neither are you."

"You've got me there." Anderson smiles. His smile drops. "She has to disappear."

# 34 Confrontation

"He is on the move again," the voice on the phone says. "He came back for a day and left again."

Jim grunts. "Did you manage to get anyone on him this time?"

"We did but he lost him."

"Damn. Do you have any idea where he's going?"

"That runaway kid hiding out here sometimes, he confronted the kid then let him stay in his room while he was gone. He wanted it to look like he was here," the voice chuckles.

"Yeah, so?" Jim is getting impatient.

"The kid is missing."

"He's a runaway. That's what they do, they run."

"McAllister was bent out of shape about it. Could be he's looking for the boy."

"Maybe, I doubt it. It doesn't feel right. He's just a runaway kid. I don't peg McAllister for a pedophile. It doesn't match his profile. He might have used the kid to make it look like he's there, but he's not about to chase after him."

"I don't think the kid left."

"What are you saying?"

"The cowboy."

Jim swore under his breath. "He is just a kid. Why did you let that happen?" His anger is mounting. Yet another victim he failed. "You get someone on him, shake down the cowboy and find out what he did with that kid. You are sure it was the cowboy?"

"No, but he's the most likely."

"Get on him."

Jim hangs up, turning his attention to Lawrence.

"You find anything on McAllister's sister yet?"

"I haven't found her yet, but I did learn something else interesting."

"What?"

"The judge who let McAllister go, I'm pretty sure he was in someone's pocket."

"I'm sure a few of them are. What does that have to do with McAllister?"

"McAllister knows where the bodies are. Hell he buried some of them. We both know you don't bury that many bodies in one place without involving a lot of people. There's some kind of killer conspiracy going on here."

"Drop the puns and get to the point."

Lawrence sneers wolfishly.

"There has to be one hell of a large organization involved."

"You are theorizing."

"I learned something about my predecessor and his obsession." His grin falters. "I don't think he killed himself. He was obsessed with something before his death. All those files he left me, a lifelong career of obsession over finding something, or someone."

"Go on."

"I dug deeper. There is something missing. One of the boxes I didn't think mattered was the key to finding the kids McAllister had. But something is still missing. I studied the rest of the files in that box. I dug into his past."

His eyes are haunted now.

"He knew."

"He knew." Jim frowns. "Knew about what?"

"All of this, the bodies. That was his obsession, and it's bigger than you can imagine."

He shakes it off.

"Forget that, I don't know enough yet. About the judge, I think he was given orders to let McAllister go. They may have killed him after and made it look like a suicide."

"How much do you know and how much can we prove?" Jim asks.

"Nothing. I'm not sure if he was paid off or blackmailed. I talked to the people who would really know if there is anything worth knowing, his house staff, ex-staff too. There is nothing on him I can prove, but there are rumours."

"Of course there are."

"There are rumours the judge may have had some unconventional tastes. He has some secrets hidden pretty deeply himself, and probably needed help hiding them."

"Shit, every scrap we uncover just makes this thing bigger and the real answer further from our reach."

Anderson's words haunt Jason. They replay over in his head.

"You just brought a big pile of crap on your family and I don't know if I can protect them. You keep messing up and one of these times it's going to hurt people."

*He's talking about David and his obsession. He's crazy. He is damned impulsive, out of control, and downright nuts; dangerous crazy and not just to himself. He has lost touch with reality.*

*It's David's mess, the damned fool, taking that woman again. But it is all on me. They're putting his mess at my feet. It's my fault because I made him what he is.*

"We can't control everyone, and a few of those we can't are asking too many questions and digging too deep. They are asking about their Jane Doe and Katherine Kingslow. But that is just an excuse. They are really chasing down the larger beast."

*Detective McNelly. He discovered there's something more than David killing women. David's fault. No, I can't put that on him, can I? That's on me. I knew I had to get rid of David, put a stop to him.*

*Kill him.*

*I just couldn't bring myself to do it. I tried to protect him all those years, both of them. Instead, I tried to get him caught, put away. It went so wrong. They weren't supposed to find the graves.*

"I came to warn you. He's your mistake and your responsibility. The management knows. They're watching and when it comes down it's going to come down hard." Anderson's words.

*If they clean up, they will do a thorough job. Not just David and that woman, me, that fat detective, everyone touching this.*

*Mom, Dad.*

*Sophie.*

*Cassie.*

*Hell, they already took the kid.*

Jason feels sick with the knowledge.

"They are going to talk to your mother," Anderson had warned. "You have to fix this before things go bad. Management will clean it up if you don't."

"I have to fix this," Jason says. "I have to do what I should have done before, make this all stop. I have to find David and end this. McNelly will give up on his Jane Doe easy enough; he probably already thinks she is dead; Katherine too, probably. But he's not going to stop until he gets David. It's personal for him.

I have to give him David, his girlfriend too, their bodies anyway. Murder suicide? I'll figure it out. First I have to find him. How?

Anderson! You don't drop under the radar of the organization."

Jason wanders the park path. It's a heavily treed park with wide expanses of manicured lawns and gardens, flowering trees and bushes, and filled with a maze of meandering paved paths to keep visitors from getting bored. The park is busy. No one seems to care who else is there. Finally, he spots it. The bench is where it was described, tucked away, almost hidden.

He sits down to wait.

He watches joggers go by, cyclists, people walking and rollerblading. A dog stops to sniff him out before its owner calls it back and it trots away.

Time stretches and so does his wait, the sun slowly moving West across the sky.

The urgent pressure in his bladder becomes too much and he gets up to slip behind a tree to urinate where no one will see him, he hopes.

He waits another few hours before his rumbling stomach pushes him to give up.

"Anderson, you bugger, you aren't coming, are you?"

Jason gets up and starts walking down the path, following the curve that puts the bench out of sight.

He stops after going some distance.

"He's old. Did he forget? No, he's sharp. No senility there. Maybe he just refuses to help."

A look of alarm crosses his face.

Jason turns and races back down the path, arriving at the bench out of breath, looking around.

A small folded slip of paper sits on the bench where he spent the past hours waiting. It is small enough to be easily missed, but he knows he didn't.

He races back to the path, looking up and down it, and just catches a glimpse of the back of a stooped over old man in a coat and hat that have gone out of fashion decades before vanishing around the bend in the other direction.

*Old man hat. Old man coat.*

"You old bugger."

Jason returns to the bench, picking up the paper and unfolding it.

It contains an address and nothing more.

"David," he says.

William McAllister leaves the path, cutting through an almost invisible deer trail where the trees and bushes are thick. His old man walk is unmistakeable. He curses his aging body and its loss of strength, his legs already feeling the strain.

Jason wanders an old used car lot. All of the vehicles have seen better days. Most are cheap. He scowls at the beat up heaps that would be better off in a salvage yard. Few look like they can handle a long trip. He doesn't dare bring attention to himself by trying to access a larger sum of money, so it's one of these or nothing. Stealing a truck would be too risky.

A tired looking salesman in a suit that looks as worn out as the cars comes trotting over with a forced smile on his face.

"Hi, I see you eyeing up that baby."

Jason considers ignoring him, still scouting the lot for something useful, debating whether the salesman will save him time or just spend too long on sales pitches for something completely useless.

"How about this one?" the salesman suggests helpfully, trying to draw Jason towards a sedan with a higher price tag and bigger commission.

"I need a truck."

The salesman pauses to think, changing course.

"I have just the thing over here." He leads Jason towards a garish attention grabber with oversized rims, aftermarket exhaust, and flames decals ripping down each side.

Jason looks at him. "Do I look twenty?"

"No, you are right, power, no flash. I know." He leads him to another truck.

It is a step above an old farm truck beater that is not road worthy enough to insure to drive on the road, but still serves a purpose on the farm.

The truck has a cap covering the box with a pull up door that closes against the top of the tailgate, making it impossible to see what's inside the box.

"Is it insurable?" Jason asks.

"It just passed inspection," the salesman says.

*Falsified, no doubt,* Jason thinks.

"It'll do," Jason says.

They go inside the small dealership building to fill out the paperwork, Jason paying cash and using false identification.

The deal completed, the salesman waves Jason off as he drives away.

"Enjoy your new truck Mr. Donaldson."

Four days later, Jason is sitting in the truck parked behind the detached garage of a home across the street from a small old home in a small town filled with small old homes.

Between the house and garage he has a view of the house across the street, but would be overlooked by anyone passing on the street. He already made sure no one was home before borrowing their yard.

He sips a coffee and chews on a sandwich he had gotten to go at a motel restaurant in the next town, watching the house across the street.

Billy tries to breathe slowly. It feels like the air is running out.

*I'm suffocating.* Panic swirls. He imagines he sees tiny lights dancing before his eyes. His eyelids are still closed; blindfold tied uncomfortably tight and the gag half choking him.

He can't get away from the stink. It's his own stink; sweat, urine, and feces. He had soiled himself a few times. It was unavoidable. The worst is the sweat, that sharp rank stink of fear sweat.

It is nothing but black. Distant sounds. He hasn't moved in hours. Or rather, he hasn't been moved in hours. He's laid there so long, tied painfully, unable to move, his arms and legs running through a series of loops of pain, numbness, no feeling, pins and needles, and back to pain.

He's been fading in and out of consciousness, or sleep, he isn't sure which, for a time that feels stretched endlessly long.

*My arms and legs are probably going to fall off. Man, this hurts! I've got to move. I've got to get out of here.*

Icy blood courses through his veins, his heart pounding too fast.

He hears movement. A scrape. A voice.

*What's he saying?*

The words are garbled. Senseless.

Ryan comes home after blowing off his anger from seeing Elaine with Trevor. He drove around until the anger finally seeped out of him. Thankfully Cassie and Jane didn't return to lecture him more.

Elaine startles when the door opens and Ryan walks in.

"Ryan, you're back."

"I'm back." He drops his bag with his clothes at the door.

Their greeting is muted, both feeling the growing expanse of distance between them and feeling awkward for it.

"Did you do much while I was gone?" Ryan asks, carefully keeping his voice neutral.

"Not really."

*It's not like I'm allowed to go anywhere or do anything.* Elaine pushes down the resentment pushing up in her. *It's not his fault. It's to keep us safe. But I'm going crazy sitting here day and night, trapped in this house.*

*I'm losing her,* Ryan thinks. *I need to do something.* He thinks for a moment.

"Do you want to go out?" he asks.

"Out?" Elaine is caught off guard. In the months they've been on the run, they have never gone out.

Ryan moves closer to her, feeling like a school boy trying to talk to his first crush. He looks down at the floor and has to make himself look up to meet her eyes.

She fidgets, looking down too before looking up to meet his eyes.

"We want to have a normal life after we get married," Ryan says. "We will always have to keep a low profile, but we can live pretty normally. We can go out like regular people. We will have enough identity changes and moves behind us. We might as well start getting used to living normal again. I think we can risk going out once in a while."

Elaine's mind is stuck. She doesn't know how to respond, what to think. Confusion pulls her in two different directions; loneliness, loss, and regret; her mixed feelings towards Ryan and Trevor.

"Where would we go?" she asks.

"Anywhere you want. The bars at these little small town motels aren't much for dancing, but we can go there. We can go someplace for dinner, or just for a walk, whatever you want."

*You are hesitating because of him,* he thinks.

He takes her hand gently. "Come on."

Elaine lets him lead her out.

Jason gets out of the car, stretching. He took a break during the night from watching the house to look after his bodily needs, finding a bathroom and again earlier this morning to get coffee and something to eat. Both times he rushed back feeling the push of nerves. What if he missed something?

For the past hour Jason stared at the house, wondering if anyone is there. They could have both gone somewhere even though it's still early morning.

At last, the door to the house opens. Jason ducks behind the truck, hoping he wasn't seen. He watches Michael leave the house, getting in a truck and driving away.

He gets in the truck quickly, following him at a discreet distance.

When Michael pulls into the slaughterhouse, joining a scattering of other vehicles in the lot, Jason drives past it, turning around down the road to come back.

Michael's truck is still parked there, empty. Others are showing up for work too.

"So, he's working at a slaughterhouse. Fitting."

Jason heads back the way they came.

Elaine is sitting in the kitchen, a now cold coffee sitting in front of her barely touched. Last night left her in a misery of confusion.

*Why do I feel this way? So guilty? Trevor was only being a friend. At first, anyway, until he pushed it too far. Now I know he wants more than friendship.*

*But Michael, Ryan,* she corrects herself, *has been more distant and secretive. He is always going on these trips, making promises for the future.*

*I need to stay with Ryan so we can be safe. I wanted to be with him. I want to be with him. Don't I? I still have feelings for him. He saved me. Because of him Ronnie can never hurt me again. I'm safe with him.*

*So why don't I feel safe? Ryan would never hurt me.*

*Because you know he might hurt someone else. You know who, what, he is. You know he's crazy. He is slipping deeper into it, talking more and more to someone who isn't there. He tried to hide it before, but now it's like he forgets I'm even there. Or maybe he doesn't care if I see him. I'm scared he's going to start again. He is obsessed with her, Cassie.*

*He is going to look for her again. And when he does, he will lose himself again.*

*He will start killing again.*

*No, he won't. He promised he won't do it, for me.*

*Trevor isn't like him. He is kind and gentle. He wouldn't hurt anyone. I wouldn't have to worry.*

*But I still love Ryan.*

*I feel like I don't know who I want to be with.*

Ryan methodically slaughters cow after cow, his rubber apron slick with blood and the slaughterhouse reeking of the cattle's blood, sickness and fear.

He tries to ignore her while he works.

Cassie stands there in his killing pit, silently watching him.

*She shouldn't be here. This is no place for a little girl.*

Sending the carcass off on the hook, he returns to the pen for another cow, herding the animal back through the path between pens to his pit.

Trevor is working in the next killing pit, both men making a point of not looking at each other. Trevor is still subdued, methodically murdering cows while silently cursing Ryan for taking the fun out of his job. It's no fun to just mindlessly kill them.

His thoughts turn to his big plans for Ryan and his woman, Elaine. He smiles.

This time when Ryan returns to his pit Cassie starts whispering to him.

"She knows you are planning to go looking for her. She does not want you to."

Ryan ignores her.

"You won't find her anyway. Even if you did, it wouldn't do you any good. She isn't me. It's too late to protect me. You failed, David. You didn't protect me. You killed me, David."

Ryan's face twists into a grimace of pain with the effort to shut her out, to not listen.

In the next killing pit, Trevor catches the pained look.

*He knows she's slipping away, he's losing her,* Trevor thinks smugly. *Look at him, making stupid faces like he's in pain.* He laughs inside, enjoying his enemy's suffering. *Soon, it is time I take Elaine for the first time. Make her mine. Make her want me. And when I'm finished with her, she will be as broken as these stupid cows and I will dump her on his doorstep.*

Ryan clenches his jaw, getting his emotions under control. *Not now Cassie. Go away. Go away.*

Elaine is startled by a knock at the door. Her pulse races and her heart pounds hard in her chest, making her chest tight with anxiety.

*Who can it be? Ryan is at work. He wouldn't knock anyway. Trevor? He should be at work too.*

She peeks out the window before opening the door.

She almost screams.

*It's him! From the courthouse! The man Michael went to visit in prison before we left.*

Tears spring to her eyes and she leans against the door quietly, feeling his presence through the door.

*What do I do?*

"I know you are in there," his voice comes through the door. "Katherine, please, I need to talk to you. I'm here to help. Michael is in trouble and he doesn't even know it. Please, let me help you."

She bites her fist, stifling the animal sound that wants to escape her lips. The courthouse comes washing over her in a cold terror. The hours spent in a hospital room under police guard, endlessly being questioned by psychiatrists and police.

The farmhouse. She can smell the damp earthy stink of the basement. It clogs her nostrils, her throat. She can't breathe. The world darkens.

*No, I can't. Please just go away. I can't.*

Jason hears the thump through the door. He tries the knob.

It is locked.

He goes around to the back, looking in the windows. From another vantage point he catches a partial view of her prone body on the floor.

He goes to the back door and looks around quickly before deftly breaking in through it.

*Easy pickings.*

Elaine opens her eyes, feeling dazed. Her head hurts. It hit the floor hard when she fainted. She blinks a few times.

"Ryan?" Someone is looking down at her. The face comes into focus.

He cups his hands hard over her mouth the moment the scream starts tearing from her lips.

"Sshh, please," Jason tries to quiet her. "Don't scream. I'm not going to hurt you. You fainted and banged your head."

She stares at him through terror-filled eyes over his hands, trying to stop the screams bubbling up her throat.

The Cowboy opens his door to stop the incessant banging on it. His eyes are glassy and vacant, his expression a drug-induced void.

He looks at the two men standing on the other side looking stern. His first instinct is to run. He barely manages to make the thought.

*I'd have to go out the window. That'll hurt.*

"Where is the kid?" one of the men asks.

The Cowboy blinks at them in confusion.

"Kid?" His mouth makes the sound of the thought in his head.

"We are with family social services. Someone called and said a kid is staying here, a runaway. We are here to take him into custody. Do you know his current whereabouts?"

*These guys reek cop. Kid? What kid? Oh yeah, that kid.*

"He's gone. New dude cleaned house, kicked him out I think. Or the kid got scared and took off. I don't know."

"We looked you up Mr. Leroy Johnson. We know your history. You like them young, boys. Where is the kid?"

Even through the haze of his high, The Cowboy, Leroy Johnson, manages to feel fear.

*If they pin this on me, I'm going back to jail for the rest of my time. I don't know what the hell happened to the kid. Shit, did I do something to him? I don't remember touching the kid. I don't think I did anything. Aw man, they'll never believe me.*

The urge to run comes and goes again. They are blocking his way out, except the window.

*Fuck it.*

The Cowboy, Leroy Johnson, turns and sprints for the window, crashing through the glass with the weight of his momentum and scrawny body, leaving streaks of blood behind where he cut himself.

The men turn and run, charging down the stairs and out the door, chasing the bleeding scrawny man down the street.

"Are you calm now?" Jason asks.

Elaine nods, staring at him over his hands still cupped over her mouth, her eyes wide with fear.

"I need you to be calm. Don't scream. The neighbours might hear and call the police. Michael talked to you about not bringing attention on yourselves, didn't he?"

She nods again.

"Okay, I'm taking my hand away. How is your head?" He lets go of her, helping her sit up.

She touches her head gingerly and winces at the pain.

"Let's get a cold compress on that." Jason takes her hand, pulling her up with him as he gets up.

Elaine wobbles a little when she gets to her feet and he steadies her.

"Sit on the couch. I'll get something for your head. Don't try to run. You are in no shape for it, and I'm here to help you and Michael. You remember me, don't you?"

She nods, mumbling a yes.

"Michael and I go back a long way."

Jason leaves her on the couch while he rummages in the kitchen for a dish towel and ice.

Elaine looks at the door, debating making a run for it. She starts getting up and a wave of dizziness and nausea washes over her. She sits back down, the motion sending shocks of pain through her head.

He returns, gently putting the ice wrapped in a towel to her head. She raises one hand to hold it in place. He looks into her eyes, seeing if her pupils are the same size. It makes her feel uncomfortable.

"You might have a concussion."

"W-what do you want?" Elaine manages to squeak out. She has never felt like a strong woman, physically, emotionally, not in any way. She never felt more helpless than she does right now.

*Please Ryan, come home. Come home now. Trevor, show up like you do. I need you.*

"I came to see Michael."

"He's not here." Elaine feels a need to protect him. She feels like she is lying for him, even though it's the truth.

"I know. He is at the slaughterhouse."

Elaine's eyes flash with surprise.

"You thought I wouldn't know? How do you think I knew where to find you? I want to talk to you alone before I see him. How are things going here for you two?"

"All right."

"Of course you would say that. How about you? Are you holding up okay? You must be going crazy here. Is he letting you work? No, he probably doesn't think it is safe yet."

His words make the loneliness she feels every day tug at her.

"How is Michael holding up? He seemed a bit … off."

Elaine looks down at her one hand in her lap. It has the urge to fidget. The other hand is still holding the ice to her head.

"What's wrong?" Jason asks. "I can see it in your eyes. Something is wrong."

Uneasy and unsure, she blurts it out, regretting it the moment the words pass her lips.

"He talks to someone who isn't there."

"He is talking to himself?"

She doesn't want to say more, but feels trapped into it.

"No. He talks to someone else. It started the day we left. I thought I was imagining it at first. He was doing it when he thought I wouldn't know. He is doing it more and more now."

Getting this off her chest lifts a weight off it, but at the same time feels like she is somehow betraying Michael. She almost says the name. Cassie. That is who she thinks he is talking to.

Jason thinks about this. *Talking to himself, okay, I can see that. Talking to someone else, now that's just crazy. Who would he be talking to? Cassie? It makes sense. He is obsessed with finding her. It led him all over the country searching for her. How many women did he think were her? He is talking to the ghost, the memory of his sister. Probably the child he didn't look after. A big brother is supposed to look after his little sister.*

This brings the unwanted memory of Sophie flooding into him; his own sister who he too failed to protect.

*Sophie. Where are you right now? How are you?* He shakes it off, pushing that memory away.

*If he is going crazy right in front of her, she might just help me stop him. I have to stop him. It's already too late to protect him, but I can still stop this before he hurts anyone else. Mom. Sophie. Dad.* Thinking about his family sends a pang of loss and pain through him. Cassie.

"I have something to show you." Jason hands Elaine a folded page from a newspaper.

She hesitates, not wanting to touch it. She takes it and looks down at it.

The headline screams out about a missing woman. Her eyes swim and she can't read the small print below. She stares at the photo of the woman.

"This is just in the next town. Pretty close to home, wouldn't you say Katherine?"

"No." The word comes out so quietly that it's almost inaudible.

"He has a sickness. He can't help it. He gets into these," he pauses, "states. A darkness inside him takes over. I think that's what scares me the most about him. When other men kill, they do it out of anger, for money or power… for pleasure. He just kills."

Elaine is shaking her head, shock making everything feel like it is happening far away.

"Did he tell you about Cassie? No, he didn't, did he? Do you know who Cassie is? Why he's so obsessed with finding her? He will never give up his obsession over her."

"His sister," Elaine says quietly.

"What?"

She looks up at him, speaking louder. "Cassie is his sister."

"Yes. Do you know who I am? Do you have any idea who I am to Michael?"

"Ryan, he goes by Ryan now."

"And you go by Elaine, I know. And before that you went by Michael Ritchot and Katherine Bennett. Before that you were Katherine Kingslow and he was Michael Underwood.

Before that he was someone else. He went by a lot of names before Michael Underwood. This is so easy for him, to just change identities, who he is, his whole life. It's not so easy for you though. It is very hard and you are very tired and lonely.

Before all those aliases, he was David. David McAllister. I'm not his real father. David, Michael, and his sister were very young when I," Jason pauses, catching himself, "when they came to be left in my care. I raised him and his sister as if they were my own."

Elaine's nerves are jangling a warning at her. *Why is he telling me all this? He killed women. The police, the lawyer, the judge, the news… they all said so. He wouldn't tell me anything if he plans to let me live. He is here to kill me.*

The knowledge she is already dead gives her a calm she didn't think she would be capable of. She looks at him steadily in the eyes.

"Where is Cassie?" she asks.

"Dead."

"He doesn't believe that. Did you kill her?"

Jason can't help but smile.

"Is that what he told you? If I killed her, then why is he looking for her? Why has he been obsessed for years with finding her?"

"I-I don't know." Elaine glances away uncertainly.

"Because he killed her. She was his first. Cassie was just little. David was only a boy. I made him dig the grave himself to bury her."

"No, that's not true."

"It's my own fault. I was raising them; I made him into a monster." He tilts his head, studying her. "I can see the vague resemblance. I can see why he thought you might have been her. After all, she was just a little girl when he killed her. What I can't figure out is why he kept you.

I mean, obviously he fell for you. But if he cares for you, he knows he has to let you go." He shakes his head. "To keep you? That was bold. Dangerous. The darkness will take over again. You don't want to be here when it does."

"He would never hurt me."

"Are you sure?"

Elaine can only stare back at him, trying to push away the doubts gnawing at her.

*Ryan won't hurt me. If he does, I have Trevor.*

The thought shocks her; that she is so quick to move on to thinking of Trevor in the same capacity as she did Ryan before; when he was still Michael; before he started acting strangely.

"Ask him what he does when he goes away on his trips," Jason says. "Ask him where he goes."

He leans in and she shrinks away. He only touches her head gently where she banged it on the floor.

"It doesn't look too bad. Look at me."

He stares into her eyes, judging the sizes of her pupils, to see if they are evenly dilated. They haven't changed.

"You are going to be just fine."

He gets up and walks to the door. "I'll be back later."

"What are you going to do?"

"I'm going to clean up his mess. I'm going to take David home."

With that he's gone, leaving Elaine reeling in confusion.

Elaine stares at the closed door. He didn't tell her his name. He didn't need to. He is famous; Jason T. McAllister, the McAllister Farm serial killer. His face and name were plastered all over the news for months.

She feels sick. Her whole world has turned upside down and she doesn't know where to be. She suffers through the day, her stress building. Finally, she looks at the clock for the thousandth time and it's late afternoon. Close enough. Too close. She picks up the phone and dials. It is answered on the second ring.

"Hi," she says in a small voice. "I need you. Hurry, he'll be home soon."

She hangs up and waits, feeling the world rushing around her at breakneck speed while she is trapped in this little bubble of time that won't move.

When it comes, the knock on the door makes her jump.

Elaine almost changes her mind.

*If I don't answer, he'll go away.* She gives in and answers the door. She looks up at Trevor uncertainly.

"You don't look so good. Are you all right?" he asks, looking concerned.

"I... It's," she falters. "I have to get out of here. I have to go somewhere. I don't know. Anywhere."

"Come on." He puts an arm around her shoulders, leading her out the door.

Elaine looks back as they drive away, wracked with guilt and torn by mixed feelings and confusion.

*Ryan, I'm sorry. I just need a little time to think before I can face you.*

He should already be home. She keeps expecting to pass his truck as they drive away.

Ryan is driving home and looking forward to relaxing his sore muscles after a hard day and feeling wrung out by Cassie's nonstop taunting him while he worked. There were a few moments he imagined the bolt gun pressed up against her forehead, her large round eyes staring back at him instead of the woeful eyes of the cow as he pulls the trigger, shooting bolts into the animal's brain with a dull triple thock.

On a whim, he turns off course, driving to the next town where there is a motel and a cold beer store. He purchases his beer and is walking back to his truck when he freezes. He is staring so hard at a woman who just walked out of the restaurant with a man that he almost drops his case of beer. He recovers it just as it slips from his grip.

The couple walk on, oblivious to his stare.

"Cassie." He almost cries out the name, but it comes out a constricted whisper instead. "It's her, Cassie. She's here, and just in the next town." He starts walking forward, about to break into a jog to catch up, and stops. "No, don't scare her off. She might not remember you."

The woman has a resemblance to Jane Doe, like a cousin might have.

He jogs back to his truck, gets in and starts it, waiting. The couple pull out of the parking lot in their car and he follows, keeping a distance behind.

Ryan follows them home. He watches them get out of the car. He sits there watching the house. She comes out again twenty minutes later wearing different clothes and gardening gloves. She starts weeding the garden.

The more he watches, the more convinced he becomes.

"I found you again."

Bursting with joy, Ryan wants to get out of the truck and run to her, scoop her up in his arms and hold her tight. *I will take you someplace safe. I will protect you.*

That uneasy feeling of being watched creeps up the woman's back. She stands and looks around. She sees the strange man sitting in a truck staring at her.

*She's looking at me. She's looking right at me. She sees me,* he thinks.

But there is no recognition in her eyes, only a sense of unease. She hurries into the house to tell her husband about the strange man staring at her, making her feel uncomfortable.

Her husband runs out of the house in time to see the truck's taillights driving away.

"It's her, Cassie! So close! I can't believe it was so easy to find her. I have to tell Elaine before I do anything."

Ryan pulls up in front of the house, barely closing the truck door in his eagerness, and bursts into the house.

"Sorry I'm late. I'll tell you all about it as soon as I've showered." He rushes through his shower, coming out almost giddy.

"I found her!"

Elaine isn't waiting for him.

"Elaine?" He is met by silence.

He moves from room to room quickly, stopping in the living room, looking lost. She's gone.

"Where?"

His face hardens.

"Trevor."

Ryan charges out of the house, the image of Trevor trying to kiss Elaine at this very door the other day burning a hot rage through his skull. He feels the curtain closing in, the world growing darker like a black cloud just blocked out the entire sky.

"No!" He pushes the darkness away, focusing on walking out the door, to the truck, climbing in, closing the truck door.

He reaches to jam the key in the ignition and is interrupted by knocking on the driver's door window. Ryan turns to look. Jason is standing there.

After he leaves Elaine reeling with the new information about Ryan, Jason sits in his truck watching the house. He watches the other truck pull up hours later and the man get out. He recognizes both him and his truck. He saw them at the slaughterhouse, arriving for work at the same time as David.

*I was right. There is definitely some serious animosity between the two. Now I know why.*

He watches Kathy leave with him, the tortured look of confusion marring her face. Soon after David, Ryan, comes home looking excited about something.

"She's not there," Jason taunts although he can't hear him.

Ryan comes barrelling out of the house twenty minutes later, his face twisted with rage.

Jason leaps out of his truck, racing for Ryan's truck. He makes it just as Ryan is putting the keys in the ignition, knocking on the window.

The face that turns to look at him makes his blood run cold. Ryan's face is a stony mask of dark rage.

"David, Ryan," Jason starts.

Ryan turns his attention back to his keys, turning them and firing up the truck.

"David, stop! Talk to me!"

Ryan puts the truck in gear.

"I know where she is!"

Ryan turns to look at him, his expression still locked in that stony cold anger.

"Talk to me."

Ryan puts the truck back into park and shuts off the ignition, getting out.

Jason instinctively steps back, keeping a distance between them.

The moment he saw Jason standing at his driver's door window, the dark veil of rage that was closing in dropped away. A surge of fear flushed through his veins and he struggled to keep his expression cold, hard. "Show no fear," he told himself.

Now, as he gets out, his legs feel like rubber and his mind is reeling with one frantic thought. How did he find me?

"Can we go inside and talk?" Jason asks.

Ryan doesn't trust his voice yet and simply nods, leading the way back inside the house.

Inside, Ryan doesn't offer his guest anything but a hard stare.

"Why are you here?"

"David," Jason starts. He stops.

"Don't call me that," Ryan says. "It's not my name."

Jason nods. "Okay, Ryan if you prefer. That detective, Jim McNelly, he isn't letting this go. He's asking too many questions, talking to people who might let something slip. This has to end before it's too late."

"Too late for what?" Ryan's lips turn up in a slow smile as realization dawns. "Too late for who?"

"They want this mess cleaned up. They-"

"You don't have to explain. I know what it means. Who exactly are you worried about?"

"My moth-"

Ryan laughs, cutting him off.

"Your mother? You? You killed my mother. You took her away from me, and from Cassie. You took everything away from us; our mother, our home, who we were. Who were we? What are our real names? Did you even know or have you refused to tell me all these years out of some twisted joke? And what about Cassie? Are you worried about her? Or have you already killed her?"

His face twists into an angry sneer, his voice rising. "Where is she? Where is Cassie? Where. Is. Cassie?" He shouts the last three words

"You know where she is." Jason can't keep the slight tremor out of his voice. "You know what you did to her. She's gone. You killed her."

"No. I found her. She was alive. You took her from me. You stole her from her family again, from me. Is she alive? Did you kill her?"

"That Jane Doe? She's not your sister. She didn't remember you, did she? That's because she doesn't know you. Let it go. For yourself and for everyone this mess touches. What, do you think you can just kidnap someone and go on your merry way and live happily ever after?"

Jason can't fight the chuckle that rises up.

"I guess you did that, sitting here playing house with one of your victims."

Ryan scowls at the use of the word 'victim'.

"It's already falling apart," Jason continues. "You've as good as lost your girlfriend."

Ryan steps forward, clenching his fists. "What have you done with her? If you've hurt her…"

Jason puts up his hands, placating.

"I only talked to her, that's all. She told me some things, I told her some things."

Ryan is on the defensive.

"Elaine knows enough of my past. I don't have to hide anything from her."

"Does she know you haven't given up looking for Cassie? Does she know you will kill again?"

Jason pulls out the article he showed Elaine, handing it to Ryan.

"What's this?" The headline screams loud. Ryan looks at the picture of the missing woman, scans the small print of the article. "Why are you showing me this?"

"I showed it to her."

Ryan's head snaps up, staring at Jason, the color draining from his face. His mind whirls, grasping for what to say.

"I know it wasn't you," Jason says. "And the authorities don't know about you. No one is looking at you for this."

"Why? Why did you show it to her?" The answer hits Ryan. "You told her it was me."

"It served its purpose. I needed to make her trust me."

He looks at Ryan thoughtfully. "How much have you told her? About us, the farm, what we do?"

"Nothing. I haven't told her anything."

"You did that right, at least." Jason pauses. "She told me about you. That you are going crazy, talking to someone who isn't there."

"You are lying. Why are you here? Really, why did you come?" Ryan glares him down.

Jason presses on, pushing him. He doesn't want to push him over the edge into the black mindless rage. He needs to know how far gone he is. How manageable he will be.

"She's scared of you," Jason says. "She says you are talking to Cassie. You are talking to the ghost, the memory, of your sister when she was a child. That is not your sister Ryan. It's nothing but a memory. You know that. Your sister lived, grew up, and I kept her hidden from you, keeping you from finding her all these years. You won't find her now."

The growing heat of Ryan's anger suddenly burns out, its dying ashes riding on a wave of shock.

The words replay in his head.

*I kept her hidden from you, keeping you from finding her all these years.*

*She's alive. He didn't kill her.*

Ryan stares at Jason hard, fighting the disorientation of shock.

*I can find her.*

He sees little Cassie standing behind Jason, frightened and so small.

*He won't hurt you anymore. I will protect you. I'll find you Cassie.*

"What do you want?" he asks, unsteadily.

"I have to clean up this mess," Jason says. "I have to stop all this, the police poking around, you. I'm here to take you home David."

# 35 Michael's Father

Jim and Lawrence sit across from Donald Downey, the man who lost his family years ago. Donald seems somehow shrunken into himself. He fidgets with his spoon, not stirring the murky coffee he had just poured cream and sugar into.

"Donald Downey, this is Jim McNelly, the detective I told you about," Lawrence says.

Donald looks up at the fat detective.

"After all these years." He breathes a heavy sigh, starting again. "I don't want to know. I don't want to hear it. They're gone, buried. That part of my life is over and in the past where it belongs."

He finally puts his spoon into the coffee, stirring it slowly and deliberately taking it out and laying it on the table.

"I went through hell when they vanished and now you want to bring that all up again. For what? Because you want to rehash some cold case? They are dead. I don't know where they are, where their mother took them. They are dead as far as I'm concerned.

It sounds cold, but I don't want them back. I am a weak man. I can't do it."

Jim is studying the man, weighing him, his slouched shoulders, drooping demeanour.

*Any other parent would have fought for their kids. They would have never stopped pushing to find them. But you just rolled over and gave up, didn't you?* He thinks.

"If we are right, they are alive; one of your kids anyway," Jim says.

"So you found her." Donald wants to look away. He wants to get up and walk out, but he can't help the curiosity burning low in his gut.

"So, how is she? I can't really blame her, taking the kids and taking off like that. That's what they said she did, the ones who weren't accusing me of killing them and hiding the bodies. Even the detectives investigating their disappearance said she ran off. I know I hurt her."

He gives a depressed ironic huff of a laugh.

"I had every intention of giving her everything; the house, everything in it. I wasn't going to fight for any of it. I found someone I thought I loved more, who was more fun, not always with her hands in something to do with kids. She punished me by taking the kids and running away. I got everything. Everything. Except my kids.

She left me too, you know, my girlfriend. Being in the spotlight was too much for her, the media hounding her, calling her a home-wrecker. The woman I broke my wife's heart over left me before the mess could die down."

"She didn't run away," Jim says.

"What do you mean? But, you found her." Donald hangs his head, rubbing the top of it as if to keep whatever is in there from coming out.

"We didn't find her, we found who we think had your kids." Jim studies him as he says this.

Donald almost looks like he cares for a moment. It is quickly replaced with his bland expression.

"So, she found a new man to support her and the kids."

He looks at them curiously. *A fat detective who does not look like he is fit enough to be a police officer, and a tall ugly reporter whose odd resemblance to a vulture seems fitting.*

"It seems odd to me, the two of you working together, a cop and a reporter."

"I'm an investigative reporter, I investigate," Lawrence says. "Sometimes I dig up something I think I should let them know." He thumbs towards Jim.

"Hawkworth already filled me in on your conversation," Jim says, "but I'm going to treat this like it's all new. I read the file. There's not much there."

Jim plops copies of the file photos on the table between them. The smiling faces of a little boy and toddler girl stare up at them next to the photo of a young woman whose smile is already too tired for her years.

"That's a real asshole move," Donald complains. He tries to not look at the photos, but as Jim intended, it is impossible. It is impossible not to feel that surge of loss stir deep down too.

"Brian and Stephanie." Jim levels his gaze at Donald. "Madelaine." He pauses to let the photos have the emotional impact he is expecting. "You were having an affair and told your wife you were leaving her. Tell me about the day they disappeared."

"I don't know when they disappeared. I only know the last time I saw them. I gave her some time to cool down before trying to talk to her about seeing the kids. It was a few weeks before I tried. A few more before anyone knew they were gone."

"Then tell me about the last day you saw them."

Donald looks down at this coffee, fidgeting with it. Finally, he looks up again.

"We went to the zoo, kind of a last thing as a family. She wanted to give the kids one last good memory. I didn't see the point. Stephanie was so young she'd never remember that day anyway. Brian probably wouldn't either.

At the end of the zoo trip we were supposed to break the news to the kids together. Madelaine insisted on that. I didn't want to. Brian might understand a little, probably not much. Stephanie was too young to understand.

It was very awkward, wandering the zoo, pretending to be a happy family. The day couldn't end fast enough. Madelaine was angry with me the whole time. It was very strained.

I didn't tell Madelaine until the end that Betty was picking me up at the zoo. I had already decided before we left home that I couldn't do it. I'm a coward, weak. I know. I've never been good with confrontations. She was furious with me for leaving her to break the news to the kids that we were separating alone.

That's the last time I saw them."

"Do you remember anything unusual about that day? Anyone showing interest in you, your wife, or the kids? Was anyone following you at the zoo?"

"No. It's a long time ago. I don't really remember, but no, I don't think so." Donald looks at Jim McNelly suspiciously. "What are you getting at?"

"We think your wife and kids were kidnapped. Although, we suspect that the kids may have been unintentional.

"They-," Donald starts and breaks off, looking confused and a little lost.

"We haven't found her remains, but we have every reason to believe your wife was murdered."

Donald's eyes drop to study the photos on the table between them. For the first time in a very long time tears burn at his eyes, turning them red and watery. He looks up from the photos at Jim.

"How-? Who-?" He's lost for words. The worse possible scenarios are going through his mind.

"The man we believe took her was rumoured to have kids, but he had no kids. There is no record of him ever having kids."

Donald swallows, trying to pull that small piece of hope from the detective's words. "You said you think one of them is alive."

Jim nods; his expression grave. It does not give the man sitting across from him any relief.

"We think the man who had them raised them as his own. We need a DNA sample from you to confirm he's your son."

"My- son- Brian."

The old man shuffles in through the heavy front door of the Bayburry Street Geriatric Home, pushing the door open ahead of him. His thin frame seems too weak for the weight of the door, but it swings easily enough.

He lets the door swing closed behind him and looks around the gaudy reception area. There is no one in sight.

Careful to lift his feet so they make no sound, he moves to a vantage point where he can see into the Director's office. It's empty.

With a small smile, he moves off in the opposite direction that she had led Jim and Lawrence previously to visit Marjory.

There, he slips through a door much like the other. Only, this one does not open to a hospital-like reception counter or soundproofed reinforced steel and glass locked door.

The bed and breakfast-style Southern plantation charm continues on past this door. Here, a secondary reception area with funereal flowers and paintings greets visitors along with well worn large cushioned chairs and once elegant tables. Two wide open doorways lead to separate wings. This is where the residents who do not need to be sedated and locked away live. This side is for those who are still sound of mind.

The old man takes the left doorway, shuffling down the hallway of the men's wing and stopping and waving at two residents playing cards. He gives them a curt nod and turns, making his way back.

One of them gives him a confused look. The other glowers, clenching his jaw angrily and bending the cards in his fist.

He is just going through the wide doorway when the Director of the Bayburry Street Geriatric Home steps out from the other wide doorway as if she had been waiting for him.

"Mr. McAllister, you know you can't just go roaming and visiting random residents without checking in. We have rules here. You must check in before visiting anyone, and you can only visit those who have you on their list."

Miss Krueger gives him a look suitable for scolding a truant schoolboy.

"Just saying hi to the chaps," William says, shuffling on through the door to the front reception area with Miss Krueger following on his heels.

"More like causing trouble and upsetting Mr. Porter. You know he doesn't like you, so why do you insist on stopping by to wave at him every time you come to see Marjory?"

"That's why." He smirks the toothless smile of a job well done.

"We haven't seen you in a few days Mr. McAllister. I'm afraid today is not a good day to see her."

William stops in his tracks, turning slowly with a scowl.

"I am here to see Marjory."

"Maybe you should come back tomorrow. She is not having a good day." Miss Krueger stands firm.

William turns, making his way to the door leading to the locked ward. "No."

He pushes his way through the door to the hospital reception area. Karen is not there today. The nurse who had tried to help Mrs. Bheals and Marjory is there instead. She looks up with a startled look at the elderly man and her boss coming in.

"Mr. McAllister, I think it would be better if you come back tomorrow when your wife might be more herself. After all, we haven't seen you in days."

He stops and turns, giving her a hard stare that chills even the hard-hearted Director of the home.

The nurse swallows, seeing the flash of fear in her boss's eyes. It gives her a new respect for the kind old man who has come to see his wife every day without fail until these past days.

He turns back without a word, moving towards the locked door and waving to the nurse to open it.

She glances fearfully at her boss, who nods the go ahead. She scrambles to comply, almost dropping the keys when her boss speaks as she is fumbling to put them in the lock.

"Maybe you should accompany Mr. McAllister."

"But, the desk. . ."

"Will still be here."

Her mind is spinning as she opens the door and her boss exits the other way, retreating away from Mr. McAllister's wife.

*She really is afraid of him. I can't believe it.*

"This way Mr. McAllister."

"I know where my wife is," he grunts, pushing past her.

They move down the hall. He pauses outside an open door, looking in at Mrs. Bheals with a frown. She looks just as she did after her attempted escape after Jim and Lawrence's visit. She is sitting slumped and motionless, strapped into a wheelchair there is no need to strap her into, staring vacantly ahead, her head leaning limply to one side and thick strings of drool hanging down from her slack mouth. The sharp intelligence is completely gone from her eyes.

William turns away, quickening his pace, hurrying down the hall to Marjory's room.

The nurse looks too, sadness passing over her face at the pathetic state of the woman.

*I have to find some way to contact her family,* she decides. *This place will kill her if I don't. It may already have, in mind anyway. I don't believe she is lost inside herself like the others. I have never seen that lost look on her face.*

She hurries to catch up to William.

William stops at Marjory's door. His body tenses and he clenches his fists. He turns to the approaching nurse, his furious look freezing her in her tracks.

"What have you done to her?" His voice is cold and low.

He moves in quickly to Marjory's side. She is strapped down to a wheelchair like the other woman. Her head is tilted, her body slumped, and her glassy eyes staring vacantly ahead at nothing.

He pulls out a cloth handkerchief and gently wipes away the thick strings of drool hanging from her slack mouth.

"Marjory, what have they done to you?"

The nurse enters the room nervously, keeping her distance.

"The Director thought she should be kept sedated for a few days," she says apologetically.

"Why?" William's age-cracked voice is cold. "What gives you the right to do this to her?"

"She was agitated, saying all kinds of stuff that made no sense."

William turns to her. "Why?"

The nurse blanches. She swallows the lump of fear in her throat.

"She had visitors. They upset her."

"Visitors. More than one." William studies her reaction. "Who?"

"I don't know. Two men. I heard they were police or something."

"What did they look like?"

"One is really fat. The other one is tall and skinny. Kind of looks like a buzzard."

William nods, his expression still grim. "I know who they are. So you decided to do this to her."

The nurse shakes her head. "The Director."

She moves closer, wanting only to run away, lowering her voice and glancing nervously at the open doorway. She whispers.

"Mr. McAllister, I think you should get your wife out of here. Your wife doesn't belong here. It's not healthy for her here."

William nods. "Leave us alone."

Lawrence looks at Jim seriously. They are driving back from their meeting with Donald Downey.

"I think we ruined that guy back there."

"Maybe," Jim says. "I can't work up much sympathy for a man who didn't even try to find his kids. You've got your story though, some of it anyway. Missing persons cold case solved. The fates of Madelaine Downey and her two children, Brian and Stephanie, revealed. Prolific serial killer Jason T. McAllister murders victim and raises her kids as his own, teaching one of them to kill, raising a new serial killer."

Lawrence turns his gaze to the road ahead. "Maybe."

"It doesn't feel complete."

"No, it doesn't."

Lawrence looks at Jim again. "Michael sure had a lot of interest in Jane Doe."

"She was a witness. So was Katherine Kingslow. He killed them both, got rid of the only witnesses who can testify against him. We have no proof he did anything. We have nothing to tie him to Jason McAllister."

"Except now the DNA from Michael's dad, proving he is really Brian Downey."

"It's not against the law to be a kidnapping victim." Jim's grimace is angry. "I know he was involved in those women who were kidnapped and murdered. I know he is involved with the graveyard in the woods. One way or another he is going down. They both are, Michael Underwood and Jason T. McAllister."

"You mean to kill him."

Jim's lips tighten in response.

There is a silent pause before Lawrence speaks again. "Jane Doe. She's his sister, Cassie McAllister, Stephanie Downey."

"You think so?"

"I'm positive. You didn't see the resemblance to the girl in the photo?"

Jim grunts. "Maybe, hard to tell. Everyone sees the resemblance when they want to. I've seen it too many times."

"I feel it in my gut."

"Let's test that theory. While they compare Michael's DNA to Donald, they can compare Jane Doe's too. We will see if we get a match."

# 36 David McAllister

Ryan knows what Jason means by taking him home. He steels himself mentally before he moves. When he moves, it's with explosive force, charging Jason and slamming him into the wall with brute savagery.

"Do you think I'm stupid? You came here to kill me."

The force knocks the wind from Jason. He struggles to push back against the younger man's strength, choking for air.

"No, not yet," he wheezes out. "Not if I can avoid it."

He breaks free and the two men stand their ground, sizing each other up. His breath is coming back.

"Right now, I want to know how bad it is. How far do I have to take it to clean up this mess? Like my father said, we clean up only what we have to. Too big, and you make bigger waves. Someone notices."

"What about Elaine?"

"She won't be found."

"You buried her." Ryan shakes with the anger filling him, the pain of loss the only thing keeping a dark curtain of rage from shutting out the world. His face twists with the pain and anger warring inside him. His hands twitch with the urge to tear the man apart, his lifelong fear of him forgotten.

"No, but you will."

"How- how did you? Did she-?" The image of her broken body fills him with pain a thousand times worse than a knife stabbing him in the heart.

"Relax. She's alive. She's with her friend, the guy from the slaughterhouse."

"Trevor." Anger burns brighter in Ryan's eyes. His fists clench into hammers ready to pound the life out of any man who gets in his way.

Jason studies his face for clues to how much he knows about Elaine's and Trevor's relationship.

"Are sure you are okay? You could have a concussion." Trevor studies Elaine's head, gently feeling the lump on her head. They are the in living room at his house.

She winces with the sharp pain brought by the slightest touch.

"I'll be fine. It's just a bump."

"Are you sure Ryan didn't do this to you? If he hurt you-…" It's a calculated threat, meant to seal her trust. He knows Ryan could not have been home yet to lay a hand on her.

He gives her a worried look.

"I just fell and banged my head. He wasn't even home yet."

"So why call me then?"

*I just needed to get away from there for a little while. To get some time to think without Ryan.* But she can't tell him this.

"I-I'm just feeling so confused. He won't be home for hours," she lies. "I didn't think I should be alone after hitting my head , just in case, and he doesn't have a cell phone. So I called you."

Trevor frowns, not believing her but unsure if she's telling the truth.

"Then you should see a doctor. Were you dizzy? Did you lose consciousness? Come on, I'll take you to the hospital."

Elaine feels a surge of panic. *I can't go to the hospital. They would ask too many questions. They might find out we aren't who we say we are. Ryan would go to jail.*

"I'm fine, really."

His stare is making her uncomfortable.

*He knows I'm lying. He doesn't know what about, but he knows. I have to tell him something.*

Hesitantly, she starts making up a story. There are some elements of truth, but she doesn't dare tell him the real truth. *I can't tell him about Jason McAllister or about Ryan and me.*

"We had a fight this morning before he went to work. We've been fighting a lot lately. I-I just needed some time. I wasn't ready to face him when he came home tonight."

"Stay here tonight, with me."

She meets his eyes, hers full of confusion and worry, his hopeful and urgent.

Ryan looks at Jason. "What are we going to do?"

"Not me, you." Jason's expression is calm. Inside he is anything but. "You are going to carry on like nothing unusual is happening. Only one man knows I'm here."

*And he spent a lifetime protecting my mother and father. He won't turn on them now, even if he doesn't feel the same loyalty to me. He was my father's Anderson.*

"Sooner or later Kathy will come back to you," Jason finishes.

"Elaine," Ryan reminds him.

Jason nods. "You are going to have to sort out your relationship yourself. We are going to have to find a way to make sure she is not a threat."

"You mean if she leaves me for him."

Jason sees the look of pain and loss in the younger man's eyes and is surprised by it. *He really cares about her.*

"Yes. She knows too much."

"She won't say anything."

"I hope not. We can't leave loose ends."

"She doesn't know anything." Ryan's look is hard, a warning.

"If she comes back to you it won't be a problem." It will also make it easier to make you both disappear.

It's Ryan's turn to nod. "What's next?"

He can't help the nervousness coursing through him. He spent his life living in terror of this man who once towered over him when he was a frightened child. Now they are sitting here, impossibly on a level field, discussing the future.

He looks at Cassie, sitting quietly in a corner, sweet little Cassie. He turns his attention back to Jason, but not before Jason noticed.

"You carry on, like I said," Jason says. "Go to work, come home, spend time with your woman."

*While you still can.* Jason can't help the regret he feels, the betrayal of the man who was a son to him.

"I have another job. I'm supposed to leave tomorrow, but I don't think I should."

"Are you worried about the organization?"

"I don't think I can leave her alone right now. Not when I have to try to get her back."

"You have to go. If you don't, it will make you look like you are not in control. Or worse, like you don't trust them."

"I'll take her with me then."

"Don't be stupid. Taking her before clearing it with Anderson will be her death. You know that."

Ryan paces like a caged animal, grabbing at his head and rubbing it hard in frustration.

"If I leave her behind I lose her, if I take her I lose her. What do I do?"

"Do what you have to."

"Are you staying here to watch her?"

"No. I have other things I need to do. I'll keep in touch. Step carefully."

"Where are you going?" Ryan looks lost. He feels lost. He needs help and he knows it.

"I have business to take care of."

*I'll be back to take care of business here.* With one last look at his son, he leaves.

Jason walks across the street and gets into his truck. He sits there for a moment, then lashes out, pounding the dash with his fist, his face twisted in frustration.

"I should stay, watch them, assess. David is a liability. It's probably too late to save them, but maybe I can keep Cassie safe, and Mom."

His thoughts turn to the kid, an innocent who got caught up in this.

"Damn!" He pounds the dash again, starts his truck, and pulls out from behind the house, driving off down the street.

Ryan stares at the closed door, indecisive.

Do I go after her? Find her? Then what? I'll beat Trevor to a pulp. She won't forgive me. But waiting here for her will be torture.

"Augh, what do I do?" He stops, clenching his fists angrily, his thoughts turning now to Cassie.

"He kept her from me. He knows where Cassie is, he admitted it. She's alive and he didn't tell me where." He starts pacing again, his movements quick and angry.

"He won't tell me. He will never tell me."

Images of little Cassie dance in his mind, the little girl playing out in the sunshine, picking flowers, running through the long grass, only her head bobbing above it visible.

Cassie shrieking. A dark pall over everything as if the clouds know to block out the light to match the mood.

Jason's angry voice yelling something he can't make out. The little girl cries out. The sharp yelp of the dog. She comes racing into the house, past him, and ducking behind the chair to hide.

Ryan is David again, just a boy. He looks down at his boy hands, not large, with the calluses that will make them hard already beginning to form from the hard farm work.

Jason comes stomping in angrily, a young man with a hot temper.

David moves, putting himself between the man and little girl. Cassie ducks deeper behind the chair, trying to hide, holding both hands over her mouth in an effort to not make a sound.

He is terrified inside, but he stands firm, blinking at Jason.

"Where is she? Where's your sister?" Jason glares at the boy.

David is speechless with fear.

Jason looks around. "Cassie? Cassie!" he barks, snarling. "She came in the barn. I told her repeatedly to never come in the barn. The barn is not a place for little girls."

He stomps off, searching the house for Cassie.

David moves to block his view, quickly waving Cassie to go. Run.

She hesitates and finally bolts, racing out the door. She stops to stare at David, her eyes haunted by something that can never be taken back. The sound of Jason's heavy feet approaching snaps her out of it and she darts outside to vanish in the gloom of the coming storm.

David stares after her, not moving. I should go with her. We can both run away right now. She saw. She saw what happens in the barn. He will kill her now.

Jason is standing over him, glaring down at him with a rage he has never seen before. He can't even blink. He is frozen in terror. It's not just rage he sees in Jason's eyes, it is fear. He has never seen fear there before.

"David. David, wake up." A little girl's voice intrudes in his mind.

He blinks, confused, looking around. He is a man again. Michael. No, Ryan, he reminds himself.

Cassie is standing before him, looking up at him.

"She needs you."

"Who?" he mumbles, unable to make sense of anything right now, where he is, who he is.

He turns at the sound of the door opening. Elaine comes in hesitantly, looking guilty. He looks at the clock. It is after midnight.

"Where were you?" he asks, his voice sounding angry in his effort to control it, to keep the fear and confusion out of it.

Elaine shifts uncomfortably. Trevor is too close. It makes her feel self-conscious. Guilty.

He rubs her arms. He has been working her all evening, trying to move her towards him, to make her fall in love with him.

"Please don't." She moves a step away. Still close enough to feel his nearness, her heart beating too fast, and her breath coming too quick. She looks up at him and he can see her arousal.

"Take me home."

"Stay here tonight." He stares into her eyes, willing her to say yes.

She looks down then looks away. "I can't. Mi-," she almost says it, almost says the wrong name. Michael.

"He's no good for you. Leave him. Stay with me, I'll look after you."

*She's like a fragile little bird,* Trevor thinks. *She's frightened. Of what? Me? Him? Or of her own feelings? Because she doesn't know what she wants? Breaking this fragile little bird is going to be fun.* He smiles, almost licking his lips.

Elaine thinks the excitement she sees in him is desire for her. It feeds her own confusing desire, sending a rush of heat through her cheeks.

"Please Trevor. I'm not ready for this. I can't betray Ryan. Take me home."

*I've already betrayed him,* she thinks.

She looks at Trevor, her eyes pained and confused.

"No." Trevor tries to take her in his arms gently and she pulls away. He stands there, giving her a little space.

"How do I know he didn't hurt you? How do I know that," he gestures to the lump on her head, "wasn't done by him? I swear if I ever find out he's hurt you…" He leaves the threat hanging between them.

"He didn't. I told you. If you won't take me home then I'll walk."

She goes to the door, hoping beyond hope for – what? She doesn't know. *Do I want Trevor to sweep me up and refuse to let me go? Do I want him to take me home to Ryan? Do I want him to let me walk out of here? Do I even want to go home to Ryan?*

*If I start walking, I can keep walking. Vanish.*

She puts her shoes on and opens the door, stepping out with one last look back. She starts walking down the walkway towards the street.

Trevor puts his shoes on in a hurry, grabbing his keys, and runs out after her. He catches up with her easily.

"Okay, I'll take you home," he pauses, "if you are sure that's what you want."

"I want to go home."

They get in his truck and sit in awkward silence for the drive. They pull up in the street a few houses down from Elaine's house, sitting there in silence.

Trevor leans in to kiss her and Elaine pulls away, making him miss. She gives him a guilty look and gets out. It takes everything she has to not look back.

She pauses before opening the door and stepping inside the house.

Trevor's face twists into a sneer of joyful malice the moment the house door closes behind Elaine.

"Almost had her that time." He chuckles and drives away.

Elaine pauses outside the door. She almost doesn't open it. Almost turns and runs back to Trevor's truck. *It's late and Ryan will probably be waiting. Worried. Angry?*

An icy finger of fear slides down her back. She has to make herself move. Open the door. Step inside.

Ryan is standing there. He turns to look at her. His face is full of fear and confusion.

"Where were you?" he asks angrily, his face hardening to match his voice.

She blinks, unsure what to say.

Ryan takes a step towards her, his body language aggressive, his muscles tense.

Elaine tenses. He sees the flash of fear in her eyes, and it cuts him like a knife stabbing him in the heart. He can't keep the pain from his eyes.

"I won't hurt you." He hates that he feels like he has to reassure her. She should know that he could never hurt her. He tries to control his voice. "I'm sorry. I sounded angry. I was worried when you weren't here; when you didn't come home. I thought-."

"I-I just needed a little time." She looks down. She can't meet his eyes. A guilty flush rises up her neck, staining her cheeks.

"You were with him." Ryan can't keep the edge of resentment out of his voice.

"Yes." It comes out barely perceptible.

Ryan is itching to step closer. He holds himself in check.

"It's okay. I understand."

Elaine looks up in surprise. Her disbelief is tempered by the fear still gripping her.

Ryan struggles to keep himself calm.

"I know you've been seeing him."

"It's not like that. He's just a friend."

Ryan shakes his head. *No, he isn't just a friend. I don't trust him.*

"He is not your friend. Can't you see that?" His eyes are begging.

She flushes. She knows. He wants more.

"I know about Jason too. He was waiting for me." He watches her reaction.

Elaine gives him a startled look. "What does he want?"

"We have to move again." *He found us and now we aren't safe. You are not safe. Cassie isn't safe.*

He finally dares to step closer to her, hesitantly taking her in his arms. "You know I will always keep you safe. I will never let anyone hurt you."

She leans into his embrace, taking comfort from it, at the same time feeling guilt rush through her with a force that makes her knees weak.

He kisses the top of her head and she winces, stiffening.

"What's wrong?" He pulls away to study her face.

"My head," she touches it lightly. "I guess I fainted when I saw him out there."

Concerned, he looks her head over, finding the lump and wincing with sympathy as he gently prods it.

"Are you okay?" He looks her in the eyes.

"I have to leave for that job tomorrow. But I can stay if you need me to," he says apologetically.

She wants more than anything to tell him to stay. "I'll be fine," she says instead.

Ryan nods. "I want you to promise me you will stay away from Trevor while I'm gone." He swallows a hard lump in his throat. "I don't want to lose you. I need you."

"You won't lose me to him."

It's not the promise he wants, but it will have to do.

They dress for bed in uncomfortable silence, an endless gulf of unsaid things between them. When they crawl into bed, turning off the lights, he pulls her close, wrapping his arms around her, a comforting embrace for them both.

"While I'm on the road I'll see about relocating us. I am afraid it means we will have to get new identities too."

Elaine says nothing, staring into the darkness in silence.

*I'll also have to see if I can find out where Cassie is,* Ryan thinks.

"I love you," he murmurs.

They both lay for a long time staring into the darkness, each alone with their own thoughts.

In the morning he is gone before she wakes up.

# 37 Michael Visits Anderson

Ryan parks his truck in front of a generic L-shaped building. He sits there studying it. The building is a nursing home.

His job is done; he met with Anderson, and came away from that meeting convinced the man has it in for him. Now he has something else he needs to do.

"You weren't easy to find. I've been looking for you for a very long time. Years."

He looks down, consulting a list hand-written on lined notebook paper. He gives a dry chuckle. There is no humour in it, only anticlimax.

"All these years I've searched for his family; ever since I ran away, hiding and running and searching. It feels kind of empty now that I found you.

Bayburry Street Geriatric Home. Marjory McAllister. That dive of an apartment. William McAllister. Cranbrook Nursing Home. The one and only, the original, The Anderson. William McAllister's Anderson.

There is only one I haven't found yet, his sister, Sophie. If anyone knows where she is, it's you, old man.

He didn't think I would figure it out. Where would Jason McAllister hide her? Where would he think Cassie would be safe? Who does he trust, who isn't locked away in a home? Who doesn't hate him? Sophie.

Okay old man, let's see if I can make you talk."

He gets out of his truck, walking up the sidewalk and into the nursing home.

Behind him, a block down the street, someone shifts inside a car. A car door opens, closing a moment later. Footsteps follow at a calm steady pace up the sidewalk towards the nursing home. A second door opens and closes and another pair of footsteps join the first.

Inside the nursing home an empty reception desk waits. The place sounds busy, the sounds of elderly men and women echo up the hall.

Ryan looks around, shrugs, and starts exploring.

The problem is I have no idea what he looks like or what name he would be registered under. Would he use his real name? Probably not, so it wouldn't help me if I knew it.

As he explores, he notices one elderly man who keeps staring at him, his eyes level and strong. It jangles his nerves.

He approaches the old man, who doesn't bother to get up.

"Do I know you?"

The old man stares up at him in silence for an interminably long time. Just when Ryan is about to give up and walk away, he speaks.

"David McAllister."

Ryan feels the warmth drain from his face. He turns pale; blinking at the old man whose steady stare makes him want to hide.

"Anderson?"

The old man gives a slight nod. "Anderson? You have me mistaken for someone else, young man."

Ryan looks around quickly and pulls up another chair, leaning in to speak without being overheard.

"You know who I am. Do you know why I am here?"

"To make trouble." The old man does not smile.

"I want to know where Sophie McAllister is."

The old man leans back. "I don't know who that is."

Ryan leans in further. "You are lying. You know the McAllisters very well. You and they go back a long way. I know how it works. Anderson is a relationship for life. A true until death do you part marriage. You kept in touch with them. You know where Sophie is."

"Why do you want to find Sophie? You've never even met her."

"That's where you are wrong." Ryan stops, staring at the old man. A look of realization comes over his face.

"She is not there anymore. She moved on." Anderson's face is a wrinkled mask of blandness.

But Ryan saw that momentary flash of worry. He smiles.

"Never mind." Ryan starts getting up.

Anderson's age-withered hand snaps out with surprising speed, grabbing him by the front of his shirt with more strength than Ryan would have given the old man credit for. He leans in.

"I have worked with little pissants like you. You are no good. Something inside you is broken, ugly and wrong. You stay away from them. You will only bring death to anyone near you," he hisses, his voice raspy with age and anger.

He pulls Ryan closer, whispering harshly at him.

"You were followed."

"How do you know?"

"Because I'm not stupid."

Ryan only smiles at the dig.

The old man's lips tighten. "Get out of here before they see you. They don't know you are here."

Ryan looks up, looking out the window in time to see Detective Jim McNelly's large frame pass by, followed by the tall skinny reporter, Lawrence Hawkworth.

"Is everything all right?" one of the nurses asks, coming closer and eyeing Ryan suspiciously.

"I'll see you later, Anderson." Ryan turns, nods to the nurse, and makes a quick exit.

Jim is at the reception, flashing his badge and talking to a nurse and an orderly. Lawrence is standing next to him looking around. They turn just as the door closes behind Ryan.

Jim and Lawrence walk through the facility, looking at withered old faces.

Anderson turns around, facing away from them.

"Who is this guy we are looking for?" Jim asks.

"I don't know. One of my sources told me he is a person of interest to us."

"Who is your source?" Jim asks it knowing that Lawrence never reveals his sources.

"You will never believe it," Lawrence grins. "One retired Sheriff Rick Dalton."

Jim stops and stares at him. "You found him."

"Yes sir, I did."

"So, what's the story on this guy?"

"When all this stuff was going down, the young women and teens going missing and found dead, the whole town deciding William McAllister was the killer. . ."

"Yeah, the whole lynch mob running the McAllisters out of town. Sounds like a bad western."

"Dalton didn't believe William McAllister was the killer. He didn't peg him as the type. But he was convinced William McAllister was guilty of something. He just didn't know what."

"And then the McAllisters vanished."

"Yes, but not before pointing Dalton in the right direction to catch the killer. The note was left anonymously, but he knew it was William. The killer was caught and sent to prison for life. End of story."

"Except Dalton couldn't let it go." McNelly knows the feeling all too well. It's what keeps him up at night, turning his stomach into a sour cesspool of acid. It drives him to drink too much, smoke too much, and eat too much crap that should not touch the inside of any man's stomach.

Lawrence nods. "He couldn't let it go. With the McAllisters gone, he searched the farm. When he found nothing, he searched it again, more thoroughly."

He pauses.

"He showed it to me."

"What?"

"It was an unidentifiable little lump. It looked like someone tried to burn it in the wood stove. He never sent it anywhere for testing, never told anyone, but Dalton was convinced it was a trophy. He was convinced it was a bone fragment, a piece of Amy Dodds."

"The little girl?" Jim's eyebrows rise in surprise.

"Dalton didn't pin that one on William either. Too clumsy he said. He thought William was too smart for that. He was convinced that was Jason's doing; probably his first victim, and that his mother tried to cover it up."

"That's exactly what we suspected too, that the girl was Jason's first victim. His first taste of blood as a kid, his own friend."

"Rick Dalton couldn't let go of his idea that William McAllister was guilty of something big; even after he retired."

"A retired sheriff has a lot of time on his hands." Jim stares at Lawrence for a minute. "Let's find this person of interest. I want to know what he has to say."

They continue their search, matching faces to a grainy copy of a photo of a man much too young for a nursing home that they studied in the car before coming in. Lawrence stops, tapping Jim and pointing. Jim looks and nods. They go to one of the nurses they talked to earlier.

"That's him, what's his name?" Jim points the old man out.

"That is Mr. Richard Andrews. Funny, you are his second visitors today. He never gets visitors."

"Who were the other visitors? Family?"

"Mr. Andrews doesn't have any family."

"So who came to see him then?"

"He never signed in. He just kind of walked in. He walked around like you did, like he was looking for someone he didn't know. They talked. It got heated, and he left. Odd thing was he called Mr. Andrews Anderson."

"What did this visitor look like?"

"He was a younger man."

Jim puts up a finger, stopping the nurse while he fishes in his pocket. He pulls out a photograph and shows it to him.

The nurse studies the mug shot of the smiling clean shaved young man with his hair cut short, Michael Underwood.

"That's him. His hair is a bit longer."

"Michael Underwood," Jim mutters with a scowl as if the name tastes bad on his tongue.

"Thanks," he says to the nurse, dismissing him. He turns and walks purposely towards the old man, his bulk threatening to barrel through anyone and anything that gets in his way. Lawrence has no problem keeping up with his long legs.

They stop, standing over the thin old man.

After a long moment of making them wait, Anderson slowly looks up.

"Mr. Andrews?" Jim stares down at him.

"Yes." Anderson stares back at him with cold intelligence.

There is no loss of sharpness in this old codger's mind, Jim thinks.

"What is your connection to the McAllisters?"

"I don't believe I know any McAllisters."

Jim pulls out the photo, showing it to him.

"This man was just here visiting you. How do you know him?"

"I don't know that young man."

Jim's lips tighten. I know you are lying old man.

"Michael Underwood. You don't know the name?"

"No."

"You know the face. He was just here. You had a heated conversation."

"I'm afraid not." Anderson doesn't break his cool composure. He has nothing to fear from the fat detective. There is only one man who he has ever felt a reason to fear.

"William McAllister. He is old like you."

"Doesn't ring a bell." Anderson lets his lips pull back in a small smile. He knows the detective is just fishing.

"Jason McAllister? Marjory?"

"No." Anderson casually shakes his head once.

As Jim questions the old man, Lawrence focuses on the home, the residents, the little details, feeling the place out.

An image comes to him. A boy, thin and hungry and dirty. He is talking to an older woman. She could be his grandmother. A young woman comes briskly around a corner of the house. She looks angry.

"This is David," the older woman says. "He came-"

"I know why he came," the young woman interrupts. She stops, staring at the boy, hands on her hips. "Go away. You can't come here."

"I just-," the boy starts, tears in his eyes along with hopelessness.

"Go away," the young woman says again, stern.

The older woman is wringing her hands, twisting a shirt she was hanging on the clothesline. She looks at the boy, then at the younger woman.

"Sophie, we can't-."

"Sophie," Lawrence says, snapping out of it, the name David ringing in his head.

Lawrence smiles, nudging Jim. Jim turns to him.

"He is looking for Sophie."

Jim turns to the old man. "Why is Michael looking for Sophie McAllister? Who is she to him?"

Anderson just smiles that little smile, saying nothing.

"I know Jason McAllister has a connection to Michael Underwood. Whatever the McAllisters are to you, it doesn't matter to me. I don't care. It is Michael Underwood I'm after. Just tell me what his connection to Jason is."

Jim already knows, but he wants confirmation.

No response, just the small smile, Anderson staring him down unflinching.

"What is his connection to Sophie?"

Silence.

"Where is Sophie?"

Silence.

"Look, if Michael is looking for her, she is in danger. He is connected to Jason, and he is a serial killer. You are not protecting Sophie by not speaking. You are putting her in danger."

Silence.

"This is no use," Jim mutters, turning away in frustration.

"We will find her on our own," he spats back at the old man, walking away. Lawrence follows him out.

When they get to the car, they both get in and sit there, deciding where to go next.

"We have to find out why Michael went to see the old man and why he is looking for Sophie McAllister," Jim says.

"That is not hard to guess," Lawrence says. "Sophie is Jason's sister."

Jim looks at him.

"What do you do when you want to find someone who is missing?" Lawrence asks.

"You talk to their family."

"Right. Let's go find Sophie. Any idea how?"

Jim starts the car. "Let's see if Beth found anything yet. If there is a record trace anywhere there is a computer, she will find it."

"You check with her. Drop me off at home. I have a few things I need to follow up on."

# 38 Looking for the Kid

Jason parks in front of the rooming house. It feels like he hasn't been back here in a long time. He gets out and walks to the front steps, noting that the grass has not been cut since he left. He mounts the steps. They creak under his weight. He sidesteps the soft spot on the porch, opening the door and going in. He is immediately assaulted by the foul stench of old garbage.

"Buggers couldn't even take the trash out," he mutters.

He looks in the living room, finding no signs the kid has been there. *Either the kid is doing what I said and leaving no signs he is here, or he hasn't come back.*

Jason goes upstairs, the stairs making the now familiar creaks and groans when he puts his weight on the right stairs. The country music is conspicuously absent.

He enters his room, looking around. The room looks undisturbed, but that does not mean much. There was little there to disturb. The bag with the boy's belongings, the books and phone that he gave him, still sits where he left it along with the note. He picks up the note, reading the jagged scrawl again.

"If I'm not here the white van people got me." He can feel the kid's terror in those words.

He puts the note down and heads back towards the stairs. A man he doesn't recognize comes out of the bathroom. He looks at Jason out of the corner of his eyes, careful not to make eye contact, and slips into The Cowboy's room.

*Looks like The Cowboy has moved on.* He isn't surprised at the fast turnover of the room.

Jason stops in the kitchen, looking at the locked basement door. He takes a step back and kicks it with the flat of his foot. The door slams open with a crunch of the lock hasp screws tearing out of the wood and the loud bang of it hitting the wall with force.

He glances up at the ceiling. There is no sound from above. As expected, no one will bother investigating the loud noise. These kinds of people don't get into other people's business.

The basement is in darkness. He flips the switch, turning the light on, and goes down. He stops at the bottom of the stairs, looking around at the cavernous emptiness of a basement one would expect to house remnants or former residents and who knows what other refuse the landlord tossed down here instead of hauling to the dump.

It had been cleared out, but there are enough scraps left behind to confirm his suspicion. Someone was set up down here doing surveillance.

Jason goes back to his room, snatching up the note again, reading it again.

"If I'm not here the white van people got me."

*The white van people.*

"What does the kid know about the white van?"

Across the street from the rooming house the curtain in an upstairs window shifts, pulling back a little and drops back into place.

Nathan throws himself backwards, banging against the wall and dropping down to a low crouch, scuttling to the corner of the dark room. The only light is what comes in through the little open door in the homemade cardboard and papier-mâché covering the window.

Nathan's long hair is tangled and greasy, his face unshaved, and his eyes wild with an animal fear. His clothes hang off his emaciated frame, his cheeks hollow and eyes bulging from their sunken sockets, making the dark circles under them darker.

He rolls his eyes to stare at the little opening giving access to the window.

He sobs and moans piteously.

Bracing himself for it, he lunges at the window, the light touching his arm and face, searing his flesh and making him scream. He stares in rapt horror, seeing his flesh smoke and crisp, melting under the onslaught like a candle melts beneath the flame.

He flips the little door closed, blocking out the light, and retreats back to his corner, sinking to the floor and cradling his ruined arm while he weeps.

"NO. NO. NO. NONONONONONONONOnonoooo."

He leaps up, scrambling to another wall, frantically snatching up sheets of newspaper and tinfoil and plastering them with white liquid from a bucket. He pastes them to the walls, rushing back for more, adding another layer. The walls are already wallpapered with many layers of newspaper and tinfoil papier-mâché.

He doesn't know why he does it. He only knows he must. The shiny metallic foil blocks out the radio signals coming from the radio towers and satellites. The words on the newsprint block in the demons writhing inside his head.

He can feel them in there now, writhing torturously, screaming and clawing, trying to get out.

He moves on to the window, putting too much pressure and feeling the false wall of newsprint and foil move, indenting in under his hand. He screams, clawing at it frantically.

"It can't touch the glass! If it touches the glass it will shatter and they will get in!" He digs his nails in, pulling it back, flattening the indent.

He falls back with relief, gasping and panting. He claps both hands over his mouth and nose, holding them tight and looking at the window in a panic.

*Don't breath! Don't breath! It will hear you!*

*It' is the man across the street. If it hears him, it might sneak up on the house.*

"It's back. How? How did it do it?"

Trembling so hard it takes him three tries to pick it up; he snatches up his special suit for going outside, pulling it on with shaking hands. He pulls on the pants, then the jacket, zipping it up. His special suit is a track suit with newspaper and tinfoil stapled to it, covering every inch of the old worn suit he had gotten from a shelter when he was homeless.

That was before Nathan's mother found him and brought him home.

He pulls on rubber boots, newsprint and foil glued to them, including the soles. Finally, he puts on his helmet. It is his masterpiece, his own design. It started as a lamp shade for one of the lamps downstairs. Now it protects him from the beams, rays, and mind controlling wavelengths. It also traps the monsters inside his head, freezing them and allowing him to think more clearly. Last, he puts on large oven mitts made of a shiny silver fabric. He feels braver now that he is dressed in his protective suit.

Ready, he clomps down the stairs noisily. The extra noise chases out the spirits hiding under the stairs.

Reaching the door, Nathan pauses long enough to call out, "I'm going out Mom, back in a bit."

The elderly woman sitting in the darkened living room doesn't answer. The lights are all off and heavy curtains drawn closed, blocking out the light outside.

He fumbles with the latch with the big mitts on, finally getting it open. He blinks against the searing white hot light of the sun on his eyes. With a quick look to make sure it's safe, he covers his eyes with his mitted hands to protect them and dashes out from the safety of his doorway, sprinting across the street and taking the steps of the rooming house two at a time. He plasters himself against the door, breathing heavily, trying to get his panting under control, his tongue lolling out like a dog.

With deliberate slowness, Ryan quietly opens the door and slips outside the nursing home, closing it behind him.

He smiles as he slips safely out of the building.

"I know where to find Sophie. He's wrong, I did meet her. It's time to pay my Aunt Sophie a visit."

Jason comes down the stairs.

*What do I do? There has to be a way to get the kid back, if he's still alive. He's innocent. He knows nothing. No, that's not true. His note, what is this about people in a white van? His writing is sloppy, hurried. Scared. Is that our people after him or someone else? He didn't strike me as a druggie, but it could be a gang or dealer trying to recruit him.*

He reaches the hallway outside the living room entrance and stops in his tracks. He turns and gapes at the strangest sight he has ever seen. A wild looking man dressed in newspaper and tin foil is standing just inside the living room staring at him with crazy eyes.

In shock, he reacts and braces himself a moment too late.

With a strange low animal sound, the crazy looking man launches through the doorway and is on him, wrapping his long arms and legs around him. The sudden collision and weight sends them crashing down, bouncing hard against the wall and rolling on the floor. The strange lamp-hat goes flying, rattling as it rolls away. The newspaper and foil covering his suit tear easily, becoming ruined.

Jason fights to break free but the man is impossibly strong, the adrenaline surging through his veins giving him super-human strength. He grapples at him, trying to get a hold of him, to punch and kick him. He slams his forehead against his attacker's face, trying to knock him in the nose and blind him, sending searing pain shooting through his own head when he misses and collides with the top of his skull instead.

Jason manages to get his feet under him, bracing his back against the wall and breaking his attacker's double arm and leg bear hug. He pushes up, pushing his attacker off. On his feet now, he tries to deflect another lunge.

His attacker's single-minded purpose wins. Moving with shocking speed, he has his hands on Jason's throat, squeezing his airway and screaming "HOW HOW HOW HOWHOWHOWHOW" over and over in an endless chant.

Jason fights to break his grip and fails. His air cut off, he weakens fast, his head feeling like it's swelling, his face reddening. His mouth opens and his tongue bulges out, desperate for air. His knees start bending. He is slowly going down.

Blackness is closing in and Jason flails, punching blindly. A wild swing strikes a lucky blow, hitting his attacker in the side of the neck, compressing the carotid artery which sends a sudden shock to his brain, making Nathan fall suddenly limp. Nathan hits the floor like a discarded rag doll, his weight taking Jason down with him.

Coughing for air, Jason struggles to roll him off. He gets to his feet.

"What the hell was that?"

Angry, he gives the prone figure a few hard kicks. He looks around quickly for something to tie him up with.

The lamp cords. He starts for the living room, making it as far as two steps inside the doorway when he hears his attacker already coming to. Without any thought for anything but keeping him down long enough to tie him up, he pounces for the nearest lamp, snatching it up and roughly tearing the cord from the wall socket.

Jason runs quickly back into the hallway and brings the lamp down on his attacker's face. Nathan looks up at him with wide eyes just in time to see the growing lamp coming down at him.

Jason pulls it back again, striking him a few more times in the head, making Nathan slump down unconscious again, blood trickling from his head now.

He turns the lamp over and savagely rips the cord out, using it to tie Nathan's hands behind his back, wrapping it so tight his skin his pulled in and slightly wrinkled, cutting off the circulation to his hands. He rips the cord out of the other lamp, using it to tie his feet. He looks around for something else to use before his attacker regains consciousness.

Finding nothing else, he yanks the T.V. forward and rips the cord out from the T.V. It takes four tries, yanking it violently, before it tears free. He ties one end around the man's neck like a leash.

Grunting, he struggles to drag the unconscious man to the stairs, propping him against the stair wall with the inner railing running up the open steps, he ties the other end off on one of the vertical rungs above, turning the cord into a noose. He checks to make sure the man can still breathe.

The now secured attacker is coming to, blinking his eyes, disoriented. His eyes come into focus and he sees Jason.

Jason stands over him, staring down at him in disgust.

"What the hell are you?"

"A-a-a-a-aa—aaaa—a," is all that comes out. Nathan stares up at Jason in wild-eyed terror.

Jason kicks him, making him grunt from the force.

"I asked you a question. What the hell are you supposed to be? Why did you attack me?"

"Ha-ha-ha-hu-hu-hu." It's an unhappy stuttering sound.

"You can't talk? You can't make words?"

"Ha-ha-ha-how? How?" Nathan's vocal paralysis breaks. "How can you? You-you were the man. Then you were the boy. But I got you. I locked you up safe, trapped you."

Nathan twitches with the need to tap his head, but his hands are tied painfully tight behind his back.

Jason leans over him, looming. "What about the boy?"

"Weak, weak, you are weak as the boy. The boy is weak. I got you. I fixed you. You can't change, Changeling. You can't leave the boy form. How did you get free? How did you be the man again?"

"You got the kid? You took him?"

"Y-yes, the boy, you. You are weak as the boy."

Jason looks at his prisoner more closely. "You are bloody nuts, aren't you? Crazy."

Nathan shakes his head, discovering he can't move much, that his neck is tied. He tries to look up. He scrunches his face like he's in pain.

"Augh," he moans. "I can feel them. I can feel them in there, trying to get out."

"Who?"

"The demons."

"The demons?"

Nathan groans again. "Yes, they do terrible things when they get out. They want out to do bad things. I can hear them."

"How do you know they didn't already get out?" Jason smirks at him cruelly.

"I can't hear them anymore. I can't hear them if they're not in my head. I know. I know what they do when they get out. They whisper to me about it inside my head when they come back."

Nathan tries to look around frantically.

"My hat, I need my hat. To lock them in, keep them quiet."

Jason remembers the messed up lampshade his attacker wore and fetches it.

"This hat?"

"Yes, yes, I need it."

Nathan sighs with relief when Jason puts it on his head.

"Now talk, you psycho freak. What did you do with the kid?"

"You know, you, him, augh." Nathan grimaces in an expression of agony. "My suit, the beams, the signals, they're getting through."

Jason kneels in front of him. Nathan watches Jason deliberately reach towards him with one hand, pinching a piece of foil in his fingers and pealing it off."

"NOOO!!!" Nathan shrieks wildly.

Jason stops, still holding the foil. "Then talk. What did you do with the boy? Did you kill him?"

"No. No no no no." He shakes his head vehemently.

"Where is he?"

"B-b-basement."

"What basement? Where?"

"M-m-my house. Ac-c-cross the s-s-street."

Jason studies him for a moment, thinking.

"What do you mean I became the boy?"

Nathan gapes at him. Of course he should know this. Is it a trick? I need to be careful, or he'll take my soul and make me one of him too. Like vampires.

"Y-y-you are o-o-one of them. A ch-ch-changeling. A m-m-monster. I saw you. You l-l-looked out the window upstairs, a man. Th-then you looked out, b-b-but you were a b-b-boy."

Jason nods, understanding now. *This guy is a bona fide lunatic.*

"If you hurt that kid, I'll put a hurt on you like you can't even imagine."

Jason gets up, starts to turn, and changes his mind. Facing his prisoner, he takes the lampshade hat off his head. He holds it between them, studying it.

Nathan looks up at him with wide eyes filled with desperation. "M-m-my hat, I need it," he mewls like a small child.

"This hat?"

"Y-y-yes."

Jason puts it on the floor before him and winks at Nathan. He deliberately stomps on it, crushing it to Nathan's horror.

Staring at his ruined hat, Nathan's mouth opens wide and he screams, the shrieks tearing violently from his throat, spittle flying, screech after agonized screech.

"Shut up or I'll rip all that crap off you," Jason says in a low dangerous voice.

Nathan shuts up, whimpering.

"Take me to him." Jason loosens the cord on Nathan's feet just enough to let him take small steps and unties the cord from the stair railing, roughly yanking him to his feet.

# 39 Trevor Mitchell is Mr. Miller

Ryan pulls into the gravel lot of a diner that seems to have been dropped randomly in the middle of nowhere, his truck bouncing and rolling over the potholes. He parks on the far end of the lot, gets out, and starts walking towards the diner.

Inside, a man sits at a booth towards the back away from the door and against a window.

He is middle-aged with thinning hair cut in a businessman style. He is wearing a cheap suit jacket, trousers, dress shirt with the top two buttons undone, and no tie.

Ryan's temporary Anderson.

Anderson watches the truck pull in, park, and Ryan get out, approaching the diner. A wry smile creases his lips as he watches. It does not reach his eyes. He turns his attention back to his coffee when Ryan reaches the door, pretending to be uninterested in the man entering.

Ryan enters the diner, pauses to look around, and heads for the booth. He slides in across from Anderson, nodding a greeting.

He looks agitated, Anderson thinks. He's uptight. He smiles inwardly, enjoying this.

"I wasn't sure you were going to show up," Anderson says, not looking up.

"I've been busy," Ryan says noncommittally.

"I know."

They pause with the arrival of the waitress to take Ryan's order and fill his coffee cup, resuming once she is out of earshot.

"There is another job lined up," Anderson says, casually sipping his coffee. "There shouldn't be anything unexpected. Mr. Miller is experienced."

Ryan stirs sugar into his coffee and takes a sip, grimacing at the painful burn of the too hot coffee.

"Is everything else going okay?" Anderson watches him, evaluating his body language.

Ryan hesitates, weighing whether or not to bring up the subject of bringing Elaine in to accompany him on his jobs. He quickly decides against it. It's too soon.

*I don't trust this guy, Anderson,* he decides. Something about him just puts him off.

"Everything is fine." Ryan thinks about what Jason told him. He trusts Anderson even less.

*He is probably weighing and judging me right now. He'll report back to his boss, his Anderson, whatever he's called. Then they'll decide if I live or die. I can run. I can go home, get Elaine and disappear. No, they'll find us. You don't walk away. You don't run away. There is nowhere you can go that they won't find you.*

"I think we need a few more moves before we can settle down. A few more identity changes, then we can settle down for good." Ryan decides his best chance is putting them at the mercy of the organization. With their help, they can vanish forever under new aliases. Without their help, they can vanish, but they'll be hunted.

*All those years on the run, and Jason always found me. How? It had to be them. They keep tabs on everyone. Hell, they knew where I've been, who I've been, in the years I dropped off the grid. When I finally contacted them, they already knew.*

Anderson nods from across the table. He was expecting this. *Michael and his girlfriend are already invisible to the rest of the world.*

*Almost invisible, except from us. You can't hide from the organization. It's about time he learned that and accepted it.*

"We can have that arranged. It's good. I think I have a new manager for you." Anderson smiles for the first time. It's not a friendly smile, more smug. "You know where to find the details of the new job."

"I do."

"We will meet again after it's done."

Ryan nods, leaving money on the table for his bill and an average tip as he gets up. He doesn't look back as he walks out despite the itch in his back to turn around.

Anderson watches out the window as Ryan gets back in his truck and drives away. "This will be interesting."

Ryan pulls up in front of the house. Getting out, he walks to the door, hesitating before opening it.

*Is she here? Or will she be with him?*

He opens the door and steps in. The house is quiet and no one comes to greet him. With his heart heavy, he goes to the bedroom to pack for the trip. He feels stiff, like he has slept for too long without moving.

Grabbing his bag, he carries it out and drops it by the front door. He heads to the kitchen to pack some sandwiches.

Ryan steps into the kitchen and stops.

Elaine is there, sitting at the kitchen table. She avoids looking at him.

"Hi," he says, feeling like there is a huge gulf between them that he is not welcome to cross. The emotional distance is like a physical force separating them.

"Hi." She still doesn't look at him.

Ryan fidgets uncertainly, then moves further in, going to the fridge and pulling out stuff to make sandwiches. He looks at her when he grabs a loaf of bread.

"Are you hungry?" he asks, starting on the sandwiches.

"No."

"I'll make you one anyway." He continues to work, the silence between them maddening. He stops before he's finished, turning to her.

"I'm sorry. Whatever it is, I'm sorry. I'm sorry for dragging you away, running away. For changing your identity and not letting you see your mom. I'm sorry for not being around enough, for- for having to take these jobs out of town. I'm sorry for everything."

*Are you sorry for kidnapping me? For keeping me a prisoner in your stinking root cellar?* Elaine feels the words in her mind like an acute pain. *Are you sorry for murdering those women? For Cassie? For that woman in the hospital, Jane Doe, who you thought was her? Are you sorry that you are still looking for her? Or that you will never find her because you killed her a long time ago?*

*Trevor hasn't hurt anyone. I don't have to be afraid he will go crazy and kill me, talking to his dead sister who is not there.*

She feels the fear, but it's clouded with doubt and guilt. *Michael would never hurt me.* The thought comes unwanted and she pushes it away. *Yes, he could,* she reminds herself.

She says nothing, only looking down at the cold half-empty coffee in front of her. She stopped drinking it hours ago.

Ryan looks at her nervously. "You know I have another one of those jobs. I told you. I need to leave soon." He pauses. "I wish I could take you with me. Soon. I'll be able to take you soon."

He stops, swallows, trying to think of how to say the next part.

"When I come back, we'll be moving again."

Elaine stiffens.

"I'll get a new job. We'll find a better house, new identities."

Elaine finally looks up at him. She is torn. Part of her wants Ryan to take her away from Trevor and the confusing emotions conflicting her feelings between the two men in her life. She blinks. Suddenly she does not want Trevor taken away. She does not want Ryan deciding her life for her, where she lives, trapped in the house alone and not allowed to go out because of his fear they will be caught. Deciding who she is.

Ryan steps closer to her. He pulls a chair closer and sits, taking her hands in his. He looks down. He can't see the reaction in her eyes.

"I know you've been seeing him. I know," he swallows, "you've developed feelings for him. But I know you still have feelings for me too. I don't want to lose you. We can still have what we talked about. A peaceful life. No more running or hiding. We can still get married, have kids."

Elaine is shaking her head slowly.

"It's not too late," Ryan says.

"I don't know what I want," Elaine finally manages.

A heavy sigh escapes Ryan. His shoulders slump and he nods.

"I understand. Maybe this trip is good. It will give you some time alone to think."

He finishes making his sandwiches, wrapping and bagging them with a couple water bottles, and leaving a sandwich for her. He picks them up and starts walking out of the kitchen, stopping in the doorway to take one last look at her.

*She's so beautiful, sitting there. Sad and beautiful. Somehow, I'll make this right.*

"I love you," he whispers and leaves.

Elaine doesn't look up. She doesn't say a word, doesn't get up to see him off. She just sits there staring at her cold half-empty coffee. Tears start sliding down her cheeks.

Ryan pulls up outside an old motel. It is the kind of place you would stay only because it is marginally better than sleeping in the ruined ashes that remain of the other fleabag motel after it burned down. It will look even bleaker in the daylight, the worst of it hidden by the dark night.

He has been on the road for two days, sleeping in only short catnaps before hitting the road again. Exhaustion pulls at him, making his head so heavy he can barely hold it up. This is where he is to meet Mr. Miller tomorrow.

He studies the place. There is only one car in the lot, parked near the office.

He takes a slow drive around the motel, casing it out. There is not a single room light on. If anyone is staying in any of the rooms, they are either out or gone to bed.

"Probably nobody but Mr. Miller is desperate enough to stay in this dump."

Ryan swings the truck back around to the road and drives off the road and across the shallow ditch, finding a secluded spot to park behind the bushes on the edge. He can still see anyone coming up the road in either direction and the front of the motel.

Shutting off the engine, he sits to wait and watch.

"Wake up David. Wake up."

Ryan blinks his eyes groggily. "Huh?" Exhaustion makes the sleep cling to him in a fog of confusion.

"David, you have to wake up."

He rubs his eyes, righting himself from his slouched position, and looks around.

Little Cassie is sitting in the passenger seat looking up at him with a serious expression.

The sun is up, the bright light glinting off the paint of the truck. Anyone driving by would have seen it glinting in the trees.

He tries to shake the sleep out of his head.

"What time is it?"

"Daytime," Cassie says helpfully.

"No, what time is it?" Ryan looks at his watch. He relaxes. "Still time."

Cassie looks at him. "You should go now."

"Why? The meeting isn't for a few hours."

She points through the trees to the motel.

There is a second car parked there now.

"Maybe you are right. I should take a look around. It will give me a chance to stretch my legs."

Ryan gets out and walks through the trees towards the motel. He does a full walk around the building, returning to the truck and getting in.

"It looks all right. I can't tell what room he's in from where the car is parked."

"You are going to see Auntie Sophie after this aren't you?"

"Yes."

"I wish you wouldn't. She probably doesn't want to see you anyway. Besides, she doesn't know where I am."

"I think she does."

"She won't tell you, David."

"Stop calling me that." His jaw clenches.

Lawrence's buzzer rings. He is on his couch surrounded by boxes and stacks of papers and files. He tries to avoid knocking any over as he gets up, stepping high to step over them, and fails. A pile leans, tips, and falls, sending files and papers skittering across the floor.

The buzzer rings again, impatiently. He reaches the door, punching the buzzer button on the wall with his thumb, holding it down to silence the noise.

"Yeah," he calls into the speaker on the wall.

"McNelly here," the voice crackles through the speaker.

Without another word, Lawrence presses the other button, sounding the buzzer below and releasing the lock.

He starts unlocking the locks on the door, finishing and watching out the peephole for the fat detective to come lumbering to his door.

He opens the door just as Jim is reaching for it, stepping back and waving him in.

"You've been busy," Jim says, taking in the mountain of boxes that has grown since he was here last. It feels like months, although it has been only days.

Lawrence closes the door, locking just a few of the locks.

"I see you added some," Jim nods towards the door.

"Can't be too safe," Lawrence frowns. "Did Beth find her?"

Jim smiles. "Of course she did. She's Beth."

"You should ask her out," Lawrence says, heading for the kitchen. "Coffee?"

"You got anything stronger?"

"I might."

Jim listens to the sound of plinking and Lawrence comes back with two glasses of ice and a bottle of rye whiskey. "Turpentine?"

"Absolutely. So what's all this?" He indicates the files.

"I'm looking for something."

"Are you ready for a road trip to visit Sophie McAllister?"

"Have the DNA results come back yet?"

"It's too soon. It could take a few weeks yet. I tried to push a rush on it, but they move in their own time."

Lawrence pours them both a glass, handing one to Jim. Jim grimaces as he swallows a mouthful.

Ryan takes one last drive around the motel, scouting it out, before he parks his truck on the side of the building. Getting out, he looks left and right before walking around the side away from the front office and around the corner to the front. He stops in front of the designated room number, takes a slow deep breath, and knocks.

His heart is pounding in his chest while he waits. The door opens. He looks up and staggers back.

Jason's pulse races and his heart pounds. If anyone is watching, if just one neighbour or passerby sees, they will call the police. The kid might not have time for him to worry about that.

Jason waited until night when the cover of darkness will help, and most people are sleeping.

Gripping the T.V. cord leash tight, wrapping it around his hand so his prisoner can't pull it free from his grasp, he opens the front door and shoves Nathan out ahead of him. Nathan wobbles, only able to take small steps with his feet hobbled to keep him from running or kicking. Jason has to help him down the steps.

"All right, lead the way. Where's the kid?"

Nathan winces and moans with the white hot agony of the stars shooting little pinpricks of light through him like little daggers, trying to kill him.

"I need my suit," Nathan whines. "They're killing me. I have to keep myself protected when the stars are out. I have a special suit for the stars."

"Shut up and walk." Jason shoves him forward and Nathan shuffle stumbles ahead.

Nathan is looking up at the sky, praying the clouds to come in and smother the moon and stars, giving him some protection from them. He can hear the moon whispering to him in its low voice. Its voice is pale like its light, lifeless. The voice of death.

He wants to cover his ears to block it out, but his hands are still tied painfully tight behind his back.

"Shut up," he moans. "Shut up." It is whispering bad things to him, drawing in the stars, making them echo its words like a thousand voices whispering in his head. "Shut up. Shut up. Shutupshutupshutupshutup."

He starts shuffle-running across the lawn, stumbling down the curb and continues his shuffle-run across the street. Jason walks fast to keep up, letting his pathetic two-legged dog lead the way. Nathan hops up the curb on the other side onto the grass, shuffle-running across to the front door of the house. He has to crawl up the steps dragging his hobbled feet up, Jason unwilling to take the risk of giving him his feet. Nathan bangs his body against the door, unable to work the knob without hands.

Jason leans past him, opening the door, and the bound man falls into the house, hitting the floor with a thud and a grunt. He rolls away from the entrance to the darkness within, yanking Jason off balance with the cord around his neck still wrapped around Jason's hand, choking himself on his own leash.

"Close the door! Close the door!" he rasps through the cord choking him.

Jason has to let go of the cord to reach the door. He does so and his prisoner lays there panting from stress and relief, finally safe from the moon and stars.

Jason walks over to the prone figure, standing over him, and roughly kicks a grunt out of him.

"Show me the kid or I'll drag your sorry ass back outside, strip you naked, and pin you down like an insect for the sun, moon, and whatever else is out there to eat you or whatever the hell you think is going to happen."

Nathan squeals like a struck pig, his eyes widening and mouth drooling with fear. He rolls, struggling to get to his feet.

Jason bends over, grabbing him by the arms, and yanking him up.

"What the hell smells so bad in here?" Jason wrinkles his nose in disgust. He recognizes the stench. Death.

Convinced now this psycho killed the kid, he lets his prisoner lead him. He has no reason to rush now.

With the demons in his head whispering vile things to him, Nathan shuffle-walks through the house, leading Jason to the basement.

*Kill him. Push him down the stairs. Trip him on the stairs. Throw yourself down the stairs with him. The man became the boy became the man. It's evil. Evil evil evil. Kill it. Kill it. Kiiillll it before it kills you. It kills. It kills the ladies. It tortures and kills them. It enjoys killing.*

Nathan tries to not listen to the voices whispering in his head, but they are incessant, the dry paper rustle of the dead and dry leaves in the fall. The sound the dead make.

They reach the basement door.

"Down there." Nathan looks at the monster that looks like a man. A quiet calm has come over him. He blinks and the blink takes a very long time. Time has slowed, seconds ticking by like minutes, still slowing down.

*Time is about to stop. That's bad. There is only one way to stop it. If time stops, it might never start again.*

Jason opens the basement door and looks down into the darkness below. There is no sound. No stronger odour of decomposing flesh wafting up.

This feels wrong. He looks to the madman.

The monster looks down to the darkness below. It hesitates.

*It knows it belongs in the dark. It doesn't want to go. It doesn't want to go home to Hell.*

The monster begins to turn its deceitful head to look at him. Without a sound, wrapped in a quiet calm, Nathan twists his body, launching himself against the monster with as much force as he can manage with his arms tied behind his back and feet hobbled.

They crash against the doorframe, the door swinging and banging hard against the wall with the bang of wood against drywall, teetering for just a split second and almost falling backwards to the kitchen floor.

Jason tries to get his balance, teetering on the precipice of falling either way. They both fall into the open black maw of the basement stairs. He hits the stairs painfully, his captive falling with him, half on top of him, half tumbling-half sliding down the stairs together to the concrete floor below.

Jason's head cracks against the concrete with a dull wet smack. The cool hard concrete against his face is soothing in that moment before the world goes black.

Two figures skulk in the dark outside the Bayburry Street Geriatric Home. They move stiffly, hunched over, keeping to the shadows, darting from bush to tree to sign to bush, finally to the wall and plastering themselves against it.

They follow the wall down and slip around the corner, stopping at a window. One tests the window, shakes its head and they move on to try the next one. Two more windows up, they score.

The window moves with a groan in the frame with some pushing. They stop and then look around, ducking down. No one seemed to notice.

The figure goes to work on the window again. It doesn't move easily, swollen in the window frame from lack of use, but it inches up a little at a time.

With the window open, he tries to climb in. First trying to lift his leg, but can't lift it high enough. He motions at his partner, whispering. "Help me."

His partner moves in, trying to lift while he tries to pull himself up, finally getting him over the windowsill head first. His partner grips his legs, easing him down inside. He puts his hands down, feeling for the floor, taking the strain off his partner when he finds it. They ease his legs down and his partner drops them, letting him fall the rest of the way with a soft thud.

He uses the window frame to pull himself up to his feet and leans out grasping his waiting partner's hand and pulling him up. With a little difficulty, they get his partner in head first through the window too. He eases him down carefully and helps him to his feet.

They turn to the bed where an elderly woman is sleeping under a too thin blanket. The light coming in from the hall through the open door reveals the faces of two geriatric men.

William McAllister stands over his wife, looking at her for a moment before he leans in, covering her mouth gently with his hand.

She stirs, mumbles, and starts shifting.

"Sshhh, Marjory. Don't make any noise. We're getting you out of here."

Her eyes are clouded with confusion, her lids and jaw slack from the drugs that are beginning to wear off. They will be back soon to dose her again.

"What did that boy do now? What trouble did Jason get into this time?" Her words are slurred, barely understandable, her voice wavering and frail.

"Ssshh, don't talk. Come on." William reaches for her arm to help her up, but it's stuck.

Anderson moves to the other side of the bed, pulling the blanket away.

"They've got her restrained." He fumbles in the dark and gets the cuff undone, releasing her arm.

"Ugh, she's soiled herself," he complains with a grimace of disgust. He scowls, meeting William's sad eyes over her. "She deserves better than this."

William releases her other arm and they help Marjory to her feet. They get her to the door and stop. William pokes his head out, looking up and down the hall.

"It's clear. Let's go," Anderson says.

"Wait, I have something I have to do." William motions him to wait here with Marjory, out of sight.

"This is a lockdown ward. It's going to be harder to get out than the home I live in. There will be alarms on the doors. When we get out, we will have to move fast."

"All the more reason I have to do this now. There won't be any coming back after we're out that door. Give me five minutes."

William steps out to the hall, keeping against the wall, and hurries down the hall towards the secure entrance and nurses' desk.

"What fool errand is he on?" Anderson mutters, watching him go. He hears a noise from the other direction and ducks back in Marjory's room.

"What-," Marjory starts.

"Quiet woman," Anderson hisses, covering her mouth. "You will give us away."

He waits; growing more anxious, then finally hears shuffling footsteps coming. A thrill of fear runs through him. We're caught! No, it doesn't sound like nurses shoes. Too shuffling.

William appears in the doorway. He pulls an old woman into Marjory's room. She stands there on unsteady feet, eyes vacant, and a thick cord of slimy drool hanging down from her slack mouth.

William shrugs at Anderson's expression.

"Mrs. Bheals. If she is senile, then so are you and I. Her family dumped her here and never came back. She belongs here even less than Marjory does. I can't just leave her."

"She is dead weight. Just look at her," Anderson frowns. "She's a walking zombie. Leave her."

"I'm not leaving her behind." William meets his scowl with a stubbornness Anderson has seen before.

"Fine, let's go. No more breaking from the plan."

The two geriatric men lead the two drugged elderly ladies out and down the hall. The foursome shuffles towards their goal, a seldom used side door on the other side of the common room.

They reach the common room and stop.

A very shocked looking nurse is standing there staring at them.

"You told me to get her out of here," William says.

It takes her a moment to register what's going on. She blinks at the four elderly people, thinking how impossible this is.

"You-, you are stealing her!"

"It's not stealing. She is a person, not a thing. You can't own her. We are breaking her out."

William stares the nurse down defiantly.

She stares back, fights an involuntary reflex to smile and laugh. It's not funny. She is scared. She thinks for a moment.

"Wait here." She scurries off down the hall in the direction they were heading.

"She is going to blow the whistle on us," Anderson says dryly. "We should kill her."

"We are not killing her."

"Why not? We can't leave witnesses."

"This isn't that kind of job. We are not killing her." William's expression is firm. He will not give in on this point.

"Fine," Anderson mutters. "This is your mess to clean up."

"That's right," William says flatly.

The nurse appears in a doorway ahead, waving them forward. They move on, stopping in the doorway. The nurse is there with an elderly woman behind her, her long hair hanging down wild and unkempt. She looks at the visitors who have come to see her.

"Do I know you?" There is no recognition in her eyes even for her two fellow residents. My family is coming to see me." She blinks and looks at them in confusion. "Do I know you? My family is coming to see me."

"Mrs. Ferguson," the nurse says. "She is too far gone to remember any of this. She'll make a good distraction. I'll tell them she got out of bed and opened the door. It wouldn't be the first time." She waves them to follow; leading poor confused Mrs. Ferguson along.

They arrive at the little used side door and stop, looking at each other.

"Go, go," the nurse urges.

William gives her a solemn nod and pushes the bar on the door. The door is locked. The sign above warns that it is a fire exit to be used only in emergencies.

Anderson looks around nervously.

The nurse is wired with stress over their escapade.

The two drugged elderly women are obliviously staring off at nothing. Mrs. Ferguson is starting to get agitated.

William waits, counting down.

Sensing something unusual going on, some of the other residents have gotten out of bed and are milling around in confusion.

As expected, with the door opener bar depressed long enough, the lock mechanism releases. Without this safety feature, the fire escape would be useless in an actual fire. He pushes the door open and the moment the connection breaks, the alarm starts wailing loudly through the facility.

Mrs. Ferguson starts wailing, holding her hands in front of her and waving them in distress. She starts pushing the other residents, trying to push through them. They start wailing and moaning. Woken by the blaring sirens, other residents are getting out of bed.

The secure entrance on the other end bangs open and nurses charge into the ward.

"Let's go!" William urges and he and Anderson lead their two charges, Marjory and Mrs. Bheals, out the door into the night, leaving the nurse to deal with the nurses and distressed patients.

"You!" Ryan stands there stupidly gaping at the man on the other side of the open door.

Trevor stares back, blinking in confusion at the visitor he was not expecting.

Ryan's shock turns to rage and he leans forward on the verge of launching himself at the other man.

"How?" Trevor hardly has any voice, fear sending a liquid chill down his spine and turning his bowels watery.

Trevor steps back, grabbing the door to slam it closed.

Fuelled by an animal rage, Ryan lunges at him with a low growl, colliding with both man and door, knocking them into the motel room.

Trevor falls to the floor, laying there staring up at Ryan in stunned fear.

"Don't hurt me."

Cassie's voice comes to Ryan, small and afraid through a veil of darkness. He sees nothing of the room around him, only the face on the floor. Trevor.

"Please don't hurt me." Cassie's voice, little, like her, so quiet he almost can't make her words out.

He is confused. Why is Cassie's voice coming from Trevor?

Cassie's voice comes from behind him now, calm and clear. "Close the door David. You don't want anyone to see."

He turns, looking for her, the world filled with a fog that will only let him see what is directly in front of his eyes. The door swims into view and he goes to it, closing it softly.

"Kill him David," Cassie says in her calm clear voice. "He hurt me."

He turns, still can't find her, and focuses on the man-face on the floor. Darkness is clouding his vision, filling his mind. He doesn't recognize the face.

"He is you David. He killed me. You killed me. Kill him David, kill yourself."

The man-face shifts and fades into the fog in his mind. Violent rage is pounding through his veins. He clenches and unclenches his fists.

Trevor stares up at Ryan. *What is he doing?* He watches him turn and calmly close the door. It sends a deeper terror through him, that calm quiet motion in a man who is oozing violence from every pore, his face a manic mask of rage. He stares up at him, standing over him, clenching and unclenching his fists.

*He is not even looking at me. It's like he doesn't see me.* He tries shifting, expecting it to draw an attack. It doesn't.

*Did he follow me here? Did he see me put it in the trunk?* Trevor glances at the closed door. *The disposal guy will be here any second. Will he think Ryan is with me? Maybe he will realize and kill him.*

"Stop calling me David," Ryan says in a low voice.

"What?" Trevor voices it before he can stop himself. What are you doing? Shut up! Don't talk!

"I am not David."

It takes every last shred of what little conscious thought he has left. Ryan looks down at his hands. Boy hands. "I. Am. Not. David." He pushes the black shroud away, trying to think.

The room slowly swims back into focus. He looks around, rediscovers Trevor and understands.

"Anderson, you sick bastard," he mutters under his breath.

Trevor stares back at him uncertainly, trapped in the indecision of fight or flight.

Ryan forces his fists to relax at his sides. He gives Trevor a slow dangerous smile.

"Mr. Miller I presume?"

Trevor nearly soils his pants. A cold sweat breaks out and his stomach lurches with nausea. *That's not him. That's not who is supposed to come.*

"I was told you are very," Ryan pauses, "experienced in this business. You know the drill, let's get this done."

He turns and walks out of the motel room, not looking back to see if Trevor will follow.

Trevor stares after him in shock. He falters, and finally gets to his feet and staggers forward on wooden legs, following him out to the parking lot.

*I'll make a run for it. As soon as I'm in my car, pedal to the floor and go.*

Ryan goes the other way, leaving him to walk to his car alone. Trevor almost makes a break for it, running for the trees, but it would be no good. Better chance in the car.

Ryan reaches his truck, getting in the same time Trevor reaches his borrowed car. Trevor turns to see, mentally sizing up the truck.

*I can't outrun that in this.* He feels his hopes sink down through his stomach. He gets in and starts driving, watching for the truck's headlights behind him after he pulls out onto the road.

Trevor drives on, half hoping to lose the truck, taking one turn and then another.

Ryan feels the presence of the package he knows is in the trunk of the car like a physical weight dragging him down.

The thought hangs on the back of his conscious mind, hovering just out of reach. He won't let it in.

He roars up on the car's bumper, tempted to ram it into oblivion. Instead he passes it, telling himself to keep to the business at hand. Deal with him after the transfer.

The truck's headlights rear up, filling Trevor's rear view mirror and blinding him as it pulls up right on his bumper. With an angry roar of the engine, it swerves off to one side and charges past him.

*What if I don't follow? That's not how this game plays. Play by the rules or you are dead. They'll find me.*

He reluctantly follows the truck down a number of winding dirt roads through nowhere. Finally the truck pulls off on the side of a road bordered by tall trees and thick bush on both sides. He stops, dutifully doing a three-point turn, and backing his trunk to the truck's back bumper.

Trevor shifts. *Last chance to run. No, he wouldn't dare kill me. He has to follow the rules too.* His hands shaking, he shuts off the engine, kills the lights and presses the button to release the trunk. He gets out, feeling his knees go weak.

Parked in position on the side of a dirt road, ready to make the transfer, Ryan watches the shadow of his enemy move inside the car against the backdrop of the headlights. The taillights stare back at him like the Devil's eyes. The car shuts off and the lights go dark. He watches Trevor get out and stand next to the car.

He gets out of the truck and walks back, meeting Trevor in the narrow space between truck and car. He lowers the tailgate, climbs up, and drags the first of his plastic barrels to the edge, dropping it to the ground with a dull thud. He jumps down, pries the lid off, and leans against the open tailgate. His job is to not touch the package during transfer. Never in view of Mr. Miller. As far as Mr. Miller knows, he never touches the package. No evidence transfer.

With trembling hands, Trevor lifts the trunk lid to reveal the carefully wrapped package inside.

Ryan feels sick. *It's the right size.* He pushes the thought back.

Trevor lifts the package carefully. He can't help but marvel how they always feel so much heavier after the light leaves their eyes. The smell of death fills his nostrils and he gags. It took longer than he wanted to arrange disposal of this one.

Ryan watches him struggle to manoeuvre the package and drop it into the barrel. He jumps down to the ground the moment Trevor takes his hands off it.

Trevor turns in surprise to find Ryan standing right behind him.

Ryan calmly looks him up and down.

"Mr. Miller, our business here is done."

Trevor has to step around him. Walking stiffly to the car, he hears the swift tread of footsteps behind him, a blinding flash of light-filled agony exploding in his head as he pauses to turn. He drops to the ground.

Ryan stands over him, tire iron gripped tightly in his fist.

"Mr. Miller, you are the package."

Ryan bends down, swinging the tire iron with all his force, again and again, blood droplets flying off the weapon, turning Trevor's head into a pulverized pulp of bone, hair, blood, and grey matter.

Ryan pushes the image from his mind. It takes every ounce of self control to not act on the impulse, instead to stand there and just watch Trevor get in his car and drive away.

He seals the barrel, lifting it with some difficulty, and loading it in the back of the truck, slamming the tailgate harder than necessary. His fist clenching as if gripping that tire iron, he turns around and gets in the truck.

He sits there for a while, just staring ahead, punches the dash with a growl, and starts the ignition, driving away in the opposite direction of Trevor.

"Anderson, you bastard." His face feels hot.

The drive is torture. Ryan can feel the weight of the barrel in back weighing down his heart. His chest is tight and his grip on the steering wheel tense.

Hours later he arrives at a secluded place in the woods. Getting out, he opens the tailgate and jumps up into the box. He grips the top of the barrel, prying the lid off, and looks in. He turns away, stepping away from it in the truck box. He sighs a low agonized gasp.

Finally, he lets the thought in. *It's her. Elaine. Kathy.* Pain tears through him, threatening to tear him apart.

He staggers back to the barrel, gripping it and gently tipping it down. He pulls the package out.

He sits there on his knees in the truck box, staring down at it, fighting the tears that are blurring his vision. His head droops to his chest.

He raises his head and reaches out with both hands, untying the rope wound and tied around the package to secure it. He almost can't do it. He gently takes the edge of the sheet and starts unrapping her.

Elaine sets the folded note on the kitchen table. There is one word written on the visible side. "Sorry." Her hand hesitates, hovering over it, ready to snatch it up again. It's not too late to change her mind.

She wipes away a tear and leaves the kitchen. She looks out the living room window, but there isn't anything there to see. A suitcase sits ready at the door with clothes to get through a few days.

She sits on the couch to wait, stiff with anxiety.

Over the next hours she gets up to look out the window again, paces, and waits. She thinks about eating, but isn't hungry. Food probably won't sit well anyway, she decides.

She looks at the time for what she is sure must be the hundredth time at least.

Finally, she lies down on the couch and lets the tears come.

"He isn't coming."

Trevor drives too fast, almost losing control on a turn. His hands on the wheel are shaking and his mind has slipped into a blind panic, leaving him with tunnel vision. His stomach is in knots and his bowels loose. It is all he can do to focus on that narrow vision of road directly in front of him.

*I thought Ryan was just some soft-headed jerk. I never thought-. I never imagined-. I-. He's one of them. I'm dead. Oh man, I'm dead. He's going to kill me. I have to take off. Oh man, what am I going to do? Just keep driving. I won't even go home for anything. Ditch the car, get my truck and go. Don't look back.*

Ryan sits back, staring mindlessly at the corpse's face. His stomach lurches and he almost vomits.

"It's not her. It's not Kathy. It's not her." He doesn't even know the words are coming out of his mouth. He grabs his hair in his fists, pulling as if he could pull out the fear, sorrow, and rage swelling inside his head. His head goes back and he lets out an inhuman wail that echoes off the sky.

He looks down at the spoiled face. She looks vaguely familiar. It doesn't matter. The only thing that matters is that she is not Kathy. Elaine, he silently reminds himself by rote.

Moving in shaky jerky motions, he re-wraps the body. He has business to finish.

Righting and sealing the empty barrel, he tethers it with the others in the back of the truck and hops down out of the box. With a little difficulty, he pulls the corpse onto the open tailgate and lifts it in a fireman's carry slung over one shoulder. He grabs his shovel with the other hand and starts walking off through the woods.

It is a long difficult hike that takes him through rough terrain a casual hiker would avoid. He walks along a narrow ridge of rock that falls away on either side to a jumble of sharp rocks and boulders and balances across a fallen tree creating a temporary bridge over an old dried up creek bed cut deep into the ground.

Ryan finally reaches his destination and gently sets the wrapped body down. Taking a moment to survey the area, he chooses his starting point and starts walking, shovel in hand, counting his steps, turns and counts, turns and counts. On it goes, a courtship dance for the dead, "Left one two three four five six, and right one two three four five six seven eight."

He stops and stabs the shovel blade into the ground with a sharp shkt sound. He puts his foot on the head of the shovel blade, using his weight to press it in further. His muscles strain with the effort of scooping and tossing aside the shovel-full of hard mud.

When the hole is large enough, he drops the shovel and brings the body, gently laying her in her new bed where the insects will slowly devour her. Filling the hole in, he carefully erases all traces anyone was ever there. Shovel in hand, he hikes back to the truck.

Hours later Ryan arrives at the truck stop where he is to meet Anderson. He doesn't bother parking at the far end or trying to be discreet. He pulls in, parking against the building.

Ryan sits there. He looks down at his clenched fists. Rage is making him feel reckless. He looks at the restaurant, looking for Anderson through the windows. He takes slow deep breaths, trying to control the violence buzzing inside him.

Play it cool. You know Anderson did this on purpose to rattle you. It's a test. They're testing you.

Ryan doesn't feel in control enough, but he can't wait any longer. It would draw too much attention just sitting here. He gets out and enters the restaurant for his interview with Anderson.

He stops just inside, looking around.

The waitress pauses and looks at him curiously, wondering if he is waiting to be seated or looking for someone he is meeting.

He does not see Anderson.

Ryan walks past the tables to the back, checking faces. He stands there dumbly for a moment. *He's not here. Why isn't he here? Andersons don't just not show up.*

He leaves, pushing past the waitress who is approaching to ask if he is looking for someone, with a curt "S'cuze me."

Consciousness swims nauseatingly before Jason. He is disoriented. Confused. Opening his eyes hurts. They won't come into focus. He tries to move and regrets it instantly, a shockingly sharp pain slicing through his head. He lets out a low groan, blinking slowly and willing the world to come into focus.

With awareness slowly returning, Jason also begins to become aware of the serious predicament he is in. He is in the dark.

*The last thing I remember ... falling ... pain. Crazy guy. Where's the crazy guy? I think he fell too. Did he land on me? Yes.*

He fumbles around, not seeing him. A wave of pain tingles through him as he tries to move. Pushing through it, he manages to sit up. He reaches up instinctively, gripping his head. Holding his head tightly between his hands seems to help so he does that.

Jason looks around and finds the crazy guy sprawled on the floor behind him and across his legs. He can barely see him in the dark. He shoves him off, feeling dizzy with the movement.

"He's still tied up at least."

Jason gets to his feet, fumbling around like a blind man, feeling walls and then the open air and finally snares a string hanging from the ceiling. He gives it a careful tug and the single bulb hanging from the ceiling clicks on.

The crazy guy on the floor is starting to wake up also. He mumbles and groans, trying to move and managing to only squirm like a caterpillar with his arms and legs tied. One of his shoulders looks displaced.

"Probably dislocated it or broke his collar bone."

Jason waits for him to be blinking and looking around, for awareness to come into his eyes.

"Where's the kid? Tell me now or so help me, I'll beat the life out of you and then beat you again."

Nathan blinks at him, blanching in terror, his eyes bulging and jaw slack with it.

Remembering what the crazy guy said earlier, Jason kneels down before him, putting himself in a position looking down at him. He smiles cruelly.

"Tell me where the boy is right now or I'll turn into you."

Nathan's eyes impossibly bulge even larger. He starts a high keening sound.

"Speak. Now." Jason's voice is sharp, forceful. He gives him a sharp slap on the cheek.

That breaks Nathan out of it. He starts muttering incoherently, stuttering and mumbling to himself very quietly as if talking to those demons tormenting him in his mind. His eyes roll and he looks across the basement.

"Behind the wall," Nathan moans piteously.

Jason turns to look, moving away as he does so the man on the floor can't attack him as easily. He sees a wall behind piles of the kind of clutter a generation or two might store in a basement and forget it's there.

"How is he behind the wall?" Jason gets up slowly, mindful of his head and sure he has a concussion. He moves to the wall and inspects it. It goes all the way to meet the other wall. The other way is blocked by the clutter.

"The stuff," Nathan is pouting now, "you have to move it."

Jason studies the pile.

Among boxes, old wicker hampers filled with junk, a rusted old bike, and a machine whose use is a mystery to him, an old stained mirror door leans against the wall. It is the only thing large enough to hide an opening big enough to fit a man.

He targets his focus on that, moving what he has to so he can move the mirror. Gripping it by the sides, he shifts it over, revealing a cut out in the drywall. It is maybe half the width of a door, narrow enough a sizeable person cannot fit. Drywall is left at the top and bottom and the edges are roughly cut. The other side is pitch black, the dim light of the single ceiling bulb making a rectangle on the floor. He leans in, peering around for a light and sees none.

"What do you do for light?"

Nathan whimpers.

Jason spots a battery powered lantern on the floor tucked by the open cutaway. It is the kind that stands on its own, a handle hanging down, the style borrowed from old oil lanterns, but in a cheap way. He tests it and it works.

Carrying the lantern, he steps across into the dark, bringing the dim circle of sallow light with him. He explores the other room. It is not what he expected. There is no other exit. Someone had walled off this part of the basement for some unknown reason, leaving no way in or out. The window is boarded up; the cracks around sealed so no light can get in or out.

The only objects in the room are old steamer trunks of various shapes and sizes. He examines one. The crack around the lid is sealed with thick layers of caulking. On top of it is what appears to be some kind of sick shrine to some strange god. The dust on it is thick, having turned long ago into that sticky film dust will become.

The others are much the same, the layers of dust of varying thickness. They are not padlocked, but the latch the locks would hold down is flipped down, the ring protruding through the eye. Anyone inside would not be able to get out unless they were incredibly strong and could push up with enough force to rip the riveted latch and hasp out of the box.

On only one has the dust been disturbed.

Jason approaches it warily, setting the lantern down. He stands before it. His mind screams at him to not look. He does not want to see what he knows is in there. This one hasn't been caulked around yet, sealing the air out. That's a good sign at least. He also doesn't smell the very distinctive stink of a corpse.

Sucking in a slow deep breath and holding it, he steels himself for the worst and flips the latch up. Nothing happens. He lifts the lid slowly.

The boy is there, motionless and pale, hogtied into a position that he is sure to have asphyxiated himself before long with the need to try to straighten his legs when they become numb and then painful from the circulation being cut off.

Tears burn at his eyes. He feels numb. The numbness is the only thing keeping him from tearing the crazy man apart with his bare hands. The anger burning in him is distant, pushed far back by the shock.

*Did he move? My eyes must be playing tricks. He's dead.*

Unable to leave the boy here to rot, he leans in to gently lift him out.

The body is pliant, soft. There are no signs of rigor mortis. As he moves him he also notes the dark bruising of the blood pooling after death is missing.

He sets the boy down and cups a hand over his mouth and nose. It's very faint, but he thinks he feels soft breaths caressing his palm.

Jason checks the boy's restraints. Zip ties!

He races for the opening, half falling out of the enclosed space in his hurry and frantically rummages for anything to cut the plastic ties with. In an open tool box with half its contents spilled out, he finds a pair of needle-nosed pliers with a notch and blade for stripping wires. It will do. He races back to the boy.

Hurriedly, he cuts the boy free and lays him out, rubbing his arms and legs roughly to get the circulation flowing and slapping his cheeks a few times, trying to rouse him.

The boy moans softly, weak.

"He's alive!" Jason almost dances around the room with the thrill of the discovery.

Picking the boy up gently, he steps back to the other side of the wall.

Nathan's eyes roll wildly at the sight of the changeling carrying itself. *It's not possible.* He starts his high keening again.

"You can stay there to die and rot," Jason spits at him as he carries the boy past him. He stops and goes back, juggling his load to free a hand enough to reach the light string, pulling it and plunging the basement into darkness. The only light now is a slowly dying lantern in the shrine of the dead beyond the cutaway in the wall. He goes up the stairs, carrying the boy.

Ryan gets in his truck, already pealing out of the parking lot while he fumbles to do up his seatbelt with one hand.

His throat is too constricted to make a sound. His whole body feels like it is vibrating with tension. As soon as he pulls onto the road, he presses the gas pedal to the floor, recklessly speeding. A single thought tears through his mind.

*If Anderson isn't here, then he's there.*

He stares ahead grimly, barely seeing the road in front of him as he races for home.

"You messed up David."

Little Cassie's voice in the passenger seat comes unexpectedly, startling him. He turns in reaction, the steering wheel turning too, and swerves across to the oncoming lane. He corrects barely in time, narrowly missing clipping an oncoming car.

He pulls the truck back into his own lane, hitting the brakes and not slowing enough as he takes a corner hard. Cassie should have been thrown against him with the inertia of the truck careening around the corner. Ryan is pushed towards the door with it, but his grip on the steering wheel helps hold him in place. He shoves the gas pedal to the floor again, accelerating and trying to push more speed out of the engine.

Cassie is unruffled by the dangerous turn, unmoved by the violent press of inertia, and seemingly oblivious to Ryan's frantic race home.

"You killed her David. You killed her just like you killed me."

"No, she's still alive. I have to get there in time. I can stop him."

"Can you David?" She smiles. "Is that a police car I see?"

Ryan blanches. If he is seen driving at this speed, they will chase him. They will call in backup. They will take him down and he won't make it home in time to save Kathy.

"Dammit, I can't slow down. I won't make it." He looks around, but doesn't see a police car. All he sees are a couple of generic models of cars, all made to resemble each other in the manufacturers' quest to win sales from the competition, and an ugly old rusting brown Oldsmobile that should have been retired from the road a long time ago.

He flies past the Oldsmobile and other vehicles, swerving around into the next lane to pass them, and quickly puts them behind them.

"That's not funny Cassie."

"You can't save Kathy, you know." Cassie is gone and in her place is Jane Doe. "Anderson won't let her live. She is a problem. Anderson doesn't like problems. He can't take a joke either and your thinking you can save me or her makes you the biggest joke of all. You brought trouble on yourself and your family."

Ryan looks at Jane. It is the Jane Doe from the hospital, her face puffy and swollen with bruising, her lip cracked. A dark collar of bruising ruins her neck.

"You did this to me David," Jane says, her voice calm and without accusation.

Ryan turns away, staring hard down the road. He can't look at her.

"Look at me David."

"No."

"Look at me David." She is Cassie again.

He can't help it. He turns to look. It is little Cassie of the barn. Little Cassie of the woods. Ruined, bloody and dirty. She still has bits of straw in her hair from the barn. A dusting of mud clings softly to her face where it had fallen and he did not brush it away.

Little Cassie who he saw die, who he dug up when his father who is not his real father, Jason McAllister, buried her in the woods.

"I'm ignoring you now," Ryan says, turning his attention back to the road.

"You kill everyone close to you David, everyone you care about." It is a new voice; one he doesn't recognize. He knows it is someone he knows.

He glances at the woman seated next to him. Her clothes and hair are out of style. Her hair is dishevelled, her dress torn. Her eyes are glazed and dry, staring at him vacantly. Her face is discoloured with bruising and a spray of blood is splashed across one cheek from her ruined mouth.

The truck swerves violently, two wheels taking air, nearly flipping over into a roll. The tires touch the pavement again, screaming and leaving a black scar of burnt rubber, bouncing hard on impact and jolting the truck the other way.

Ryan fights for control and the back spins around to replace the front. Finally the truck shudders to a stop, crooked and facing the wrong way across two lanes of the road, wheels smoking and surrounded by the stink of burnt rubber.

"Mommy?" he almost says, catching himself and stutters out, "M-m-mom?" He reels with shock. His head swims with it. The world outside the truck no longer exists. "Mom? Mom. What's my name, Mom? What's my real name? What's my real name?"

The seat next to him is empty.

Ryan snaps out of it. He shakes his head to clear it, trying to push away the dark fog enveloping him.

The fog pushes back and he realizes where he is. Turning around and straightening out, the truck engine growls as it charges forward, devouring the road ahead.

He ignores their taunts for the rest of the drive, Cassie and Jane Doe taking turns tormenting him from the passenger seat.

"What the hell," Jim mutters after the truck that goes flying past him on the highway. He's in a hurry."

"He's late for something," Lawrence jokes. "If Jane Doe is his sister, maybe Michael didn't kill her."

"Maybe, but maybe he did. Do you still think she's alive? That Aunt Sophie is harbouring her?"

"If he didn't kill her, if Jane Doe is Cassie, then Jason might have tried to protect her from Michael."

"At the prison, when Michael met with Jason McAllister, he demanded to know where she is. The guard heard him yelling through the door, demanding to know where Cassie is. Jason McAllister has her, or at least knows where she is."

"She's with Sophie McAllister."

"I guess we'll find out when we get there."

Lawrence looks at Jim. "How long?"

"Until we get there? A while."

"What happens after we find her? After you get Michael and Jason for the bodies in the woods? How long are you going to keep this up?"

Jim's hands tighten on the steering wheel.

"Until I find the bastard who killed my wife."

"It wasn't either of them."

"They killed someone's wife."

Jason carries the boy in, gently laying him on the couch. Worried, he checks him over. The boy is still breathing. Shallowly, but still breathing.

Leaving him there, he races upstairs, taking the stairs two at a time and barges into his room. He grabs a few things and starts leaving, pausing in the doorway. He turns back, grabs the bag of stuff he bought the kid, and leaves, hurrying down the stairs.

Gently picking the kid up, surprised at just how little he weighs, Jason carries him outside and sits him in the passenger seat of the truck, buckling his seat belt and tilting him away from the door to close it.

He gets in on the driver's side, gently repositions the boy leaning against the passenger door and making sure his head is comfortable.

"It's time to bring David home."

He starts the truck and pulls away.

When Ryan finally pulls up in front of the little house they rented, he is so exhausted he can barely keep his eyes open. His face is droopy with it. He is unwashed and unshaven and long ago stopped feeling the gnawing pangs of hunger. He drove through the night and much of the day without stopping to rest to get here.

Numb with fatigue, he half stumbles out of the truck, jogging up the walk to the door on legs that don't want to move.

His throat catches as he bursts into the house. He is greeted by silence.

*They got her. Anderson got her.* Pain swells inside him, filling him up until he feels he will pop like an over-filled balloon with it. He stumbles to the couch, his legs giving out as he reaches it, letting himself fall to sit on it heavily. His head drops and he covers it with his hands, fighting the wail of sorrow that is pushing up his throat.

Elaine appears, stepping out from the bedroom doorway.

Sensing a presence, Ryan looks up. He stares at her in shock and confusion. It takes him a long moment to realize she is really there. She isn't a ghost like Cassie and Jane Doe, haunting and tormenting him.

He catches the guilty look on her face before she can hide it. Elaine was never good at hiding her feelings.

"You look rough," she says, not moving to approach him. The tension in the air is thick.

"You are still here." His voice is quiet, defeated.

Elaine misunderstands the meaning. She nods and swallows. She thinks he knows she was leaving, that he means that she did not leave him for Trevor.

"I'm sorry," she manages. She had cried herself through her loss and self pity hours ago. She had come to terms with where she is and who she is.

Elaine looks down. She can't meet his eyes. "I want to go home. I want to go home to my mother."

Ryan nods slowly. *I can't keep her here. I can't keep her a prisoner of who I am, what I am. Can she go back? Is it too late? Will Anderson let her?*

Elaine takes his silent nod as acceptance.

"A man came to see you while you were gone," she says. "I think he was your boss at the slaughterhouse. I think you got fired."

Ryan tenses. "Who was it?"

"I don't know. He didn't give me a name. He only said that they don't need you anymore."

"What did he say exactly? What were his exact words?"

"He said tell Ryan that his services are no longer needed."

The sight of the color draining from his face sends a tingle of fear through her.

"What did he look like?" The words come out choked.

"Like a business man. More like a used car salesman kind of business man. Middle-aged, hair thinning and cut short. He had a cheap suit jacket, trousers, and dress shirt, no tie.

Ryan? What's wrong? Why are you sweating like that? You look sick." She finally breaks free from the doorway, crossing the gulf of safety space she kept between them to come to his side and look at him worriedly.

"Pack a few things, fast, we have to go." Ryan is already on his feet, moving with nervous jerky motions.

She follows him to the bedroom where he pulls his duffel bag from the closet and starts hurriedly shoving random clothes into it.

"Where's your bag?" He pushes past her, grabbing her suitcase from the closet and stops at the weight of it. He looks at her and she meets his look with a guilty one before looking down. He sets it down by the bedroom door. "Grab anything else you need."

"What's wrong? Why do we have to leave in a hurry? Is it the police?"

The thought comes to her. *If I waste time, hold us up, they might get here before we leave. They'll lock him up, maybe me too as an accessory, but we won't have to run and hide anymore.* She flushes with guilt over thinking of letting him get caught.

Ryan pauses long enough to look at her, his eyes steady and serious. "Worse." He goes back to frantically packing.

His weighted tone and the fear in his eyes send an icy dread down her spine.

As soon as the duffel bag is full, he zips it and snatches it up, grabbing her suitcase on the way out to the living room.

"Come on, we don't have any time."

"What's going on? Please, Ryan, you are scaring me."

"I'll explain on the way." He drops the bags at the door, turning and crossing quickly to her, reaching to grab her and drag her along.

He stops, looking down at his outreaching hand, and drops it to his side.

"I won't force you to come with me. Not ever again. It's your choice."

Elaine stares at him, seeing the depth of his fear, his loss, the fear of losing her and worse, fear for her safety.

"Ryan-."

He cuts her off.

"Kathy, you might as well just call me David, or Michael if you prefer. That's what you knew me as first. I was David growing up. At least that's the only name I remember. I don't know my real name. These identities are useless to us now."

He expects the voices of Cassie and Jane Doe to start whispering in his head, "Run David Run," over and over, hissing and swarming over each other. They are strangely silent.

Kathy stares at him, blinking in shock, almost wavering on her feet. She steels herself, making a decision. *Michael is the one person who will never hurt me.* She moves past him, picking up her suitcase and standing there waiting for him.

Michael is shocked and thrilled, but they are still in danger. Anderson was already here. He hurries to her, grabs his duffel bag, and she follows him out the door to his truck. He tosses their bags in the box and they get in.

Half in the truck, Michael stops and stares down at the steering wheel. A note is taped to it. He pulls it off, reading it silently.

You can't hide from us.

*Anderson is toying with us.* He crumples it up and throws it out the door onto the road. Pulling himself inside, he closes the door and starts the truck, driving away, this time taking care to not bring attention to them.

"Where are we going?" Kathy asks.

"To see my aunt."

"You have an aunt?"

"Sophie. I have a lot to tell you."

As they drive out of town, they pass a weathered truck with a cap covering the box. The truck is approaching from another road.

Jason recognizes Michael's truck ahead. He follows it, carefully keeping at a distance that isn't obvious.

The boy who now calls himself Billy is sitting in the passenger seat. "Are we following that truck?"

"Yes."

# Part Seven

# An Ending

# 40 Sophie

Michael turns up a gravel road, following it for miles and passing farms until it turns to mud. He turns into the long drive of a farm some distance down the mud road.

"Are you sure this is it?" Kathy looks at the road doubtfully. The road would be impassable every time it rains, the mud sucking vehicle tires in and miring them.

Michael frowns. He isn't sure at all.

"It's been a long time. I was a kid when I found her. Even if it is the right place, she might not even live here anymore."

He pulls up in front of the house. It is not a large farmhouse, larger than the McAllister farm, not as old, and neatly kept.

They are greeted by a medium sized brown dog, who trots over, tail wagging and letting off a few loud barks when they get out.

The dog nuzzles Kathy's leg and she pets him.

Michael looks around.

A middle-aged woman appears, walking around the house. She stops in her tracks, staring at them in surprise, recognizing Michael immediately. She breaks from her surprise.

"What are you doing here?" Her tone is not friendly.

A little girl appears from behind her, following her, and stops to stare wide-eyed at the strangers.

"Go in the house," the woman commands, not turning to look at the girl. The girl turns on her heel and runs back around the house.

"Sophie," Michael says, almost choking on the name with the sudden rush of the memory of his other visit to this house. She had turned him away then.

Sophie's eyes and the line of her mouth are hard.

"I told you never to come back here."

Kathy stands back, watching them uncertainly, feeling awkward.

"I don't know where else to go." Michael looks past her, searching for something. "She's here, isn't she?"

"There is no one here for you. You need to leave now."

Michael's stance shifts. He has no intention of going anywhere. "I know she's here. He has nowhere else to take her. Where is she?"

The door creaks open and a young woman pushes her way out, arms laden with an over-filled laundry basket, using her back to push the door open while she turns through the doorway with the basket, stepping from the house. The door bangs shut behind her, pulled closed by a spring.

"Sophie-," She stops, staring at the three people gathered outside. The color drains from her and she blanches. She starts trembling and stands there frozen.

"It's okay Cassie," Sophie says, her voice still cold and hard, "he won't hurt you. Not ever again."

Michael feels the pull, the need to rush to her, to grab her up and hold her, to realize she really is there and to protect her. He shifts forward with the need.

Seeing the shift in his posture, Cassie drops the basket, flinching and on the verge of running.

"Cassie-," Michael manages to croak out.

"Cassie, go inside the house and put on tea. The green tea. See if we have tea biscuits too. We have company." Sophie's voice is calm and commanding. It has not lost its hard edge.

Cassie nods, trembling with fear, and stumbles back into the house. She catches one of the kids on the way to the front door, stopping him and taking him back out of sight with her.

*Green tea. How does she think it's safe?* Cassie fumbles in the kitchen, putting the kettle on the stove for tea. It is more than a request. It is a code. Tea biscuit is the cue she isn't really talking about tea, although putting on a pot of tea is a cover for the code.

Orange Peko would have meant to be on alert. Black tea means run. She picks through the tea boxes, moving the Orange Peko tea and the Earl Grey. She reaches for the green tea, pausing, her hand hovering between it and the Chamomile. The Chamomile is special.

*I can make this all go away with the Chamomile.*

She grabs the green tea, replacing the others, closing the door, and brings it to the counter.

She listens to the hissing ticking of the kettle as it warms, looking back at the cupboard and its now hidden teas.

Michael stares after Cassie after the door bangs shut and the house swallows her up.

"David." Sophie says his name sharply, bringing him back to her.

Michael looks at her. She is carefully keeping her distance.

Blinking, Michael looks at Sophie again, this time with curiosity. A cow lows forlornly somewhere in the distance.

It reminds him so much of the little farmhouse, but larger and newer. Everything better kept. A clothesline is strung across two poles, laundry hung and flapping in the breeze.

A medium sized brown dog chases a ball thrown by a boy.

A girl, smaller, methodically weaves long grass around two sticks, tying them together. A grey kitten mewls at her, looking for attention. A shadow hangs over everything. Clouds fill the sky, blocking out the sun.

He focuses on the kids. *It's not them. Different farm. Different kids.*

"Hey, wake up. It's not who?"

Lawrence coughs and blinks, waking up, feeling disoriented.

"Did I fall asleep?"

"You were mumbling something about it not being them. Not who?" Jim takes his attention off the road long enough to glance at Lawrence, his meaty fists gripping the steering wheel.

"How much longer until we get there?"

"Not long."

"I think we should speed up. I have a feeling he's already there."

"Who? Michael?" Jim's hands tighten on the wheel.

"Maybe, or Jason. I don't know."

"Like father, like daughter," Michael says.

"Close. I clean up a different kind of mess."

Michael's eyes widen.

Sophie looks at Kathy.

Kathy is still staring after the young woman, Cassie, with a shocked look, reeling from seeing her again. Jane Doe. The woman who shared a root cellar with her and escaped, leaving her behind. She feels dizzy.

"Go inside," Sophie says to Kathy. "Help Cassie with the tea."

Kathy looks at Michael uncertainly and he nods. She goes in reluctantly, leaving them outside alone.

Stepping into the house feels alien to Kathy, walking into a stranger's home where they clearly are not welcome. She wants nothing more right now than to turn around and leave, just get in the truck with Michael and drive away. She hesitates, then moves further into the house, feeling awkward.

Sophie waits for her to be out of earshot before speaking.

"My father was more of a waste disposal expert."

"So, what do you do?"

"I make problems go away."

Michael looks down at his feet, at the closed door, and back at his aunt, if she can be called that. Jason McAllister wasn't his real father, so Aunt Sophie isn't his real aunt.

"I'm a problem aren't I?"

She nods, her expression still cold and emotionless. "You are out of control. I should have dealt with it a long time ago."

"Fa-," Michael catches himself, "Jason said the same thing. Are you-?"

"Your Anderson called me in to clean up your mess."

Michael glances at the closed door again. "The guy at the slaughterhouse."

Sophie shakes her head. "You and your friend in there."

Michael tenses, concentrating on loosening his fingers to stop them from tightening into fists. "But-."

"Your Anderson has a sick sense of humour."

They look at the sound of a truck coming up the driveway.

"Are you expecting someone?" Michael asks.

The kettle starts whistling shrilly and Cassie turns the stove off. She looks back at the cupboard once more before she drops the tea bags into the tea pot, pouring scalding water over them.

The little girl who had been outside comes into the kitchen, looking up at her hopefully. "Can I have a cookie?"

"Yes," she says absently.

Kathy joins her in the kitchen, standing to the side awkwardly and feeling lost.

Cassie looks at her.

Kathy clears her throat, not sure she can trust her voice. "Jane-."

"It's Cassie."

Kathy nods, looking down guiltily.

"Back at the McAllister farm, you didn't come with us," Cassie says. "You could have escaped. Instead you stayed. Why?"

"I-I don't know. I just couldn't I guess."

"Did you have a chance to stop him? Before he came after us?"

Kathy can't meet her eyes. She nods so slightly it's almost imperceptible. She tries to swallow the lump growing in her throat and can't. She feels like it will choke her. That might be a good thing right now.

"He killed her. Connie. When he caught up to us, he grabbed her and shook her like a dog shakes a damned rabbit. He was like a wild animal."

"I-I'm sorry."

"You stayed with him. You went with him. Did you protect him too?"

Kathy nods, a tear rolling down her cheek, followed by another. "He-he won't hurt me." Her voice is small. "He won't hurt you either. You are his sister. You know that, right?"

"So Sophie tells me."

"Do you remember your father?" Kathy looks at her finally, her eyes looking red and bruised with the pain filling her heart.

"Yes and no. I have a few vague memories of the man Aunt Sophie says raised me, the man who brought me here, Jason McAllister. I have no memories of my real father.

Sophie told me what happened. Everything. She offered to help me find my real father. She said I could go back, reunite with him and live a normal life."

Kathy nods. "What are you going to do?"

Cassie looks at her curiously.

They turn at the sound of the door opening, footsteps and voices.

"Kill him," Cassie says softly, her face calm and placid.

Kathy looks at her quickly. *Which him?* Her attention is drawn back to the approaching people.

"That's Jason's truck," Michael says.

"Who is that with him?" Sophie asks.

Michael squints to see in the distance. "It looks like a kid."

"Not another one." Sophie's tone is annoyance.

They wait for the truck to reach them and stop. Jason gets out, the boy climbing out the other side.

The runaway, Billy the Kid, looks around curiously. He eyes Michael and Sophie warily.

"They won't turn you in," Jason says.

"Another stray pup?" Sophie complains, shaking her head with disapproval. "You know they don't approve."

"I couldn't leave him. He wasn't safe."

"From them? That's your own doing."

"That's what I thought too. Turned out a wack job lives across the street. He is obsessed with the kid. He had him locked in a trunk like a coffin."

Michael is eyeing Jason warily.

Billy studies his surroundings, pretending he doesn't hear. It's usually safer that way. The dog trots up to check him out and he pets him idly.

"If he's not on their radar, he's safe with us."

Sophie softens imperceptibly. "What's his name?"

"He's going with Billy."

"Billy, do you like cookies?"

Billy shrugs, not looking at her.

"Let's go in for tea."

Michael goes in first, feeling a rush of worry and the urge to protect both Kathy and Cassie.

Billy follows, scouting out escape routes as he goes.

Sophie and Jason come in together last.

"You've made a pretty big mess of things," she says.

"Yes, I have."

Sophie nods towards Michael ahead of them. "Anderson called me in to clean up your mess."

Jason nods. "I suspected that might happen. I came to clean it up myself."

Sophie pauses, making him stop, looking up at him.

"I'm taking David home," Jason says.

Her eyes flash understanding. "The girl too?"

"Depends how much she knows."

Sophie shakes her head, leaning in. "It doesn't matter. We've moved past that. They want the whole mess cleaned up."

"Including me."

Sophie nods. "You have both become liabilities."

They walk on, catching up to Michael and Billy stopped at the kitchen doorway. They stop, Jason joining Michael, both staring in surprise. Billy edges towards the hallway wall, looking for a clear path in case he has to run.

In the kitchen, Cassie is staring at Michael with the guarded look of a rabbit facing the wolf. Her breath is coming in short quick breaths, her stance defensive. Kathy is staring at the other people in the kitchen in confusion. She turns to look at Michael, meeting his eyes with uncertainty, and blanches with fear when she sees Jason behind him.

"You've always been a hack, coming in the most obvious way when you could have come in unseen," William McAllister growls, stepping forward. He almost smiles at the looks of shock on Michael's and Jason's faces.

He turns to Sophie. "You invited them?"

"No, they just showed up."

William scowls and grunts. "That's going to make this harder."

He gives Michael and Jason a hard glare. "Bloody fools better behave themselves or I'll put them down myself."

Behind him the elderly Anderson, once a man who evoked fear in Jason in his youth, is fussing over two elderly women.

"Mom, Dad," Jason says in shock.

Marjory turns, her face fluttering to confusion and then a smile. She pulls away from Anderson to shuffle over to Jason and hug him.

"We don't have time for reunions," Anderson snaps gruffly. "That damned detective is on his way, Jim McNelly."

"We're already packed," Sophie says. "We were just waiting for you to show up."

Anderson nods. "Let's go."

Michael, Jason, and Kathy follow in confusion as they all file out of the house.

Michael and Jason look towards their trucks.

"Leave them," William snaps, "they know what you are driving. You got anything; toss it in the back of the truck."

They see the truck now, parked on the side of the open garage, half hidden from view by a large tree. It's an extended cab, newer. It will blend in well with the other vehicles on the road. They go to their trucks, grabbing the bags and tossing them in the back.

Anderson pulls a car out of the garage and William starts ushering the old women to it.

Michael stops Cassie on the way to the car. His eyes burn with a desperate need.

"What happened to you after," he pauses. *After I killed you.* He can't say it. He hopes she was too young, that she remembers nothing. "When we were kids, after the farm, where did you go?"

"I don't want to talk about it right now."

She gets in the car, leaving him standing there staring after her.

"We need to go," Jason urges him on, steering him to the truck with Kathy.

"What do we do now?" Cassie asks. They are crammed together into three vehicles, following each other like a mini convoy. She is in the vehicle with William and Marjory McAllister, Anderson, and the surprisingly keen old Mrs. Bheals, former resident of the Bayburry Street Geriatric Home.

"There is only one thing we can do," Anderson says. "We keep hiding the bodies."

# 41 Gone

The ancient brown Oldsmobile creaks and groans and rattles as it rolls over the driveway into the farmyard. It rolls up to stop in front of the house, the engine stuttering as Jim shuts it off. It starts ticking almost immediately as it begins cooling down.

"Looks pretty quiet." Lawrence looks around.

"Let's see if anyone is home."

The doors growl and squeal on their hinges as they get out, the car rocking from the released tension on the springs with McNelly's weight lifted out.

They mount the stairs and knock on the door, listening. There is not a sound from inside. They wait, knock again, and exchange a look.

"Someone might be hurt inside."

"Could be. We do have reason to suspect two serial killers are in the area, headed for his location."

Jim tries the door. It is not locked.

"Country people, they never lock their doors."

They go inside and look around. At first everything looks normal, like the residents may have simply gone out for the afternoon.

The go into the kitchen. They see the teapot and Jim walks over to it. He feels the outside. He looks at Lawrence.

"It's still warm. It looks like we interrupted tea."

"They knew we were coming," Lawrence says.

"Let's keep searching."

They move on to the bedrooms, splitting up to search.

"Jim!" Lawrence calls from another room.

Jim follows his voice to another bedroom.

"Check it out." He points to the closet shelf.

There is a clear difference between the thin layer of dust at the edge of the shelf and a dust free space on the shelf. It would fit a suitcase.

"Damn," Jim mutters.

"We missed her," Lawrence says.

"We missed them," Jim corrects him. He pulls out one of the dresses hanging on a hanger. "This is not the same size clothes that are hanging in the other bedroom. There were two women living here."

"Kids too. Looks like a boy, maybe ten, and a girl, younger."

"That's not all."

Lawrence looks at Jim curiously. Jim holds up a comic book. Billy the Kid.

"I found this downstairs. This was at the rooming house, in Jason McAllister's room."

"So, you think this is where Jason McAllister went."

"It makes sense. Who can you trust more than family?"

"If you are right, that puts Jason and Sophie McAllister on the run with Michael Underwood and Jane Doe, aka David and Cassie McAllister."

"The unsolved kidnapping of Brian and Stephanie Downey is solved, but we've lost them again. That case isn't closed yet, and neither is my case on Michael Underwood." Jim's jaw works, his lips puffing out his moustache in thought.

"So where do we go from here?" Lawrence is still bothered by the sense of foreboding he felt. His dream of this place was no dream. It looks exactly like it did only he has never been here before.

"I think I'll be taking a little vacation."

Lawrence looks at Jim in surprise. "You've never taken a vacation."

"I have a lot of time banked, maybe enough to find Michael, or David, or Brian, whatever I should call him. I'm going to find Michael Underwood no matter what it takes."

Lawrence nods understanding. "I can work from the road. Most of my stories are there."

Jim frowns. "You are still chasing ghosts, aren't you? He didn't leave you his files, you inherited his obsession."

"I guess we both have our own obsessions then. I have a feeling they're tied together more closely than we think."

"So when we get back, we follow our leads and see where it goes."

"You might just find your ghost," Lawrence says quietly, "whoever killed your wife."

A chill runs down Jim's back. Suddenly he has the feeling Lawrence knows something he isn't telling him. "Let's get out of here."

END

# Killing David McAllister

## Book 4: The McAllister Series

# Part 1

# Safety

# 1 Promises

"Did you mean what you said? That you are going to kill him?" Kathy asks, looking at Cassie.

Kathy still feels the shock. It fills every fibre of her being, numbing her and pushing the world away to some distant place. She feels like she is trapped in a bad movie.

"Did I mean what?" Cassie does not look at her. She can't. Every time she looks at Kathy she is filled with anger.

"At the farm; you said you are going to kill him. Did you mean it?"

"I meant it." Cassie glances at her and quickly looks away.

Kathy swallows, thinking.

*Do I ask? What will she do, kill me? Isn't that what I want? To die? To get this all over with? The only way out of this is death.*

"Who did you mean?" she asks, hesitating. "Which one of them are you going to kill?"

"Does it matter?"

Kathy feels nauseas. *I don't know who I want it to be,* she thinks.

"I feel like this is unreal," Kathy says. "I thought you were dead."

"I'm not. No thanks to you."

"That's harsh."

"You deserve it."

Kathy's throat constricts and her eyes burn with the tears that threaten to come.

"It's time to go." The voice has the raspy tremor of age.

They look up at Anderson's intrusion. Kathy is anxious he somehow knows what they are talking about.

Cassie gets up and walks away without looking back.

Kathy watches her go. "She hates me," she says softly.

"She has good reason to," Anderson says.

He reaches one age-gnarled hand down to help her up.

She reaches up, taking his hand and letting him help her up, surprised at the strength in his withered muscles.

They walk to the vehicles together, where everyone is waiting.

Anderson moves to walk next to William.

"We have to drop off your Mrs. Bheals somewhere at the first chance," Anderson whispers to him. "We have too many people involved in this already. I don't think I can do anything for that woman David brought, but we can get rid of the old woman before it's too late for her."

William nods.

"I couldn't leave her there. You saw the place. What it's like; the patients. She doesn't belong there. There is nothing wrong with that woman's mind. I don't know why she was in that place."

"Family probably wanted to put her where she can't trouble them," Anderson says. "It happens when you get old."

"What about the kid?" William asks, his eyes shifting to look at the kid following Jason.

"I don't know. I have to find out." Anderson's face is grim.

*I don't want to tell them the kid is probably going to have to be disposed of,* he thinks. *But, William probably already knows that.*

# 2 Open Doors

Jim McNelly is sitting at a small battered table in a very unpleasant run-down motel room. The ugly wallpaper has stains he would rather not try to identify. The carpet is a worn down shag that never should have happened, and the décor a nineteen thirties thrift store match. The room has a decidedly disagreeable odor reminiscent of the curious stink of death.

His cell phone rings.

"McNelly," he gruffs into the phone.

I pulled some strings and got those DNA samples pushed through."

Even distorted by the bad connection, Beth's voice is a ray of sunshine in the dreary room.

"Beth, I could kiss you right now."

"Jim, that's sexual harassment."

She is teasing, of course. Beth knows he does not mean it as anything more than a metaphor to express his thrill at the news.

"Save it for internal," he jokes back. "What are the results?"

"We have confirmation," Beth says. "The match came back. There is a ninety-nine point six percent chance Donald Downey is the father of the Jane Doe."

Jim blinks back the tears that suddenly come to his eyes. He feels stupid for it, even with no one here to witness it. He swallows. His voice has just the hint of a tremor when he speaks again.

"What about the other one?"

The silence waiting for Beth to respond is torture. Finally she speaks, hesitantly.

"Michael Underwood is Donald Downey's son."

The rest of her words come from far away, hollow and empty while Jim's world drops out from under him and he stiffens with a slow smouldering anger. Her voice grows more distant with each word.

"Michael is Brian Downey. Jim, you did it. You solved the cold case of the disappearance of Brian and Stephanie Downey. I don't know if we will find anything confirming if they are also David and Cassie McAllister."

When he does not respond, she says his name into the silence of the phone, waits, and repeats his name.

"Jim."

"Jim."

"Jim."

He snaps out of it, shaking off the shock enveloping him to focus on the phone call again. The shock is as pointless as the crimes he investigates. He knew it was coming, the DNA would confirm what they already know, but hearing that confirmation is still jarring.

*It's not closure*, he thinks. *There will be no closure. Not until I find Michael Underwood and take him down.*

"Beth," he manages into the phone.

"Jim, if you can find Jason McAllister and get him to confess, or get Michael to give you a statement, you will have this. You will have Jason McAllister on kidnapping Madelaine Downey and her children, and the murder of Madelaine Downey."

"Have you had any luck tracing any of them?" Jim's voice still has an edge to it.

"No. Sophie and William McAllister have vanished off the grid. There has been no action on their bank accounts and credit cards."

"You aren't telling me something. I can hear it in your voice. What are you leaving out, Beth?"

Jim is met by silence.

On the other end, sitting at her desk in their shared office at the small precinct, Beth's red-nailed fingertips go nervously to her mouth. She starts chewing her lacquered nails, a habit she never had before.

The discovery of a massive multi-generational hidden graveyard in the woods brought out a host of new nervous ticks for her as new revelations are revealed.

*I can't tell him,* Beth thinks. *He will completely lose it. He already lost it over finding out Michael played him; that his partner, Michael Underwood, is a fictitious identity; a clever con.*

"Beth, don't hide it from me. There is more. What is it?"

"Jim," her voice is hesitant, her mouth open to make herself keep breathing, and her eyes anxious.

"Marjory McAllister vanished."

"What do you mean she vanished?"

"She is missing from the nursing home."

"How? What happened?"

"There was a commotion at the nursing home. One of the patients got up and pressed the emergency release on a fire exit in the lockdown wing for Alzheimer patients. When the alarm sounded it was chaos. The alarm sent an automatic signal to emergency and fire trucks were dispatched. There were fire crews coming in and out of every door clearing the building. When they finally sorted the patients all out and put them back to bed two patients were missing."

"Marjory." Jim's voice is definitive. He pauses. *It's probably irrelevant,* he thinks. "Who else?"

"A Mrs. Rose Bheals. She has no relation to the McAllisters."

"Probably an accident or a diversion," Jim decides.

"You don't think Marjory vanishing is an accident, do you?" Beth asks.

"No. William visited his wife very day. He is not going to vanish without taking her with him."

"He kidnapped his wife." Beth's voice still holds the strain of the shock she felt when everything fell in her lap.

She taps her gnawed on red-painted fingernails on a thin closed file on her desk.

"He broke her out," Jim says.

Jim remembers the care home with its very un-charming attempted false Southern charm. The frightening Miss Krueger, Director of the Bayburry Street Geriatric Home, and the cold mental ward hospital feel of the lockdown ward with the moaning and wailing patients wandering in states of confusion and distress.

"Beth, remind me to never get old."

"What?"

"Never mind."

"Jim," Beth's voice is hesitant again, unsure.

"What is it?"

"There is something else."

The line goes silent. Jim is just about to speak when Beth's voice comes back. She speaks quickly, in a hurry to get the words out before she changes her mind.

"I ran the DNA through some database searches with other departments in other jurisdictions."

*I don't like where this is going,* Jim thinks.

"Jim, I got multiple hits."

# Other books by L.V. Gaudet:

## The McAllister Series:

*Where the Bodies Are*

Are you ready to step into the twisted mind of a killer? What kind of dark secret pushes a man to commit the unimaginable, even as he is sickened by his own actions?

A young woman is found discarded with the trash, left for dead. More bodies begin to appear, left where they are sure to be found and cause a media frenzy.

The killer's reality blurs between past and present with a compulsion driven by a dark secret locked in a fractured mind. Overcome by a blind rage that leaves him wallowing in remorse with the bodies of victim after victim, he is desperate to stop killing.

The search for the killer will lead to his dark secret buried in the past, something larger than a man on a killing spree.

*The McAllister Farm*

Take a step back into time to meet the boy who will create the killer and learn the secret behind the bodies in Where the Bodies Are.

William McAllister is a private and reclusive man who does not like to have attention drawn on his family. His family history is as dark as the secret hiding in the woods.

Just as he begins to bring his troubled son into the family business, a serial killer starts preying on local young women. The McAllisters quickly find themselves drawn into the spotlight when the town decides William McAllister is the killer.

The attention is a threat to both William McAllister's profession and his family. He has no choice but to find the killer himself.

He might not like what he learns.

*Hunting Michael Underwood*

Hunting Michael Underwood follows on the heels of book one, Where the Bodies Are, bringing the first two stories and their characters together as the search for the killer continues.

Step deeper into the twisted mind of a killer as he slips further into madness.

Michael Underwood has vanished and everyone is searching for him. Detective Jim McNelly is determined to not stop until he finds him. Working with the detective, Lawrence Hawkworth is still chasing the bigger story he knows is behind the bodies. Jason McAllister knows he must stop the killer he created before he goes too far. He may be the only one who can stop him.

Unable to let go of his barely remembered past and the search for his sister, the killer goes looking for Jason McAllister's past and his family.

*Killing David McAllister*

Sometimes the only way to stop a monster is to kill it. He has gone by many names, but he was raised as David McAllister, and finding what he is looking for is not enough to quiet the darkness inside him.

Other Books:

Garden Grove

Who wants to stop construction at the new Garden Grove residential development? Everyone, it seems. Garden Grove is a hotbed of complications from costly mistakes and petty vandalism to sabotage and the poisoning of the work crew.

While the construction crew struggles to stay on schedule, they face growing problems and, with them, an increasing sense of unease.

A group of local housewives drawn into the growing mystery uncover a secret that brings Garden Grove deeper into a new mystery connecting all the suspects.

When all attempts to have the site shut down permanently fail, two long time local elderly residents step up their own efforts. Each with their own family secrets, the pair of quirky old birds are pitted against each other and their longstanding family feud is brought to the boiling point.

The mystery deepens with the discovery of old human remains that have their own dark past recently planted at the jobsite.

## The Gypsy Queen

(1952)

When a young man with an enthusiasm for get rich quick schemes discovers an old abandoned paddle wheel river steam boat, he has dreams of the riches and glamour she will bring.

His best friend and unwilling business partner sees only rot, decay, and their ruination in the old boat.

Struggling to rebuild her, they are pitted against everyone from the Shipbuilders' Union to the local casino boss. Meanwhile, strange accidents and a sense of dread falls on those who enter the boat as she awakens with a hunger for her ounce of blood.

The Gypsy Queen's dark past will not be forgotten.

# About the Author

L.V. Gaudet is a Canadian author, a member of the Manitoba Writers' Guild since 1993, the Horror Writers Association, and Authors of Manitoba.

L.V. grew up with a love of the darker side; sneaking down to the basement at night to watch the old horror B movies, Vincent Price being a favourite; devouring books by Stephen King, Dean Koontz, and other horror authors; and has had a passion for books and the idea of creating stories and worlds a person can get lost in since reading that first novel.

This love of storytelling has this author working writing and editing into a busy life that includes a full time job, family, and doing the little things to help the writing community including offering encouragement to others in the online writing community and volunteering time helping with the Manitoba Writers' Guild Facebook presence, proofreading for the HWA newsletter, and visiting schools for I Love to Read month.

L.V. Gaudet currently lives in Winnipeg with two rescue dogs, spouse, and kids.

# Hunting Michael Underwood

The McAllister Series Book 3

Detective Jim McNelly is furious. Detective Michael Underwood disappeared without a trace with the only living witness to the McAllister murders. Worse, Michael is not who he pretended to be. And then the other shoe fell.

Jason T. McAllister, tried and convicted of the kidnapping and murders of multiple women and the prime suspect behind the bodies discovered in the woods behind the McAllister farm, is being inexplicably set free. He will not spend the rest of his life in prison.

Jim is determined to find Michael Underwood, bring him down, and discover the truth about who he really is and what his connection to Jason McAllister is.

Working with his long time friend, the notoriously unscrupulous investigative reporter Lawrence Hawkworth, Jim will not stop until he finds Michael and the answers to the bodies found in the mass graveyard in the woods behind the McAllister Farm.

Jason McAllister knows he must stop the real killer behind the murders he was convicted for. As the killer spirals further into madness, Jason is the only one who can stop him. But, he needs help. He is going to have to talk to his father, William McAllister, the man who taught him how to hide the bodies.

Michael Underwood and Katherine Kingslow are on the run. A victim of domestic abuse and only known survivor of the McAllister Farm killer, Kathy has lapsed into Stockholm syndrome. Now she is torn between her need to be with her captor and fear of his escalating psychotic episodes.

Everyone is hunting for Michael Underwood.